With Signs & Wonders

Happy birthday
for dear
Manjack
Love ever
R

With Signs & Wonders

AN INTERNATIONAL ANTHOLOGY
OF JEWISH FABULIST FICTION

EDITED BY DANIEL M. JAFFE

INVISIBLE CITIES PRESS
MONTPELIER, VERMONT

Invisible Cities Press
50 State Street
Montpelier, VT 05602
www.invisiblecitiespress.com

Library of Congress Cataloging-in-Publication Data

With signs and wonders: an international anothology of Jewish
fabulist fiction / edited by Daniel M. Jaffe.
p. cm.
ISBN 0-9679683-5-6 (alk. paper)
1. Short stories, Jewish. 2. Jews—Social life and
customs—Fiction. 3. Supernatural—Fiction.
I. Jaffe, Daniel M.

PN 6120.95.J6 W58 2001
808.83'935203924—dc21   2001016615

MANUFACTURED IN THE UNITED STATES OF AMERICA

Book design by Tim Jones
for Sterling Hill Productions

FIRST EDITION

For my grandparents:
Dorothy Mann Rosenberg and Israel (Irving) Rosenberg
Toby Sharlin Jaffe and Morris Jaffe

Contents

ACKNOWLEDGMENTS

I AM EVER GRATEFUL to Joel Bernstein, senior editor of Invisible Cities Press, who invited me to compile this anthology. His advice, flexibility, humor, and warmth made the project an experience of joy. My thanks to Professors Leo F. Cabranes-Grant of Wheaton College, Leonor Figueroa-Feher of the University of Massachusetts—Boston, and Stephen A. Sadow of Northeastern University for their general advice, referrals to authors and texts, and overall enthusiastic support. I am likewise grateful to Cynthia Ozick, Dina Rubina, Rose Moss, Tehila Lieberman, Joyce Lieberman, Jonah Jaffe, Louise Popkin, Marsha Pomerantz, Mark Schaefer, Dick Cluster, Ann Shultz, Masha Neplechovitsj, and Andrea G. Labinger for directing me to various authors, texts, and cultural understandings I might otherwise not have encountered.

Much appreciation to Susan Lee-Belhocine of Oxford University Press for her background advice on general editorial matters, as well as to Kim Davis, Linda Woolford, and again (and again and again) Leo F. Cabranes-Grant for invaluable suggestions concerning the introduction.

To Grandma Dot, Mom, and Dad, my deep gratitude for the value of *L'Dor V'Dor*, From Generation to Generation.

INTRODUCTION

And the Lord brought us forth out of Egypt with a mighty hand,
and with an outstretched arm, and with great terribleness, and
with signs, and with wonders.

DEUTERONOMY 26:8

THE RECORDED TRADITION of Jewish fabulist literature
begins with the Bible: through one miracle after another God creates the
universe, creates mankind from dust, destroys much of creation with a
flood, saves the Jewish people—Moses' shape-changing rod in Pharaoh's
court, the Plagues, the parting of the Red Sea, pillars of fire and smoke.
Eve chats with a snake; Abraham, Moses, and others converse with God;
Jacob wrestles with an angel; Joseph has prophetic dreams; Ezekiel has
mystical visions; Jonah is swallowed by a great fish and lives to tell of it.
The Bible may be regarded variously as a historical chronicle, an imagined cultural foundational myth, a metaphor for psychological experience, or a mix of these. Nevertheless, the fact remains that biblical
storytelling relies heavily on the fabulist.

Subsequent religious texts written to interpret, elucidate, and elaborate upon the Bible—the Babylonian and Palestinian Talmuds and the Midrash—explored the fabulist dimension of the Bible through legends, tales, and fables. In the Middle Ages and later these stories made their way into rabbinic and even lay Jewish folklore. Supernatural creatures such as golems, dybbuks, and demons became part of Jewish storytelling.

In thirteenth-century Spain the Zohar appeared and became the foundation of later kabbalist mysticism. In their attempts to gain insight into the nature of God and creation the Zohar and other kabbalist texts explored, among other issues, the mystical nature of sexual expression, the transmigration of souls, and the nature of Satan, devils, and demons. Kabbalist mysticism flourished in sixteenth-century Sephardic Safed in Palestine, particularly through the teachings of Isaac Luria, who claimed that the mysteries of creation had been revealed to him by the prophet Elijah. This study and influence of mysticism later contributed to the widespread seventeenth-century belief in the false messiah, Sabbatai Zevi of Turkey. In the following century the Kabbalah influenced the rise of Chasidism, an ecstatic movement founded in Eastern Europe by the Baal Shem Tov. The movement's most influential storyteller was the Baal Shem Tov's great-grandson, Rabbi Nahman of Bratslav, whose oral Yiddish narratives merged kabbalistic symbolism and mysticism with the motifs of Eastern European folktales. Chasidic storytelling, particularly as recounted by Martin Buber and Elie Wiesel, continues to capture the modern imagination.[1]

Twentieth-century writers from around the Jewish world have continued working in this fabulist tradition, adapting and incorporating earlier stories, motifs, styles, and forms, modifying them, taking them in new directions. A few examples: Israel's S. Y. Agnon and Poland's I. L. Peretz both wrote in Hebrew and Yiddish, and drew upon earlier Jewish fabulist

---

1. Lengthy discussions of the history of Jewish literature, including fabulist traditions, can be found in Howard Schwartz's introduction to *Gates to the New City*, ed. Howard Schwartz (New York: Avon Books, 1983), 1–108; David Stern's introduction to *Rabbinic Fantasies*, eds. David Stern and Mark J. Mirsky (New Haven: Yale University Press, 1998), 3–30; and Gershom Scholem's *Kabbalah* (New York: Meridian, 1978), 8–86.

texts, folk legend, and myth in order to create a modern form of fabulist story. Writing in Hebrew, Israel's Shulamit Hareven re-creates, in her *Desert Trilogy,* the biblical era, filling in gaps of the recorded history to achieve very much what midrash does, although not in traditional midrashic form. Samir Naqqash, who has lived in Iraq, Iran, India, and Israel, writes in Arabic; he includes belief in signs and the spirit world in his work. In his short story "Prophecy of a Madman in a Cursed City," for instance, he explores what it means to be chosen as a prophet against one's will.[2] In his Yiddish stories Isaac Bashevis Singer of Poland and the United States frequently explored the occult, drawing upon traditional Eastern European Jewish folklore. Writing in German in the former Czechoslovakia, the Austrian Franz Kafka portrayed the reality of modern existence through stories whose realities feel unreal, dreamlike, not rationally explainable. Italy's Primo Levi, known largely for his autobiographical accounts of concentration camp internment, also wrote stories of fantasy and science fiction, taking fabulist tradition in a different direction. Clarice Lispector of Brazil, considered perhaps the finest short-story writer in the Portuguese language, explored the surreal and fantastic.[3] Great Britain's George Steiner stretched the limits of the Talmudic parable in his "A Conversation Piece,"[4] and Bernard Malamud, Cynthia Ozick, Stanley Elkin, and Woody Allen of the United States have each taken the fabulist tradition in a different direction, applying distinctive sensibilities, often with tremendous humor. As these examples indicate, the surreal, the magical, the spiritual, the mystical, the off-kilter unreal have continued in Jewish literature throughout the world.

It is this millennia-old tradition that provides the foundation for the fiction collected in this anthology, which is intended as a sampling of contemporary fiction informed by Jewish fabulist tradition. This book is

---

2. Samir Naqqash, "Prophesies of a Madman in a Cursed City," trans. Ammiel Alcalay, M. Joseph Halabi, and Ali Jimale Ahmed, in *Keys to the Garden*, ed. Ammiel Alcalay (San Francisco: City Lights Books, 1996), 111–124.

3. See, for example, Clarice Lispector, "Where You Were at Night," trans. Alexis Levitin, in *Soulstorm* (New York: New Directions, 1989), 114–130.

4. George Steiner, "A Conversation Piece," *Proofs and Three Parables* (London: Granta Books, 1993), 100–114.

not meant to be canonical or otherwise definitive. In fact the book is, to a certain extent, designed to be very much the opposite: one of its goals is to bring together authors who are not (yet) universal literary household names.

Nevertheless, several are, indeed, among the most honored writers in their respective countries: Steve Stern, known specifically for his Jewish fabulist fiction, is the 1999 winner of the National Jewish Book Award for Fiction in the United States; Moacyr Scliar of Brazil, also known as a Jewish fabulist and widely published in English in the U.S., has won awards in Brazil and elsewhere and seen his work translated into more than half a dozen languages; Angelina Muñiz-Huberman, noted particularly for her kabbalist-influenced stories and also widely published in the U.S., has won numerous prestigious literary awards in Mexico and elsewhere; Dina Rubina has twice been nominated for the Russian Booker Prize and has won literary awards in the former USSR, Israel, and France; Teresa Porzecanski is one of the most prolific and esteemed writers in Uruguay, and has won numerous domestic and international awards and fellowships; a volume of Cyrille Fleischman's French-Jewish-themed stories won an award from the Académie Française. Together with these impressive international writers, many of the others included in *With Signs and Wonders* have won prizes, awards, and literary grants, although the authors are at earlier stages of renown.

The works presented here by thirty-one authors and translators were originally written in more than half a dozen languages: English, Hebrew, Spanish, Portuguese, French, Russian, and Finnish. And collectively the anthology's authors and translators have grown up or otherwise lived in nineteen countries: China, Uzbekistan, European and Siberian Russia, Ukraine, Lithuania, Finland, Germany, Belgium, France, Iran, Israel, Morocco, Canada, the United States, Mexico, Cuba, Brazil, Argentina, and Uruguay. Works variously reflecting Sephardic (Spanish), Ashkenazic (Central and Eastern European), and Mizrahic (North African and Middle Eastern) Jewish experience are included. How different are the sensibilities from this broad range of languages, countries, and traditions?

How similar? In her study of international Jewish folklore, *Cuentos Judíos con fantasmas & demonios* (Jewish Tales of Ghosts & Demons), the Argentinian writer Ana María Shua came across hundreds of similar stories "in which the names of fairies, princesses, knights and shepherds were in Yiddish or Hebrew or Ladino. The princes ate lots of potatoes if the stories came from the Ashkenazic tradition and lots of rice if they came from the Sephardic tradition."[5] Is this similarity surprising given that our notions of the fabulist all stem from the same Bible, Talmud, Midrash, and early body of kabbalist literature?

The stories in *With Signs and Wonders* are varied in terms of style and subject, as well as in their approach to the fabulist. In some, one mystical or magical moment becomes a character's turning point. In others, the entire story is pervaded by a magical or mystical sensibility. In still others, there is a discrepancy between the ways in which various characters perceive the spirit world, some taking magic and the supernatural for granted, others reacting with surprise and doubt. The variety of responses to the fabulist very much echoes the range of biblical characters' varied reactions when encountering God, angels, miracles. And of course, as when reading fabulist elements in the Bible, one can read the fabulist aspects of the anthology's stories literally or as metaphor.

Traditional motifs appear strongly in several stories. Galina Vromen's "Sarah's Story" is a retelling of the Akedah (the biblical tale of Abraham's binding of Isaac) from Sarah's point of view, and echoes Hareven's trademark re-creation of biblical settings; this piece is midrashic in its effort to fill in biblical gaps, to elucidate a biblical story through speculation and elaboration. Moacyr Scliar's "The Prophets of Benjamin Bok" explores the struggle endured by a modern man who has been chosen to give living voice to the ancient prophets, and reminds one of Samir Naqqash's story (referenced above).[6] In his "Tsuris," about a rabbi who explains the alleged Yiddish derivation of the word *dinosaur*, Steven Sher

5. Ana María Shua, *Cuentos Judíos con fantasmas & demonios* (Buenos Aires: Grupo Editorial Shalom, 1994), 27–28.
6. Scliar's story also brings to mind a story by Steve Stern, "The Lord and Morton Gruber," in *Lazar Malkin Enters Heaven* (New York: Viking, 1986), 59–86.

satirizes the fabulist midrash even while acknowledging its power. John Shepley reshapes a centuries-old myth in "A Golem in Prague."

Angelina Muñiz-Huberman's "The Tower of Gallipoli," a story about Sabbatai Zevi in his seventeenth-century Turkish prison, feels almost as though it were written through the sensibility of a late-medieval kabbalist—yet with a contemporary sensitivity to homosexual love. Gloria De-Vidas Kirchheimer's "A Case of Dementia," Tehila Lieberman's "Anya's Angel," and Ruth Knafo Setton's "The Cat Garden," stories about young people in the United States and Israel who question their parents' mystical beliefs, can be read as contemporary variations on kabbalist tales that integrate the real with the supernatural. Kabbalist belief in the power of words and the nature of the universe play a central role in Yakov Shechter's "Midday," in which an Israeli uses kabbalist ritual to attempt a crime. In Teresa Porzecanski's "The Seder," preparation of the seder meal turns into a spiritual encounter with history. A deceased woman's spirit cares for her family by advising the non-Jewish housekeeper in Daniel Ulanovsky Sack's "Home Cooking." And kabbalist notions about the transmigration of souls inform both my "Sarrushka and Her Daughter," about a Ukrainian Jewish girl with the ability to absorb others' souls and memories, and Mark Apelman's "A Visitor's Guide to Berlin," in which a guidebook author discovers more residents of Berlin than just the living.

Kafka's influence can be felt in several of the anthology's stories. In Porzecanski's "Rochel Eisips," an Uruguayan is asked to deliver, to a person she has never met, a letter whose contents she never learns. The protagonist of Dina Rubina's "Apples from Shlitzbutter's Garden" finds herself in a slightly off-kilter reality that evokes a heightened state of spiritual consciousness. In Marjatta Koskinen's "Dies Irae," dream visions of a far-off town keep intruding into the Finnish protagonist's daily life.

The varied styles found in twentieth-century Yiddish and Hebrew fabulist literature are also reflected in a number of stories here. The protagonist of Deborah Shouse's "A Portrait of Angels" is the only one who sees an angel. In Joan Leegant's "The Tenth," the unexpected completion of a minyan by an improbable presence forces a rabbi to contemplate the nature of soul and the possibility of divine intervention into daily life. Joe Hill's "Pop Art" tracks the life of an inflatable plastic teenage Jewish boy and his flesh-and-blood, non-Jewish friend. A Siberian Bigfoot is characterized in Yizhak Oren's "The Cat Man." In Steve Stern's "The Tale of a Kite," a flying Chasidic rebbe causes the non-Chasidic Jewish community of Memphis, Tennessee, to worry about his influence over their children.

Stern's story brings to mind the Pied Piper of Hamelin. Indeed, the influence of numerous non-Jewish literary sources can be felt throughout the anthology. The magic and magical realisms of *A Thousand and One Nights* as well as the works of Salman Rushdie, Gabriel García Márquez, Isabel Allende, and others find expression in Avi Shmuelian's "Moonstruck Sunflowers," a novel excerpt about a Jewish character wandering through a magic-filled Iran, and in my own "Sarrushka and Her Daughter." Juan Rulfo's imagined world where spirits coexist with the living can be sensed in Koskinen's "Dies Irae," in Apelman's "A Visitor's Guide to Berlin," and in Cyrille Fleischman's "One Day, Victor Hugo . . . ," in which a group of twentieth-century Parisian Jews welcome into their midst a suddenly present Victor Hugo.[7] Rebecca Boroson's "The Roussalka" puts a Jewish twist on the old Russian myth of the seductive water nymph. Shechter's "Midday" feels Camus-like in its existential mood, and Eugene Seltz's "Compelle Intrare" overlays the supernatural onto a late-twentieth-century murder mystery.

In at least one case a story here represents the influence of Jewish fabulist literature on a non-Jewish writer. Responding to my question as to whether he were Jewish, Joe Hill wrote: "Bernard Malamud had a famous line in one of his stories. He said, 'All men are Jews.' I think, though, that he was speaking metaphorically; you're not wondering whether I'm metaphorically a Jew, but whether I'm actually a Jew. I'm

---

7. The latter recalls Woody Allen's short story "The Kugelmass Episode," about a contemporary Jewish New Yorker who becomes involved with Madame Bovary. See *Side Effects* (New York: Random House, 1980), 41–55.

not. 'Pop Art' I wrote on impulse, out of a desire to honor Malamud and Singer, two writers who have cast a very deep and lasting influence on my work."[8]

In terms of underlying theme, at least half the authors in *With Signs and Wonders* investigate the borderland between the real and the mystical or otherwise question the nature, the very existence, of mystical experience, angels, and otherworldly beings. Other themes explored in these stories include: the mystical nature of desire, the legacy of the Holocaust, generational conflict over tradition, food as a link to heritage and ancestors, the mystical power of language, response to God's call, the nature of Jewish identity, relations within and among various Jewish communities, relations between Jews and non-Jews, and Jew as outcast or "other." Fabulist forms of storytelling can accommodate a broad range of investigations and express varied imaginations.

Fabulist fiction. What is the appeal of the fabulist? For writers, movement away from realism gives the imagination a different kind of freedom, allows us to make sense of the world on our own terms rather than through standard rationalities. We can distort reality so as to highlight aspects of it. The cultural historian and literary critic John Thiem explains that "one of the main advantages of magical realism as a literary mode lies in its extraordinary flexibility, in its capacity to delineate, explore, and transgress boundaries. More than other modes, magical realism facilitates the fusion of possible but irreconcilable worlds."[9] Indeed, all fabulist approaches permit writers (and readers) to break free from empirical rules of order, although we must come up with new rules for the universes we create. Every chaos has its underlying organizational principles.

Whereas all fiction is an answer to "what if?", fabulist fiction takes the questioning even farther by challenging the assumed premises, by start-

8. One thinks of non-Jewish Jorge Luis Borges, several of whose stories reflect a fascination with Jewish Kabbalah. See the Introduction to Ilan Stavans's *Tropical Synagogues* (New York: Holmes and Meier, 1994), 15–20.

9. John Thiem, "The Textualization of the Reader in Magical Realist Fiction," *Magical Realism: Theory, History, Community*, eds. Lois Parkinson Zamora and Wendy B. Faris (Durham: Duke University Press, 1997), 235–248.

ing with the premise "if only . . ." If only angels existed, if only magic played a role in the world, if only one could converse with God.

Fabulist fiction goes so far as to suggest that alternate realities might, indeed, exist—perhaps not the specific alternate realities rendered in a given story, but some kind somewhere. To write fabulist fiction is to assert the possibility of alternate ways of being-perceiving-living. Are conceptualized possibilities unreal because they are intangible? Is God?

When engaging with fabulist fiction, we return to satisfactions felt in childhood upon hearing fairy tales that confronted us with our innermost childhood terrors—abandonment, isolation, loss of parent and love, powerlessness in the face of cruelty.[10] For adults, fabulist literature wrestles with fundamental concerns of adulthood—the nature of death; reaction to ethical and moral evil; duty to parent, family, ancestor, history; (in)ability to control our own destinies, to make sense of ourselves and the surrounding world. When reading about off-kilter realities, we recognize the frequent senselessness of our own and feel reassured that we're not out of our minds; we're merely somewhere within the continuum of understanding. In this tangible world where "might" often does make "right," at least our hopes can be sustained through Bible, myth, legend, and story in which God triumphs over Satan and provides secure guidance (even if we don't want it), where angels participate in our lives, the evil eye is thwarted, a golem comes to the rescue, souls linger on earth after death. The fabulist offers a connection to the divine and the hope for messianic redemption one day, if not now.

As in all cultures, storytelling—fabulist or otherwise—is as old as our culture itself, a fact that has prompted, in the minds of at least two of our great writers, a potential religious dilemma. In the preface to her collection *Bloodshed and Three Novellas,* Cynthia Ozick notes that Ibn Gabirol, an eleventh-century Spanish Jewish philosopher and poet, worried: Might Jewish storytelling violate the Bible's Second Commandment, that against idol worship? We create characters in stories, give them life, empathize with them, care about them, laugh and cry with them, learn from

---

10. See Bruno Bettelheim, *The Uses of Enchantment* (New York: Vintage Books, 1989), 3–19.

their behaviors and contemplations. To the extent that we adore stories and their characters, to the extent that we "idolize" them, are we creating graven images? Are fabulist stories, in particular, violating the Second Commandment's prohibition against making "the form of anything that is in heaven above, or that is in the earth beneath, or that is in the water under the earth"?

Ozick ponders the question, the link between storytelling as magic and idol worship as magic. She explores the issue in "Usurpation," a story that she describes as "an invention directed against inventing—the point being that the story-making faculty itself can be a corridor to the corruptions and abominations of idol-worship, of the adoration of magical event."[11] Thus Ozick demonstrates the potential scope and power of story, the capacity of story to contemplate, and be critical of, its own nature—and the capacity for story to help readers contemplate their own.

In furthering Ibn Gabirol's and Ozick's inquiry, I would, in typical Jewish fashion, reframe and redirect the question by means of another question: Might not the Jewish penchant for story, particularly for fabulist story—whether as part of Talmudic debate over a point of law, or as kabbalist straining to grasp the unfathomables of the universe, or as post-Holocaust contemplation of the modern human condition—might not Jewish fascination with the imaginary, in whatever language we speak and wherever we live, actually be one of the cornerstones of our multimillennial ability to endure?

---

11. Cynthia Ozick, preface, *Bloodshed and Three Novellas* (New York: Knopf, 1976), 11.

Selected Bibliography

Agosín, Marjorie, ed. *The House of Memory: Stories by Jewish Women Writers of Latin America.* Translation edited by Elizabeth Rosa Horan. New York: The Feminist Press, 1999.

——, ed. *Passion, Memory and Identity: Twentieth-Century Latin American Jewish Women Writers.* Albuquerque: University of New Mexico Press, 1999.

Alcalay, Ammiel. *Keys to the Garden: New Israeli Writing.* San Francisco: City Lights Books, 1996.

Allen, Woody. *Side Effects.* New York: Random House, 1980.

Bettelheim, Bruno. *The Uses of Enchantment.* New York: Vintage Books, 1989.

Buber, Martin. *Tales of the Hasidim.* Translated by Olga Marx, with a foreword by Chaim Potok. New York: Shocken Books, 1975.

Cheyette, Brian, ed. *Contemporary Jewish Writing in Britain and Ireland: An Anthology.* Lincoln: University of Nebraska Press, 1998.

DiAntonio, Robert, and Nora Glickman, eds. *Tradition and Innovation: Reflections on Latin American Jewish Writing.* Albany: State University of New York Press, 1993.

Elkin, Stanley. *The Living End.* New York: Avon, 1996.

Glatzner, Nahum N., ed. *Franz Kafka: The Complete Stories.* New York: Shocken, 1971.

Hareven, Shulamit. *The Desert Trilogy.* Translated by Hillel Halkin with the author. San Francisco: Mercury House, 1996.

Howe, Irving, and Eliezer Greenberg, eds. *A Treasury of Yiddish Stories.* New York: The Viking Press, 1954.

Kalechofsky, Robert, and Roberta Kalechofsky. *Echad: An Anthology of Latin American Jewish Writings.* Marblehead, Mass.: Micah Publications, 1980.

Kramer, Chaim. *Crossing the Narrow Bridge: A Practical Guide to Rebbe Nachman's Teachings.* New York: Breslov Research Institute, 1989.

Levi, Primo. *The Mirror Maker.* Translated by Raymond Rosenthal. New York: Schocken, 1989.

Lispector, Clarice. *Soulstorm.* Translated by Alexis Levitin. New York: New Directions, 1989.

Lyndon, Sonja, and Sylvia Paskin, eds. *The Slow Mirror and Other Stories: New Fiction by Jewish Writers.* Nottingham, U.K.: Five Leaves Publications, 1996.

Matza, Diane, ed. *Sephardic-American Voices: Two Hundred Years of a Literary Legacy.* Hanover, N.H.: University Press of New England, 1996.

Malamud, Bernard. *The Stories of Bernard Malamud.* New York: Farrar, Straus & Giroux, 1983.

Neugroschel, Joachim, ed. and trans. *The Great Works of Jewish Fantasy and Occult.* Woodstock, N.Y.: The Overlook Press, 1986 (originally published as *Yenne Velt*).

Ozick, Cynthia. *Bloodshed and Three Novellas.* New York: Knopf, 1976.

Sadow, Stephen A., ed. *King David's Harp: Autobiographical Essays by Jewish Latin American Writers.* Albuquerque: University of New Mexico Press, 1999.

Scholem, Gershom. *Kabbalah.* New York: Meridian, 1978.

Schwartz, Howard, ed. *Gates to the New City: A Treasury of Modern Jewish Tales.* New York: Avon Books, 1983.

Shua, Ana María. *Cuentos Judíos con fantasmas & demonios.* Buenos Aires: Grupo Editorial Shalom, 1994.

Singer, Isaac Bashevis. *The Spinoza of Market Street.* New York: Farrar, Straus & Giroux, 1979.

Stavans, Ilan, ed. *The Oxford Book of Jewish Stories.* New York: Oxford University Press, 1998.

————, ed. *Tropical Synagogues: Short Stories by Jewish-Latin American Writers*. New York: Holmes & Meier, 1994.

Steiner, George. *Proofs and Three Parables*. London: Granta Books, 1993.

Stern, David, and Mark J. Mirsky, eds. *Rabbinic Fantasies: Imaginative Narratives from Classical Hebrew Literature*. New Haven, Conn.: Yale University Press, 1998.

Stern, Steve. *Lazar Malkin Enters Heaven*. New York: Viking, 1986.

Thiem, John. "The Textualization of the Reader in Magical Realist Fiction." In *Magical Realism: Theory, History, Community*, edited by Lois Parkinson Zamora and Wendy B. Faris. Durham, N.C.: Duke University Press, 1997, 235–48.

Wiesel, Elie. *Four Hasidic Masters and Their Stuggle Against Melancholy*. Notre Dame, Ind.: University of Notre Dame Press, 1978.

Wisse, Ruth R., ed. *The I. L. Peretz Reader*. New York: Schocken, 1990.

Brazil's MOACYR SCLIAR is known particularly for his Jewish fabulist fiction. A dozen of his novels and short-story collections have been translated into English. His short stories are now available in one volume, *The Collected Stories of Moacyr Scliar* (University of New Mexico Press, 1999), and an autobiographical essay in English can be found in *King David's Harp: Autobiographical Essays by Jewish Latin American Writers* (University of New Mexico Press, 1999). Scliar's work has been translated into more than half a dozen other languages as well, and has been adapted for television, film, theater, and radio. Perhaps his most famous novel is *The Centaur in the Garden*, the story of a centaur born into a Russian Jewish émigré family in Brazil. Scliar has won prizes in Brazil and elsewhere, and recently served as a visiting professor at Brown University. A retired public health physician, Scliar lives in Porto Alegre, Brazil. "The Prophets of Benjamin Bok" is from his 1979 collection, *The Dwarf in the Television Set.*

ELOAH F. GIACOMELLI has translated five of Moacyr Scliar's novels and six collections of his short stories; the stories are now available in *The Collected Stories of Moacyr Scliar* (University of New Mexico Press, 1999). Her translations from the Portuguese have appeared in many American and Canadian literary magazines and anthologies. A retired educator, Giacomelli resides in Vancouver, Canada, where she continues to translate Portuguese-language literature.

The Prophets of Benjamin Bok

MOACYR SCLIAR

Translated from the Portuguese by Eloah F. Giacomelli

THE PROPHETS DIDN'T INCARNATE themselves in Benjamin Bok all at once. At first it wasn't even a whole prophet that took control of him. Parts of a prophet, more likely. An eye, a finger. Paulina, Benjamin's wife, was later to recall the strange dilation of a pupil, the convulsive tremor of the thumb of his left hand. But Benjamin Bok, a small, thin man with a bald head and a hooked nose, a very ugly man— and to make matters worse, going through a midlife crisis—and afflicted with a gastric ulcer—Benjamin Bok, poor Benjamin Bok, was regarded —in fact, had always been regarded, even during his childhood—as having a nervous disposition. His parents, in a constant state of alarm, had been overprotective toward him, partly because he was an only child, but mostly because he was so nervous. The boy didn't eat well, he slept restlessly, he had nightmares. His parents kept taking him from doctor to doctor. Leave the boy alone, the doctors would tell them, and he'll get better. But Benjamin's parents didn't leave him alone until he married. And even so, they never ceased to remind Paulina that Benjamin needed to be looked after.

Thus, knowing about her husband's nervous disposition, Paulina didn't attach much importance to what—as she later came to realize—could be interpreted as premonitory signs, and she remained unconcerned even when Benjamin Bok began to intersperse Hebrew words in conversation (which he would do in an odd, raucous voice, a voice that wasn't his). Paulina didn't question her husband about this matter, but had she done so, she would have found out that he *had never learned Hebrew*. Benjamin's parents, assimilated Jews, had never made an issue of it despite the fact that the boy had always enjoyed reading the Bible.

One day Benjamin flew into a tantrum. He kicked a small coffee table to pieces—right in front of his children, two girls aged eight and ten. Paulina became furious. But she still didn't realize what was happening to her husband.

Finally it was Benjamin himself who became aware of his situation during a social gathering of coworkers in a *churrascaria*.

Benjamin was an accountant (in reality, something like a manager) in an investment company owned by Gregório, a childhood friend. Gregório, a burly, expansive man, liked to give parties; he wouldn't let the end of the year pass without taking all his employees to a *churrascaria* for a Brazilian-style barbecue.

While Gregório was gabbing away, Benjamin, seated beside him, had his eyes fixed on the remainders of the barbecued meat strewn across the table.

"Dry bones," he cried out suddenly.

Gregório stopped talking, and everybody turned to Benjamin. Dry bones, he repeated, like an automaton. What the hell, Benjamin? said Gregório. Why have you interrupted me like this? And what's the big idea, this dry bones crap?

Benjamin mumbled an apology, and the incident was soon forgotten. But it wasn't him who had said that, of this he was sure; the voice wasn't his. At home, already in bed, it occurred to him that *Dry bones, I heard the word of the Lord . . .* was one of Ezekiel's prophecies. The prophet had spoken through Benjamin's mouth, right there in the *churrascaria.*

Benjamin was a malcontent. He couldn't resign himself to being a mere employee, but he had no desire to become a boss. He was always disparaging the government, but he didn't think much of private enterprise either. He had the reputation of being an oddball, so nobody in the office was surprised at the oddity of his behavior in the *churrascaria.* But everybody commented on that dry bones incident. It didn't occur to anybody to connect those words with Ezekiel's prophecy.

Days later Benjamin Bok went into Gregório's office. Without a word he took a Magic Marker out of his pocket and proceeded to trace Hebrew letters on the newly painted wall. Flabbergasted, Gregório looked on.

"But what the hell are you doing?" he bellowed at last.

Benjamin then turned to Gregório and stared at him.

"You've been weighed in the balances and found wanting," he then said.

"Weighed in the balances? Found wanting?" Gregório was puzzled. He didn't know that he had just heard the prophet Daniel speaking, and that Benjamin, as he sat on the floor amid the large vases that decorated the office, was in fact in the lions' den.

Gregório asked Paulina to come to his office for a private talk. Benjamin is bonkers, he said without beating around the bush, we'll have to commit him to a hospital, there's no other way. Breaking into tears, Paulina said that she recognized that her husband wasn't well, but a hospital would be the end of him. Besides, perhaps the whole thing was due to exhaustion. Benjamin works too hard, she said in a tone of voice in which Gregório detected a clear accusation. Subdued, and somewhat remorseful, he conceded that perhaps it wasn't a case for a mental institution.

"But," he was quick to add, "something has to be done. I can no longer put up with this situation, Paulina. The firm is buzzing with gossip. I become discredited, you must understand."

Paulina was again in tears: Ah, Gregório, if you knew what I've been going through, she sobbed. I can well imagine, he said, but so what, Paulina? Let's get down to the nitty-gritty: What's the problem? What's the solution? I haven't got all day. We already know what the problem is, so let's tackle the solution.

After considering various solutions, they opted for the one that seemed the most practical, at least for the time being. Gregório would give Benjamin time off for a vacation. Paulina was to take her husband to a seaside resort in the state of Santa Catarina.

At first Benjamin didn't want to hear about a vacation, much less about going to the beach. I get nervous having nothing to do, he said. Besides, I dislike beaches, I'm allergic to sand.

Gregório then intervened and threatened to make an issue of it—he would even fire Benjamin if it came to that. Reluctantly, Benjamin acquiesced. They left the children with Paulina's mother and went to the seashore.

The hotel where they stayed was nearly empty, for it was the off season.

During the first few days Benjamin seemed to be getting better. He would rise early in the morning, do calisthenics, have breakfast, then read for a while—mostly the Bible, in which he was again very interested. At ten o'clock in the morning they would go down to the beach and stroll among the rare vacationers. In a rather talkative mood, Benjamin would reminisce about his childhood and recall funny incidents that had occurred during their engagement. The sea air can do wonders! Paulina whispered into the mouthpiece when she phoned Gregório to keep him posted.

On the days that followed, however, Benjamin was again in a state of perturbation. He had become very quiet; he slept restlessly. In his sleep he mumbled incomprehensible things. One night he leaped out of bed screaming: Be gone, you wretch! Leave me alone! Paulina had to shake him awake. He was beside himself.

Paulina didn't know what to do. She was afraid of an unpleasant scene at the hotel; she considered returning to Porto Alegre, but she didn't dare to take any steps without first consulting Gregório. She phoned him.

"I don't want Benjamin here, not in the condition he is in!" shouted Gregório. "He is to stay there until he gets better. Don't bring this nut here, I already have plenty of other worries."

Paulina returned to the bedroom. In the semidarkness, with the shutters closed to keep the heat out, Benjamin was lying motionless in bed. Paulina went up to him.

"He wants me to return to Porto Alegre," groaned Benjamin. "He wants me to announce that the days of the firm are numbered. Because of Gregório's, and other people's, iniquities."

"He, who?"

"You know who." He pointed to the ceiling. "Him. He won't leave me alone."

"Perhaps we'd better go home," said Paulina, trying hard not to cry.

Benjamin leaped to his feet. "No!" he shouted. "I don't want to. I don't want to go back! I don't want to prophetize! I want to stay here, sunbathing!"

He gripped his wife's hand: "Why can't I be like everybody else, Paulina? Why can't I lead a normal life?"

Weeping, they hugged each other. Paulina then helped him back to bed, and then she, too, lay down. She fell asleep. When she woke up, it was already night. Benjamin was not in bed.

"Benjamin!"

She made a dash for the bathroom: he wasn't there, either. Seized by a sudden foreboding, she opened the door to the terrace.

A figure was running down the moonlit beach. It was Benjamin. At times he would stop to gaze at the sea; a moment later he was running again, at times in one direction, at times in another, as if not knowing where to go.

Paulina knew what he was searching for. The fish. The prophet Jonah was searching for the gigantic fish that would swallow him and take him to his destination.

Benjamin began to take off his clothes. Naked, he then proceeded to advance toward the sea.

Tearing down the stairs, Paulina ran to the beach, which was only a short distance away from the hotel.

"Benjamin! Don't, for God's sake, don't!"

He was standing still, with the water waist high. She entered the sea and tried to lead him away, but he kept resisting, and finally he gave her a shove; she fell, and a wave dragged her away from him. At that moment the hotel staff arrived on the scene. With great effort they managed to take Benjamin back to his room.

A doctor came and gave him an injection. Shortly afterward, he was asleep.

The next morning Benjamin couldn't remember a thing. But he seemed fine, although tired and depressed.

They spent a few more days at the seashore, with Benjamin getting increasingly better. Paulina was convinced that he was cured. Maybe it was the dip in the sea, she thought. Or maybe it was the injection.

They returned to Porto Alegre. I feel great now, Benjamin would say again and again. He could hardly know that the prophets were readying themselves for a new attack.

Gregório had a partner—Alberto, the son of old Samuel, the firm's founder, now deceased. Alberto, a shy, absentminded man, had a degree in economics, but gardening was his passion. His dream was to develop a new variety of begonia, which he would name after himself. Before dying, old Samuel had asked Gregório, whom he had promoted from manager to partner, to look after his son. Which Gregório did for several years, but with growing impatience. Prodded by his wife, ambitious like him, Gregório started to devise a plan to rid himself of his partner.

Benjamin, who suspected that something was afoot, had his suspicions confirmed when he overheard, by chance, a conversation that Gregório had over the telephone. It was a long-distance call from São Paulo, where Gregório had a mysterious informant who would tip him off about such things as investment opportunities, new regulations still in draft form, imminent bankruptcies. Then a few days later Benjamin saw Gregório in conversation with Alberto. He was trying to persuade his partner to trade his interest in the company for shares in business enterprises in São Paulo.

"Your profits will be much higher, Alberto. You won't have to work anymore, you'll be able to live on the returns of your investments. You'll be able to spend the rest of your life puttering around in your vegetable garden."

"Flower garden," corrected Alberto.

"You bet, in your flower garden. So? What do you think? Wouldn't it be great?"

Benjamin was outraged. Gregório knew very well that the sharp rise in value of those shares was only temporary: the market was jittery, unstable. Poor Alberto was being lured into a trap.

But it was really none of his business, Benjamin thought to himself. Besides, it was all one to him whether he had one boss or two bosses; it really made no difference to him whether he had to work for Gregório or for Alberto.

He went back to his office and closed the door. Before reaching his desk, he stopped: he was feeling dizzy. It was starting all over again—that thing with the prophets. With his eyes closed, his teeth clenched, his face congested, he stood there motionless for a few minutes. He then opened his eyes and made for the door, but before he had time to open it, he had to stand still again. The same weird sensation was now returning, but with greater intensity.

Two prophets. Two prophets were trying to gain control over him at the same time. Two fierce prophets—Elijah and Amos—were fighting and jostling each other in a scramble for what little space there was inside poor Benjamin Bok. They were scrimmaging inside his chest, inside his belly, trampling his entrails with their sandaled feet, their shouts resonating in his skull. At last, having apparently reached a settlement, they literally pushed Benjamin out. He went staggering down the carpeted corridor, and he opened the door of Gregório's office.

"You accursed man!" he shouted. "You want to seize your partner's share of the business just like King Ahab seized the vineyard of his subject Naboth!"

(It was Elijah speaking.)

"Woe to those who tread on the heads of the poor," he went on. "Woe to those who are unfair to the meek! Woe to those who falsify the balances by deceit! Woe to those who sleep in beds of ivory!"

(It was Amos speaking.)

Flabbergasted, Gregório watched him. Benjamin then started to sputter some garbled words. Inside him they were fighting again, the two prophets. Finally Elijah shouted: "I'll say no more. I'm leaving now. I want my chariot of fire so that I can climb up to heaven!"

Gregório made a dash for the phone and dialed the number of a psychiatric clinic. An ambulance came. Benjamin didn't want to go, and he started fighting with the orderlies. Then all of a sudden he calmed down, and with docility he let himself be led away. Had he convinced himself that the ambulance was the chariot of fire?

At the psychiatric clinic Benjamin got to know the man who received the Holy Spirit.

"No, it's not a dove at all. It's more like a butterfly. It enters me through my right nostril and then it keeps flitting about inside my head. It's terrible."

He also got to know the woman in whom Buddha had once incarnated himself: "Just imagine my suffering—me, skinny like this, with that enormous roly-poly inside me."

And there was the mulatto upon whom saints were in the habit of descending; and there was the student who received Zeus. Everybody suffered. Everybody—except for a bearded, longhaired man, who seemed tranquil. He was not possessed—he *was* Jesus Christ. I do envy him, the man who received the Holy Spirit would say with a sigh. I'm afraid I've been allotted the very worst of the Holy Trinity. I don't know what God the Father is like, but he can't possibly be as jittery as this butterfly.

Benjamin, too, envied Jesus Christ—the limpidity of that gaze, the splendor of that face. If only I could be like him, he would say. He would do anything to be able to rid himself of the prophets. As a matter of fact, the worst part of the whole experience was the expectancy, for once the prophets took possession of him and started speaking through his mouth, he no longer suffered; he became nothing but an empty carcass—a kind of armor that the spirits utilized.

One day he told Jesus Christ that he envied him.

"If your intention is to take my place," said the mental patient, smiling all the time, "desist from entertaining any such notion. There is one and only one Son of God—me."

"No, that's not what I meant, you misunderstood me," explained Benjamin. "All I want is to rid myself of these prophets."

"The first step," the other man went on, "is for you to become a Christian. I could even make an apostle out of you, there are openings for apostles. Sell everything you own, distribute the money among the poor, and follow me. Together we'll then traverse the roads of the earth, leading men to their salvation."

He took a scrap of paper and a pencil stub out of his pocket.

"Let's make an inventory. What do you own? A car? A house? Clothes?"

No, none of that had anything to do with what Benjamin had wanted to say. Nobody understood him, not even his psychiatrist, a young man named Isaiah. The coincidence of this name didn't escape the notice of Benjamin. Nor of the doctor, for that matter. Deep down, the doctor would say to Benjamin, what you fear is the prophet that I represent. What you're afraid of, Benjamin, is that I, the prophet Isaiah, will start fighting with your prophets.

Benjamin didn't believe in any of it, but he wasn't one to question the opinion of a doctor with postgraduate work in the United States. So he would listen to the psychiatrist in silence; when it was time for occupational therapy, he would carve little wooden horses; and when it was time for recreation, he would compete in a Ping-Pong tournament. And he would take his medicine conscientiously. The worst of it was that the drugs gave him an allergy—a skin disease that quickly ulcerated. Here I am in the same condition as Job's, he thought, alarmed, but upon remembering that Job was not a prophet, he sighed, relieved.

Upon being discharged from the hospital, Benjamin found another job. For many years he led a tranquil life. That prophet thing seemed definitively over.

Then one day he disappeared.

Full of despair, Paulina notified the police. She then went to every single hospital in town—including the mental hospitals—and she ran ads in the newspapers, and put notices on the radio. She even went to the morgue. With revulsion and horror she looked at the corpses that a sinister-looking attendant had taken out of the freezer. Luckily, Benjamin was not among them. But he was nowhere to be found.

Years later the mailman delivered a yellow envelope to Paulina—mailed in Rio, but obviously originating from a foreign country. It contained nothing but a picture—a snapshot, badly out of focus, showing a smiling and somewhat fatter Benjamin Bok, in a safari outfit complete with a cork hat similar to the one the explorer Livingstone used to wear. He was sitting on a folding chair, on a barren plain. Beside him, lying on the ground, a huge lion. Standing somewhat farther away, a little black boy looked on curiously. And there was nothing else. No letter, not even a dedication on the back of the picture.

However, it didn't take long for Paulina to deduce the meaning of the message. At first she thought of Daniel in the lions' den, but Daniel had already had his turn. No, what was represented there was a version of Isaiah's prophecy: *The lion will lie with the sheep, and a child will lead them.*

Benjamin Bok had finally found his peace.

Avi Shmuelian was born in Rafsanjan, Iran, and now lives in Jerusalem. He has engaged in many occupations, including construction worker, restaurant owner, porter, skin diver, and hypnotist. Also an artist, Shmuelian studied at Jerusalem's Betsalel Art School. His first novel, *Moonstruck Sunflowers,* was published in 1992 and has been compared, by the Israeli novelist David Grossman, to the work of Gabriel García Márquez.

Marsha Weinstein has translated the fiction and nonfiction of Israeli authors David Grossman, Shulamith Hareven, Meir Shalev, Albert Swissa, and Ronit Matalon, among others. Also a photographer, she currently lives in Jerusalem.

Moonstruck Sunflowers

(EXCERPT)

AVI SHMUELIAN

Translated from the Hebrew by Marsha Weinstein

FOR YEARS MULA YOUSSUF had harbored a desire to see the sea, ever since the time Haim Dalal had used incantations to bring rain to Rafsanjan. Those had been years of relentless drought. After three barren winters the wells and aqueducts—which flooded the fields and even the city, when all was right—were nearly dry. With the onset of summer the sun had shortened the distance between itself and the drought-stricken, had scorched the carcasses of beasts in the fields, had seared the parched trees. When it had dried even the tears in the eyes of the citizens, when a burning dust had gathered on everything, the Muslims turned to the Jews and asked that they use their powers to bring forth rain.

Haim Dalal, who had only just learned the secret of commanding ghosts and spirits, sat with the other founding fathers in his house amid the ruins. They scoured the old tomes, combing their crumbling leaves until they came upon something about a reservoir. Finding King David's lament for his beloveds, Saul and Jonathan, they read: "O mountains of Gilboa, no dew, nor rain be upon you, nor fields of offerings. . . ." One of those present asked: Where then, did the rains that did not fall on the Gilboa, fall? Haim Dalal sent his twin sons, Joshua-Two-Wives and Arai Diono, to the dried-out river, and they brought him a startled frog. He filled four clay bowls with water and placed them in each of the four corners of the yard, sprinkled salt on the frog's back, and then set the frog loose in the center of the yard. Instantly the frog leaped into the northernmost bowl of water. Thus he determined that the rains of the Gilboa had fallen for thousands of years in northern Persia, forming the Lake of the Kuzars.

That very day he gave the Muslims a parchment of eagle's skin on which were written explicit names and he told them to slaughter an ass in the fields, put the parchment between its teeth, immolate the decapitated head with the talisman in its mouth, and scatter the ashes over the waters of the northern lake.

That summer a party set out from Rafsanjan bearing the ashes of the ass's head, and at the end of autumn they scattered the ashes over the waters of the sea. At the onset of winter grey clouds gathered above the city, endless rains fell, and raging floodwaters threatened to obliterate the city, as in the first days. With no letup—the clay houses dissolving around their inhabitants, the city sinking like an island in a stormy sea until none came and none went—the Muslims turned again to Haim Dalal, this time asking that he call off the siege of the city.

Haim Dalal, who, with his family, had found refuge in the synagogue in the lower city, passed through the door of the house of prayer, burying his head in his long coat for protection against the rain and cold. He climbed the tower in the city wall. Alone, gazing at the turbid, turbulent waters, he stood shrouded in thought. To get to the heart of the matter he took up his childhood habit of sticking a finger in his mouth and sucking it for hours. When at last he climbed down, drenched and trembling, he confronted those who awaited his judgment with these enigmatic words: "The waters themselves are wise; their power is hidden within them." Right then and there he ordered the carpet weavers to weave a flying carpet, according to his design.

In the synagogue that Saturday he took aside the young Mula Youssuf, the only Jew with green eyes, and told him to prepare for the day when the flying carpet would be ready, as he was to fly to the lake and scatter above it a powder for the dispersal of clouds. When the weaving of the carpet was done, the winter ended and the clouds vanished, revealing the faces of the citizens, which were as grey as the clouds. In the days to come, the carpet would give Haim Dalal a place to sit cross-legged, but the longing to see the sea would stay with Mula Youssuf, and it was this longing that brought him from the crossroads at which he found himself, to the sea.

When at last he stood on a cliff overlooking the sea, it seemed to him that he was seeing a familiar sight. Even when he went down to the seaside fishing village, the sea could not teach him anything new—neither by its appearance nor by its properties. All was as he'd read in the Bible, even the mirage he saw at sunset: an enormous metallic bird landing on waves at the edge of the horizon. He compared what he saw to God's chariot, as described by Ezekiel in his prophecy. The next day, when the bird appeared again, he turned to the fishermen, whose language he did not know and, with gestures, asked what this could mean. The fishermen, who were busy salting fish and laying them out to dry on palm fronds, rose as one, leaned forward, spread their arms out to the sides, skipped around in a circle and, with gestures, explained to him that he had seen a *tayara*. Years later Mula Youssuf would be the only Jew in Rafsanjan to believe Arai Diono when he returned from serving in the army of the Reza Shah and spoke of having seen with his very own eyes metal flying machines that could rise as high as the clouds, even with all the Jews of Rafsanjan inside them. All the others just laughed and called him mad.

Mula Yousssuf joined a caravan of camels bearing sea salt to Rafsanjan and this time he was determined not to stray from the path. Yet by the first day his mule was trailing behind the camels, unable to keep up. Only at midnight did he manage to catch up with the caravan. The next day Mula Youssuf lifted her long ears and whispered magic words into them, then stroked special places on her long face, as Sariav had taught him. Within a few days the beast had learned the ways of camels and was carrying Mula Youssuf on her back at the head of the caravan. When he was but two hours' ride from the village of Meherabad, near the city of Bam, the sky filled with thousands of humming bees, which landed at the outskirts of the village. When he had seen quite enough of the bees, Mula Youssuf tugged at the mule's reins, and turned toward Bam.

IN THE DAYS WHEN Mula Youssuf was journeying far from Rafsanjan, an eye-healer came to town—a Dr. Yakoubian. Hassan Choupori the town crier, who had the longest pipe and the biggest mouth and was the tallest of the Rafsanjanis, made his rounds down the main street and through the maze of alleys, spreading the news at the top of his lungs and drawing after him a crowd of the curious.

Without warning the many Muslims who were stricken with trachoma, the blind and the half-blind, gathered in the upper synagogue. The eye-healer and his assistant Raphael Kermoni sat themselves in the center of the courtyard and began to receive patients who were still on their feet, one by one. At first they treated the mild cases who came and stood between them, each in turn. Raphael Kermoni would press their backs to the bloated belly of Dr. Yakoubian, who would yank them by the scalp and drip red iodine into their eyes.

Among those who were treated with iodine was Ali Paloo, a face so familiar among the Jews that he often got confused at the mosque, praying "Sh'ma Yisrael" when entreating Allah to keep him from going blind, for since the trachoma epidemic his sight had deteriorated with each passing year. While the other patients saw the world as a sinking sun and whimpered as if salt had been thrown in their eyes, Ali Paloo endured the searing pain, straightened his back, and stood at the head of the line of severe cases, to request more treatment. In the meantime the eye-healer and his assistant ground copper sulphate with dried tortoise eggs and medicinal herbs. When all was made ready for the operations, they called to the blind to pass under their hands.

The first was Ali Paloo. He kneeled. Raphael Kermoni stood over him, legs spread, and yanked his head back. Doctor Yakoubian tested his new method on him: First he poured black powder into his eyes, then passed a long, heated needle between his eyelids until smoke rose from them. A quick, sharp pain pierced Ali Paloo's brain, passed to his heart and from his heart spread in needles of heat to each limb of his body and like an echo back to his head, until it was no longer possible to keep him from shaking. They bound his hands and legs like those of a terrified beast being brought to the slaughter.

Seized with fright, the other blind people fled for their lives, stumbling over one another. The eye-healer hid his disgrace in trembling hands as he lay cloth compresses smeared with vaseline on the seared eyes of Ali Paloo; then he and his assistant gathered up their bundles and the hat full of coins. That very day they vanished from Rafsanjan, leaving behind Ali Paloo shuddering on his back like a drugged cockroach.

The worshippers who arrived for afternoon prayers were overcome with dread, fearing what would happen should the matter become known to the Muslims of Rafsanjan. They passed a long pole between the bound hands and legs of Ali Paloo, hoisted him aloft, and carried him to the dim room of Rivka Katchali. They stood out on the balcony for afternoon prayer, then sat down to ponder their plight. Not finding a solution, they determined to delay their decision until the day of the solar eclipse. The next morning they placed a large and deep copper tray in the synagogue courtyard, filling it with water they had drawn from the Paayab. They stood around it, entranced, gazing at the pale countenance of the sun. Baba Bozorg, the elder among them, pointed at the quivering stain and stated gravely, that this was the solar eclipse. The worshippers passed their hands over their faces in blessing, then spilled the sun on the garden. They then gathered in the synagogue to discuss how to remove the stain of disgrace left by Dr. Yakoubian.

When a week had passed, Ali Paloo was put on the back of an ass and, accompanied by Hassan Choupori the town crier, sent to the hospital of the "English" in the county seat of Kerman to get false eyes. By mistake, he arrived at the old hospital. There they opened Ali Paloo's eyelids, which had coagulated, dug out his sockets, and replaced his eyes with two painted dove eggs. When chicks burst from them, they tried painted wooden balls, but these were slowly gnawed by worms. After other unsuccessful attempts, his caretakers left him to the mercy of the "English." There, attended by the Jews of Kerman, he waited months for the arrival of two eyes, ordered from the land of the "English": one blue and one black, with metal weights for stabilizers. Later, when Ali Paloo would be asked how it was that his eyes were two different colors, he would answer that he was half-Muslim, half-Jew. When he had adjusted, Ali Paloo returned to Rafsanjan, where he made a living turning off lights on the Sabbath in the homes of the Jews, who passed him from hand to hand.

One Sunday, as he sat on a stool in the store of his friend the cobbler, cradling the end of his walking stick, his eyes were suddenly drawn out by a magnet in the shape of a horseshoe which, in his search for nails, the cobbler had unwittingly passed before Ali Paloo's eyes. Thereafter, the removal of Ali Paloo's eyes with the cobbler's magnet became a stunt that greatly amused his friends. Later it became a source of income. Enlisting Hassan Choupori, they bought from the old Muslim grave digger an ancient owl that could turn its head all the way round like a spirit, and a parrot, which Ali Paloo taught to speak, and grew a watermelon in a glass bottle. They went from village to village posing as a band of magicians, and made a fortune presenting the wonder of the removable eyes and the bottled watermelon with the owl on top. When the parrot would ask: "What's the time? What's the time?" the owl would turn its head like the hand of a clock. Ali Paloo walked about without eyes, aroused the pity of the onlookers, and collected money in a hat. He promised that if they gave generously, the cobbler would climb into the bottle and eat the watermelon. Meantime Hassan Choupori would strut around on stilts so tall he could pull fog from the sky and obscure the eyes of the skeptics. Thus it was that the cobbler could prove he had entered the bottle and got out again: he did it while the crowd was lost in a fog.

One day, when they arrived at the village of Meherabad, near Bam, they found a surprise waiting for them in the form of Dr. Yakoubian. As they entered the village, Hassan Choupori noticed a large crowd gathered in the square. Raising his head, he picked out Dr. Yakoubian in the center of the crowd. After a brief consultation the band decided to retrace their steps and wait in ambush at the edge of the village. The next day they caught Dr. Yakoubian and his assistant Raphael Kermoni. They bound them together, back to back, until they were as one. Then they smeared sugar water on their eyelids, left them there beside a bees' nest, and went on their way.

The next day, those who passed on the road from Meherabad found the bloated carcasses of the two healers. The bees' venom had left marks of advanced decay, and the two had been cleft in twain by the pressure of the ropes. The villagers dug a deep pit and poured into it the sticky mass of deadmen along with a few bees that were still sunk deep in the sockets of their eyes, and sealed the pit with clumps of earth. Spring water gushed from the bowels of the earth and the sides of the rocks at the base of the freshly dug grave. Flowing downhill toward the valley, it watered the fields.

One day Hassan Khoury, an old, blind man who was born with his eyes closed, came upon the spring. The instant he doused his face with the spring water his eyelids opened, sprouted lashes, and stayed open two whole days and nights for fear of closing, never to open again. On the third night he succumbed to his body's weariness. He lay on his back beside the spring, asleep with his eyes open, and dreamed the first dream he had ever dreamt in his life: The eye-healer stood on a hill like a white, gleaming angel, and spread his wings over countless hovering bees. His assistant hovered nearby, drawing a trail of dizzy bees after him. When the eye-healer had reached the utmost height he stood, weightless, on the chest of Hassan Khoury; in the terrifyingly soft voice of the dead, he demanded a fistful of bees in exchange for granting him sight, lest his eyes refuse to close, forcing him to witness the deeds of men even if he turned his head away. When Hassan Khoury woke he sacrificed countless bees, mashing them on the grave, and began to see like any man. That very day he appropriated the site, erecting a marble monument and an impressive, high-domed structure, as befits a holy place.

The rumor of the wondrous healing powers of the waters of Ein Yakoubian spread through the county, bringing pilgrims from far and wide. The number of visitors and the mashing of bees were so great, that many supplicants fainted from inhaling the venomous fumes that rose off the grave. The situation became so dire that only Hassan Khoury, who was immune to all poisons, could enter the mausoleum. He stood at its doorway and, in exchange for a modest sum, took sealed jars of bees and sacrificed them gleefully on the grave. Within a short time the waters of the spring had become poisoned, and any careless enough to swallow water when washing their faces died on the spot.

At that time there was a great shortage of bees, and those in need of even one stinging bee had to pay bee hunters in gold ingots, on which was embossed the visage of the Reza Shah.

Though Mula Youssuf's heart grew heavy, he had the strength of beasts. He left behind plains and mountains, villages and towns. So anxious was he to return to Rafsanjan that he skirted towns and took shortcuts. In the end, he lost his way. He would point himself in the direction of one town, but find himself in another; turn down the path to Bapht— and be greeted by the gates of Sirjan. Yet he kept on. He would close his left hand around the ring, and keep on. When he entered a town, he would stay only to buy fodder for the animals and provisions for himself. One time he needed kerosene, to fix Shaheen's shoes. Another time he sought a harness-maker and a rope-maker. He would quickly acquire what he needed, then continue on his way.

One evening he came to an oasis, and stopped there for the night. In the morning, he found it difficult to rise.

He said to himself: "It is mere idleness getting the better of me."

He forced himself to sit up, but instantly his head became light and dizzy. He thought: "The sun is unusually hot today."

Stealthily, slowly, a chill came over his body, and he trembled. Pain pounded in his head and brought tears to his eyes. It spread to his neck and his armpits and his groin. By nightfall he was burning with fever, hallucinating. At midnight, when the moon rose, he saw tiny figures dancing among the date palms. He said: "If these are spirits, I must have reached Rafsanjan."

Later he was blessed with many visitors. Montazeri, sailing on the ocean, riding on a tree stump, extended his hand to him, then grew distant. He also saw Sariav, a cock chasing him. The figures and shadows flickered, disappearing into abysses and behind peaks, returning to his side, prating in his ear. The most bothersome was Mula Rahamim, who chided him in sign language, sitting on his chest and pressing his bones until, no longer able to breathe, he wheezed and fainted.

He was awakened in the afternoon by voices which he took to be imaginary. He was encircled by the blurry figures of soldiers. One said: "The man's burning with fever."

Another corrected him: "He's dying."

Mula Youssuf's eyes closed.

"He's dead."

Alarmed, he tried to open his eyes to show that he was alive. One of them rested a hand on his forehead and said: "Wake up, Mula Youssuf, wake up. I am the Messiah . . . I am the Messiah . . ."

Years later, when Arai Diono came to Mula Youssuf and confessed: "I'm crazy, I'm crazy," Mula Youssuf would answer by saying: "Once upon a time you told me that you were the Messiah, and I believed you, for I was ill."

Indeed, so grave was his illness that those who cared for him despaired, and at the end of two weeks grew doubtful whether he would ever awaken. But one evening he surprised them. He opened his eyes and, seeing a clean-shaven soldier with the face of a youth leaning over him, asked if he really was the Messiah—then promptly fell asleep again.

The next day he woke, his body bathed in sweat. He tried to find a comfortable position. His limbs were so stiff that he could not move his hands. He let his eyes wander, trying to fix his gaze on something. He saw smooth clay walls plastered with palm fronds. He realized he lay in a bare room, at an oasis. He slept fitfully, vaguely remembering voices and blurred figures, until at last they melded together and stood before him in the person of a farmer. In those days Mula Youssuf could rise from his mat and lean against the clay walls. The farmer would come and go tirelessly, tending him in silence. He would dissolve various powders in water, support his head and bring the balm to his lips. He would bring him fruits to eat and quench his thirst with camomile tea.

One morning he awoke to the sound of neighing and whinnying. He rose and found his belongings. They had been there beside him all along, resting against the wall. He walked out of the room, happy. Shaheen and the mule were drinking from the trough in the stable.

He went up to the mule and lovingly stroked her back. She trembled in response. Shaheen received him calmly, as if they had never been apart. He thought: "How sated and happy are the beasts. They have been lovingly tended."

He remembered the farmer. He said: "I must thank him for his deeds."

He did not find him in the granary or in the meadow. He went back to the clay hut. Not a soul was in its four rooms. He went out. He saw countless sunflowers in full bloom. They encircled the house on all sides to the horizon. Nothing but sunflowers and the farmer's hut.

He sat in the doorway of the room on a straw mat and waited. Hours passed. Besides him and the beasts, who waited nearby, not a soul was in sight. Nothing moved; nothing stirred. Even the sunflowers stood as if eternally bent in morning prayer. They did not turn their faces toward the sun, or follow its movements.

For hours Mula Youssuf sat sunk in thought, trying to recall what had happened to him. There were days missing since he had come to the oasis, and he didn't know who it was that he had seen. Had the spirits of Rafsanjan forgotten their custom of helping him in time of trouble? Who was the Messiah? Why did he appear in a soldier's uniform? Where had the farmer gone?

All that day the farmer did not appear; neither did he come that night. At midnight the moon rose, and the sunflowers followed its movements until dawn. In the morning they again stooped in prayer, unmoving.

"Moonstruck sunflowers," thought Mula Youssuf, and added: "The laws of nature must have lost their force, if sunflowers can turn toward the moon." He rubbed his hands together. He noticed that the ring was missing; it seemed curious to him that someone would have coveted the ring, but not the rest of his belongings. Later he found food and drink in abundance; he understood that he was not to leave the hut until the farmer returned. Nights and days he waited, never diverting his thoughts from the sunflowers. Those were moonless nights, and they, forsaken, went back to staring at the sun. The sun scorched their leaves, dried them and bent their stalks.

Mula Youssuf went to look at the heads of the sunflowers before they buried their faces in the earth. He lifted one and tore a handful of seeds from its face. He cracked open a few. They were tawny-hulled, and white inside. Eating a few seeds, he said: "If I continue to wait, signs of day and night will also appear before me. I will set out before waiting becomes my existence, as idleness is for the mule."

He went to the stable and fed the beasts sunflower seeds in anticipation of the journey. This time he piled all his sacks and bundles on Shaheen's back. Astride the mule, leading Shaheen by the reins, he sadly distanced himself from the withering sunflowers.

REBECCA BOROSON is editor of both the *Jewish Standard* and the *Jewish Community News* in New Jersey. A former fiction reader for *Redbook* and Book-of-the-Month Club, her nonfiction has appeared in the *New York Times, Woman's Day, Glamour,* and elsewhere. Boroson's fiction frequently explores fabulist themes.

The Roussalka

REBECCA BOROSON

THIS IS THE STORY my grandmother told me.

She was a young girl, lately married to the most learned and pious man in the village. But she was not happy. She liked to sing, and he would have no singing. She liked to dance, and he would have no dancing. She liked to walk in her bare feet and feel the earth, and he made her wear stiff, heavy shoes.

She was an orphan, and the match had been made for her by the women of the village. She had had to accept it; no other man would take her without family and a dowry, except her long, shining hair—and even that was cut, as was the custom, at marriage.

But it was the wrong match, the wrong match, and every day was heavier than the day before, so that she stopped wanting to sing and dance, and the stiff, heavy shoes began to feel like her skin.

One fall day, collecting kindling for the fire, she happened to pass the river, and saw in it her image—a drab thing, more drab against the season's reds and golds, even against the river's greeny brown. In the river, she thought, the stiff, heavy shoes would bear her down, and that would be the end of all her misery. So she lay down her bundle of twigs and began to walk into the water.

But when she had gone out as far as her breasts, she was surprised to see a ray of green hair across the water. It is a roussalka, she thought, and if she had been a Christian, she would have crossed herself, for roussalkas are water nymphs who lure men to their deaths. But she was going to her death anyway, so she was not afraid. She said to the creature, whose face was obscured by the watery green hair, "Roussalka, roussalka, let me pass. I have my journey to make."

She saw the hair move in the water, shaking like green water snakes. And then the water snakes parted and revealed a head, and then the head rose up out of the water upon a body.

And now my grandmother was truly surprised, because she saw (roussalkas don't wear clothes) that this was a male roussalka, something she had never heard of. And the male roussalka began to sing, as sweet and green a song as she had ever heard. And he put out his hands to her and said, "Come. I will share your journey." And holding his hands (green hands they were, she told me), she walked farther and farther into the river, until it was past her lips, and her nose, and her eyes.

Under the river was the roussalka's home, and there was always music in it. My grandmother became renowned among all the roussalkas for her singing and dancing. She was never happier in her life, and she lived there a hundred years.

Now time, among the roussalkas, spreads out, so that one of our seconds, which we hardly sense and almost never enjoy, becomes a full and sweet year. So really, my grandmother had been under the water in the roussalka's home for no more than a hundred human seconds. It was enough (human) time for a man of the village, who happened to be passing, to see her sink. He dove in and pulled her out.

When she awoke, she was lying on the big bed in her husband's house, and the roussalka, invisible to all but her, was at its foot, weeping green tears.

"No," she said to him and to anyone who would listen. "I am not staying here. I want to go back to my home, to my husband." And she reached out her hand to the creature no one else could see.

"Your husband is here," said a man she hardly recognized, a man with a black beard and a stooped back, and he bent down to her and took her hand into his.

"No," she said, pulling away, "my green husband," and for the next two days, she was told afterward, she raved in that fashion.

But the longer she lay on that bed, the less she could see of the roussalka, and by sunset of the second day he was not visible at all. As soon as she was let up out of bed, she went looking for him, but as her husband had sent a small boy to follow her and make sure she did not do herself harm, she could not walk into the water.

So she walked along the river, searching for him, even after her belly began to swell with my mother. And after my mother was born, she would nurse her by the river, never taking her eyes from the water for fear she would miss him. But there was never a trace of him, not a single green hair floating on the water, not a strain of his green song.

Day after day she kept vigil, mute in her misery, but by and by, as she watched and listened to the river, her own song broke out, and her feet kept time, and her hair grew back in elflocks.

Her husband, who was not a bad man, or a stupid one, was so relieved to see her restored to life that he encouraged her to dance and sing (when she cared to) and to go without shoes (but only in the house). He even said she did not need to cut her hair (and liked to watch her smooth it, mornings, with a tortoiseshell comb).

So living in his house became more bearable. And as more babies came, she had less time and opportunity to look for her roussalka. After some years the family left the village and came to this country, and there was no way ever to find him again.

Every time she told me this story she would say to me, "Remember always to sing and dance. It's the only way to stay alive. Now go and play, my little green child. . . ."

Born in New York, JOAN LEEGANT has spent most of her adult life in Massachusetts, where the Massachusetts Cultural Council recently awarded her an Artist's Grant in Fiction. From 1978 through 1980 she lived in Jerusalem. Formerly a practicing attorney, Leegant now teaches writing at several colleges in the Boston area. Her short fiction has appeared in *Nimrod, Columbia, American Literary Review, Kalliope,* and *Response: A Contemporary Jewish Review,* and her personal essays have been published in various books, including *New Kosher Cuisine for All Seasons* (Ten Speed Press). Several of Leegant's stories have been finalists in contests; "The Tenth" won third place in *Nimrod's* Katherine Anne Porter competition.

The Tenth

JOAN LEEGANT

AFTER FIFTY-ONE YEARS as a rabbi Samuel Steele had believed—until that morning—that when it came to the often elusive tenth man needed to complete a minyan, he had seen everything. Drag queens. Blond farm boys with names like Swenson, Nordstrom. A former monk who sometimes wore his robes. He gazed out the big window of the study in what he was sure would be his last shul—small, sparsely attended, and, like almost all of its members, dying—and watched Beaconswood Avenue come to life. He had been wrong.

The steady flow of pedestrians had already absorbed all but one of the handful who'd made up that morning's quorum, conducting them like a gentle stream into the everyday world. It was a beautiful day, one of the first of real spring, the season always late getting to Boston, as if it had to stop somewhere else along the way. Birds, green leaves, a blue sky, like a postcard. The trolley stopped on the corner with a loud clang, the car Nathan Lefkowitz should have been getting on. Instead Lefkowitz, at eighty-six the oldest of Samuel's congregants, lay sleeping on the couch behind him, recovering. It was Lefkowitz who had been charged that morning, as he had for the past forty years of mornings, as far as Samuel could tell, with finding the tenth man. They could pray without a full quorum but most of the men, some weeks all of them, were saying the kaddish, which could only be said with the requisite ten. And what else could they do for their dead now but pray?

The door of the trolley flew shut, and the car lumbered on. Samuel glanced over at Lefkowitz, who was covered with a thick blue banquet cloth, the only thing Samuel could find in the closet, left from the days when the shul still put on functions. At six forty-five that morning Lefkowitz had posted himself outside the shul, standing by the door, as was his custom, counting. By ten to seven there were eight of them, including Samuel; by five minutes of the hour they had nine.

Taking no chances, Lefkowitz had immediately begun to make the rounds, starting with the trolley stop. There he would have politely inquired of any of the men if they were Jewish and, if so, could they help form a minyan. Samuel watched him from the study window, as he did every time the older man ventured out, his small and ancient form draped in a gray raincoat. He admired Lefkowitz's style. He had been privy to a variety of techniques in his day, from strong-arm tactics laying the guilt on reticent Jews to the ultimate in discretion that verged on code, so much so that it was sometimes impossible to know what religion was involved, or even that it was religion at all. He appreciated Lefkowitz's straightforward manner.

Having no luck at the trolley stop, Lefkowitz turned around and began walking to the other end of the block. He passed Samuel at the window but didn't look up. At the other end, they both knew, was a less promising source, an apartment building heavily populated with college students. Samuel had never actually seen Lefkowitz at work there—the building was out of view—nor had he ever approached it himself. But he had heard enough to imagine. To guess that the handful of rumpled students who emerged at that hour probably didn't live there and had instead spent the night in someone else's apartment having too much to drink, or smoking marijuana, or being in love, or something simulating it. It was hard to know. The two or three souls Lefkowitz had managed to pick up there in the year since Samuel had arrived invariably fled before the singing of *Adon Olam,* at the first sign of anyone removing a tallis and preparing to conclude lest, God forbid, they might have to face anyone, talk about themselves.

The street was perking up, more trolley clangs, more traffic. That morning, however, astonishingly, shockingly, Lefkowitz had been successful at the student apartment building: a set of Siamese twins.

Recruitment hadn't been involved. According to Lefkowitz's account after the service, he hadn't even opened his mouth when they stepped out of the doorway and said, *You're from the synagogue up the street, aren't you?* Lefkowitz was in the middle of telling this to Samuel when suddenly his face turned ashen and he began to tremble. Samuel helped get him onto the couch, then went to the kitchen for a cup of orange juice. By the time he got back, Lefkowitz was asleep. That was over an hour ago.

Now Lefkowitz was coughing himself awake. Samuel went to the couch, handed him the juice. Lefkowitz pulled himself up, the blue banquet cloth sliding toward the floor, and sipped. Samuel rearranged the cloth over Lefkowitz's legs, took the empty cup. "Did I tell you what they said to me as they came out of the doorway?" Lefkowitz said, as if he were dreaming, not an hour, not even a minute, having passed.

Samuel sat on the edge of the couch. Of course Lefkowitz was shaken up; they had all been shaken up. Not given to talk, especially not to anything resembling hysteria or gossip, the other men had left quickly, keeping their words brief, hushed, covert. *Poor fellows, God help them, see you tomorrow.*

But Lefkowitz was taking it the hardest. And why not? He was the one who'd first seen them, the one they talked to. "'You're from the synagogue up the street, aren't you?'" Lefkowitz said. "That's what they said, Samuel."

"And then what happened?"

"I couldn't utter a word. Though they seemed nonplussed, like they were used to it." Lefkowitz paused. "I don't know how they live."

Samuel nodded. Who could imagine such a life, forever side by side with another? Where the line between where one began and the other ended disappeared halfway down? Or had never even existed?

Lefkowitz went on. "Finally, I began to recover my senses. But before I could think of what to say, they asked if they could come to the minyan." Lefkowitz's eyes, a faded gray that thirty years before might have been pale blue like the material now covering his legs, seemed to be pleading with Samuel, as if Lefkowitz were afraid he'd made some terrible mistake. "So I asked if they were Jewish."

"And?"

"They said yes. But I couldn't tell who was talking. One of them or both. It was like one voice coming from two people, or two voices speaking at once. Or maybe one was speaking and the other gesturing. I couldn't tell, it was so confusing."

Samuel put his hand over Lefkowitz's. More than anything, they all feared confusion: the tricks the mind played, the lapses that happened without them knowing. But who wouldn't have been confused, the two of them standing in a doorway chatting with poor Lefkowitz as if coming upon such a tenth were the most natural thing in the world?

"The walk back is a blur," Lefkowitz said. "I don't know how we got here." He waved his free hand aimlessly. "All through the davening I'm thinking: I never saw them walk, how did they walk, one pair of legs, two half bodies on top, two arms?" The hand came down, limp, onto his chest. "But they must have walked in front of me. They were holding the door when I got here."

Samuel pressed Lefkowitz's hand. "Maybe you kept your eyes down, Nathan. Maybe you looked away, not to make them feel like a pariah." Lefkowitz turned, shook his head. "When in your life did you ever stare at the misfit, the cripple, the crazy person?" Samuel insisted. "You were fed it with your mother's milk like the rest of us: Don't make a mockery of the stranger, a spectacle of the infirm."

Lefkowitz made a sad smile. "Paganism, that's what my father called it. The side shows at the circus, the veterans without legs that we looked at in the street." He paused, remembering. "By him, one look made it into a freak show, one glance and we were as bad as the barbarians who made midgets dance on tables. Always, we were one step away from idolatry."

"You're not losing your mind, Nathan. I'm telling you, you looked away. Wild horses couldn't have made you watch those two unfortunates."

AFTER POURING Lefkowitz another cup of juice and making him nibble on half a tuna sandwich that Samuel's wife, Ellie, had packed for lunch, Samuel put Lefkowitz in a cab with instructions not to even think about returning at dusk for *mincha*.

"We'll miss you but we'll manage. You have to rest," Samuel said at the door of the taxi. His disorientation, his near-faint, and, most distressing of all, his certainty that the fright he'd had was somehow his own doing, that he should not have engaged in conversation with the two young men: this, Samuel knew, was what Lefkowitz was thinking as the cab pulled away, Lefkowitz looking at him from the window, imploring, as the car melted into the traffic. Because at eighty-six one did not gloss over such disturbances of the ordinary. Nothing was chance.

Back inside, Samuel went into the sanctuary, the lights still on, the room just as he had left it when the service had concluded. He walked to the *bimah* at the front, climbed its single step, stacked up the prayer books scattered along the table next to the wooden ark holding the shul's two Torahs, picked up someone's gloves, a box of cough drops. He glanced around the room. Except for the makeshift ones he'd managed to pull together in the military—an unused supply tent in Korea, a store-room on an air force base on Cape Cod—this was the smallest shul he'd presided over, and the one he liked best. The whole place had a cluttered feel, a kind of intimate disorder he'd found himself craving after years of sterile spaciousness in his suburban posts. When the job came up, it made sense. They were moving to Brookline anyway, where Ellie had family and where they could tell themselves they were retiring so they would-n't have to think about retiring somewhere else.

He put the gloves and cough drops on a little table that looked like a castoff from someone's redecorated living room, edging the gloves up against a pile of loosely folded tallises. Extras, for guests. Had the visitors worn any? He didn't know. The topmost one slid to the floor, one of the slippery types, smallish, for bar mitzvah boys. He picked it up, folded it, the silky fringes slipping out of the neat square as soon as he placed it back on the pile. With no sexton to keep things in order things accumu-lated: unclaimed gloves, a menorah left standing until Pesach, more and more volumes scattered about. After a while he and Ellie would come in on a Sunday and spend the day putting away, organizing, dusting the bookcases in the study that had surely once been stately but, like every-thing else, were now chipped and marked, the shelves sagging.

He picked up a paper that had fallen between the lectern and the wall, a flyer for a lecture somewhere. *Kabbalah: Lessons for Today.* But he had no complaints, didn't need a custodian, new bookcases. That could wait for the next rabbi, if there were one. A young fellow, or maybe a girl nowa-days, straight from the seminary and hungry for a job, whose task it would be to revive the place, bring in young people, maybe the Russians who were filling out the neighborhood.

He nudged the lectern against the wall. Meanwhile, his congregants had no interest. The business of a Hebrew school, bulletin boards with colorful pictures of Queen Esther in the spring and Noah's Ark in the fall, fund-raisers and budget meetings and politics: who wanted that any-more? They'd had enough in their time. That's why they'd hired him, their last old rabbi: to run a quiet place, services three times a day, the latter two at dusk—one before dark, one immediately after—a little *drasha* in between if he had something to say, a page of text together if he didn't. It was as though all of them, himself included, had stumbled upon a pre-cious secret: that a dying shul, rather than being a depressing last gasp, the hollow-eyed harbinger of the disappearance of some little pocket of Jewish life the way it was so somberly and miserably described in the magazines and newspapers, was, actually, a rich reward. A place, even, of spiritual peace, where they could utter comforting and well-worn recitations without the distraction of worrying about the future. Any future.

He walked to the ark and carefully opened the doors. The Torahs, ancient sisters, rested side by side undisturbed. They had not been removed that morning, there had been no reading, but he had never relinquished the habit of checking. No one's eyesight was as good as it used to be, and the last thing anyone wanted was to be responsible for a Torah slipping out of its perch and landing on the floor, a sacrilege that carried with it the penance of a forty-day fast. Though he had never heard of such a thing being enforced.

He checked each Torah's footing, the ends of the spindles snug in their well-worn grooves. What if the visitors returned the next day when there was a reading? When the young man they'd hired to chant it came in? Avi, from Brandeis.

He ran his hand along the first one, over the faded brocade cover that looked like a nightgown worn by a newborn baby, the kind that slipped softly over the head and tied just below the feet. It had been a great relief to find at the shul not only one but two Torahs so dressed, the uncomplicated cloth a welcome relief from the silver-plated armor that had encased the Torahs in his more prosperous congregations, suits of mail that had made them not only terribly heavy to lift but like objects of war, things to be shielded and guarded against. As if the silver casings were meant not to protect the sacred scrolls from without, but to keep anyone from penetrating within.

He moved his hand to the second Torah, over the soft brown cloth that was probably velvet but had been worn so thin it was impossible to be sure. A baby's nightdress, yes, but also a shroud, for these were old men's Torahs, vessels draped the way they would all be draped in the end: in plain, worn cloth—their own tallises—with no need for fine jackets or ties or properly shined shoes.

Gently he closed the doors of the ark, stepped off the *bimah,* and walked along the rows of benches, three to a row, like park benches with wooden seats and straight backs, armrests on the ends. For these, too, he was grateful. He hated those long fixed pews, the ones with the pockets in front. Like church, they were to him, and a shul was not a church. The older he got, the less tolerant he was of such imitation. Predictably, like all old men, he was stretching himself backward in time, back to his childhood shul, cramped, dusty, books piled up in every corner like this one and where, next to his father, he had absorbed the rhythms of how and where and when to pray, if not necessarily always why. Praying became to him as involuntary as taking in air and letting it out, as much a part of him as talking, seeing, tasting. Eat. Sleep. Breathe. Pray.

He walked the rows, checking for fallen eyeglass cases, a stray wallet, a set of dropped keys. Slowly he walked, scanning, until he came to the third row, the last bench on the right, closest to the door. He stopped, looked on the floor, the seat, the arms.

This was the place reserved for guests, where that morning they had sat. He let himself down onto the bench and studied the seat as if a sign were about to appear, carved, in the wood. When had he noticed them? Unlike Lefkowitz, who had seen too much, he had had only a glimpse.

He looked up at the *bimah*. He hadn't seen them during the service, his back to the congregation as he hunched over the lectern. On days when there was no reading there was no need for him to turn around. Instead he would concentrate on the sounds behind him, focus on the contents of the eastern wall in front of him.

He squinted up at the wall's decorations. A pair of copper plates etched with shepherd scenes, a cheap painting of dancing Chasidim, an out-of-date poster of ruby-cheeked kibbutzniks happily loading bushes of oranges, an inset of Jerusalem bathed in a sentimental golden glow. He never really looked at these when he was davening, fixating instead on random details—the flying black coat of a Chasid, the garish glow of the Dome of the Rock—isolated images that would get themselves insinuated into his prayer. He stared at the oranges, bright, like crayons. He had looked at them all through the morning prayers. Now, from his place on the bench, it surprised him to see them inside their own picture, part of a whole scene, as if they had some other life to go home to when he wasn't up there with them.

He turned to the doorway. Could he have seen them before the service? When Lefkowitz disappeared from view on his way to the student apartments, he left the study window and began to put on his tefillin, as he did every morning, privately. It was his moment alone with the memory of his father, on whom he had first seen the black leather straps and little boxes containing—he'd believed then, a little boy of two or three—a piece of God. Each morning now he would try to dwell with his father, conjure his face, summon his voice, an expression, a few words; try to feel him, the looming presence he'd stood beside every morning of his early life, his father's huge tallis sweeping over him and sheltering him like a great white sail.

He turned back to the *bimah*. Before and during the service he had not yet seen them. But he had sensed them. Felt, at the start, hunching over the lectern, that someone was there. For a fleeting moment he'd thought it was his father. Then the sensation vanished, and he was alone.

He got up, walked back up the *bimah,* looked out into the row where he had just been sitting. It wasn't until the very end, then, when they'd finished singing *Adon Olam* and he'd turned around and begun the casual ritual of removing his tallis and unwinding his tefillin, that he finally saw them.

Saw them standing and smiling, dark hair, clean shaven, pale shirts, white maybe. They were looking straight at him, the backs of the benches in front of them only partially obscuring their lower half. In the next instant they were moving in perfect unison toward the door. And then, in a single, swift motion, a pivot, like a great bird preparing for flight, they were gone.

A horn blared outside, a trolley jangled its bell. A collision averted. He knew what he had to do.

He stepped off the *bimah,* strode out of the sanctuary. There were a hundred questions. Who were they? Why had they come there? Would they come back? But there were other questions, too, terrible questions, brutal questions he had not allowed himself to think before. How should they be counted? Were they one man, or two? The tenth, or a ninth as well? Were they even a man at all?

He stood before the bookcases in his study, questions parading across his brain like an occupying army and defying his desire to give a simple, compassionate response—of course they should count, of course they should participate, what does it matter!—rude guests that arrived unbidden, filing in one after another: Could they stand on the *bimah* for an honor? Could they come up to the Torah the next day and make a blessing? What if they traced themselves to the Cohanim, the priestly class who were permitted no deformities, whose descendants were bound by special rules?

And as for how many they were, did the soul of a man reside in his heart, of which each of these young men, thankfully, possessed his own, or the brain, of which, likewise, there were two?

Or was it instead at the site of his procreational and most primitive power, the locus of the covenant of Abraham, whose exquisite and excruciating bloodletting seal took place simultaneously to the bestowal of his name? A site at which these most blameless young men had been granted only a single shared strength.

Slowly he pulled out a thick text. He had no choice. If nothing else, he had learned in his seventy-six years that there was never a simple answer to anything, that even compassion was a layered thing. That a pair of Siamese twins were not necessarily two, or even one, when it came to counting in a minyan, or when it came to formulating any rules by which to live. And that their appearance that morning could not be passed over or forgotten, that it carried with it a host of deliberations, arguments, even fears, trailing it like a small but insistent wake.

THE TWINS were not in shul the next morning. Nor did anyone need to find a tenth, a full quorum having assembled outside Samuel's study well before starting time. No one mentioned the young men, asking instead after Lefkowitz, who hadn't made it in.

At seven sharp Samuel took his place at the lectern, told himself to call Lefkowitz after the service, opened his prayer book, and began. He stared at a dancing Chasid. Behind him the men murmured and chanted, loosely linked singing, a string of bells in a breeze.

He turned a page. A vague cloud hovered over him, something tugging at the back of his awareness. Disappointment. He was disappointed that the young men hadn't come back. Although he'd worried how Lefkowitz would take it, and about everyone's capacities for restraint, for the ability not to stare, he'd hoped they would return. He had done his homework and found enough to bring them fully into the ritual. They could count in the minyan as two, be given honors at the Torah, participate in all ways. He was going to welcome them, embrace them, fold them into their circle of old men who themselves were already moving toward the peripheries of life. What better place for such guests than among those for whom even the most extreme oddities hardly mattered anymore? Among them, they could be ordinary Jews, ordinary human beings, their strangeness lifted, removed.

Instead, that morning they had Avi, the Brandeis student, who'd brought a friend: Jeff? Josh? He couldn't remember. He closed his eyes to the Chasid, trying to concentrate. A sound rose up behind him; they were singing the *Sh'ma*. Recently he had estimated he'd said the *Sh'ma* ninety-six thousand times in his life, three services a day, once more at night before falling asleep, and countless times of fear when, in his fright, he called out God's name. Never, of course, would he expect an answer. Though lately he'd discovered in himself a shameful desire, a wish to have, just once, a glimmer. A sign.

He put his hand over his eyes and murmured. The disappointment cloud lowered itself over him, dragging on his shoulders like a cloak. Of course the strangers hadn't returned; he had been foolish to expect them. Just as he had been foolish to think he could somehow contain them by resolving his legalistic puzzles. He had sat in his study the day before proving to himself the compassion of the tradition, even with its dogged insistence on the law. What did it mean, he'd asked himself, a thick volume of Talmud open before him, that a two-headed man had appeared before Solomon asking to inherit doubly from his parents and that Solomon had ruled against him? That the man was decidedly one?

He had pulled from the bookshelves Rashi, Ibn Ezra, Maimonides, stacking the yellowed texts on his desk until he found an answer: The application of the law should amplify the store of good in the world. By declaring the two-headed man, driven by greed, to be one, Solomon reduced the sum of evil in the world; but declaring the visitors to be two, each to count in the minyan, doubled the store of good.

He found more. Three hours later, the afternoon sun diffuse and tired, he read in the crisp white pages of a looseleaf binder the painful modern precedent: a pair of mortally ill Siamese twin babies. Was it permissible to perform a surgical separation that meant certain death for one in order to give the other a chance for life? The answer was riddled with doubt but on one issue was certain: two lives, two persons. Then, a postscript. Despite heroic medical efforts, four weeks later, two burials.

Exhausted, he had closed the binder and called Ellie to pick him up, watched for her from the study window. Fifteen minutes later she drove up.

He gave her a light kiss on the cheek. She smiled, looking into the rearview mirror. What would he do without her?

"How was your day?" she said, watching the mirror.

More than ever, he wanted to tell her everything. About the visitors, Lefkowitz's fright, the terrible medical case. She was a compassionate listener, plus, a Talmudist's daughter, she had a fine mind, a first-rate education.

But he would refrain. In all his years, through half a dozen pulpits and hundreds of personal encounters, he had been scrupulous about guarding his tongue, vigilant for the dangers that came of too much talk. Even when the hearer was his most beloved wife.

"Fine," he said as she pulled out into the traffic. "And yours?"

She smiled, watched the road. "Okay. Thelma Greenspan called, they're back from Florida. I said we'd come by this evening."

He nodded. After so many years they both knew the rules. Respecting the boundaries was by then second nature. Though he never failed to remember that keeping a marriage alive under such conditions was no small thing.

BEHIND HIM it had become quiet. Avi and his friend were on the *bimah,* opening the doors of the ark. He stepped away from the lectern and positioned himself behind Avi, who took out a Torah and led them off the platform in a little procession.

The men reached into the aisle with their tallis fringes to touch the scroll. He'd been a fool the day before, poring over his books, contorting himself over precedents. Did he think the strangers had come to the shul to demonstrate the inclusiveness of the tradition? He had used the law thinking he was welcoming them but, really, he was trying to dismiss them. Dismiss their strangeness, their power.

They were winding around the back, passing Lefkowitz's customary seat. He glanced at the empty row, Lefkowitz's blue velvet tallis bag still on the bench from the day before.

Lefkowitz. Now he knew what Lefkowitz had been worried about. The shul had no sign out front, nothing to identify it but a faded Jewish star carved in the stone over the door, so worn it barely signaled anything. Set back from the street, indistinguishable from the rest of the block, it would hardly be noticeable to a stranger.

Then how was it those particular strangers seemed to know before Lefkowitz even spoke that he was from the synagogue up the street?

Of course: Lefkowitz had been thinking of Elijah. Elijah, who was said to come regularly down to earth to perform miracles. There had to be a thousand stories, a thousand tales. Elijah in the forest, Elijah on a train, Elijah as a beggar, a child, a woman, intervening to rescue from poverty, heal disease, arrange a marriage, avert a stillbirth.

And complete a minyan. If he wanted to look it up, go to the fancy computerized system at Brandeis and type in *Elijah,* and next to it *minyan,* he would get a hundred entries, five hundred entries. And why not? The imagination was unlimited and, as Ellie would say, so was the misery of the peasants in Europe who made all those stories up, the products of wishful and magical thinking, fodder for old men and little children. Not that it did those peasants a lot of good, she would add, Elijah's miracles miraculously absent in 1939.

He followed Avi down the middle aisle, past the third row and the empty bench by the door. The guests were absent, Lefkowitz was absent, even his father seemed absent. Putting on his tefillin in the study earlier, the men rustling just outside his door, he'd found it difficult to summon his father—his face, the color of his hair, whether he'd always worn eyeglasses—as if the sensation of the day before, his father in the sanctuary with him, had scared his father's spirit away. As if his father, like Lefkowitz, had had a shock and needed to rest.

The processional over, he took a seat in the first row while Avi continued up the step to where Bernie Freedman, a regular, at sixty-seven the baby of the shul, waited with Avi's friend. Gently they removed the Torah's cloth covering and slowly unrolled it to the right place, took their places by the table, and Avi began.

He closed his eyes, listened to the street sounds, the trolleys still intermittent. Unlike Ellie, he wasn't so sure. Who said Elijah was absent in 1939, hiding, as some claimed, like God? Who was to say that every one of those who lived wasn't a miracle? Life and death, poverty and riches; might there not be otherworldly guides to help conduct humanity back and forth between opposite worlds?

A cluster of birds had converged at the window as though to investigate Avi's chanting. He opened his eyes. A streak of color flew off a branch. Was it so outlandish? If Elijah could come to Bavaria, to Kraków, to Minsk, why not also to Brookline, among old men grateful for a quorum, not likely to flinch?

Avi's friend was taking a turn, his chanting surprisingly smooth for such a young man, as if he were seeing not words on the parchment but pictures. The sea, waves, clouds. Anyway, it didn't matter if he or Ellie or

Lefkowitz or anyone else believed whether such figures roamed the earth. You couldn't identify them and, even if you could, there was nothing you could do about it.

They stood. The Torah reading was over. Bernie Freedman held up the scroll for all to see then, with Avi's help, rolled it up, slipped on its faded dress. They opened the ark, placed it next to its silent companion, and closed the wooden doors.

Slowly Samuel walked up the single step for the concluding prayers. No, he knew what really lay behind Ellie's fierce refusal, her vigorous denial of such otherworldly possibilities. It was fear, raw fear. The same fear that had caused Lefkowitz to tremble and he himself to bore like a beetle into his dense books until his eyes burned. Terror at ever having to see unwittingly such figures at work, acknowledge the finger of God so close at hand.

THE SERVICE over, Samuel went out onto Beaconswood with the others, shook their hands, and waited for them to blend into the pedestrian traffic. Then he walked up the street to the student apartments. He stood in front of the redbrick building, a few scrawny blades of grass forcing themselves out of the little patch of dirt, competing with candy wrappers and Coke cans. What was he doing there? He looked at the glass door. He could try to open it but even if he succeeded, what would he do? Stand in the tiny vestibule on top of old newspapers and magazines, sandwiched between two doors, looking like a loiterer, a thief, someone coming to steal their packages and mail?

Packages and mail. The door opened easily and he stepped inside, a row of tarnished gold buttons on the wall. Evans. Iannino. Winter. Katz. What was he looking for, two names written side by side broadcasting the presence of Jewish Siamese twins? Steven-Stuart Schwartz? Was he crazy?

A noise, a knob rattling: the inside door opened with a whine. A girl with a backpack, Miss Evans or Miss Iannino, thinking he was a Peeping Tom, an intruder, a pervert, who'd call the police and have him arrested immediately.

"Need some help getting in?" She was holding the door open for him, smiling. Reckless girl, letting him in like that. He could be a criminal or, at the very least, a suspicious-looking old man with a beard. Clean shaven all his life, recently he'd grown an unruly feathery sort of thing that Ellie said made him look wild eyed, like the aging Albert Einstein, or Heschel. Now a sweet-looking girl was letting him in as if he were some legitimate resident who simply had forgotten his key.

In a second she was out the door and he was inside, in a drafty-looking stairway, the building hushed, as though asleep. He squinted at the name by the door nearest him, NESTOR, J., typed in the little slot over the buzzer. What did he think he would learn at these doorways at eight o'clock on a Thursday morning?

The door opposite Nestor, J., opened. He turned, waiting to be scrutinized, evicted. Instead, a young man, twenty, twenty-one, softly closed the door behind him and smiled. Sweatshirt, jeans, sunglasses in his hand, he was heading for the front door and the street.

"Excuse me," Samuel said, and heard his voice echoing loud in the foyer. "I'm looking for someone, maybe you can help me? Twins, they were here yesterday."

The young man thought for a second and shook his head. "Don't think so. You're sure they live here?"

"I don't know, just that someone met them here, walked with them down the street."

The young man paused, pointed with his sunglasses to the stairs. "A couple of brothers live on the second floor, maybe it was them. They look kind of alike." He shrugged. "That's all I can think of. Good luck." He put on the glasses and was out the door.

Samuel stood alone in the hall. Of course they didn't live there; otherwise the young man would have noticed. And if they were visiting, he would have to interview everyone in the building. And then what? Explain why he was looking for them?

Why was he?

The outer door opened and a man tossed a stack of newspapers into the vestibule. He had to leave, he didn't belong there. He pulled open the heavy doors and went out onto the walk.

The street had come to life, the air like a newly opened box of ladies' dusting powder. He looked all the way down Beaconswood, the trolleys out in full force, young people with backpacks and light jackets waiting at the stop. The whole city, the whole world, it seemed, had awakened to a fresh new day while he had been inside looking for—what? Was he an old man whose grip on reality was slipping?

He walked up the path to the sidewalk, trying to take in the freshness, a scent maybe of flowers somewhere, then abruptly turned and looked back at the student apartments.

The doorway. There was something wrong with it. It was the doorway from which Lefkowitz said they had stepped just as he'd walked up. It was too narrow, a railing on either side, barely wide enough for one. And it was shallow, not deep enough to hold anyone comfortably for more than half a minute. Even he, a small man, would have had a hard time balancing himself on the little step, feeling himself tipping forward, the door urging him from behind. It didn't seem possible they would have been standing in the doorway, waiting. Could they have waited outside?

He stared at the glass. Why would they be waiting at all? Waiting for what?

Lefkowitz. Lefkowitz! He had forgotten to call! Lefkowitz, who the day before had had the fright of his life. Where was Lefkowitz? He had never missed a day at shul without calling, without making sure someone knew where to go for the tenth man. Samuel had told him to stay home for *mincha* last evening but not for the morning service today. It had to mean only one thing. That Lefkowitz was sick, or dying.

And that they were not Elijah at all but the Angel of Death, who had come for the one person who was certain to appear on that day, in that time, in that place. Lefkowitz. Was it so impossible? Who was to say? Who knew except the dead, and the dead never talked to the living. Only the living talked to the dead, and got no answers. Or so he had thought.

He turned and hurried down Beaconswood. If it was a beautiful day, which it was, he must not take the time to notice. If the birds were out in record number, as they seemed to be, and if it looked as though the bluest sky and the softest air had settled, finally, around him, he mustn't stop to appreciate it. Neither the strange young men nor Lefkowitz had returned to the shul that morning, and such unexplained coincidence, such disturbance, such a sign, must be registered and not forgotten or overlooked or sidetracked, regardless of the weather. Or life.

He pulled open the door of the shul, got to his study, fumbled with the desk phone. Shaky, he found Lefkowitz's number on a sheet in the top drawer and dialed, listened to three rings, four, five, then began mumbling the *Sh'ma*. If Lefkowitz didn't answer, he would call Bernie Freedman, who still worked, went to an office where someone would have to answer the phone. After that he would call Ellie, wait for her outside, and watch for her in the humming spring air he would force himself to ignore.

EUGENE SELTZ was born in Siberia, where he studied applied mathematics in Tomsk. He later studied poetry writing at the Gorky Institute in Moscow, and emigrated to Israel in 1991. Two books of his poetry have been published (one in Russia, one in Israel); a collection of his short stories, *Compelle Intrare,* is forthcoming in Israel. Two other stories from the same collection have appeared in *Kontrapunkt,* a Russian-language literary journal based in Boston. "Compelle Intrare," the collection's title story, is Seltz's first story to appear in English.

DANIEL M. JAFFE has translated numerous Russian short stories and essays as well as the Russian-Israeli novel *Here Comes the Messiah!* by Dina Rubina (Zephyr Press, 2000). In 1999, he received a Massachusetts Cultural Council Professional Development Grant in support of his literary translation work.

Compelle Intrare

Eugene Seltz

Translated from the Russian by Daniel M. Jaffe

There exist, down here, realities which seemingly incline to the unknown, through which egress from thought seems possible, and toward which speculation streams. Conjecture has its compelle intrare *('compulsion to enter,' Latin). If one passes certain places and before certain objects, one cannot do otherwise than to stop as prey to dreams, and to permit one's spirit to advance in that direction. None could avoid encountering this deceased without meditating.*

VICTOR HUGO, *The Man Who Laughs*

SANDOR KOGAN WAS ONCE a soldier. And a good soldier at that. Although he didn't serve in the crack troops unit (a trifle interfered—no driver's license), he took part in local wars and proved himself to be a great soldier overall. Right up to that awful wounding.

Sandor had been born in the small provincial town of Atlit on the Mediterranean seashore. His entire childhood was spent at the foot of a Crusaders' fortress, a structure that was the only reason for Sandor's small town to be included on all the country's tourist maps. Here he grew up amid the cruel games of peers, here he learned to be friends with and be at loggerheads with them, here he first noticed certain oddities in himself. More accurately, his childhood friends pointed out these oddities to him, and then his parents did as well. The oddities manifested themselves as intense moments of concentration resembling dumbfounded confusion. This concentration would suddenly take possession of the boy while he was looking at something that moved. Any movement—be it an ocean wave, a bonfire flame, or the countryside flying by through a car window—would bring Sandor to a state of prostration from which he could not easily extricate himself. Through his stare, he'd somehow become so absorbed into the movement that he'd completely renounce the outer world. His eyes would be wide open, his breathing suppressed. He wouldn't be paying attention to outside sounds, wouldn't hear when hailed by name. He would only keep staring.

When this eccentricity became the basis for ridicule by his school chums, Sandor began, with courageous persistence, to fight it. And he won.

True, when he turned eighteen, he was positively unable to pass the driver's licensing exam, although he made a host of desperate attempts. The examiners' verdict was severe: diffuseness of attention. Sandor Kogan didn't even suspect back then that within this paradoxical formulation (could attention really be diffuse?) lay his entire fate—not so much his life, actually, as his death.

THE FIRST Tuesday of December 1993 on a beach in the wilds not far from Caesarea, the corpse of a young girl was discovered. She was lying on the sand, pressing a cold palm to her chest. Her clothing—jeans and a white woolen sweater—were clean, actually pressed. The policeman, leaning over the girl's body, was frightened to discover that her hair smelled of delicate perfume.

Hearing about yet another corpse, Investigator Z. realized that he'd lost. Definitively and irrevocably. This was the sixth such death in the past three and a half months. All six victims had been found not far from the sea, all six were young people, former or current university students. And that was all that linked them. They hadn't known each other, had no common acquaintances, lived in different cities. Their paths had never crossed. All this had been proven during the investigation. Four young men and two young women perished by the sea, in foul weather, for an unknown, and consequently, mysterious reason.

SANDOR'S PARENTS had repatriated to the Holy Land from Hungary at the end of the 1950s, leaving behind a large house in the country near Kaposvár. His father was in love with fishing. In Hungary he'd go to Lake Balaton every Sunday. After moving to Israel, the family settled by the sea. Father insisted on this—he regarded the moist sea air as beneficial to the health. He suffered from asthma and frequent bouts of nostalgia. It was during one such bout that Sandor was born. Otherwise he'd have had a completely different first name, one more in keeping with his primal Jewish surname.

All the same, Sandor Kogan was a good soldier. And he would have become a good officer if not for that idiotic bullet.

INVESTIGATOR Z. felt that he was coming down with something. Many are familiar with that loathsome state when you know an illness is setting in, yet you can't stave it off. It inexorably conquers your entire system, cell by cell, despite your heroic resistance. Sort of a light rehearsal for death.

Z. felt his thoughts about this case becoming too obsessive, but he just could not withstand them. They surrounded his brain as if it were an enemy fortress, and they were beginning preparations to storm it.

Ach, if only these six instances had resembled murder even just a little. For here lay the precise source of the investigator's defeat—in the fact that all six had died a natural death. Not a single trace of force had been discovered on their bodies, not the least little scratch. Their former lives had been ordinary to the point of banality, resembling hundreds of thousands of others. They consisted of a succession of well-known amusements natural to young people, amusements that were a melding of equal parts pleasure and death defiance.

THE BULLET was indeed idiotic. It happened in the middle of Gaza during the breaking up of a Palestinian demonstration. Back then Sandor commanded a division of ten soldiers. They'd been transferred to Gaza from the West Bank.

By that time his second year of army service was coming to an end. For such an experienced warrior, the breaking up of a demonstration was a routine operation, involving the clear-cut sequence of two or three well-rehearsed military measures. A megaphone, an armored troop carrier with a water cannon on top, Plexiglas shields for protection against rocks, several tear-gas grenades—and the demonstration is dispersed. And so it was this time, too. The Palestinians ran off in various directions. The soldiers, huddled up in the armored troop carrier, started smoking. A respite was at hand. At that moment a shot rang out.

As would later become clear, a thirteen-year-old lad had done the firing. He was sitting on the roof of a mosque with a homemade low-caliber rifle. He had only one cartridge (also homemade, by the way). And that cartridge was a fateful one.

The bullet entered the left temple, exited the right. Senior Sergeant Sandor Kogan's head was shot right through.

EACH OF THE six corpses had been identified fairly quickly. The public began to grumble. The press raised a ruckus. After these deaths had formed a pattern, the newspapers literally lay siege to the police station where the investigative group worked. Z. took up the habit of locking himself in the toilet away from the journalists and sitting there for hours on end. "I've got a strong butt. It doesn't care what it sits on," he said.

The siege ended only when one of the dear little yellow news rags published an interview with the scandalously famous astrologist and clairvoyant Zevi Brunstein. The charlatan announced that a terrible new epidemic was spreading and that the above-mentioned sixth death was only the first warning bell. "A horrid disease," preached the oracle. "It's sparked by microbes that make their way to earth from the cosmos by penetrating holes in the ozone layer. Its consequences will be catastrophic. They'll surpass the consequences of AIDS many times over."

After that sensation, the journalists switched to scientists and doctors, leaving the police in peace.

SANDOR KOGAN survived. Half a year in a clinic, seven extremely complicated neurosurgeries, and his left eye was a thing of the past.

Sandor accustomed himself rather quickly to his one-eyed state. Where his irrevocably lost left eye had been, they inserted a glass prosthesis so fine that recognition of his maiming was difficult even under those circumstances when a fellow conversationalist would stare him straight in the eye.

After leaving the hospital and registering his disability status, Sandor declined his father's suggestion to return to Atlit, and he rented a small studio in the settlement of Orot—four kilometers from Caesarea. Here, one might say, he withdrew, leading the life of either a hermit or outcast.

His military pension was quite sufficient. Sandor spent the first half of each day at the beach, which he reached by bike; and the second—sitting at home by the window and staring intently at either clouds or the occasional car passing along the highway.

PATHOLOGISTS WHO were used to just about anything became lost in conjecture. The postmortems revealed that two of the youths had died from ruptured spleens. What's more, there were absolutely no indications of what had caused the ruptures. The remaining young people had been stricken by totally unprovoked ruptures of the heart muscle.

"Of course this is idiocy," Professor Plotkin said to Investigator Z., "but it all gives the impression of someone having climbed inside the heart and having burst it from within."

"Who?" asked the investigator, understanding full well the foolishness of his question.

"Cut it out! If I knew who, I'd have received the Nobel Prize by now."

SANDOR GAVE himself over once more to intense contemplation, to his old childhood eccentricity, at which no one dared laugh anymore. Well, there was no one to do the laughing. Sandor didn't share his private vice with anybody. When his glance encountered a moving object, he seemed to penetrate its fundamental secret, the very essence of its movement, its primary impulse. Sandor not only saw the very nature of this expression of life, but he clearly grasped why it was taking place. And this imparted to his gaze a certain power, one of elastic vitality: he realized that whoever knew the cause was the absolute sovereign of the effect. It seemed to him that his healthy eye was doing the work of two—of itself and its murdered colleague. He regarded his vision's flow as a hot beam (crimson with lackluster gold veins) of destructive force, which was merely lying in wait for a predesignated command, cipher, or key in order to begin functioning.

Sandor didn't go out of his way to limit communication with people. Nevertheless, his inactive outer life did not offer him the opportunity to find true friends, stable ties, pleasant camaraderie. Besides, more and more frequently he'd catch his fellow conversationalists paying guardedly alarmed attention to him. At first this didn't bother him, but then he realized that he'd have begun to "diffuse his attention" even during a conversation; that is, even in front of witnesses, this impolite concentration would sometimes take possession of him. As a result, Sandor gradually reduced all his acquaintanceships to rare, almost accidental encounters, and so as not to be severely oppressed by loneliness, he got a cat.

"ONLY ONE thing links these six: they all died from an unknown cause." Investigator Z. had long tired of racking his brains over this mystical problem and was trying to bid it farewell forever, arguing with himself for the nth time that it was irresoluble. "All were healthy. Ages—from twenty to twenty-three. Four men and two women. All found not far from the sea. Each went there alone, without friends, and died there at night, without witnesses. No traces of any kind. Sixty-seven people were interrogated, twelve of them were brought into the case as suspects. But all turned out to have ironclad alibis. You couldn't bring charges anyway—nobody had been murdered, right? Maybe all died out of spite! They simply went to the beach at night and croaked, as if just to frustrate a senior police investigator! *Ach,* it's time to wind up this nonsense! Whatever, the higher authorities won't let me open a criminal case: the expert examination failed to support the elements of murder.

"Yet there's some sort of devil-making here! Six healthy young people die from ruptured spleens or heart attacks by the seashore. In foul weather. On various beaches. They show up when the shore's emptiest, like zombies. They show up properly dressed, like they know they have to go there in order to die.

"Hypnosis? I don't really believe in it. Unknown narcotics? Doubtful. A sect? Nonsense. Those young people had outgrown their knickers already.

"Then what? To hell with this job!"

WHENEVER SANDOR Kogan fell into his private state, both his eyes became similarly glassy. From the side it was a rather terrifying spectacle. But few saw Sandor Kogan from the side.

One evening he was sitting at the window and reading a book by lamplight. It was just after ten o'clock. His right eye was working well. He'd managed to grasp several paragraphs immediately, and simultaneously to see all that was happening beyond the limits of the page. A light breeze fluttered the curtain. The cat lay on the windowsill. Her soft fur fluttered as well. The cat's name was Ness. She was obsessively tidy and preened her thick coat to a mirrorlike sheen. Sandor had acquired Ness from a neighbor, who asserted that her mama had been a pure-blooded Persian. The cat's identical gray eyes proved the exact opposite. But it was all the same to Sandor.

The fluttering of the yellowish white fur forced the owner to tear himself away from his reading. He ran a hand across his eyes, shook his head, and started looking at the cat. A minute later he was looking at her without blinking. His living eye gradually filled with a glassy sheen. A wave of hot energy flowed over his brain.

He unexpectedly remembered Gaza, remembered his soldier friends, the armored troop carrier's dusty surface. The Palestinian boy's bloodied corpse swiftly rose into consciousness—the photograph they'd shown him in the hospital. "He's the one who shot you," the commander said back then. "He won't be recovering, but you—come on, get well!"

"YOU'VE GOT a visitor," the duty officer said as Z. was getting ready to go home.

A tall, tanned young man walked into the office. His face was tense, his movements fitful. He was clearly agitated.

"I saw her," he said from the doorway, jabbing a finger at the photograph of the girl found day before yesterday on the beach. "I saw her several months . . . half a year . . . before . . . her death . . . I looked at her—and then . . . she died . . . I'm the one guilty of everything . . . And those young guys, too . . . I probably looked at them, too . . . in the summer . . . or spring . . . I can't remember . . . It's all my doing! . . . You understand or not? It's my doing . . ."

THEN SANDOR saw the shooting. Yes, he saw the bullet leave the shotgun's rusty barrel, saw it cut through the thick air, saw it approach, slowly rotating around a horizontal axis, saw it softly enter his—Sandor's—left temple. . . . The vision was so real that Sandor felt a sharp pain in his head.

He came to and looked at his watch. Just after ten. Sandor had spent no more than a few seconds in his stupor.

Ness was dozing, not paying her owner the least little attention.

"YOU UNDERSTAND, it's some mystical thing. The guy's gone completely nuts." Investigator Z. was sitting in a café with Professor Plotkin. It was Friday—two old friends having their usual get-together.

"That girl who died a month ago—he saw her in the summer on the beach at Caesarea," Z. continued. "And he says he's the one killed her. So I ask: 'How? Exactly how did you kill her?' And he answers: 'I couldn't stop staring at her while she played beach ball.' I say: 'So, and?' He starts fussing, sobbing, and talking all kinds of gibberish about some cat with gray eyes, about Gaza, a Palestinian boy . . . You know, I felt right away this guy wasn't in his right mind. He's probably read too many reports from *Criminal Files* . . . I hate journalists."

"And you're certain he's totally uninvolved."

"I checked it out. He doesn't know the victims' names or where they lived; he knows literally nothing about them. And their friends and relatives don't recognize him as even the faintest, most casual of acquaintances. In short, after an absurd half-hour conversation, I recommended he see a doctor."

"You're too crude. Although for a policeman that's more a virtue than a failing. And it didn't enter your head to explore his past?"

"Sure it did . . . I'm not as dense as you think. He lives in Orot, rents a large apartment there in one of the old buildings. Doesn't work anywhere . . . receives a disability pension. Wounded during the Intifada. In the head, if you ask me. It all comes to the same thing. He's simply insane. I say to him: 'So okay, you can't tell *how* you killed them. Then explain to me *why* you killed them?' And he wrings his hands and cries, 'Oh, if only I knew why!' No two ways about it, he's insane."

IT HAPPENED to him for the first time. For the first time he saw something real in his daydreams. And that reality horrified him. But not because of the cruel and godless form it took, not at all—but because of its substance. Formerly, he would remember his army service with pleasure. It was as if there were nothing else for him to remember. The army was the only period in his life stuffed with notable events, like a featherbed's down. But this time he suddenly felt that the soft, warm featherbed had turned into a coarse straw mattress. For Sandor Kogan, the bloodied face of the Palestinian boy—his ill-fated killer—became a black symbol, a symbol of death.

"WHAT IS IT with your habit of oversimplifying!" Plotkin ordered another bottle of beer. "That's not to say that maybe he's really insane. There's still so much of the unexplainable in human nature that in your place I wouldn't have jumped to conclusions.

"Just listen, I have a story: At the end of December nineteen sixty-seven in Krasnoyarsk back in Siberia, there was an unfortunate incident. A Zaporozhets sedan was following along an ice-covered local road when the brakes went, and it smashed into a truck heading in the opposite direction. The tragic thing was that the truck was hauling a huge fir tree to be set up in the town's main square. The stump and middle part of the tree lay in the truck's long flatbed, but the top stuck several meters out the back.

"As a result of the collision, the tree practically split the Zaporozhets in two. The windshield, the driver (a fat middle-aged guy), the front and backseats were strung onto the ice-covered coniferous axis like beads onto a thread.

"The military hospital where I used to work wasn't far from there. I was a surgeon with the highest qualifications, by the way, but not a pathologist. Anyway, that's not important. The truck driver called for help, we arrived at the site, we moaned and gasped and then sawed the tree from both sides and carried the poor guy—a knotty tree stump in his chest—right off into surgery.

"And four months later he left for work. The newspapers wrote up this unique operation in great detail. I was the hero of the day. Although I still can't understand how the top of that fir, with a diameter of about ten centimeters if not more, didn't cause any serious injuries to the guy's internal organs. Just a punctured lung, a rib fracture—mere trifles."

Two WEEKS later the cat suddenly disappeared. Sandor searched the entire district, questioned all his neighbors, combed neighboring fields and construction sites—all in vain.

Ness showed up one overcast November morning on the deserted beach where Sandor was in the habit of whiling away his lonely hours, staring at steam from the chimneys of an electric power plant.

The cat lay in the sand. Her formerly clean yellowish white fir stirred with every puff of wind. The identical gray eyes stared fixedly at the sea. Ness was dead.

Sandor carried the stiffened little body home and buried it at one of the construction sites during the night. Had someone else been in his place, he'd definitely have paid attention to the fact that dead Ness was extraordinarily clean and tidy, as if before dying, she'd gone to a kitty hairdresser. Someone else would definitely have posed the question:

What did she die of? And would definitely not have found an acceptable answer.

But that's—someone else. Sandor, on the contrary, regarded Ness's death as fitting. He already knew the cause of her death. He had already resigned himself to the discovery that shook the depths of his soul, he already realized that it was the vision, that same terrible vision from his past life, that turned out to be the very command, cipher, or key to the emanation of energy from his single eye.

He forced himself not to think about the war, not to remember Gaza. But the memory would slip out from under his control. The vision would fall upon him suddenly, would catch his fevered brain unawares. It sometimes happened while he was looking at the sea, sometimes while he was observing people on the beach. He knew this would all end badly. He tried shutting his healthy eye, wore thick dark glasses, forced himself to look only at books. Nothing helped. At the moment of sudden concentration his entire body would freeze up. He'd be unable to stir and, like a condemned man, would watch the nightmare through to the end. The same terrifying nightmare every time, the only one he had, the one he knew down to its smallest detail.

Finally, reading in the newspaper about the deaths of the girl and the five others, Sandor went to the police.

"BUT THAT's not the most important thing," Professor Plotkin continued. "This man, formerly a supplier or warehouse manager, abandoned his job after the operation and a few years later became the most famous soothsayer and clairvoyant in the country. At that time this kind of activity wasn't particularly encouraged, but everybody knew about his miraculous abilities. Every single day an incredibly long line formed at his apartment. They wrote to him from all corners of the incredibly huge empire. And then a few years later he died. Called his wife one evening and told her that he'd die the next day at noon. That's exactly what happened."

"No way," said Z. "It's all mysticism. And believe you me, I've seen crazies in my day. . . . This guy who burst in on me day before yesterday was one of them for sure. At first he got all excited, waved his arms around, gushed with spit, and then when I suggested he go to a doctor, he suddenly shut up. He gave me a fixed stare like he was burning his look right through me, then he flinched, softened up somehow, and asked, 'So you think it's worth going to a doctor?' I said I was absolutely certain. 'Well, okay. I'll give it a try.' And with those words he went away as quiet as could be. . . . You're telling me he's not insane?"

"Possibly. Possibly," the professor muttered and asked the waiter for the bill.

THEY PUT Sandor in a psychiatric clinic. In one of the best—as a disabled veteran.

He spent more than a year there, behaved peacefully, lived in a private room, didn't go out anywhere, only read books and listened to the radio.

He died several months after Investigator Z. took his well-deserved retirement. However, the latter didn't know about all this, since he left to live abroad with his younger daughter.

Sandor Kogan died from an extensive brain hemorrhage. The nurse on call summoned the doctor at two o'clock in the morning. Sandor lay in his bed, carefully covered with a regulation sheet. He lay straight, quietly at attention like a true soldier. His face was turned to the room's yellowish white ceiling. The corners of his lips were slightly opened in a strange smile. His healthy right eye was tightly closed, almost screwed up. But the left, on the contrary, was wide open and gleamed with a cold glassy sheen. Light from the desk lamp, refracted in the dead pupil, reflected a formless yellow patch on the ceiling.

"I don't understand at all," said the treating physician. "Physically, he was completely healthy. His pressure was fine, his heart strong, all indicators were normal. Could it just be the wound? . . . No, it couldn't be! . . . Strike me dead, I can't understand it!"

After they removed the deceased, the doctor discovered under the pillow a book by the Belgian mystic Claude Bouaille. It was called *Inscrutable Paths*. A photograph served as a bookmark—it depicted a bloodied youth lying on dusty asphalt beside the large wheel of some sort of military vehicle. The doctor opened the book and read: "Russian Field Marshal Kutuzov, while still a young officer, received a terrible wound in one of his battles. A bullet, shot from a musket, pierced through his head—from temple to temple. But Providence wished Kutuzov to remain alive and initiate the downfall of Napoleon Bonaparte. As is well known, Kutuzov died in Poland in 1813, and so did not wait for the triumphant conquest of Paris by Russian forces. However, he fulfilled his mission to the last.

"A fine literary example of this same phenomenon was demonstrated by the Latin American writer Gabriel García Márquez in the novel *One Hundred Years of Solitude*. Colonel Aureliano Buendía shot himself in the heart and remained intact and unharmed. The bullet passed through his body without causing the suicide the least little harm.

"The human body contains several safe pathways through which any foreign object may pass without obstacle, not causing any damage whatsoever. These pathways, per the will of Providence, sometimes change their configuration so as to preserve a person from unavoidable, it would seem, death.

"But Providence acts selectively. It preserves from death only those who, as a consequence, become its true instrument. And then not for long. When the instrument goes out of commission, it self-destructs."

Two WEEKS before his death Sandor requested that a mirror be brought into the room.

"It's too long since I've seen myself," he told the doctor. "I hope that's not contraindicated?"

GLORIA DEVIDAS KIRCHHEIMER's fiction has appeared in numerous literary journals as well as in several anthologies: *The Tribe of Dina* (Beacon Press), *Shaking Eve's Tree* (Jewish Publication Society), *Follow My Footprints: Changing Images of Women in American Jewish Fiction,* and *Sephardic-American Voices: Two Hundred Years of a Literary Legacy* (both University Press of New England). Under the name Gloria Levy, she made one of the earliest recordings of Sephardic folk songs in the United States for Folkways/Smithsonian. She is coauthor (with Manfred Kirchheimer) of *We Were So Beloved: Autobiography of a German Jewish Community* (University of Pittsburgh Press). She is the recipient of a Fulbright Scholarship and of the Elias Canetti Prize for Fiction in the 1998 National Sephardi Literary Contest. "A Case of Dementia" is taken from her recently published short-story collection, *Goodbye, Evil Eye* (Holmes & Meier).

A Case of Dementia

GLORIA DEVIDAS KIRCHHEIMER

My father, who is not given to introspection except about his pension plan, came to believe that my mother was having a breakdown.

How did he reach this conclusion? His prior experiences with breakdowns were mechanically or municipally related: toasters, subways, the work ethic of civil servants. Within his category of mental aberrations, disrespect for one's parents or husband ranked high.

He whispered over the telephone and I had to strain to hear. Mother had been "hysterical." She had called him names: "tyrant," "dictator," "monster."

In a household where contrariness on the part of its females was regarded as a sign of grippe (the culprit was offered a glass of water and made to lie down), outright criticism was unthinkable. I feared for my father's sanity; Mother was on the road to health. With delight I pictured the scene. Mother brandishing a pot in which she had cooked thousands of delicacies for him, or waving a slipper or—most appalling—rending her clothes after the fashion of her Egyptian countrywomen.

She used to tell me stories about the Arab quarter, the bazaar, the harems, the Arabic girls who taught her to put kohl on her eyes and henna in her hair and amulets around her neck. She swore to me that she had given up her Egyptian ways the moment she touched Ellis Island. But I wondered. Her eyes were so large, so dark. She could play the tambourine and gyrate demurely in a rudimentary belly dance.

And now forty years of submission to my father had finally erupted, accelerated by his retirement. A man who had commanded a large staff on three continents was now reduced to questioning my mother on the wisdom of refrigerating a grapefruit and interrogating her about every telephone call she made or received. To a person accustomed to having his employees toe the line, the sight of Mother leaving him in the middle of the day to attend a meeting of the charitable organization of which she was president constituted dereliction of duty.

I asked if I might speak to her. I wanted to congratulate her. For her benefit he said heartily, "Everything is fine, fine." Then again in a whisper, "Don't say anything." Then, "Honey, it's your beloved daughter," a curiously archaic mode of referring to me.

"Leave me alone." I heard Mother's voice in the background. "Leave me in peace."

"Everything is under control," my father said loudly. Then, *"Ne dis rien,"* as though along with her reason, she had also lost one of her mother tongues.

To me Mother said, "Is this a life?"

Ignoring the question, I said it was all to the good that she had finally exploded.

"I'm sick. It was terrible."

"Yes, but—"

"I was tearing my hair," she added, as if to convince me of her dementia. She had in fact said to me recently and quite cheerfully that I must not be surprised if she should go berserk. "Berserk," she had repeated, relishing this exotic word that she knew only from newspaper accounts about seemingly normal persons like herself. "This is Alcatraz," she said, perhaps confusing the George Washington Bridge, which she could see from her window, with the Golden Gate. Earlier she had prepared a six-course meal for my father, with instructions, before leaving for a meeting. He had accused her of abandoning him and threatened to go on his own to the old-age home. "I prepare everything for him. Hand and foot . . . Is this the thanks? No, I don't want coffee now—" He must have made her some, a peace offering. "Half a cup then. Hmmm. Not bad. So how are you?" she asked me. "You're lucky. You can come and go as you please. Women's lib."

"Women's lib," Father echoed gaily over the extension phone. "Didn't I just make her a cup of coffee?"

"FOR BETTER, for worse, and this is worse," he complained when next I phoned. "Of course I didn't say anything, I didn't want to upset her. Monday a meeting, Tuesday a benefit, Wednesday a luncheon—"

What energy, I thought, picturing Mother in her rakish felt hat, those great dark eyes, the snappy leather briefcase.

"What would public opinion say? A wife who leaves home every day. I ask you, is this natural? She is so high strung. What should I do?" And lest I think he was actually consulting me, he said, "I will speak to the rabbi."

Ah, not that. An unctuous, platitudinous man whose yeshiva was Madison Avenue. But so great was my father's reverence for "the office" that it did not matter what kind of person filled it as long as he displayed the appurtenances. I pictured Claude Rains, *The Invisible Man,* playing the part, skullcap bobbing merrily, prayer shawl sweeping the furniture. Respect for the office was what mattered to my father. Thus, when President Nixon was forced to resign, my father felt sorry for him. After all, he was

The President. The only office exempt from respect was that of Labor Leader, for to my father it was synonymous with Racketeer, his memory still fresh from the unionization of his clerical staff. This rabbi had already proven himself a keen judge of the human heart by recommending a Caribbean cruise to an insurance agent whose wife's derangement was clearly manifested in her refusal to prepare a box lunch for him every day.

How was mental illness treated in the Old Country, in Turkey, Greece, Egypt? The afflicted person was said to have had the evil eye cast upon him or her. By having a special incantation performed, the person lost the hex and was cured. The incantation, in Hebrew and Ladino, was first a recitation of all the victim's maternal forebears, followed by a heavily symbolic story about the prophet Eliahu. The person administering the spell must always be a female. It must be learned not through instruction but through eavesdropping while it is being performed. If the woman reciting it begins to yawn uncontrollably, the spell is working. During my childhood it had been performed with great efficacy by my mother as an all-purpose cure, equally good for melancholia and viral infections, though over the years it had gradually been replaced by penicillin.

One day I discovered, tucked into the drawer where I kept my tennis socks, a gaudy glass bead that I recognized as the charm against the evil eye. It was crudely painted with concentric circles, in the middle of which was a blue dot, presumably the iris, rimmed in (bloodshot) red, the whole resembling a bulging eye suffering from glaucoma. Designed to outstare the evil eye, it had been hidden there for my protection by my mother.

To MY FATHER'S great relief, the rabbi renders the verdict that my mother is suffering from overwork and needs to curtail her activities outside the home. "Psychiatry, shmuckiatry," my father says. "A racket. They make money so families can split up. Look at the divorce rate."

I look and wonder how my parents have stayed together for so long. Was she ever truly happy? Was he ever different? Always the despot, benevolent but always contemptuous of any ambition she might have entertained (though he boasted of her capabilities behind her back). A woman who might have gone to college or held an important position. Now she administers thousands of dollars, supervises dozens of volunteers, a woman who writes and edits reports, deals with printers, rabbis, caterers, immigrants, and bureaucrats. Why has it taken her so long to revolt?

"Everything is under control," he says in the middle of our phone conversation, signaling my mother's arrival home. "How's the weather there?" as though I were in Palm Beach instead of three miles downtown. "Darling, I was just saying that your daughter is almost as pretty as you." He laughs that nasty laugh I've heard so often.

"This is not a life," she says to me, answering her own question from an earlier conversation. "You know your mother is nothing but a vegetable? Come for dinner or I won't be responsible. . . ."

No help for it. I leave my office early and rush uptown to pay my call on the unhinged woman.

A barefoot female opens the door and greets me by singing a song in Italian. Not Hello, glad to see you, but instead a song about a sprig of violets plucked from a mountainside, sung in a strained alto—she has never reconciled herself to being a soprano manquée. She is braless and disheveled, her slip hangs down below a crooked hem. She sashays across the room, ending her song, and with scarcely a pause for breath starts reciting a long poem in French about a noble wolf. On the table there is food for ten though we are only three tonight. One never knows who will drop in, and truth to say, in the old days people were always dropping in and staying. "Is this my daughter?" she asks after ending her poem, upon which my father gives me a meaningful look.

A loud street noise startles us and Mother quickly licks her index finger and touches her throat three times, uttering a few expletives in Arabic.

"Isn't she cute," Father says to me with an agonized smile.

Mother points to him. "Dr. Jekyll and Mr. Hyde."

I am very relieved. There is nothing untoward in her behavior. She is quite herself. "How like yourself you are," I say, quoting Strindberg to her.

"I knew you would understand." Tucking her arm under mine she says, "Only what is written in French is poetry, and only what is sung in Italian is music. The rest is holy—the Hebrew—or harsh—the German." Her cultural cosmos has no room for the Scandinavians.

"Strindberg was a Swede, Mom."

"Smorgasbord," she says, leading me to the kitchen.

"When do we eat?" Father taps on a glass with a fork. "Let's have a little service around here."

"Do you know that he can't even boil water?" Mother asks.

"What good is boiled water?" he says.

"À boire, à boire, par pitié!" she cries. A drink, a drink, for pity's sake. Father pours some wine and, not to be outdone, recites a short poem in French about a shipwreck. The dinner ends with conviviality. They appear to be making eyes at each other and I leave soon after dinner, not wishing to be de trop.

DISTRAUGHT, my father has violated the hallowed custom of the parent waiting for the child to call and phones me to say that in his time women were stoned for desertion.

"Desertion? You mean adultery."

She phoned him from the street and refused to say where she was.

We must call the police. This is alarming.

"All she said was she had a ticket."

"A ticket? Train, bus, plane—?"

"A matinee. I ask you, is this right? Without consultation?"

"Without permission you mean," I say, emboldened.

"Of course I would have given my permission. I am a reasonable man. I don't know what to do anymore."

"Perhaps—" dare I say it? "—it would be good for *you* to talk to a psychiatrist."

"God forbid. Charlatans. They are worse than chiropractors. They are all in cahoots. No. I have an idea. You are going to laugh at it." He hesitates while I clear my throat. "My father, may he rest in peace, would turn over in his grave if he were alive. But I am a desperate man."

Not a Caribbean cruise.

Not garlic hung around the neck.

Not a walnut shell inscribed with Hebrew characters, to be placed under a pillow.

His solution is that I, the daughter, must perform the evil eye exorcism upon my mother. Ah, no—this is the twentieth century. I remember myself as a scoffing, irreverent child, sick with stomachaches, chicken pox, strep throat, giggling as my mother performed it at my bedside, tolerant and loving even as I mimicked her yawning.

"Really, Dad—"

"It worked for you, didn't it? You got rid of the measles. And when I had pleurisy . . ."

Yes, this is our answer to the Ashkenazim. The evil eye incantation in lieu of chicken soup. "But I don't know it. I never memorized it."

"If you are not willing to help your own mother . . ."

"All right, but it's absurd. In this day and age." My bravado masks the strain of superstition that prevents me from ever breaking a chain letter *(The last person who broke this chain suffered a cerebral hemorrhage)*. Why take a chance?

ONE LATE afternoon a stylish woman in her midthirties, dressed in a suit and carrying an attaché case, hurries to—a board meeting? A conference? A senate subcommittee hearing or a lecture hall to address a gathering?

This woman is going to cast a hex over the evil eye. Not in a village hovel or a stucco house with no plumbing overlooking the Mediterranean, but in a thirty-five-story apartment house with the thin walls, plastic palms, and peeling paint that are de rigueur in new buildings. Closed-circuit television reveals to the doorman a professional woman of the new breed, the kind who understands corporate law and makes decisions affecting his life. The woman's lips are moving. She is babbling a spell whose origins are lost in twelfth-century Spain.

The victim opens the door cheerfully. How to reconcile polyester with exorcism? Is there a connection? Mother shrugs. "If it will make him happy . . . I threw him out. We can't have a man listening. What a lovely evening. What a shame to stay home. I would rather go to Lord and Taylor. You need a new raincoat. Why do you wear such dark colors?" She fingers my suit. I am reminded of my father's "You are almost as pretty as your mother."

"Now, Mom, you know I think this is ridiculous. All this ancient mumbo jumbo."

This unleashes a monologue in French by Racine, about honoring one's ancestors, all while she plies me with food.

"And besides," she finishes, "it always worked when *I* did it."

I pick up the gauntlet and stamp around. "Well, I suppose it can't hurt."

We lower the blinds and take the telephone off the hook. I feel as though I am about to perform the Black Mass. Mother lies down on her bed. The Arts and Leisure section from last Sunday's *Times* is on her night table, along with a dog-eared copy of proverbs by La Rochefoucauld.

"Salt," she prompts me.

I go into the kitchen and pour about half a teaspoonful into my right hand. Mother's eyes are closed. Will something dreadful happen if I don't do it right? *The last person who broke the chain died a horrible death.*

"Take your time, honey," she says. "I'm very comfortable."

I raise my right hand and make a pass over her face. I begin to recite in Ladino, with my American accent: *"Vida, daughter of Allegra, whose mother was Miriam . . ."* I feel a lump in my throat. I am blessing my mother. *"Before her was Fortuna who was the fruit of Esther . . ."* A veritable amazonland from which men are excluded. Women's lib, I hear my father say. Mother sighs. Words come into my head, Hebrew blessings learned as an unwilling Sunday school student. I am swaying now as I chant. Twenty floors below us trucks rattle down the avenue, a few bars of disco music float up and die away.

There is a smile on Mother's face; her eyes remain closed. Now again in Ladino: *"Eliahu walked down the road, clad in iron, shod in iron. Three keys he carried: one to open the gate, one to lock it, and one to ward off the evil eye."* I smother a yawn and repeat the line about the three keys. I see him clanking down a country road, dusty trees—poplars, cypresses—the prophet in medieval garb, fooling the authorities, fooling the evil eye, casting away doubt and evil from the people of Israel. *"How many are the daughters, how many are the names, how many the signs and wonders?"* I am so tired. I can hardly raise the hand holding the salt over Mother's face. Wearily, yawning, I trace a six-pointed star across her face, a name for each point of the star, a blessing for each name, miracles for each succeeding generation, a logarithmic explosion of miracles for my mother.

She opens her eyes and nods kindly at me, at my hand. I open it, press the index finger of my left hand to the salt so that some grains adhere to it. She sits up and I place my finger gently in her mouth, applying the salt to her palate. I do this three times, reciting a threefold blessing in Hebrew that I do not remember ever having heard before. My eyes are tearing. Violently I throw the salt over her left shoulder. I am yawning uncontrollably. Mother reaches out and embraces me.

"How do you feel?" I ask, not knowing what to do with the rest of the salt on my palm.

"Wonderful," she says. "For once your father was right. I never felt better in my life."

Born, raised, and educated in Argentina, DANIEL ULANOVSKY SACK continued his graduate studies in Paris and, later, in Cambridge, Massachusetts, as a Nieman Fellow at Harvard University. He is a journalist with the Buenos Aires newspaper *Clarín* and also the editor of *Latido,* a journal of cultural exploration. His book *Los desafíos del nuevo milenio* (Challenges of the New Millennium) (Editorial Aguilar, Buenos Aires), containing interviews with thirty-five scholars from Claude-Lévi Strauss to Norman Mailer, was published in 1999. "Home Cooking" is his first published fiction in any language.

LOUISE POPKIN holds a Ph.D. in Spanish and Latin American literature and is a lecturer in Spanish at the Harvard University Division of Continuing Education. Her translations of Latin American prose, poetry, and drama—particularly from Uruguay and Argentina— have appeared in a number of anthologies and in literary journals, such as *Triquarterly, Kenyon Review, Mid-American Review,* and *Beacons.* She resides in Montevideo, Uruguay, for part of each year.

Home Cooking

DANIEL ULANOVSKY SACK

Translated from the Spanish by Louise Popkin

EUSTAQUIA WAS THE FIRST to sense something odd.

Just the day before, as she dusted the mirror in the dining room, she had thought her Indian complexion looked lighter and that her wrinkles were almost gone. Her hair no longer hung straight down to her waist: it was fluffy and held its shape, as if she had been to the beauty shop downtown. What a peculiar feeling: nobody was around, yet somebody was. Good Lord, she had better cross herself. And the scent of magnolias . . . but wait a minute, it's too early . . . Why, yes, they had been in bloom the day that everyone sat there looking at the poor *señora,* the women drinking tea, and the men coffee.

And then that very evening little Miss Fanny, still in black, mentioned the kidneys in wine sauce Mama used to make. The best part was that sweetish taste from the onions. Not onions, green garlic, Raquel insisted. And Don David said I'd do anything to make them happy, and he promised to ask Aunt Sarita for the recipe or, if she doesn't have it, Simona Finkel, that lady who takes orders for knishes.

After dinner it was time for their nightly ritual. They listened to their favorite soap opera on a local radio station, read a few pages in their books, then okay, how about a kiss now, and you're off to bed. At eleven all the lights went out in the big old house and in the faint glow of the crescent moon, you could barely see the linen still hanging on the clothesline in the rear courtyard, the one the maid's rooms opened onto. Eustaquia really disliked the idea of leaving the sheets out there all night, but they were still damp and she wasn't about to bring them in so they could get all musty. Not that I'm superstitious, but everything gets so clean in the sun and Lord only knows what might be out there at night.

Once David saw that the girls were asleep, he could let down his guard. Better they should go out, he told himself, that way they can't see me cry. But why am I crying, when it feels like she's still around? And Eustaquia tossed and turned in her bed. With a little garlic and a bit of onion, too—all finely chopped—a dash of red wine, some lemon juice and two teaspoons of sugar. You dice up the kidneys real small . . . Oh, and use the clay pot, Eustaquia, and keep the cover on, so they'll soak up the sauce. And don't overcook them; more than half an hour and they're as tough as shoe leather. No, ma'am, no more than half an hour. And I won't forget the salt. Salty like my sweat, water . . . there now, let me get up . . . Yes, of course I'll fix them.

As soon as the sun was up she rinsed out the sheets again without explaining why. It's a gorgeous, sunny day, my dears, and I've got a surprise for you. Go get your papa, he'll be taking you to the park for a walk. And I'm off to the butcher shop: Don Andrés, you make sure those kidneys aren't too big, now; and I don't want them swimming in blood, either.

Fanny and Raquel had a fabulous time. Their walk began at the flower bed with the calendar, the one where they write each day's date with tiny plants that jump around like magic. There's a man who comes at night,

Papa said. I don't believe you; how can they keep moving them, when they take so long to grow? With their father's permission, the two girls were all dolled up: Instead of their usual black, they had on pale pink chiffon dresses and little tan straw hats. Their shoes weren't ideal for the park, but they just loved the sheen of the patent leather. And how can I say no to them, isn't it bad enough they have no mother? To the pond? Okay, but keep your hands out of that filthy water; three tickets for the boat ride, please. Oooh, look at that little monkey; wow, there are two of them. Watch out, they might have rabies, and what if they bite? Oh, come on, Papa, just one little bag. I told you, it's almost time for lunch. Well, okay, but don't overdo it; that candied popcorn is no good for you; it'll just give you a tummyache.

When they got back to the house, Don David tried his best to be mistaken: that smell couldn't possibly be what he knew it was. Darling, don't do this to me, why won't you understand? But the girls were ecstatic: "It's Mama's dish, those kidneys with all that yummy gravy to soak up." But Eustaquia, you said you didn't know how to make them, that the *señora* never taught you. And may I die and go to hell if I lied, sir. I got up today and bought the kidneys, and this is how they turned out . . . I didn't want to make them, but something told me I had to . . . And that's the honest truth—I swear by the Father, the Son, and the Holy Ghost— so please, Don David, don't scold me. No, I didn't read it anywhere; I don't even know how to read.

They ate the kidneys in silence. The grown-ups, that is. The girls, on the other hand, were in high spirits and gulped down two whole servings apiece, 'cause Mama told me when we were all grown up she'd teach us how, only we were still too little. For now, she'd say, just the caramel candies.

After a few weeks that kidney dish was back on their weekly menu. Every Tuesday and Saturday Eustaquia would fix it, and when they smelled the sweetish aroma of the onion and green garlic, no one remembered that the recipe had simply reappeared out of the blue. And little by little life in the Berstein household seemed to return to normal.

Although David held on to his dark ties and handkerchiefs, Fanny and Raquel stopped wearing black for good. School took up a major part of the girls' time, each first in her class, just as Mama would have liked. And every Saturday, there were movies and every Sunday, tea over at Aunt Sarita's, since she was all alone in life.

I hadn't given it any thought until now, but it isn't good for the girls to grow up without a mother; and you really loved your sister, so why not? Besides, embarrassing as it is to say this, I'm attracted to you; you're so much like her. As for Sarita, well, she wasn't saying yes or no, and that was driving David mad. Please God, I can't deal with bringing the girls up on my own. And I'd sooner die than admit it to anyone, but, well . . . a man has his needs, and at this stage in life I'm not about to go running around.

Sarita was terrified but she knew that in due time, she'd say yes. Even the rabbi from the Paraguay Street synagogue approved of the match; he didn't see anything wrong with her having her first man at age forty-something. Dear God, why were pleasure and fear always so inseparable?

That afternoon she had promised to help Raquel and Fanny with their homework. The three of them were in the dining room learning that Argentina extended from Jujuy all the way down to the Southern Territories. And thanks for the hot chocolate, Eustaquia, and those warm teacakes with the poppy seeds. But for heaven's sake put down that tray, your hand is shaking.

"Do you feel sick? You're looking a little peaked."

"It's just that while I was dusting, I was sure I saw something. It reminded me of when . . . No, don't mind me, Miss Sarita. I must be tired, there's been too much to do. That's all it is."

Why, Eustaquia, whatever is the matter with you? Why are you getting so worked up talking about this? Look, my dear, go have a cup of tea and lie down for a while. I'm sure your blood pressure is down. And don't worry about dinner, I'll see to it. No, ma'am, please don't send me to my room, there's something I have to tell you. Let me explain. Whenever I look in the big mirror, I feel like I'm out of my mind. And maybe I really am. Because my head shakes on its own, as if I were saying no. Is that me shaking it? I say no, but my reflection in the mirror says yes. But it's saying no, Miss Sarita.

"You're talking nonsense, my dear. And, look, you're burning up with fever. Now, you go straight to bed; by tomorrow you'll calm down, and you'll feel much better. I've told David that this house is too big for you to take care of by yourself. Nobody can stretch themselves that thin."

Raquel and Fanny went on with their homework. And Sarita started dreaming up dinner. Why not make a real feast and prove that she, too, could be a housewife? Down with the idea that single women are okay at baking teacakes but next to useless when it comes to real cooking, because after all, if it's only me, I may as well keep it nice and simple.

By now the aroma of chopped basil was wafting into the dining room, where the girls sat gabbing away. So was the sound of the chicken frying with the onions and a red pepper. Something felt familiar, though they weren't sure just what. For all that was left of Mama was their fondness for those kidneys, thanks to Eustaquia, who had learned to cook them. Hunger, that hunger mingled with their homework, and the enigmatic flavors.

"Papa, Eustaquia's sick and she's got a fever. She's burning up. Aunt Sarita's sent her to bed and started dinner."

David didn't notice what was happening. In his eagerness, his mind failed to recognize those familiar smells; he figured she was cooking up some new dish. Of course, he was happy. Why, he was even glad when Eustaquia got sick: he assumed she had done it on purpose, to give Sarita a chance and let them be a family of four again. And so he dressed for the occasion, going up to his room to put on a colorful tie.

In the kitchen the banging of the pots and pans resounded to the rhythm of obsession. She had to prove she could do it, that everything would work out for the best. The chicken was crisp; the carrots and sweet potatoes were browning in a cast-iron skillet in the oven; and the cream, mixed with the basil, was all ready to be poured over the platter, right before it was served.

David came into the kitchen with a mischievous look about him. For the first time he dared to touch her the way a man touches a woman. Just on the arm, to be sure, but how good it felt. Shhh, just for a little while, let me get the feel of your skin. And she said okay, but I'm scared. Don't look at me: the rush of adrenaline, all those hangups. And right then and there, that first kiss. Stolen, yes, but the real thing.

All at once David came back to his senses. Why, it's that chicken in basil cream sauce she used to make for our birthdays. Now I recognize it, Sarita, it smells exactly the same. Thank you. And then it was come on, everyone, let's eat. How odd: The girls were hungry one minute, and full the next. David, torn between his compassion and his queasiness. Sarita, still in a festive mood, and still oblivious. Then Fanny took the plunge: Aunt Sarita, this tastes really bitter. My tummy hurts.

"I wonder if the cream spoiled. Or maybe the chicken they sold us was bad."

The breasts and drumsticks started turning black. Only David tried to eat another mouthful, and he couldn't swallow it. He hid it under the tablecloth so he wouldn't hurt her feelings. But Sarita was already in tears, a mixture of stifled sobs and retching; she had to spit out what didn't belong to her.

Meanwhile, in her room facing the rear courtyard, Eustaquia babbled on in her sleep. And be sure not to pour the cream over it until after you've added the basil; otherwise, it'll all turn bitter. Don't worry, ma'am, I understand perfectly; they mustn't be mixed. Why, yes, of course, I'll make it, *señora*.

JOE HILL lives in Massachusetts. In 1999 he won the A. E. Coppard Prize for Short Fiction. Another of his stories was runner-up in the Willamette Short Fiction Contest in 2000; the story will be published in the *Clackamas Literary Review* in spring 2001. Hill's fiction has also appeared in *Palace Corbie* and *Implosion Magazine*.

Pop Art

JOE HILL

MY BEST FRIEND WHEN I was twelve was inflatable. His name was Arthur Roth, which also made him an inflatable Hebrew, although in our now-and-then talks about the afterlife I don't remember that he took an especially Jewish perspective. Talk was mostly what we did—in his condition roughhouse was out of the question—and the subject of death, and what might follow it, came up more than once. I think Arthur knew he would be lucky to survive high school. When I met him he had already almost been killed a dozen times, once for every year he had been alive. The afterlife was always on his mind; also the possible lack of one.

When I tell you we talked, I mean only to say we communicated, argued, put each other down, built each other up. To stick to facts, *I* talked—Art couldn't. He didn't have a mouth. When he had something to say, he wrote it down. He wore a pad around his neck on a loop of twine and carried crayons in his pocket. He turned in school papers in crayon, took tests in crayon. You can imagine the dangers a sharpened pencil would present to a four-ounce boy made of plastic and filled with air.

I think one of the reasons we were best friends was because he was such a great listener. I needed someone to listen. My mother was gone and my father I couldn't talk to. My mother ran away when I was three, sent my dad a rambling and confused letter from Florida about sunspots and gamma rays and the radiation that emanates from power lines, about how the birthmark on the back of her left hand had moved up her arm and onto her shoulder. After that a couple of postcards, then nothing.

As for my father, he suffered from migraines. In the afternoon he sat in front of soaps in the darkened living room, wet eyed and miserable. He hated to be bothered. You couldn't tell him anything. It was a mistake even to try.

"Blah blah," he would say, cutting me off in midsentence. "My head is splitting. You're killing me here with blah blah this, blah blah that."

But Art liked to listen, and in trade I offered him protection. Kids were scared of me. I had a bad reputation. I owned a switchblade, and sometimes I brought it to school and let other kids see; it kept them in fear. The only thing I ever stuck it into, though, was the wall of my bedroom. I'd lie on my bed and flip it at the corkboard wall, so that it hit, blade-first, *thunk!*

One day when Art was visiting he saw the pockmarks in my wall. I explained, one thing led to another, and before I knew it he was begging to have a throw.

"What's wrong with you?" I asked him. "Is your head completely empty? Forget it. No way."

Out came a Crayola, burnt sienna. He wrote:

So at least let me look.

I popped it open for him. He stared at it wide eyed. Actually, he stared at everything wide eyed. His eyes were made of glassy plastic, stuck to the surface of his face. He couldn't blink or anything. But this was different than his usual bug-eyed stare. I could see he was really fixated.

He wrote:

I'll be careful I totally promise *please!*

I handed it to him. He pushed the point of the blade into the floor so it snicked into the handle. Then he hit the button and it snacked back out. He shuddered, stared at it in his hand. Then, without giving any warning, he chucked it at the wall. Of course it didn't hit tip-first; that takes practice, which he hadn't had, and coordination, which, speaking honestly, he wasn't ever going to have. It bounced, came flying back at him. He sprang into the air so quickly it was like I was watching his ghost jump out of his body. The knife landed where he had been and clattered away under my bed.

I yanked Art down off the ceiling. He wrote:

You were right, that was dumb. I'm a loser—a jerk.

"No question," I said.

But he wasn't a loser or a jerk. My dad is a loser. The kids at school were jerks. Art was different. He was all heart. He just wanted to be liked by someone.

Also, I can say truthfully, he was the most completely harmless person I've ever known. Not only would he not hurt a fly, he *couldn't* hurt a fly. If he slapped one and lifted his hand, it would buzz off undisturbed. He was like a holy person in a Bible story, someone who can heal the ripped and infected parts of you with a laying on of hands. You know how Bible stories go. That kind of person, they're never around long. Losers and jerks put nails in them and watch the air run out.

THERE WAS something special about Art, an invisible special something that just made other kids naturally want to kick his ass. He was new at our school. His parents had just moved to town. They were normal, filled with blood not air. The condition Art suffered from is one of these genetic things that plays hopscotch with the generations, like Tay-Sachs (Art told me once that he had had a granduncle, also inflatable, who flopped one day into a pile of leaves and burst on the tine of a buried rake). On the first day of classes Mrs. Gannon made Art stand at the front of the room and told everyone all about him, while he hung his head out of shyness.

He was white. Not Caucasian, *white,* like a marshmallow, or Casper. A seam ran around his head and down his sides. There was a plastic nipple under one arm, where he could be pumped with air.

Mrs. Gannon told us we had to be extra careful not to run with scissors or pens. A puncture would probably kill him. He couldn't talk; everyone had to try to be sensitive about that. His interests were astronauts, photography, and the novels of Bernard Malamud.

Before she nudged him toward his seat, she gave his shoulder an encouraging little squeeze and as she pressed her fingers into him, he whistled gently. That was the only way he ever made sound. By flexing his body, he could emit little squeaks and whines. When other people squeezed him, he made a soft, musical hoot.

He bobbed down the room and took an empty seat beside me. Billy Spears, who sat directly behind him, bounced thumbtacks off his head all morning long. The first couple of times Art pretended not to notice. Then, when Mrs. Gannon wasn't looking, he wrote Billy a note. It said:

> *Please stop!* I don't want to say anything to Mrs. Gannon but it
> isn't safe to throw thumbtacks at me. I'm *not* kidding.

Billy wrote back:

> You make trouble and there won't be enough of you left to
> patch a tire. Think about it.

It didn't get any easier for Art from there. In biology lab he was paired with Cassius Delamitri, who was in sixth grade for the second time. Cassius was a fat kid with a pudgy, sulky face and a disagreeable film of black hair above his unhappy pucker of a mouth.

The project was to distill wood, which involved the use of a gas flame—
Cassius did the work while Art watched and wrote notes of encouragement:

> I can't believe you got a D- on this experiment when you did it
> last year—you totally know how to do this stuff!!

And:

> My parents bought me a lab kit for my birthday. You could
> come over and we could play mad scientist sometime want to?

After three or four notes like that, Cassius had read enough, got it in
his head Art was some kind of homosexual . . . especially with Art's talk
about having him over to play doctor or whatever. When the teacher was
distracted helping some other kids, Cassius shoved Art under the table
and tied him around one of the table legs in a squeaky granny knot, head,
arms, body, and all. When Mr. Milton asked where Art had gone, Cassius
said he thought he had run to the bathroom.

"Did he?" Mr. Milton asked. "What a relief. I didn't even know if that
kid *could* go to the bathroom."

Another time John Erikson held Art down during recess and wrote
KOLLOSTIMY BAG on his stomach with indelible marker. It was spring before it faded away.

> The worst thing was my mom saw. Bad enough she has to
> know I get beat up on a daily basis. But she was really upset it
> was spelled wrong.

He added:

> I don't know what she expects—this is sixth grade. Doesn't
> she remember sixth grade? I'm sorry, but realistically, what are
> the odds you're going to get beat up by the grand champion of
> the spelling bee?

"The way your year is going," I said, "I figure them odds might be
pretty good."

HERE IS how Art and I wound up friends.

During recess periods I always hung out at the top of the monkey bars by myself, reading sports magazines. I was cultivating my reputation as a delinquent and possible drug pusher. To help my image along, I wore a black denim jacket and didn't talk to people or make friends.

At the top of the monkey bars—a dome-shaped construction at one edge of the asphalt lot behind the school—I was a good nine feet off the ground, and had a view of the whole yard. One day I watched Billy Spears horsing around with Cassius Delamitri and John Erikson. Billy had a Wiffle ball and a bat, and the three of them were trying to bat the ball in through an open second-floor window. After fifteen minutes of not even coming close, John Erikson got lucky and swatted it in.

Cassius said, "Shit—there goes the ball. We need something else to bat around."

"Hey," Billy shouted. "Look! There's Art!"

They caught up to Art, who was trying to keep away, and Billy started tossing him in the air and hitting him with the bat to see how far he could knock him. Every time he struck Art with the bat it made a hollow, springy *whap!* Art popped into the air then floated along a little way, sinking gently back to ground. As soon as his heels touched earth he started to run, but swiftness of foot wasn't one of Art's qualities. John and Cassius got into the fun by grabbing Art and dropkicking him, to see who could punt him highest.

The three of them gradually pummeled Art down to my end of the lot. He struggled free long enough to run in under the monkey bars. Billy caught up, struck him a whap across the ass with the bat, and shot him high into the air.

Art floated to the top of the dome. When his body touched the steel bars, he stuck, face-up—static electricity.

"Hey," Billy hollered. "Chuck him down here!"

I had, up until that moment, never been face to face with Art. Although we shared classes and even sat side by side in Mrs. Gannon's homeroom, we had not had a single exchange. He looked at me with his enormous plastic eyes and sad blank face, and I looked right back. He found the pad around his neck, scribbled a note in spring green, ripped it off, and held it up at me:

I don't care what they do, but could you go away? I hate to get the crap knocked out of me in front of spectators.

"What's he writin'?" Billy shouted.

I looked from the note past Art and down at the gathering of boys below. I was struck by the sudden realization that I could *smell* them, all three of them, a damp, *human* smell, a sweaty-sour reek. It turned my stomach.

"Why are you bothering him?" I asked.

Billy said, "Just screwin' with him."

"We're trying to see how high we can make him go," Cassius said. "You ought to come down here. You ought to give it a try. We're going to kick him onto the roof of the friggin' school!"

"I got an even funner idea," I said, *funner* being an excellent word to use if you want to impress on some other kids that you might be a mentally retarded psychopath. "How about we see if I can kick your lardy ass up on the roof of the school?"

"What's your problem?" Billy asked. "You on the rag?"

I grabbed Art and jumped down. Cassius blanched. John Erikson tottered back. I held Art under one arm, feet sticking toward them, head pointed away.

"You guys are dicks," I said—some moments just aren't right for a funny line.

And I turned away from them. The back of my neck crawled at the thought of Billy's Wiffle ball bat clubbing me one across the skull, but he didn't do a thing, let me walk.

We went out on the baseball field, sat on the pitcher's mound. Art wrote me a note that said thanks, and another that said I didn't have to do what I had done but that he was glad I had done it, and another that said he owed me one. I shoved each note into my pocket after reading it, didn't think why. That night, alone in my bedroom, I dug a wad of crushed notepaper out of my pocket, a lump the size of a lemon, peeled each note free and pressed it flat on my bed, read them all over again. There was no good reason not to throw them away, but I didn't, started a collection instead. It was like some part of me knew, even then, I might want to have something to remember Art by after he was gone. I saved hundreds of his notes over the next year, some as short as a couple of words, a few six-page-long manifestos. I have most of them still, from the first note he handed me, the one that begins *I don't care what they do,* to the last, the one that ends:

> I want to see if it's true. If the sky opens up at the top.

AT FIRST my father didn't like Art, but after he got to know him better he really hated him.

"How come he's always mincing around?" my father asked. "Is he a fairy or something?"

"No, Dad. He's inflatable."

"Well, he acts like a fairy," he said. "You better not be queering around with him up in your room."

Art tried to be liked—he tried to build a relationship with my father. But the things he did were misinterpreted, the statements he made misunderstood. My dad said something once about a movie he liked. Art wrote him a message about how the book was even better.

"He thinks I'm an illiterate," my dad said, as soon as Art was gone.

Another time Art noticed the pile of worn tires heaped up behind our garage and mentioned to my dad about a recycling program at Sears, bring in your rotten old ones, get 20 percent off on brand new Goodyears.

"He thinks we're trailer trash," my dad complained, before Art was hardly out of earshot. "Little snotnose."

One day Art and I got home from school and found my father in front of the TV with a pit bull at his feet. The bull erupted off the floor, yapping hysterically, and jumped up on Art. His paws made a slippery zipping sound sliding over Art's plastic chest. Art grabbed one of my shoulders and vaulted into the air. He could really jump when he had to. He grabbed the ceiling fan—turned off—and held on to one of the blades while the pit bull barked and hopped beneath.

"What the hell is that?" I asked.

"Family dog," my father said. "Just like you always wanted."

"Not one that wants to eat my friends."

"Get off the fan, Artie. That isn't built for you to hang off it."

"This isn't a dog," I said. "It's a blender with teeth."

"Listen, do you want to name it, or should I?" Dad asked.

Art and I hid in my bedroom and talked names.

"Snowflake," I said. "Sugarpie. Sunshine."

How about Happy? That has a ring to it, doesn't it?

We were kidding, but Happy was no joke. In just a week Art had at least three life-threatening encounters with my father's ugly dog.

If he gets his teeth in me, I'm done for. He'll punch me full of holes.

But Happy couldn't be housebroken, left turds scattered around the living room, hard to see in the moss-brown rug. My dad squelched through some fresh leavings once, in bare feet, and it sent him a little out of his head. He chased Happy all through the downstairs with a croquet mallet, smashed a hole in the wall, crushed some plates on the kitchen counter with a wild backswing.

The very next day he built a chain-link pen in the side yard. Happy went in, and that was where he stayed.

By then, though, Art was nervous to come over, and preferred to meet at his house. I didn't see the sense. It was a long walk to get to his place after school, and my house was right there, just around the corner.

"What are you worried about?" I asked him. "He's in a pen. It's not like Happy is going to figure out how to open the door to his pen, you know."

Art knew . . . but he still didn't like to come over, and when he did, he usually had a couple of patches for bicycle tires on him, to guard against dark happenstance.

ONCE WE started going to Art's every day, once it came to be a habit, I wondered why I had ever wanted us to go to my house instead. I got used to the walk—I walked the walk so many times I stopped noticing that it was long bordering on never ending. I even looked forward to it, my afternoon stroll through coiled suburban streets, past houses done in Disney pastels: lemon, tangerine, ash. As I crossed the distance between my house and Art's house, it seemed to me that I was moving through zones of ever-deepening stillness and order, and at the walnut heart of all this peace was Art's.

Art couldn't run, talk, or approach anything with a sharp edge on it, but at his house we managed to keep ourselves entertained. We watched TV. I wasn't like other kids and didn't know anything about television. My father, I mentioned already, suffered from terrible migraines. He was home on disability, lived in the family room, and hogged our TV all day long, kept track of five different soaps. I tried not to bother him, and rarely sat down to watch with him—I sensed my presence was a distraction to him at a time when he wanted to concentrate.

Art would have watched whatever I wanted to watch, but I didn't know what to do with a remote control. I couldn't make a choice, didn't know how. Had lost the habit. Art was a NASA buff, and we watched anything to do with space, never missed a space shuttle launch. He wrote:

> I want to be an astronaut. I'd adapt really well to being weightless. I'm *already* mostly weightless.

This was when they were putting up the international space station. They talked about how hard it was on people to spend too long in outer space. Your muscles atrophy. Your heart shrinks three sizes.

> The advantages of sending me into space keep piling up. I
> don't have any muscles to atrophy. I don't have any heart to
> shrink. I'm telling you. I'm the ideal spaceman. I *belong* in
> orbit.

"I know a guy who can help you get there. Let me give Billy Spears a call. He's got a rocket he wants to stick up your ass. I heard him talking about it."

Art gave me a dour look, and a scribbled two-word response.

Lying around Art's house in front of the tube wasn't always an option, though. His father was a piano instructor, tutored small children on the baby grand, which was in the living room along with their television. If he had a lesson, we had to find something else to do. We'd go into Art's room to play with his computer, but after twenty minutes of *row-row-row-your-boat* coming through the wall—a shrill, out-of-time plinking—we'd shoot each other sudden wild looks and leave by way of the window, no need to talk it over.

Both Art's parents were musical, his mother a cellist. They had wanted music for Art, but it had been letdown and disappointment from the start.

> I can't even kazoo,

Art wrote me once. The piano was out. Art didn't have any fingers, just a thumb, and a puffy pad where his fingers belonged. Hands like that, it had been years of work with a tutor just to learn to write legibly with a crayon. For obvious reasons, wind instruments were also out of the question; Art didn't have lungs, and didn't breathe. He tried to learn the drums but couldn't strike hard enough to be any good at it.

His mother bought him a digital camera. "Make music with color," she said. "Make melodies out of light."

Mrs. Roth was always hitting you with lines like that. She talked about oneness, about the natural decency of trees, and she said not enough people were thankful for the smell of cut grass. Art told me that when I wasn't around, she asked questions about me. She was worried I didn't have a healthy outlet for my creative self. She said I needed something to feed the inner me. She bought me a book about origami and it wasn't even my birthday.

"I didn't know the inner me was hungry," I said to Art.

That's because it already starved to death,

Art wrote.

She was alarmed to learn that I didn't have any sort of religion. My father didn't take me to church or send me to Sunday school. He said religion was a scam. Mrs. Roth was too polite to say anything to me about my father, but she said things about him to Art, and Art passed her comments on. She told Art that if my father neglected the care of my body like he neglected the care of my spirit, he'd be in jail and I'd be in a foster home. She also told Art that if I was put in foster care, she'd adopt me, and I could stay in the guest room. I loved her, felt my heart surge whenever she asked me if I wanted a glass of lemonade. I would have done anything she asked.

"Your mom's an idiot," I said to Art. "A total moron. I hope you know that. There isn't any oneness. It's every man for himself. Anyone who thinks we're all brothers in the spirit winds up sitting under Cassius Delamitri's fat ass during recess, smelling his jock."

Mrs. Roth wanted to take me to the synagogue—not to convert me, just as an educational experience, exposure to other cultures and all that—but Art's father shot her down, said not a chance, not our business, and what are you crazy? She had a bumper sticker on her car that showed the Star of David and the word PRIDE with a jumping exclamation point next to it.

"So Art," I said another time. "I got a Jewish question I want to ask you. Now, you and your family, you're a bunch of hard-core Jews, right?"

I don't know that I'd describe us as *hard-core* exactly. We're actually pretty lax. But we go to synagogue, observe the holidays—things like that.

"I thought Jews had to get their joints snipped," I said, and grabbed my crotch. "For the faith. Tell me—"

But Art was already writing:

No, not me. I got off. My parents were friends with a progressive rabbi. They talked to him about it first thing after I was born. Just to find out what the official position was.

"What'd he say?"

He said it was the official position to make an exception for anyone who would actually explode during the circumcision. They thought he was joking, but later on my mom did some research on it. Based on what she found out, it looks like I'm in the clear—Talmudically speaking. Mom says the foreskin has to be *skin*. If it isn't, it doesn't need to be cut.

"That's funny," I said. "I always thought your mom didn't know dick. Now it turns out your mom *does* know dick. She's an expert even. Shows what I know. Hey, if she ever wants to do more research, I have an unusual specimen for her to examine."

And Art wrote how she would need to bring a microscope, and I said how she would need to stand back a few yards when I unzipped my pants, and back and forth, you don't need me to tell you, you can imagine the rest of the conversation for yourself.

I rode Art about his mother every chance I could get, couldn't help myself. Started in on her the moment she left the room, whispering about how for an old broad she still had an okay can, and what would Art think if his father died and I married her. Art, on the other hand, never once made a punch line out of my dad. If Art ever wanted to give me a hard time, he'd make fun of how I licked my fingers after I ate, or how I didn't always wear matching socks. It isn't hard to understand why Art never stuck it to me about my father, like I stuck it to him about his mother. When your best friend is ugly—I mean bad ugly, *deformed*—you don't kid them about shattering mirrors. In a friendship, especially in a friendship between two young boys, you are allowed to inflict a certain amount of pain. This is even expected. But you must cause no serious injury; you must never, under any circumstances, leave wounds that will result in permanent scars.

ARTHUR'S HOUSE was also where we usually settled to do our homework. In the early evening we went into his room to study. His father was done with lessons by then so there wasn't any *plink-plink* from the next room to distract us. I enjoyed studying in Art's room, responded well to the quiet, and liked working in a place where I was surrounded by books; Art had shelves and shelves of books. I liked our study time together but mistrusted it as well. It was during our study sessions—surrounded by all that easy stillness—that Art was most likely to say something about dying.

When we talked, I always tried to control the conversation, but Art was slippery, could work death into anything.

"Some Arab *invented* the idea of the number zero," I said. "Isn't that weird? Someone had to think zero up."

> Because it isn't obvious—that nothing can be something. That something that can't be measured or seen could still exist and have meaning. Same with the soul, when you think about it.

"True or false," I said another time, when we were studying for a science quiz. "Energy is never destroyed, it can only be changed from one form into another."

> I hope it's true—it would be a good argument that you continue to exist after you die, even if you're transformed into something completely different than what you had been.

He said a lot to me about death and what might follow it, but the thing I remember best was what he had to say about Mars. We were doing a presentation together, and Art had picked Mars as our subject, especially whether or not men would ever go there and try to colonize it. Art was all for colonizing Mars, cities under plastic tents, mining water from the icy poles. Art wanted to go himself.

"It's fun to imagine, maybe, fun to think about it," I said. "But the actual thing would be bullshit. Dust. Freezing cold. Everything red. You'd go blind looking at so much red. You wouldn't really want to do it—leave this world and never come back."

Art stared at me for a long moment, then bowed his head and wrote a brief note in robin's-egg blue.

> But I'm going to have to do that anyway. Everyone has to do that.

Then he wrote:

> You get an astronaut's life whether you want it or not. Leave it all behind for a world you know nothing about. That's just the deal.

IN THE SPRING Art invented a game called Spy Satellite. There was a place downtown, the Party Station, where you could buy a bushel of helium-filled balloons for a quarter. I'd get a bunch and meet Art somewhere with them. He'd have his digital camera.

As soon as I handed him the balloons he detached from the earth and lifted into the air. As he rose the wind pushed him out and away. When he was satisfied he was high enough, he'd let go of a couple of balloons, level off, and start snapping pictures. When he was ready to come down, he'd just let go of a few more. I'd meet him where he landed and we'd go over to his house to look at the pictures on his laptop. Photos of people swimming in their pools, men shingling their roofs; photos of me standing in empty streets, my upturned face a miniature brown blob, my features too distant to make out; photos that always had Art's sneakers dangling into the frame at the bottom edge.

Some of his best pictures were low-altitude affairs, things he snapped when he was only a few yards off the ground. Once he took three balloons and swam into the air over Happy's chain-link enclosure, off at the side of our house. Happy spent all day in his fenced-off pen, barking frantically at women going by with strollers, the jingle of the ice cream truck, squirrels. Happy had trampled all the space in his penned-in plot of earth down to mud. Scattered about him were dozens of dried piles of dog crap. In the middle of this awful brown turdscape was Happy himself, and in every photo Art snapped of him he was leaping up on his back legs, mouth open to show the pink cavity within, eyes fixed on Art's dangling sneakers.

> I feel bad. What a horrible place to live.

"Get your head out of your ass," I said. "If creatures like Happy were allowed to run wild, they'd make the whole world look that way. He doesn't want to live somewhere else. Turds and mud—that's Happy's idea of a total garden spot."

> I *strongly* disagree,

Arthur wrote me, but time has not softened my opinions on this matter. It is my belief that, as a rule, creatures of Happy's ilk—I am thinking here of canines and men both—more often run free than live caged, and it is in fact a world of mud and feces they desire, a world with no Art in it, or anyone like him, a place where there is no talk of books or God or the worlds beyond this world, a place where the only communication is the hysterical barking of starving and hate-filled dogs.

ONE SATURDAY morning, mid-April, my dad pushed the bedroom door open and woke me up by throwing my sneakers on my bed. "You have to be at the dentist's in half an hour. Put your rear in gear."

I walked—it was only a few blocks—and I had been sitting in the waiting room for twenty minutes, dazed with boredom, when I remembered I had told Art that I'd be coming by his house as soon as I got up. The receptionist let me use the phone to call him.

His mom answered. "He just left to see if he could find you at your house," she told me.

I called my dad.

"He hasn't been by," he said. "I haven't seen him."

"Keep an eye out."

"Yeah, well. I've got a headache. Art knows how to use the doorbell."

I sat in the dentist's chair, my mouth stretched open and tasting of blood and mint, and struggled with unease and an impatience to be going. Did not perhaps trust my father to be decent to Art without myself present. The dentist's assistant kept touching my shoulder and telling me to relax.

When I was all through and got outside, the deep and vivid blueness of the sky was a little disorientating. The sunshine was headache bright, bothered my eyes. I had been up for two hours and still felt cotton headed and dull edged, not all the way awake. I jogged.

The first thing I saw, standing on the sidewalk, was Happy, free from his pen. He didn't so much as bark at me. He was on his belly in the grass, head between his paws. He lifted sleepy eyelids to watch me approach, then let them sag shut again. His pen door stood open in the side yard.

I was looking to see if he was lying on a heap of tattered plastic when I heard the first feeble tapping sound. I turned my head and saw Art in the back of my father's station wagon, smacking his hands on the window. I walked over and opened the door. At that instant, Happy exploded from the grass with a peal of mindless barking. I grabbed Art in both arms, spun, and fled. Happy's teeth closed on a piece of my flapping pant leg. I heard a tacky ripping sound, stumbled, kept going.

I ran until there was a stitch in my side and no dog in sight—six blocks, at least. Toppled over in someone's yard. My pant leg was sliced open from the back of my knee to the ankle. I took my first good look at Art. It was a jarring sight. I was so out of breath, I could only produce a thin, dismayed little squeak—the sort of sound Art was always making.

His body had lost its marshmallow whiteness. It had a gold-brown duskiness to it now so it resembled a marshmallow, lightly toasted. He seemed to have deflated to about half his usual size. His chin sagged into his body. He couldn't hold his head up.

Art had been crossing our front lawn when Happy burst from his hiding place under one of the hedges. In that first crucial moment Art saw he would never be able to outrun our family dog on foot. All such an effort would get him would be an ass full of fatal puncture wounds. So instead he jumped into the station wagon and slammed the door.

The windows were automatic—there was no way to roll them down. Any door he opened, Happy tried to jam his snout in at him. It was seventy degrees outside the car, over a hundred inside. Art watched in dismay as Happy flopped in the grass beside the wagon to wait.

Art sat. Happy didn't move. Lawn mowers droned in the distance. The afternoon passed. In time Art began to wilt in the heat. He became ill and groggy. His plastic skin started sticking to the seats.

Then you showed up. Just in time. You saved my life.

But my eyes blurred and tears dripped off my face onto his note. I hadn't come just in time—not at all.

Art was never the same. His skin stayed a filmy yellow, and he developed a deflation problem. His parents would pump him up and for a while he'd be all right, his body swollen with oxygen, but eventually he'd go saggy and limp again. His doctor took one look and told his parents not to put off the trip to Disney World another year.

I wasn't the same either. I was miserable—couldn't eat, suffered unexpected stomachaches, brooded and sulked.

"Wipe that look off your face," my father said one night at dinner. "Life goes on. Deal with it."

I was dealing all right. I knew the door to Happy's pen didn't open itself. I punched holes in the tires of the station wagon, then left my switchblade sticking out of one of them so my father would know for sure who had done it. He had police officers come over and pretend to arrest me. They drove me around in the squad car and talked tough at me for a while, then said they'd bring me home if I'd "get with the program." The next day I locked Happy in the wagon and he took a shit on the driver's seat. My father collected all the books Art had got me to read, the Bernard Malamud, the Ray Bradbury, the Isaac Bashevis Singer. He burned them on the barbecue grill.

"How do you feel about that, smart guy?" he asked me while he squirted lighter fluid on them.

"Okay with me," I said. "They were on your library card."

That summer, I spent a lot of time sleeping over at Art's.

> Don't be angry. No one is to blame,

Art wrote me.

"Get your head out of your ass," I said, but then I couldn't say anything else because it made me cry just to look at him.

IN LATE AUGUST Art gave me a call. It was a hilly four miles to Scarswell Cove, where he wanted us to meet, but by then months of hoofing it to Art's after school had hardened me to long walks. I had plenty of balloons with me, just like he asked.

Scarswell Cove is a sheltered, pebbly beach on the sea, where people go to stand in the tide and fish in waders. There was no one there except a couple of old fishermen and Art, sitting on the slope of the beach. His body looked soft and saggy and his head lolled forward, bobbled weakly on his nonexistent neck. I sat down beside him. Half a mile out the dark blue waves were churning up icy combers.

"What's going on?" I asked.

Art bowed his head. He thought a bit. Then he began to write. He wrote:

> Do you know people have made it into outer space without rockets? Chuck Yeagher flew a high-performance jet so high it started to tumble—it tumbled *upward,* not downward. He ran so high, gravity lost hold of him. His jet was tumbling up out of the stratosphere. All the color melted out of the sky. It was like

> the blue sky was paper, and a hole was burning out the middle
> of it, and behind it, everything was black. Everything was full of
> stars. Imagine falling *up*.

I looked at this note, then back to his face. He was writing again. His second message was simpler:

> I've had it. Seriously—I'm all done. I deflate fifteen or sixteen
> times a day. I need someone to pump me up practically every
> hour. I feel sick all the time and I hate it. This is no kind of life.

"Oh no," I said. My vision blurred. Tears welled up and spilled over my eyes. "Things will get better."

> No. I don't think so. It isn't about whether I die. It's about figur-
> ing out where. And I've decided. I'm going to see how high I
> can go. I want to see if it's true. If the sky opens up at the top.

I don't know what else I said to him. A lot of things, I guess. I asked him not to do it, not to leave me. I said that it wasn't fair. I said that I didn't have any other friends. I said that I had always been lonely. I talked until it was all blubber and strangled, helpless sobs, and he reached his crinkly plastic arms around me and held me while I hid my face in his chest.

He took the balloons from me, got them looped around one wrist. I held his other hand and we walked to the edge of the water. The surf splashed in and filled my sneakers. The sea was so cold it made the bones in my feet throb. I lifted him and held him in both arms, and squeezed until he made a mournful squeak. We hugged for a long time. Then I opened my arms. I let him go. I hope that if there is another world, we will not be judged too harshly for the things we did wrong here—that we will at least be forgiven for the mistakes we made out of love. I have no doubt it was a sin of some kind, to let such a one go.

He rose away and the airstream turned him around so he was looking back at me as he bobbed out over the water, his left arm pulled high over his head, the balloons attached to his wrist. His head was tipped at a thoughtful angle, so he seemed to be studying me.

I sat on the beach and watched him go. I watched until I could no longer distinguish him from the gulls that were wheeling and diving over the water, a few miles away. He was just one more dirty speck wandering the sky. I didn't move. I wasn't sure I could get up. In time the horizon turned a dusky rose and the blue sky above deepened to black. I stretched out on the beach and watched the stars spill through the darkness overhead. I watched until a dizziness overcame me, and I could imagine spilling off the ground, and falling up into the night.

I DEVELOPED emotional problems. When school started again, I would cry at the sight of an empty desk. I couldn't answer questions or do homework. I flunked out and had to go through seventh grade again.

Worse, no one believed I was dangerous anymore. It was impossible to be scared of me after you had seen me sobbing my guts out a few times. I didn't have the switchblade anymore; my father had confiscated it.

Billy Spears beat me up one day, after school—mashed my lips, loosened a tooth. John Erikson held me down, wrote COLLISTAMY BAG on my forehead in Magic Marker. Still trying to get it right. Cassius Delamitri ambushed me, shoved me down and jumped on top of me, crushing me under his weight, driving all the air out of my lungs. A defeat by way of deflation; Art would have understood perfectly.

I avoided the Roths'. I wanted more than anything to see Art's mother, but I stayed away. I was afraid that if I talked to her it would come pouring out of me, that I had been there at the end, that I stood in the surf and let Art go. I was afraid of what I might see in her eyes; of her hurt and anger.

Less than six months after Art's deflated body was found slopping in the surf along North Scarswell beach, there was a FOR SALE sign out in front of the Roths' ranch. I never saw either of his parents again. Mrs. Roth sometimes wrote me letters, asking how I was and what I was doing, but I never replied. She signed her letters *love*.

I went out for track in high school and did well at pole vault. My track coach said the law of gravity didn't apply to me. My track coach didn't know fuck-all about gravity. No matter how high I went for a moment, I always came down in the end, same as anyone else.

Pole vault got me a state college scholarship. I kept to myself. No one at college knew me, and I was at last able to rebuild my long-lost image as a sociopath. I didn't go to parties. I didn't date. I didn't want to get to know anybody.

I was crossing the campus one morning and saw coming toward me a young girl with black hair so dark it had the cold blue sheen of rich oil. She wore a bulky sweater and a librarian's ankle-length skirt; a very asexual outfit, but all the same you could see she had a stunning figure, slim hips, high ripe breasts. Her eyes were of staring blue glass, her skin as white as Art's. It was the first time I had seen an inflatable person since Art drifted away on his balloons. A kid walking behind me wolf-whistled at her. I stepped aside, and when he went past, I tripped him up and watched his books fly everywhere.

"Are you some kind of psycho?" he screeched.

"Yes," I said. "Exactly."

Her name was Ruth Goldman. She had a round rubber patch on the heel of one foot where she had stepped on a shard of broken glass as a little girl, and a larger square patch on her left shoulder where a sharp branch had poked her once on a windy day. Home schooling and obsessively protective parents had saved her from further damage. We were both English majors. Her favorite writer was Kafka—because he understood the absurd. My favorite writer was Malamud—because he understood loneliness.

We married the same year I graduated. Although I remain doubtful about the life eternal, I converted without any prodding from her, gave in at last to a longing to have some talk of the spirit in my life. Can you really call it a conversion? In truth, I had no beliefs to convert from. Whatever the case, ours was a Jewish wedding, glass under white cloth, crunched beneath the boot heel.

One afternoon I told her about Art.

That's so sad. I'm so sorry,

She wrote to me in wax pencil. She put her hand over mine.

What happened? Did he run out of air?

"Ran out of sky," I said.

TEHILA LIEBERMAN grew up in New York in an Ashkenazic family and a Sephardic congregation. She lived in Israel for five years, during which time she studied at the Hebrew University in Jerusalem. Currently she is a writer in residence at the Writers' Room of Boston. Lieberman's short stories and essays have appeared in *Nimrod, Colorado Review, Salon Magazine, Literal Latté, SideShow,* and the Travelers' Tales Guides anthologies *Women in the Wild* and *A Woman's Path.* She won the *Colorado Review*'s Stanley Elkin Memorial Prize for fiction; several of her stories have been finalists in literary contests. "Anya's Angel" was a finalist in three separate literary competitions.

Anya's Angel

Tehila Lieberman

MY MOTHER ONCE TOLD ME that the way she understood it, we were living in the only existing physical universe, which was but the palest reflection of the many nonphysical universes that existed. That there was, however, a through flow between the worlds, and just as some spirits and acts of the divine trickled down to us, so did our actions affect the other layers of worlds.

It was late when she said this, past midnight. She was sitting in the kitchen, a notebook in front of her. She had decided suddenly to study Kabbalah. She couldn't talk to my father about these things. He had built a reputation on his agnosticism and his particular bent had grown a name, had turned his name into a noun. So when I would come upon my mother in the kitchen at all hours of the night, her glasses sliding down her nose, the books open before her, it was like coming upon her in an affair, only worse; a body is much more easily disengaged than angels and demigods and the remnants of worlds that now clung to her. I was watching her transform and wondered if perhaps she was going to die, if she knew and was not telling us that she would be leaving us and needed to map out the realms into which she thought she might step. I wondered if perhaps it was to escape us, if we exhausted her—the constant stream of my father's scholarship, my own incessant wanderings and returnings; if having been only partially alive by the side of my father for years, she was finally claiming a territory onto which he would not follow her, one that would remain exclusively hers.

As she moved away from us she became gradually more alive, and I was caught in the ironic moment of knowing what she must have felt at the first signs of my unstoppable separation—at the unstoppable separation and adulthood of her only son—a quickening of heart, an excitement at the wings she saw sprouting, and then the growing wound on her own skin as those wings lifted, flapped, tore me just a little more from her breast. So, too, observing her in her long gowns from the Moroccan markets she had visited with my father, her hair coming down out of a loose barrette, I felt that I had to let her go, that if I intimated that in any way I needed her to be the rock against which I was to kick off yet again, she would return and I would have her grounding, her growing weightedness on my conscience.

So I held still and let her drift away. As did my father in his silent, impenetrable way, and she looked down at us, both accusing and relieved that we could have so little need of her, as if perhaps we had been tricking her all along, holding her hostage when in fact we could handle our own angst, our own lost steps in the world.

Sometimes I was tempted to crawl under her wing and hide from my father's stern disapproval of me, of my lack of commitment to any discipline. Especially when he would emerge from his silence, from his cave of a study, his tall frame bent from hours of hunching over a desk; when he would blink at us, remember slowly who we were, then launch into a lecture perfect in its logic, flawless in its arguments about how I was wasting my life, how in doing so many things I was actually doing nothing.

"It is an illusion, Adam," he would say, "that one can in this way acquire wisdom, acquire any kind of universal perspective. If you truly want to understand, to know, to be able to see, choose one discipline and master it. In it the entire universe will be reflected."

These were the moments when I wanted to draw close to my mother, stand in her growing light, and say something to my father about my soul's work. But ultimately I couldn't, because whether or not it was all folklore, or held, in fact, great stores of truth, I wanted no part at this time in my life in discourses on soul sparks and states of consciousness. I had been surrounded for too many years with lofty and cerebral endeavors, and it had left me with a corporeal hunger, with a desperation for earth and bodies and skin and water, for rocks carving the soles of my feet and bodies entangled in mine.

And so I'd been traveling. I couldn't get enough of fields racing by the windows of trains, of mountains red, pale, hung with clouds, or swallowing whole enormous suns. There was something, too, in the leavings, the departures—one's life in one's palm, the pulse of a rushing train. It was so clear to me at times that this was the true wealth and some of the most important knowledge and it was silent and inarticulate.

Anya knew it, as we sat on the train up to Machu Picchu, her head on my shoulder, a thick striped blanket we had bought in a local market draped over both of us. Anya knew it and so much more.

BETWEEN MY various journeys I would usually come back to New York, and, because my stays were brief and often centered on the need to earn money for the next trip, I would stay in the large Riverside Drive apartment my parents had purchased near Columbia so that my father could move between his home study and his office without having to see too much of the world. For as long as he could manage it he avoided Broadway with its teeming life, walked up Riverside instead, then cut to West

End until it ended, until for a few short blocks he was thrust onto Broadway and into the world. He would hurry—I had seen him do this—looking neither left nor right until the gates of the university swallowed him and he headed to the safety of his office. He had grown step by step, paper by paper, post by post, with bits of my mother's lifeblood stuck to him at every step, into the eminent biblical critic of his generation, as erudite and dry as the parchments he studied, as the urns and manuscripts he flew all over the world to see. He had translated and analyzed one of the alleged authors of the Old Testament, had, it would almost seem sometimes from the way he spoke, sired him, and in the process—especially as I continued to produce nothing that he considered worthwhile—abandoned me in his favor. I couldn't have won, I would tell myself sometimes. How could I compete with long tractates on the vestments of priests, the burned pleading of temple offerings, the purple linen, the cedar, the silver? This son of my father's constructed for him the world he most wanted to see, ran his fingers up and down goblets and candelabras, recited genealogies.

Until her recent venture into the very mysteries that my father sought to dissect, my mother had eased her own loneliness by reading incessantly, anticipating the occasional trips they would take with a hunger that betrayed how very bound she felt, and throwing dinner parties for my father's circle of colleagues. To many of their generation, she seemed the quintessential academic wife. Bright and articulate, she had given up pursuing her own Fulbright in Semitic languages to marry my father and move with him from one postdoctoral position to another until he was tenured at Columbia. She was respected and even loved in the circles in which they moved. But when I would see her at these parties, her drink in her hand, her faraway expression, it was so clear to me that hers was a life unfulfilled. Her stifled wanderlust was apparent in the way she dressed, in the dangling earrings she wore, which she'd found in various foreign markets, in the way she had filled the living room with the treasures she had picked up. Watching her move across that large room that held, along with its conventional sofas, long bits of wall hung with Tibetan masks, antique Persian copper trays, Spanish ceramic plates that conquered every pristine corner of wall, I thought, I am living out her unspent passion, and felt simultaneously a great expansive love for her and a contracted sense of myself as I realized that I'd become a very predictable cliché. Of course I was no less predictable where my father was concerned. Son of the eminent scholar, with no academic aspirations, having never held down a respectable job, I knew in every breath, in every silence, in every pause that I had disappointed him.

Their friends oddly enough adored me—especially the wives. Their own children had marched passionately or willingly into careers in academia, or medicine, or science, all of which were respected in this world as long as one was in the forefront of research. I was the local renegade, the gypsy, and the wives in particular—though they never would have overtly encouraged this for their own children—seemed to goad me on. As if having lived alongside their retreating husbands, having hushed their children for years so as not to disturb his work, I was what they had secretly wished for their sons—an escape, a chance at living fully alongside a woman, at being engaged in a life.

It was on one of my brief jaunts home between trips, as I was counting the days until Anya's arrival, that I had encountered my mother studying the mystical texts late into the night. I was waiting tables at a restaurant on Columbus Avenue and would return at two or three in the morning to find her at the kitchen table thumbing through huge books worn with use, their Hebrew letters curling and dancing their mysterious secrets across the page. Sometimes I would join her, draw her into a conversation about this or that, pull her toward me until again she had weight, gestures, until her old vocabulary returned, until she included me in her glance. But usually I just kissed her, shut my door, and lay on my childhood bed, my body exhausted, my mind alive and dancing with thoughts of Anya, feeling a sharp intake of breath as I remembered the stakes of our dance, then the return of calm as I forced from my mind thoughts of the cliff from which we were hanging and saw instead the sun coming up over Cuzco, Anya's hair on the pillow, time slowed and tasted.

I had met Anya on the outskirts of Cuzco, where I had rented a house for a few months and she in her daily walks had wandered. I was outside fixing a broken shutter when she wandered by, an unexpected vision in this Inca memory of a city. She was long and pale and thin and would have been mistaken for Russian nobility at a different time. Her bearing was regal but at the same time had a naturalness that made her seem at home in this untamed landscape. She said hello as if I didn't surprise her, as if she'd been encountering versions of me all her life. I invited her in for coffee and knew in the first few moments after she'd entered my house that I would fall in love with her.

We were sitting at my kitchen table, between us a large window with its view of the mountains above the red-tiled roofs of the city. I had asked her how long she'd been here, where she'd been before, and she began to tell me that she'd been in Cuzco for about a month, that before that she had traveled through the Greek Islands, but in my mind I was already touching her lips, held by the long line of her arms, waking up next to her in the overcast morning, falling asleep with my head in her lap as we sped on night trains, being with her—a terra firma to cling to, to love. But when I opened my eyes, as if she'd read my thoughts, she made a motion as if to brush something away and told me that she was dying. She had been diagnosed—she spoke quickly as if to get this dreaded speech behind her—approximately eighteen months before with a rare form of leukemia. It was currently in remission but the doctors had told her the next time it surfaced, that would be it. She had opted, since they knew it was ultimately fatal, not to combat it again with all of the aggressive therapies, but wanted instead to try to live this last stretch as fully as she possibly could. And so she'd been traveling, and where for years she had worked hard to juggle her two somewhat incompatible loves for archaeology and poetry, she was now devoting herself exclusively to the poetry. The archaeology, though—she paused, then laughed—was not really allowing her to abandon it, as increasingly her poems were describing particular places with their many layers of time and civilizations, their rituals, their symbols, their views of the world.

She paused, looked out the window, then back at where I sat not moving.

"What about your family?" I asked, though somehow I already knew that there was no family in the picture.

"I was raised by my grandparents," she answered. "My parents died in a car crash when I was very young. My grandparents are not terribly well. They just know that I'm traveling. I don't want them to know yet."

I wanted to reach across the table, take her hand, but I didn't. "Have you been traveling alone this whole time?"

"No." She looked away. "I was with someone for many years. His name was Hans. We had met on a dig. When I was diagnosed, he left his work to travel with me. We traveled through the Middle East, then the Greek Islands. We settled for a while in Santorini. But then I asked him to leave. I didn't want—I don't want to do that to anyone."

She stopped awkwardly and I stopped asking questions. We just sat there for a long while in silence looking out the window that held a view of the colors ripening, softening, of the afternoon dropping down the slopes and into the valley.

"Come," I said on an impulse. I grabbed a bottle of wine, some bread and cheese, and led her out to the rocky hilltop a few yards from my house. We broke open the bread and cheese and had a strange picnic in silence. As the sun disappeared and the darkness grew around us, I could see a growing vulnerability, small glimpses of fear and sadness crossing her face, hints of the relentless battle she was waging to keep her face turned toward life.

When she said she wanted to go, I walked her to the small house she had rented in the center of town. I had been in love before, been entangled in various relationships of more or less intensity, but never had I felt such a sharp sense of recognition, as if this were some missing piece. I understood for the first time the word *destiny* as if until now I had been tossing it lightly from palm to palm and only now had sprung open its ponderous door and was entering it, the winding cavelike structure that it was. Entering it with this woman whose spirit was much larger and braver than mine, whose body could not take itself for granted, whose soul had taken stock of such a large chasm. I wanted to hold her, to kiss her, but I was afraid more than I might have been otherwise to tread those boundaries. I touched her cheek, brushed some hair back from her face, asked her if she wanted me to stay.

"No," she said after a moment in which she looked away as if she were wrestling with the question. I immediately regretted having asked, realizing at that moment that her debate was not about sleeping with me or not sleeping with me but rather about something much more painful, much larger.

"Good night." I kissed her forehead. "I will come to see you tomorrow."

But in the middle of the night there was a knock on my door and she was there. "Damn it," she said as she let me put my arms around her, as she buried her face in my chest.

She stayed with me that night and the night held all of the complexities of what was to come—of bodies very much alive and drawn to one another, then the long hours that followed in which I held her as one would hold a child, and the gift of her trust, of the intimacy of her sleep, felt both precious and unbearable. I knew that it was going to take much more strength than I had to be with her and then to let her go—let her go on living the way she'd chosen to live—let her, when the time came, die and leave me with whatever memories we had created, tethered to this landscape, to all the questions about what might have been.

WE LIVED together for a couple of months in what was for me, and I think for Anya, one of the strangest and in many ways most extraordinary stretches of time I'd known. We lived passionately and economically. By that I mean that there was an economy in the way we dealt with everything. Our days were spent separately and then together seeking the wisdoms and pleasures of where we were. Anya avoided the hot stretches of the day, using those hours to write in the house she still kept in the center of town. Instead she ventured out, first in the early-morning hours when only the carts were stirring, and then later when the sun lowered itself behind the houses. She would walk for hours then, not wanting to miss the shift of light on the soft whites of the buildings, the growing shadows, the lifting winds. We would meet in the evening, bring together food we had bought in the market, and prepare a feast to take outside, often joined by the children who lived nearby. With all their semblance of normalcy those days and weeks demanded from me an enormous discipline. If I was to truly honor the path she had decided to take, I couldn't break down and think about what was to come, the unimaginable terrain that would never again contain these moments, this head on my shoulder. So that when the thought of losing her—of this being borrowed time—would surface, I would still it. I became adept at stilling it because she would not let those monsters surface, steal huge parts of her day, force her to see the shortness of her time rather than the fullness she was determined to inhabit.

Each day when she left the house, I pulled out my journal and wrote. Nothing profound—just descriptions of villages and boat rides, sketches of daily life in Cuzco, images that still returned at unexpected moments of some mountain vista in Nepal. But when I heard her coming, I hid my work. Partly because I didn't want in any way to encroach on a domain so preciously hers, but also—and perhaps this was more the point—having read some of her work, I felt like a complete novice, both in the writing itself and in the breadth of experiences that I had to bring to the page.

Then one day—I hadn't been paying it much attention—I realized that my money was running out. Anya had enough to keep going but not enough for the two of us, and I wouldn't allow her to waste any of it supporting me.

"Come to New York," I said. "It will take me just a short while to put some more money together."

"I don't want to die in New York."

She was leaning against me, my arm tightly around her shoulder. We were sitting on the train up to Machu Picchu. We did this ride periodically.

I wasn't sure anymore whether it was that spectacular destination or the climb together high into the clouds that we preferred, but it had become a ritual of sorts for whenever one of us needed some perspective. Indeed it was hard to imagine Anya in New York, or in any other big city, having only known her against the backdrop of Cuzco. Still, I couldn't imagine leaving her alone for long, and after some time I managed to convince her to join me. We contracted that I would leave in a few weeks and that she would follow several weeks later, once I'd had a chance to settle and find a job.

EVEN AFTER all the traveling I had done, the transition to life in New York was difficult. And to make matters worse, with every day that passed I was growing increasingly uneasy about having asked Anya to come. With every day that I wandered through the city amid the sea of faces hurrying I knew not where, exhausted or despairing or hungry for things that I knew were meaningless for Anya, with every evening that I spent in the restaurant amid the chatter and the mindlessness, with every night that I returned to the strangeness of my parents' household that felt as if it could not contain for a moment longer their new and unexpected dance away from one another, I found myself wondering what I had done in imploring Anya to join me.

What had I imagined? My mother's embrace that could hold anyone, love anyone to wellness? My father's—what? He was emerging less and less from his study. He seemed to be working even harder, as if in nurturing the new young stars in the department, he was being pursued by intimations of his own mortality and was determined to uncover yet another layer, yet another detail heretofore unknown.

As he continued to withdraw, my mother seemed that much more preoccupied. She would study her books late into the night. In the morning she was often gone when I awoke. She would return apologetic and smiling, as if I had caught her at something. I found myself wondering if perhaps there could be someone else, but no, it violated everything I thought I knew of my mother.

But then one day I happened to return from work in the early hours of morning and spotted her. I had run into an old friend at the restaurant, someone I hadn't seen in years. He had waited around until the end of my shift and then we had found a bar and talked until dawn. When I returned home a little before six, the building was still asleep. Only the doorman stirred briefly when he saw me. But as I entered the elevator to go upstairs, I suddenly saw my mother coming out of one of the downstairs apartments. I stepped out of the elevator only to see her turn back suddenly, as if she'd forgotten something and knock on the door she must have just left. I moved a bit closer. The door opened. It was dark in the apartment behind her, and I couldn't make out who she was talking to. It was none of my business, I told myself, but I was already coming up behind her, tapping her gently on the shoulder. She started, then turned and hugged me. "Adam."

Staring out at me was a very old man with a long white beard. He smiled at me over her shoulder. He was a small man, a cross between an elf and a rabbi. He must have been in his nineties. His eyes sparkled with life, in great contrast to his body. His features exuded—I would say light if it didn't sound odd and magical, so I will say an almost impossible and unnatural kindness. My mother stepped back and introduced us. The old man nodded at me. I had the sense, although his expression remained kind and smiling, that he was assessing me in some way. I don't know what it was he saw but he looked puzzled. My mother and I said good-bye and rode up in the elevator silently. When we reached our door, she motioned that we should sit and we sat down side by side on the floor in the hall. Again it grew clear to me that had she been born into my generation, she, too, would have been a world traveler, a global nomad, sitting like this awaiting a train, about to tell some fabulous story to her travel companion. But at this moment I was her companion and she began to tell me a story.

The man she'd been visiting was a rabbi, originally from a part of Russia in which there once had been a large Jewish community. The local synagogue had organized people to take care of him until now, but at the moment there was no one. She would go and have tea with him early in the morning, straighten his apartment, make sure his bills got paid. He had introduced her to some of the kabbalistic ideas, and that's what had gotten her intrigued. He didn't think it was a good idea that she studied it, but she was intrigued nonetheless.

"Where's his family?"

She looked away, fighting back tears.

"You know of course," she began, "about the roundups the Germans conducted in the small villages and shtetls, marching the Jews out to the forests, stripping them of their clothes and jewelry, forcing them to stand around the rims of pits—"

She paused.

"His whole family was killed in one of those."

"How did he manage to escape?"

"He happened to be in the States raising money for an orphanage he had just established. He wanted to go back and see if he could save any of his extended family, but his relatives here forbade him to go, told him there was nothing he could do, that if he went he was sure to die, too. Anyway, according to some witnesses, right after the group of people that included his parents, wife, and children were killed, it suddenly started to pour, thunder and lightening and torrential rains. The SS guards who had carried this out didn't even bother to fill in the pit but left to return to their barracks. It later reached him that a local man from the nearby village had seen a little girl, who matched the description of his youngest child, crawling out of the pit and running into the forest. He spent years after the war trying to locate her, but to no avail."

My mother began to cry silently. I sat there imagining that I was this man, left in this world without everyone he had once loved. I saw that child, digging her way up through twisted limbs, climbing out of that human pile, and running without a mother, without a world, toward some unknown fate.

THE NEXT day the doorbell rang. It was the rabbi, looking for my mother.

She's not here," I told him. I asked him if he would like to come in for tea. "No thank you," he answered softly and with a strong Yiddish accent. My father stepped out of his study briefly. The two men looked at one another. Then the rabbi turned to leave.

What I think my father must have seen was a religious old man—the symbol for him of what stood in his way between fact and logic and tangible, scholarly proof and the minds of some people, including possibly now my mother. What I think my father may have seen was obstinacy in the face of what he considered such overwhelming evidence.

What I saw were the two poles of my own confusion, my own lack of answers, and perhaps, more to the point, my own avoidance of the questions that somewhere had been a subtext in my upbringing.

"He visits other worlds," my mother said the next day. She had returned from the small Cuban diner on the corner and was sitting at the kitchen table, her glasses half steamed by the *café con leche* she had taken to go. She herself made wonderful cups of coffee but when her wanderlust struck and there was no imminent travel, she would do, she said, whatever she could to salvage the pleasures of traveling. Sometimes she'd go to the Cuban place and sit and contemplate the faces and listen to the conversations around her. Other times, like today, she would order the coffee to go and sit at the kitchen table as if she were awaiting some bus or plane.

"What do you mean?" I asked her.

She looked over her shoulder as if to make sure that my father wasn't approaching.

"He tells me that as he has gotten older, he has begun to visit other dimensions. He says that he has 'seen' all the souls of the members of his family but cannot find that one daughter. If she were alive, she would be middle aged by now, probably have grown children of her own."

I wondered if perhaps my mother was going to go off and search for this woman, whether it would be in the guise of this mission that she would take her first steps away from us.

"Why are you looking at me like that?"

"Are you going to go and look for her?"

"I don't know." She looked away. So she had at least considered it.

"He looked for years. There are agencies devoted to these searches— no, I don't think I could do anything that hasn't been done."

"WHAT DO you think about all this?" I asked my father later that day. I knew even as I stood there that this was the wrong thing to do. It felt like a profound betrayal of my mother. Was I so desperate to find even the smallest common ground with this man that I would sacrifice my understanding of my mother, the knowledge that this was not only about my mother's compassionate soul nor about a spiritual journey so much as the beginning of her own independent journey? Was I so in need of his approval that I would betray that deeper certainty that my parents were spinning away from one another, that their concern over me and my fate was no longer going to hold them together? That my mother was starved, starved to think, to explore, to arrive at her own conclusions. That she was slowly drifting away from him and that my father was oblivious. As I stood there knowing all this and awaiting with dread my father's response, I knew that I had betrayed her. I knew that if he moved any closer to me with this dark invitation, I would feel worse.

"What I think," he began, "is that ultimately we are biological animals. The so-called spiritual hungers that individuals and groups have felt and expressed over the ages have served a very clear function for survival."

For once I was grateful for the intellectual sun that ruled this man, that he had not jumped at my invitation, that he had not kindly or unkindly joined me in questioning my mother's judgment.

NEW YORK was beginning to wear on me. I went down to the Village to hear some jazz, wandered in and out of various neighborhoods in search of something. But nothing moved me. Nothing left a mark, as if I were saturated, as if I were engaged elsewhere and couldn't take anything in.

Then the day I was both anticipating and dreading finally arrived. Anya's flight was landing early in the morning. I went to pick her up in my father's old Volvo. As she came toward me down the long hallway I could see that she was paler than I'd remembered, tired and thin. We held each other for a long while, grateful, and also scared. We were silent in the car. She put her head on my shoulder and sighed. I looked out the window. I wanted to be driving by something beautiful, to show her from the first moment that there was something that I could offer her here, but there was nothing but drab highway, flat landscape, housing projects coming up on the right.

"Your mother sounds lovely," she said. "I'm excited to meet her."

Anya of the boundless hope, Anya who still found a way to insist on joy. I was feeling with every moment more unsure of the wisdom of having brought her here.

"Perhaps I can ask her to lend us some money and we can go back a bit sooner."

She looked at me, surprised. "I thought you made it a point to always do this independently, to never ask them or anyone else for money."

"That's true," I said. "But it doesn't feel right suddenly to have taken you from your traveling, from spending as much time as possible in Cuzco."

"You know," she said "I've taken a turn for the worse since you left."

"Nonsense," I said quickly. "You look wonderful."

She was quiet. When I looked over at her, she was staring forward. She looked angry.

"Can we stop please?" she said

"Stop where?"

"Anywhere. It doesn't matter. Just stop."

I pulled over to the side of the highway. Cars were hurtling danger-ously by us.

"Look, Adam," she said, "some things have changed since you left Cuzco and I need to know whether or not you are going to be able to change with them. I have taken a turn for the worse. It's true that I tried as long as possible to do as much as I could but I don't want to escape it anymore. I'd better start looking it in the face because it's demanding that I do so. Yes, I love places like Cuzco, but what I realized after you'd gone was that by letting you in I had already made a choice—a choice I hadn't been ready to make with Hans—to let myself ask you for what I need, to accept your care and support, knowing what awaits you. This is a responsibility that I didn't want to take, that I didn't want to give to anyone. But it happened."

She looked away from me, out the window past the buildings, past the highway and trees.

"What I need now is to be accompanied, not rushed past the dark moments as if they weren't happening, but truly accompanied. I don't know what I am going to feel in the time ahead. I don't know what it will be like. All I know is that I want someone to accompany me, to help me look it in the face, help me perhaps make some sense of it. And that it doesn't matter if it's New York, if it's Cuzco, or if it's Paris."

I nodded. I couldn't speak. I pulled back onto the highway, took her hand, held it all the way to my parents' house. I will never again be able to drive that stretch of highway without feeling the feelings of those moments. As if I had entered a weather system. As if from that point in the road the air grew thick with souls, with hovering souls seeking accompaniment, with souls putting the living to a test. I will always remember how every turn in the road brought a turn in my convictions that I could do it—that I would fail—that I would find my way intuitively—that I would falter as I was faltering now, leave her to a lonely journey.

My mother greeted Anya as if she'd always known her, as if she'd always held her so closely and tightly. The table was filled with a rich assortment of cakes she had picked up at the Hungarian pastry shop. My father also greeted her warmly then began asking her all about Cuzco—questions he had for some reason never directed to me. I saw her face softening. I saw her take in these walls of my life. I saw the bounty of my mother's love. I saw my father—and this was the strangest part—engaged in conversation with her as if she were an equal, as if she were someone of interest. He was asking her about the digs she had worked on and as she answered him, it emerged that she had worked on an important dig in Syria that had unearthed some biblical pottery. He grew animated in a way I had never seen. For Anya, briefly, strangely, we were becoming a family. I began to relax. One moment at a time, perhaps I would be able to do this. Perhaps this house could hold her, we could hold her, give her what she needed. When the doorbell rang, I wondered for a moment who it might be. It was an unlikely hour for visitors. Perhaps the rabbi, I thought, but then no, he had never come back since that day he had encountered my father. But when I opened the door, it was the rabbi.

"Who is it?" my mother called from the kitchen.

Before I could answer, she was turning the bend into the living room with Anya right behind her. I saw Anya stop short as soon as she saw the rabbi. Perhaps she, too, was aware of the sense of light around him. I heard a soft intake of breath and knew suddenly that I would lose her, too, that whether or not it was his intention, the rabbi was going to strip me of the women who had sustained me.

I saw Anya recover, lowering her head in a greeting that spoke of respect and humility. I looked at the rabbi. He was riveted to her face. He was growing paler and paler. I saw a mixture of pain and recognition and joy and disappointment. Then suddenly, his eyes dimmed and he slumped to the floor. My father rushed in and together we pulled him to the couch, propped some pillows under his head. My mother ran to the kitchen and returned with some strong chemical, waved it opened under his nose.

When he came to, he couldn't take his eyes off Anya.

"What is your name?" he asked, almost afraid of his own voice.

"Anya Vasileva."

"And your mother's name?"

"Tatiana."

"Tatiana? No, your mother's name was Malkah. And what happened to your mother?" His voice was almost a whisper.

Anya's eyes grew teary. "She died in a car accident when I was three."

His brow furrowed. He shook his head.

"No."

I looked over at my father. It was impossible, as always, to read his expression.

The rabbi closed his eyes. Anya was beginning to tremble. I wanted to reach out and hold her, wrap my arms around her, take her to my chest and hold her but she shot me a look that said no—not in front of him. I found myself suddenly wanting my father's cool, cerebral rationality. I wanted a different explanation, an intellectual refrain running through my head to diffuse this terrible sense of destiny unfolding before me.

The rabbi extended his arms as if reaching for Anya and, without any shyness, she bent down to embrace him. It was impossible, I knew. Anya was not Jewish. Her family was Russian Orthodox. And she was too young to be his daughter. My mother turned to me as if she'd read my thoughts, as if we were thinking in unison, and whispered, "Perhaps his granddaughter?"

"IT'S IMPOSSIBLE," I told my parents later that night when Anya had collapsed into an exhausted sleep and the rabbi, exhausted, too, having sat in our kitchen for hours drinking cup after cup of tea and holding on to Anya's hand, had, at my mother's coaxing, finally fallen asleep on the couch. My parents, I realized, looked comfortable in the same room for the first time in a long while. It was as if Anya's arrival had shifted something, had pulled them, however briefly, back onto that joint ground on which they had once created a protective place.

"As far as I know, her parents . . ."

"Who knows? Who knows?" my mother interjected. "Perhaps that is why you ended up in Cuzco—to bring her back here. Perhaps that has been the purpose of your travels—to find Anya, to bring her here."

"Hannah." My father looked angry. "Her parents were Russian Orthodox, not Jewish. Her last name has no known Jewish genealogy. Perhaps she bears some physical resemblance to his daughter. Perhaps he reacted that way because he wants more than anything, has been waiting perhaps, to close this chapter of his life."

"Perhaps," my mother said, retreating. "And perhaps it doesn't matter. If this will grant him even the illusion of family, if this will grant her the illusion of family . . ." Before she could finish her sentence she stopped, came around the table, and put her arms around me as if she had suddenly realized that I was about to lose Anya sooner than I had bargained for, that if this evening was any indication, this brave woman and this brave old man needed one another in some way that none of us could fully explain.

AND THAT was in fact the way it was. Anya began to spend a great deal of time with the rabbi. Sometimes I would accompany her to his apartment and he would welcome me lovingly. Still, I felt that I was losing her to more than her imminent death. Her death was mine and hers. We had negotiated around it, resolved it, and I now had to wrestle with it in a new way. But when I saw him, when I saw the vastness of his presence, that sense of light, of worlds beyond this, I thought, Anya is right to prefer him now. What did I have to offer but the reckless chase after a few more collected moments, a few more sunsets over villages, train rides into Peruvian clouds?

"That's not true," she said to me that night when I confessed all of these thoughts. "That's just not true. These are hints, I think, of some other beauty."

"You are beginning to sound like my mother."

Still, in a burst of clarity and in what was perhaps some new maturity I decided to try to keep the clamoring of my own needs out of it, to step back and let Anya have whatever it was she needed. And I was the only one who seemed to be at a loss for a role. My father was growing close to her in a way that with every day surprised me more. She had shown him her poetry and its layers of civilizations, its language that shifted from ancient to modern, had so excited him that he had taken it to colleagues and was on a crusade to have her work recognized and published in some prestigious journals in both the Bible and literature faculties. My mother was feeding her as often as she could, creating colorful and sumptuous displays of food that could only tempt, often talking with her long into the night, conversations that would hush and stammer when I approached, then rush forward again with my retreating step. From the bits and pieces I overheard, there was nothing that I was not supposed to hear; it was just that my presence reminded them briefly of who they really were, how they were really connected. Without me they were a mother and her long-lost daughter, catching up, breathless, telling their tales.

The nights were excruciating. Anya would come and lie by my side, and I felt that this was all that was left me for me to do—to hold this long and shrinking body, to rock it to sleep—then to lie with my eyes open lest the Angel of Death surprise us in our sleep, step out of the shadows of this childhood room that still contained mementos, souvenirs of when time only marched forward and never looked back, and never lost its footing.

THEN ONE day—I don't know what it was—I was sitting on the couch in the rabbi's small and dimly lit apartment. He and Anya were drinking schnapps and playing a game of chess by the light of a small table lamp. I was looking at her, at the line of her back, the thinness of her arms, the sudden lack of steadiness as she got up for a glass of water. I thought, she doesn't have much time, and whether or not this man was in any way family, there were other people who might want to see her.

"Anya," I said that night, "your grandparents—"

She nodded before I could complete the sentence.

"You can write to them, call them, whatever you like. And—" she hesitated.

"Anyone else?" I asked.

"Hans—do you think you can find Hans?"

I felt a palpable pain.

"Where is he?" I asked.

"Ouia, on Santorini."

At first I thought that I wouldn't, that I would allow myself perhaps that one act of selfishness, of self-preservation. But when with every day I saw her energy flagging, I regretted that choice and initiated a flurry of activity to find this Hans Uldrich, expatriate of Holland, citizen of Anya's heart. I contacted the Greek embassy, which helped me track down the telex of the administration of Santorini.

WE RECEIVED a message back saying that Hans was on his way, would be there as soon as he could. I called Anya's grandparents in Chicago. Their voices broke when I told them Anya was with us. Hans had contacted them months ago when he was searching for her, had told them that she was ill. They'd been so worried and hadn't known where to find her. Anya's grandmother was recovering from a bad bout of the flu, but they would catch a flight as soon as they could.

Anya was declining rapidly. She barely had the strength to go downstairs. Instead the rabbi would come up to see her, set up a chess set next to her bed, teach her a few words in Yiddish. I would bring them cups of tea, sometimes just sit and read. One day as he was moving a pawn across the board, I heard him say to her nonchalantly, smiling, "Chanaleh"—this was what he called her—"I have seen Malkah. She is well."

With every day now Anya's energy was dwindling. She was luckily not in much pain but was beginning to have trouble breathing. We would gather in the kitchen at night to debate what to do. Anya felt strongly about avoiding hospitalization and wanted no "extraordinary measures" taken. With the help of the doctor we had found for her when she had first arrived, we convinced her to agree to some oxygen. The rabbi now barely left her side. He held her hand, bent close to her, and whispered things in her ear that none of us could hear. Her lips would curl up into a smile. I don't know if they were tales, bits of the past he believed they shared, or intimations of what was to come, but she seemed to need him more than ever. We called her grandparents, held the phone to her ear. I couldn't understand a word of the Russian but when the conversation ended, she was very upset. I took her into my arms, stroked her back, her hair, felt the bones of her face on my shoulder, felt her shaking, felt for the first and only time the tears that she had never before let come.

"We will look after them," I assured her, and she held me with what felt like all of her remaining strength.

The doctor came again. He emerged from her room before he could remove from his face the expression that told us that she was very close to the end. We increased the oxygen. I found myself hoping that she would hold on until her grandparents arrived, even until Hans arrived. At night my mother would convince the rabbi to go and catch "even a little sleep," and we would take turns sitting by her bedside. One night I must have dozed on my shift. When I awoke, I remember looking at the clock; it was four forty-four. I looked over at Anya. Her eyes were closed. She could have been sleeping but I knew inexplicably that she was gone.

I lay my head on her chest and started to cry, at first silently, then louder and louder until I was wailing like a child. My mother rushed in, my father right behind her. She took me in her arms and held me. Eventually my mother led me out, switched on a small lamp in the kitchen, and put on a pot of strong coffee. Outside the window a thin yellow light was emerging from behind the dark buildings. The sounds of morning, of a city awakening, were beginning to lift, to fill the familiar spaces that they always occupied. We were still sitting there numb, only intermittently aware of the spreading bands of light, of the crawling movement of time, when the doorbell rang. When I opened the door, a tall man with long blond hair stood there. He was much the way I'd imagined him— Hans. The minute he saw our faces, he knew that she was gone. I led him to the bedroom and left him there alone. When he came out, pale, barely meeting my eyes, I felt my heart going out to this man whose heart had broken, was breaking again, here in this room with people he didn't know. I led him up the back stairs to the roof. The sun was just coming up. I pulled out a cushion I kept hidden up there, put it on the highest perch of the roof, and turned to go.

"Stay here as long as you like."

"Thanks," he said. I knew that whatever I felt about him, I was ultimately the one who had accompanied her on this last stretch, that if I had wounds and questions and worries to address, his were no less deep.

WHEN HANS came down, my mother poured him some strong coffee. As he was beginning, at her insistence, to have a little something to eat, my mother jumped up.

"The rabbi—we must tell the rabbi."

She left to go downstairs and returned a few moments later with the rabbi. He was hunched over, his eyes blurred with tears. He nodded at us, then walked slowly on my mother's arm into Anya's room and stayed there with her for a long while. Hans, my father, and I were left in the kitchen, an awkward and unlikely group. After a few moments my father mumbled something and got up and left. He was struggling to control the emotions that were beginning to erupt despite his efforts. I heard the door to his study close. Hans and I sat together for what felt like hours. His gaze was fixed out the window, his body turned away from me, tense. But still we sat together, as if she would have wanted this, as though without it some part of her might be lost.

I'VE BEEN in Santorini for several weeks now. At first I thought that perhaps I should go somewhere else and not step onto this bit of land that had once held Anya in another couple. That I had enough to contend with in the sea of emotions that was just beginning to overwhelm me, to flood me with moments I hadn't known I'd recorded, with the tangibility of her absence, with the knowledge that this finally was the absence that is hinted at in every good-bye, in releasing our skin from another's skin, in the sun scratching its way downward leaving its blood streaks like memories. She was gone and more palpably with me.

When Hans suggested that I come and spend a few weeks, though, it felt somehow right, and we flew together in a long and overflowing silence. I knew that Anya's grandparents would arrive in New York and that my mother would give them all that she had of Anya—stories, memories, the gift of her poems. That she would expand and contain their grief, so that by the time they left they would not feel so alone; they would have become family. I knew that in one form or another, at least temporarily, she was going to leave my father, and that this leaving would launch the next part of their lives. I knew all this and I did not want to be there. And so I accepted Hans's invitation and together we took the night flight to Athens, then slept on either side of a lifeboat on the crowded fifteen-hour boat trip to Santorini. He found me a room on the outskirts of the village and we met in the evening at one of the bars frequented mainly by villagers, but also by some of his friends.

I don't know exactly what I did with those days—sat and watched the sun on the water far below my daily perch, where the big tourist ship circled in search of the new port, the goats scampering up and down the rocky slopes. There were so many questions. An emptiness that had always been there now was big enough to swallow me. And the strangeness of all the events—coincidence or not? And if not, how to explain it? And where did it leave me? A vehicle, a form of transport? Life, death riding on my back to their destination as if I were not of them, but merely a carrier, a barge.

Still, I resisted the two poles that had become my parents—to define it as sheer coincidence in the randomness that was the universe, or to see it as some cosmically determined event. There was something lost, I thought, in the knowing, in dressing oneself in one or the other set of answers. The life, the sense of possibility was in the questions, in the territories not yet known, and in the movement between them with the accompanying sense of expansiveness, of a largeness of view.

I had, in one moment of overriding emotion, gone to see the rabbi several days after Anya died. I don't know what I'd intended to ask him, even if I'd intended to ask him anything, but I had felt a sudden desire to see him, to sit perhaps for a few minutes longer with a bit of Anya. When no one answered, I tried again, but I knew even as I knocked louder and louder that he was gone, that he had died like the other member of an entwined couple, like a soul that has lost its interest in the world. I went to get my mother, then the landlord. We found him as I imagined. He had died in his sleep.

Hans and I were meeting in the evenings, a strange echo to my days with Anya. We would meet at one outdoor bar or another and watch the sun erupting over the water, the white houses aglow. He would ask me hungrily for stories of Anya those last months. I did not ask the same. But it was growing clear to me how little we have of someone. I had this piece. He had that piece. I coveted his piece and it was clear from the questions that he asked, from the expressions that crossed his face, that he coveted mine.

There was some ritual we were performing here and for the time being, it seemed to be one we both needed. It grew clear, too, that Hans's impulse for me to come and the fact that I was not yet ready to leave were both born of our attempts to exercise some control over that greater parting that had spun itself too quickly with its own mad logic and had left us both feeling, each in his own way, discarded and irrelevant.

Everything in my life felt up for grabs, every question, every assumption. But a few things were growing gradually clearer. With every day that I spent with Hans and with his circle of friends, I saw the more clearly what I might become. I saw that he had not yet recovered from Anya's death, but also that he was keeping that pain alive, that it had become an excuse for some inability to move. I saw the people with whom he surrounded himself, each with his or her own life story, with his or her particular pain, looking to blur it in the Greek sun, in the sweltering bodies that poured in predictable waves out of Europe. I saw how their stories had become legends, elaborated over the years or cut to a cryptic sparseness.

It was becoming clear to me, though I felt powerless yet to act on it, that traveling for traveling's sake would no longer fulfill me. That I would wander and sit and climb and drink with little or no satisfaction. That my life would feel purposeless. The people I would meet would seem to be running from themselves. Their stories would tire me, would grow tired as they told themselves. It was growing increasingly clear to me that there were some things I wanted to do. I wanted to walk into my father's study and tell him what I had learned about the preciousness of time to accompany another soul—how many years we had wasted, were wasting. I wanted to take from their secret place the various pieces I'd been writing and see where they would go.

I was thinking about this one day on my ledge, watching the sparks of light dancing on the water, the fishermen's boats going out with their frayed nets. Perhaps it was the sparks, or the particular cast of light, but I suddenly remembered one of my mother's discourses on the movement between worlds, on the way in which our every action created an angel, was reflected in a world of angels, and suddenly, for the briefest second, I thought I saw something hovering just above my head. I thought I saw wings beating hard against the air, a face tense with the tremendous effort it was taking to remain in one place. He seemed to be trying desperately to move, to want with every spark of his being to move, and I thought, very soon I will move on, very soon I will release him, because maybe he wanted to fly to Anya, or maybe he just wanted to fly.

GALINA VROMEN was raised in the United States and spent ten years as a foreign correspondent for Reuters News Agency in Israel, the Netherlands, and Britain before settling in the Tel Aviv suburb of Hod Hasharon in 1993. She is currently a staff translator and copy editor for the English edition of the Israeli newspaper *Haáretz* and teaches English at the Open University in Tel Aviv. Her fiction has appeared in a number of publications, including *Reform Judaism, American Way,* and the *Jerusalem Review.* She is the author of a guidebook to Vienna, published in Hebrew in 1997.

Sarah's Story

GALINA VROMEN

THE MOUNTAINS SOAKED in the oncoming darkness, turning black against the orange sky as I ground the grain for tomorrow's bread.

In the distance Abraham approached, more slowly than usual, bent over his walking stick, his neck craning from side to side like a hungry bird. His headdress and robes billowed around him so that he seemed to sway unevenly, although he moved quickly for a man his age.

When he reached me, he bent and touched my shoulder in greeting and I tilted my cheek to meet the knotty hand he had already withdrawn. I continued grinding while he went inside. He coughed up phlegm and rummaged for a cloth before emerging to wash himself by the flat stone where we keep the water jugs.

I rose to prepare dinner. My knees ached as I stood; my legs could no longer straighten completely. My back, too, refused to reach its full height. The earth these days seemed to beckon, pulling my body down as if about to claim it.

"I almost lost a sheep today—the foolish beast tried to cross the canyon when I wasn't looking—but I got her back," he told me, patting his beard dry.

I nodded in sympathy and put the soup on the fire to boil.

"Isaac not back yet?" he asked.

"No," I said.

"Good."

I looked up in surprise.

"It will give us a chance to talk," he explained, meeting my gaze.

"What about?"

"You must promise not to be upset," he said, sitting on the mat beside me.

I was startled. "Why, what am I going to be upset about? Has Isaac gotten into some mischief?"

"No, nothing like that. You must listen to what I have to say calmly to the end, without interrupting."

"Abraham, what is it?" I said, annoyed at his presumption that he—or I—could rule my emotions.

"Sarah, Sarah, my good wife, we have been through so much together."

"Yes," I answered, but it was more a question than an affirmation. What could he want from me now? What new notion had he gotten into his head? Maybe it had nothing to do with Isaac. Maybe he was thinking of getting a new wife.

"Last night I had a dream. More precisely, a vision—from God."

My eyes searched Abraham's face, my heart filled with fear. Heaven knows, we have enough to be grateful to God for. He has given us happiness, with each other and with Isaac. He has given us of His bounty and I pray in thanks to Him every day, as I should. Like most people, I have a straightforward relationship with Him: I pray and He either answers or

He doesn't. But with Abraham things are more complicated. God is always coming to him with demands. Of course, it is a great honor, but deep in my heart—this is difficult to admit—I think Abraham is overburdened by God. My husband considers me too ignorant to understand, but when you hear my side of the story you will understand that I have come to know far better than Abraham the mystery of God's ways. Sitting by the fire that day, however, I was terrified.

"What did God want?" I asked Abraham.

"Well, He told me to take Isaac to a mountain in the region of Moriah and—sacrifice him."

"What?" I said incredulously.

"Sacrifice him, like a lamb."

"Are you mad?" I said, so startled I dropped my usual deference for my husband. "Is God mad?" I whispered. I peered at his face for a glimmer of hope. But he clenched his sharp jaw, just visible under his sparse white beard, and his nostrils flared in determination, offering me no comfort.

"I don't know, Sarah. The truth is I don't know. I didn't mention it this morning, because I had to think about it, try to figure God's reasoning. We waited so long for Isaac, wanted him so much, and now," his voice broke in bewilderment, "God is asking us to give him up."

"Are you sure you understood right?" I rushed to interject, my voice suddenly shrill and insistent. "Maybe God meant something else, maybe the vision has another interpretation."

"No, no Sarah. I am . . . ," he hesitated, overcome with emotion, "absolutely sure of the vision." Holding back tears, he added hoarsely, "And out of love of God, I must obey Him, just as you, out of love for me, are obliged to obey me. Oh Sarah," he sobbed.

I put my arms around his thin shuddering shoulders, trying to comfort him. I myself was tearless. My mind was racing. "How can it be? Can He really want us to do this? Why? How can He be so cruel?" Huddled on the mat, we clung to each other in misery as layers of night washed over us.

After a while I rose and silently served Abraham his soup in one of the green earthen bowls he had brought me when we first settled on our land. My mouth was too sour with rage to eat. "Please give Isaac some soup when he comes. I cannot stand to face him. I am going to bed." I went inside and lay down, drained and numb.

On my bedding I thought about Isaac, the miracle of my old age. No one can imagine how fervently I had prayed for his birth. No one can fathom the jealousy with which for years I had watched women suckle babies—such jealousy that once, when Hagar, our servant, was feeding her son, I found myself imagining the baby biting off her teat, leaving the breast badly gashed and oozing blood. I was so humiliated at the time by my thoughts that I ran to a field and vomited. Afterward I lay in that field for a long time, with my eyes closed, trying to calm myself. But the cacophony of the bugs was as insistent as the dull longing in my hollow womb. I opened my robes and looked at my pitiful belly, already sagging with age like the toothless smile of a beggar. Much as I love my husband and wanted him to have a son, even if I could not give him one, it drove me crazy to see Hagar with their son Ishmael. I know I agreed to the whole arrangement—I even encouraged it—but afterward it took all my restraint not to kill her.

When I became pregnant, I didn't realize it for six months. When Isaac was born, I would wonder for hours at the light brown tufts of his hair, fine as threads of a spiderweb, catching the light in all the colors of the rainbow as he suckled at my breast. Later I was stunned by his dogged determination in learning to walk. He would totter, drunk on the elixir of mobility, his eyes fearless from effort, defying my predictions of his imminent fall. A few years later, while running after a sheep, he scratched his face badly in the brambles. I cried for hours when I realized a few months later that the tiny scars on his translucent conch skin would never disappear. Recently the child had been melting away, like clay streaming down a mountain in the flash floods of spring. He was turning all gangling sinew, an excess of arms and legs mysteriously held together by bulbous knots of shoulders, knees, and hips. The tufts of dark hair tentatively sprouting under his arms and on his chest made him seem more vulnerable than manly. Like clay, he would re-form into something else, the same and yet different, and I would still love him. These days he brushed me aside if I tried to kiss him. But I could tell—by the slight hesitation before he pulled away—that he did not entirely reject my affections. He still liked to tell me in his careful, pedantic way about whatever he had noticed while tending the sheep. If he saw a plant new to our region, he would bring it to show me. It was through him, rather than from Abraham who was much more reticent, that I first heard about the plagues that visited our neighbor's sheep, or the birth of a new calf.

But what was I doing, reminiscing pleasantly after what Abraham told me?

God is impossible, I thought to myself. How can He be so unreasonable? We judge our own success in life by our ability to learn the art of moderation, knowing how to ask in moderation, knowing how to give in moderation. But God is immoderate, both in what He gives us and, now, in what He is asking us to give up.

Suddenly I imagined the scene. Abraham tying up Isaac. Would the child resist? Abraham would talk to him, try to soothe him at first. Then the look of horror in Isaac's eyes as he realized what his father planned to do. Would he call for me and scream in terror as Abraham grabbed his neck? Would Abraham hesitate a moment before pressing a glistening knife to the throat? I saw the vein in Isaac's neck, convoluted and pale blue, always bulging at the slightest provocation. It was the vein that had strained when he had first tried to hoist himself over the wall near our encampment; that had throbbed as he screamed, more from outrage than from pain, when he fell on the other side. It was the vein that pulsated when he lugged jugs of water and when he called out to his father in the field. It was the vein I stroked when he occasionally still lay his tired head on my lap as he had loved to do as a child.

I envisioned the knife descending toward the vein. First the gleaming metal squeezed against the meager fat on his neck, like a hand gripping a thin arm in fear. Then a line as it cut through the skin—a clean cut. A last scream. Then blood. Rich, dark, fresh. At first oozing hesitantly, then gushing. The child whimpering, each whimper prompting a fresh spurt.

Would the blood cover Abraham's hand? Would he hold Isaac as he died or turn away?

Over and over the scene surged through my mind. Abraham's fingers grabbing the soft skin. Visions of the wound ripping open flashed like a never-ending lightning storm against a red sky of blood.

I tried to stop the visions. But they were replaced by yet more horrible ones. Abraham lighting a fire under the limp body. The flames blackening Isaac's slim, pale chest, licking the cavity under his ribs to mere bone, then ash. The dark curls on his hair in flames, his eyes sizzling to nothingness. Would Abraham turn away and weep? Or would he stand, facing the fire, leaning on his stick, and mutter "It is God's will" in a litany against pain? Would it work? Could one diminish pain with such words?

No, I concluded. If this is God's will, then He is an outrage. I, for one, will not do His will. If Abraham insists on fulfilling the demands of such an unjust God, I will take Isaac away, we will run as far as we can.

But I could think of nowhere to go. Abraham was sure to use all his resources to track us down. He would send messengers and scouts far and wide to apprehend us. And in the end, I knew, he would succeed—with God's help or without. No, there was no place to run. I had to think of something else.

The shadows from the fire outside leaped and dimmed on the tent wall like my feverish thoughts. I twisted and turned, discarding one idea after another. I considered telling Isaac what his father planned, in hopes the boy would resist. But Isaac would either bow to his father's will or he would have to kill Abraham. Knowing Isaac, he would probably honor his father and agree to his own death; for he adored his father no less than Abraham adored God. It was too cruel to fathom—Isaac knowing his father was ready to kill him, like that very occasional lamb at the slaughter that, sensing its fate, ceases bleating, and arouses our pity more than the scores of other beasts that cry out for mercy.

I considered killing Abraham myself but feared my will would desert me at the last moment; for, truly, I loved Abraham, fool though he was in succumbing to his vision. Besides, I could see no way to do it. Grab a knife and drive it into his heart? He was no longer a strong man, but then neither was I as strong as I had been. He was sure to resist, fend me off, perhaps even kill me.

I was amazed at my own thoughts, astounded that God could bring me to such despair that I would consider killing my own husband. God heaps nightmares on us as carelessly as a child pours sand on a colony of ants.

As I tossed and cried, dismissing one thought after another, I heard Isaac approach the fire outside the tent.

"Isaac, I want to go look at some sheep in the Moriah region. I've heard say they are especially good for breeding. I want you to come with me," I heard Abraham tell him.

Isaac sounded pleased. "Shall I gather provisions first thing in the morning and get the donkey ready?"

"Yes, we'll leave at sunrise."

"Well, then I'd better get some rest."

Abraham wished his son good night and soon turned in himself. He lay by me, tried to hug me from behind. But I stiffened. How can you? my mind protested. Soon I heard him snoring, sleeping soundly. How peaceful perfect faith is! It must be easier to sacrifice your son if you believe in perfect causes. But where does perfect faith end and utter madness begin? How are we to know the difference? It is the doubters like me, who through some lack of grace or some excess of vision, either do not see enough or see too much, who cannot sleep. Abraham is resigned. I am not. But Isaac is no less my son than Abraham's. Doesn't God have to ask if I, too, agree to this sacrifice? I do not and I will not. I don't know how I will stop Abraham, but I will.

In the morning Abraham rolled out of bed just as the dusty light of early morning filtered into our tent. He coughed, stumbled outside, and splashed water on his face. He went to the woodpile and began to chop up branches, loading them onto the donkey while Isaac boiled water for tea, got food for the beast, and awakened the two servants who were to accompany them.

I was already alert, having been unable to sleep all night. I lay taut and tense, waiting for them to leave. Isaac, bless him, came in to kiss me. I pretended to sleep, as I did not want him to see the terror in my eyes. I feared that if I allowed myself to look at him, I would grab him and refuse to let him go and he would come to know the true purpose of his trek to Moriah. So I only moved slightly and murmured a bit so he should know that his kiss had been, somehow, acknowledged. My heart cried as I inhaled his must with the kiss, trying to imprint on my mind that sweet-smelling mixture of sheep, burned wood, sweat, and the trace of mint from the morning tea still on his lips.

Abraham came in also to kiss me. He stood and looked over me lovingly, imagining me to be peacefully slumbering. I opened my eyes, stinging from lack of sleep. "How can you?" I hissed at him.

He shrugged. "What I must do is harder than what you must do. You just have to resign yourself to our fate. I, by my own hand, must implement it."

"What foolishness. You think because what you must do is difficult that it is somehow right. I will never forgive you, Abraham, or that God of yours. No mother would," I whispered. "I will not let you do it."

He shrugged again. He scowled, his jaw pointed firmly forward, his lips narrowing like a closed oyster shell in that stubborn look I had known in him all our life together. "Peace be upon you," he said quietly and left the tent.

No sooner had they left than I rose from the bedding, washing and dressing as fast as my clumsy limbs allowed. I rebraided my long gray hair and put on a white robe. The color accentuated my skin, which was darker than my son's and had gone spotty and rough like a lizard's with age. My frame, always small, had become more brittle and spare with time so that the robe hung on me as loosely as on a peg. I grabbed a small bag of flour from the storage hut, filled a leather water flask, and strapped both on my back. I dug up money from the hole under our bedding where Abraham hid our coins. I took all there was.

"Do not wait for me tonight," I told one of the shepherds who normally helped Abraham. "I'm leaving you in charge here until Abraham or I return."

I set out as the sun finally made its full face visible over the horizon, bathing me in its light. Despite my distress, I closed my eyes to greet it. At this hour its warmth was still welcome, although I knew I would curse its heat well before the day ended. I figured Abraham had to be heading northeast toward Moriah and soon I picked up his tracks. My every joint ached with the effort. "Never mind," I muttered to myself, shaking the pebbles out of my sandal with each step, my feet almost ankle deep in sand. "I'll get used to this. Old bones are always stiffest in the morning. The important thing is to keep up." I looked ahead, where Abraham, Isaac, and the servants fell from view and reappeared again as they made their way through the dunes.

It was early spring; the tenderest grass spread across the sand, thicker in the gullies where the winter rains had collected. It looked as if an almighty hand had sprinkled the hills far and wide with a layer of fine green dust. There was nothing around but sky, sand, grass, and that un-dulating speck of humans in the distance to which I remained riveted like a hungry dog to a dangling bone.

By noon I was gasping for breath, my ankles and fingers were swollen, but at least my bones no longer ached. I was covered in dust. I could feel the grains of sand lodged deep in my wrinkles. My throat was parched al-though I had made generous use of my water flask all morning. "How much farther can it be to the Moriah region?" I wondered.

It turned out to be another two days. I will never know how I managed to keep up with the men. But I did. I suppose I should be grateful that Abraham has aged no more gracefully than I have; the trip must have been difficult for him, too, and it must have been he who slowed down the others. I was so exhausted at night that when a beetle crawled across my forehead and headed down my cheek as I rested, I did not even lift an arm to brush it away. My back throbbed dully on the hard ground; my fingers were so swollen I could hardly grasp the water flask for a drink.

On the second night they bedded down in a nomad settlement. I set up my far more modest camp just out of their hearing. Fortunately, in the course of the day I had come across a caravan loaded with merchandise from the south of Sinai. I stopped the leader, hoping he might sell me a blanket, which he did. Then, being an adept merchant, he tried to sell me fabrics as well, some marvelous pieces such as I had never seen before. I was about to reject the idea, for I think it is foolish for a woman with as many wrinkles as I to bedeck herself with finery. But then it occurred to me that some magnificent fabric might be just what I needed to carry out the plan that had been forming in my head as I stumbled across the desert in pursuit of my son. So I bought some white gossamer cloth and some brilliant blue fabric, both of which were intertwined with threads of the most delicate gold.

On the third day Abraham had awoken and was staring at the distant mountain when I spotted him from my own camp behind a nearby bush.

Instantly I knew that this was the mountain he planned to climb to carry out his mad mission. I folded my blanket and scurried away just as Abraham was unloading the wood from the donkey and instructing the servants to await him. I passed a tent at the end of the settlement that was out of sight and sound of Abraham's camp. Before it, I found a young man fixing a cutting tool. He was unusually tall, with red hair that curled and cascaded down his shoulders.

"I wonder if you might help me," I said.

He looked up, startled. Before he could dismiss me, I rummaged in my clothing for the bag of coins I had hidden in my bosom. "You must do as I tell you and you will be handsomely rewarded."

He shrugged in a movement at once indifferent and inquisitive.

I beckoned him to follow me, signaling him to keep quiet. We came within sight of Abraham, who, having left the servants behind, was proceeding up the mountain alone with Isaac. "You must help me up the mountain, after those two men. But they must not know of our presence."

Rock by rock, we wove our way up the mountain. I could feel my heart pounding, my head, too, first from the effort, then also from the heat. My strength almost failed me but the young fellow was of the helpful, unimposing sort: he pushed me when I needed pushing, and pulled—

gently—when I needed to be pulled. I was grateful for his silence. By the time we reached a plateau near the top, I was shaking from exhaustion. "Now what?" he asked. He had to wait for me to catch my breath before I could answer.

"Now we wait a bit," I whispered, still gasping. Abraham was just a stretch above us. There was a rustling in the bushes near us. "What's that noise?" I asked in a whisper.

"Probably a mountain goat," the young man whispered back. "Would you like me to try to catch it for our lunch?"

I was about to reject his idea, as a feast was the last thing I could imagine at the time. But then it occurred to me that a mountain goat might serve us well. "Do you think you can catch it without harming it?"

"I can try," he said.

"Do. But be quiet," I instructed him. He leaped into the bush, rope in hand, and emerged a few minutes later, slightly scratched on his arm but with the animal—a ram, as it turned out—in tow, the rope around its neck.

"Please tie it to a tree," I instructed him. When he was done, I took the rich fabric I had bought out of my bag. "Wrap yourself in this," I told him.

"What is this?" he said. "Are you mad, woman?"

"This is what I am paying you for. Put it on, let the cloth puff around your neck." When he had done so, I gave him a piece of gossamer to add at the last moment. Then I told him what to do. He proceeded ahead of me.

Truth be told, he followed my instructions perfectly. The white cloth was almost like a cloud, billowing around his face, and the gold threads made the blue cloth blinding as it caught the full sun of midday. Nothing could have looked more angel-like than that nomad, with his brilliant red hair. "Abraham, Abraham," he called out.

"Here I am," Abraham answered.

The nomad stepped into the clearing. "Do not lay a hand on the boy," he said. "Do not do anything to him. Now I know you fear God, because you have not withheld from me your son, your only son."

My savior said his lines in a marvelous sonorous voice, just as I had ordered him to, then backed away and allowed himself to be hidden by the thicket. I stood not more than three arm lengths away, holding on to the ram.

When the nomad—I never learned his name—had moved away, I let the animal go. The poor beast was so overcome by freedom that as it bounded to the top of the mountain, its horns caught in the thicket. Abraham seized it and offered it as a sacrifice to God. So the ram lost that precious freedom to be alive. But my son, my beloved son, regained his.

And whenever Abraham retells the events of that strangest of days, as he so likes to do, I remain silent and nod solemnly, particularly when he reminds all who will listen that God works in mysterious ways.

DANIEL M. JAFFE grew up in New Jersey and now lives in Massachusetts. His short stories and essays have appeared in dozens of literary journals, magazines, and anthologies, including *Response: A Contemporary Jewish Review, The Greensboro Review, The Florida Review, Christopher Street, Soviet Jewish Affairs* (United Kingdom), *The Abiko Quarterly* (Japan), *Fiction and Drama* (Taiwan), and *All the Ways Home* (New Victoria Publishers, 1995). His translation of the Russian-Israeli novel *Here Comes the Messiah!* by Dina Rubina was published in 2000 (Zephyr Press). He is the recipient of a fellowship from Princeton University for language study in Russia, as well as a Massachusetts Cultural Council Professional Development Grant. Jaffe's first novel, *The Limits of Pleasure,* will be published in fall 2001 by Southern Tier Editions, an imprint of the Haworth Press.

Sarrushka and Her Daughter

DANIEL M. JAFFE

And I, like a soundless continuous scream
Over the buried thousands and thousands,
I am each old man shot here,
I am each child shot here.

YEVGENY YEVTUSHENKO, "Babi Yar"

WHILE SEATED IN THE SHADOW of the brown monument at Babi Yar, I learned of a mother and daughter, the mother dead and buried in a markerless grave like so many others in Ukraine, the daughter, perhaps alive and still fulfilling her duties on earth. Their story was told to me by a girl no more than twelve or thirteen, a child with a wide face and lapis-blue eyes.

She approached from the foot of the monumental tower of bodies and sat down beside me on a flat gray stone, where she proceeded, while shifting uncomfortably and slowly unwinding her black braids, to tell of a time fifteen years before Babi Yar was to become party to deeds inspiring monument, symphony, and poem. She told me a tale of Kiev—a city then nursing wounds from foreign invaders, from domestic ones, from convulsions that had nearly rent the capital in two.

OLD SARRUSHKA MOISEEVNA, a thin, bent woman just a few years over one hundred, frail but with knees strong enough to support her soup-carcass of bones without a cane, had never married the man her papa had chosen, had never wanted another body to invade her own. She had felt winters grow more harsh over the decades, had seen food grow more scarce, had watched wars of various labels drift beneath her apartment windows, had wearied of sewing red linings into her white coats and dresses—one week wearing them as designed, the next week wearing them inside out in the hopes that rifle-bearing patriots guarding the streets below would permit the color-coded citizenness to pass undisturbed. She had watched double-headed eagles flee to the skies and hammer-crossed sickles rise from beneath the earth in their place, had seen her parents die, had read that her brothers were killed, that her nephews and in-laws were massacred in the west or frozen in the east. Remaining steadfast and determined never to abandon the cold-water flat of her youth, she gradually grew lonely and longed for a child.

One Yom Kippur afternoon, having descended from her third-floor apartment high above the corner of Mezhigorskaya and Nizhni Val, she walked not to the bakery for her weekly bundle of three rolls, but hesitated, turned, and went instead to Number 29 Shchekovitskaya Street, a pink synagogue in her neighborhood of Podol, hoping to hear the Service of Remembrance, the prayers chanted in memory of the dead, to listen to them, sing them in her heart for those who had died before her, and to memorize the verses so that one day, after she had departed this life leaving no one alive to chant on her behalf, she could recognize the lilt intended for other ears in heaven's breezes and, in hearing those somber strains, would at least know that she, too, once had lived.

In the synagogue yard on a moss-covered tree stump she sat and listened to sharp voice cracks pierce the building's windows and walls, heard the words she had never learned to read; she hummed the rhythms softly. Then she crept to the synagogue steps, knelt at the entrance, bowed her head in prayer. Unable to think of words to convey the trembling in her heart, she opened her mouth, moved her lips in silent meditation.

A robed figure stepped out from among doorpost shadows. Cloth sandals flapping on dusty feet, he stroked his dirty-snow beard with a translucent hand, asked whether old Sarrushka were ill from hunger or had drunk too much sacramental wine the eve before.

"I pray," she whispered.

"Then come inside, read an entire book of prayers."

"I have only one left unspoken," she whispered again. "Company now; to be remembered after I am gone."

The translucent figure rested his hands on her head, mumbled in a tongue she did not understand, then said, "Go, tomorrow morning, to the Dnieper's banks."

She brought her lips to the fringes dangling in the robe's creases, kissed them, clutched them to drag herself erect, and hobbled away. The next morning she found on the Dnieper's banks a drifting basket woven of freshly mown hay and pitch, bearing an infant inside, one whining to be clutched to old Sarrushka's dried fig of a breast.

She coddled her newborn daughter and spoke to little Pamya of all that she had observed in her more than one hundred years, and as her baby grew into childhood old Sarrushka taught her to interpret the length of cuts on fingers, the thickness of calluses on toes, the shape of scabs on knees. Pamya scurried about all day, now in the playground, now on the sidewalks, now in parks, now at school, and she would re-count to old Sarrushka, in rushed, breathless gusts, as they lay side by side every night in bed, the excitement of fire-escape pigeon dances, of Tsentralnyi Park squirrels working with greater industry than Pamya had ever seen in neighborhood shops, of mysterious alphabets and numbers she was learning. The girl spoke, as well, of historical events that in old Sarrushka's memory had taken different shapes. For years their daily ritual continued.

One evening after a dinner of barley and onion gruel, Pamya refused to recite for Sarrushka the day's events, yanked out the pink bows from her hair, untangled thick braids from on top of her head, shifted uncomfortably at the table, and stood, quaking at the sight of a moist red spot on her warm wooden chair. Sarrushka smiled and embraced her daughter, explained a new mystery of nature. Relieved, Pamya pressed her lips to the forehead of her mother, and the old woman bolted upright with sudden new knowledge—sudden sights, sudden sounds of Pamya's day: how Pamya had helped peel layers from the purple cabbage head of the sunburned lady downstairs, how Pamya had helped diaper, in courtyards off Kreshchatik Avenue, babies on benches and had held and rocked them as if her own, how she'd listened politely to fairy tales about murderous Grandpa Frost of the North and evil Baba Yaga of the forest, stories told by white-kerchiefed grandmas who insisted upon the existence of dangers forewarned by fable and myth. From that evening forward Pamya never needed speak to her mother at nighttime as they lay in bed; she had only to kiss her forehead to relate the discoveries of the day.

While running up steep, cobblestoned St. Andrew's Hill one spring afternoon, Pamya came upon a doll of rags that had fallen into the gutter. She picked it up in wonder about the owner, kissed the doll on its faint red lips, felt no answers tingle on her own.

"I must find out who lost her," Pamya said that evening during dinner. "She was part of some little girl's past."

Sarrushka peered across the table at her growing daughter, a spring finally bubbling up from the earth.

Pamya hunted for the doll's former owner, carried the doll all around town, displayed her overhead like a May Day parade banner, marched throughout Podol to every school and playground, even to meetings of young Party faithful in their red-kerchief yokes. Finally, as Pamya rested with the doll by the statue to Bogdan Khmelnitsky—old liberator of Ukraine and destroyer of the Jews—a weeping woman in black recognized the doll, ran up and grabbed it, hugged the clump of grimy rags to her breast, invited Pamya to a funeral service for a daughter who had died of consumption.

At midnight old Sarrushka accompanied Pamya to pay respects at St. Sofia's Cathedral, a museum for the public during the day, a secretly functioning church at night. Pamya watched flat frescoed characters hunt and dance, walked on floor tiles of Mideastern crescents and King David's stars, and for a moment joined the Russian Orthodox stepping on Muslim and Jew.

The bereaved mother, holding a newborn in one arm, waved Pamya to her side with the other, pointed to the rag doll on the shoulder of her dead daughter. The girl was half Pamya's age, dressed in frilly white, lying in an open coffin trimmed with pink bunting, a band of white cloth wrapped around her sallow brow, her head resting on a pillow and tilted forward so she could face her little breast where a small icon was propped, a painting of the Iverskaya Madonna, Baby Jesus in her arms. Old relatives moved from among candles flickering beside the coffin's head and feet, shuffled forward, pressed their lips to the dead girl's white-cloth band to bid a farewell kiss.

Pamya, too, touched her lips to the cloth band, then felt a current of shock course through her body. She jolted upright, bent suddenly forward, her shoulders hunched from an unfamiliar weight. She turned in panic to the dead girl's baby sister cradled in her mother's arm, reached out to touch the small round face, kissed the infant lightly on the lips, and Pamya felt the weight leave her, felt a warm lightness drift throughout her body, puffs of steam released from a boiling pot.

The baby's eyes widened for a moment at Pamya's touch and kiss, her face glowed with an icon's Byzantine halo, then the child fell asleep, and with eyes shut she murmured—this infant who did not yet know how to speak—about the night her now-dead sister had sewn the dolly together from scraps, of her sister's chest pain in the days before her death, of her sister's birthdays celebrated years before.

All whispered of Pamya's magic.

From that night forward Pamya felt drawn to suffering and death, would rush to place her hands on the sunken belly of a dying street beggar, to ripple her slender white fingers along his protruding tanned ribs as if strumming a harp, to bring her ear close to his mouth to catch the precise timbre of his very last breath, and then to touch her lips to his brow. She rushed about in hospital corridors on the heels of bustling nurses, poked her pencil-nub nose into this ward and that, pressed her tender lips full on the mouths of as many women as possible who were dying—in childbirth, from botched abortions, from food poisoning, from cancers too long unnoticed then too long untreated, from tuberculosis, from beatings by drunken husbands—and then, heavy with memory, Pamya lumbered about to find newborns whom she could kiss and entrust with the departed's life treasures.

For years Pamya lived in order to help neighbors defeat the loss of death, and old Sarrushka lived in order to care for her daughter.

Then one autumn the shape of the universe changed for Ukraine—another Napoleon, one who munched strudels instead of eclairs, cast his shadow over the east, advanced across plains and through forests, sent web-flopping goose-soldiers along the dirt roads to Kiev, filled the capital with cannon and guns, drew tight a noose that would choke and slowly kill. Hunger of flesh as much as starvation of spirit changed the face of the city: lawyers and plumbers and shopkeepers turned into grubs writhing for tossed morsels of potato or bread; little boys formerly enchanted by mysteries of the Baal Shem Tov transformed into flea-bitten alley cats scrounging at night for escape holes in fences, for mice to gobble raw; old scholars collapsed unnoticed on sidewalks, grew so thin they turned into transparent doormats; mothers learned to lasso toddlers who risked floating to heaven because of their bellies' bloating; and those who still had teeth gnawed and swallowed Muscovite coins in the mistaken belief that fat on the body was a safe place to store wealth. It was a time when miracles filled Aryan eyes: Jewish torsos disappeared completely from beneath necks, shrank into nothing, left visible only long, greedy faces and dangerously sharp hooked noses; Gypsy bodies, too, dissolved with the morning dew, faded into large swarthy ears dangling perverse rings of black magic; psychiatric hospitals reconfigured into centers for fumigation of societal pests; and wooden houses of worship to a passé God turned into funeral pyres sacrificing human trash.

The devastation spurred Pamya on to continue her ministrations of kissing the dead and dying. She slept less and less to extend the workday for her mission, until old Sarrushka refused to allow her daughter to set foot from their home, feared the strain on Pamya's health. They sat every evening well after dusk, huddled together to share each other's warmth—the apartment's only heat—and listened for the sonorous ring of cast-iron church bells whose tolls might swaddle Kiev in peace, but heard instead shrill concerts playing from the ravine known as Babi Yar, sonatas and symphonies that reverberated across the steppes, orderly concertos, repeated refrains of staccato-noted runs followed by in-evitable long rests, *rat-a-tat-tat* serenades, machine-gun music, occasion-ally accompanied by a choral high-pitched note.

It was the chorus that drew Pamya from the apartment, the arias that Sarrushka could not block out of her daughter's ears by scratching the walls and forming earplugs of mildew and mold. During an intermission from Babi Yar one night, Pamya broke free from her mother's pleading shields, followed the strains of silence to the black ravine.

She crept over wooden fences, below barbed wire, slid along a blood-coated field, saw red everywhere, bright red in moonlight like a lover's expectant wetted lips, red slowly turning purple into a capillary-crushed black eye. She crawled along the thickening dark crust that smothered every pore in the earth's skin, that would, when finally peeled away, leave the earth barren and scraped.

Once she reached the edge of the ravine Pamya flung herself on the heaving mass of earth, clawed through the yellow sand, through the stench that clubbed her about the face; she twisted among the Ukraini-ans shot in revenge for partisan bombings, the captured Soviet sailors of the Dnieper fleet, the local soccer team that had dared to defeat the in-vaders'. She wormed among the Jews and Gypsies who had displayed the arrogance of being Jews and Gypsies. She crawled and slithered among ten thousand corpses, some bleeding from the head, some from the chest, some not bleeding at all because their veins had already emptied, and Pamya convulsed from ten thousand tremors of shock, of fear, of pain.

As her fingertips and lips grazed the clammy twisted neck of one, then the protruding split shin of another, she witnessed a parade of grateful soccer fans, the ceremonial awarding of a medal for bravery, the secret baptism of a firstborn grandson, the marriage of a youngest daughter, Sunday afternoons building castles in the sand, Sabbath-evening dinners with four generations at the table, ten thousand packages of moments remembered.

She ran from the ravine that was Babi Yar, ran with lungs exploding to the Dnieper for soothing, but it had turned as red as the ancient Nile, partly from blood draining along tributaries from the ravine, partly from shame at continuing its flow. Pamya dove into the Dnieper, swam deep until completely immersed in the copper-tasting blood, swam deep until she could match her pulse to the throb of the river's. She dragged herself onto shore, slept while the pores of her skin closed shut around droplets of Dnieper red, while the follicles of her hair thickened and swelled magenta, while her eyes turned deep burgundy, her teeth stained pink.

Old Sarrushka, alarmed at her daughter's long absence, trudged about the city in search of the young woman's crumpled form, then found her, asleep among new-grown reeds at the river's edge. Old Sarrushka, weak and slight as her 120th birthday approached, carried her heavy daughter on creaking shoulders and back, dragged the young woman home and lay her limply in bed, spoon-fed her soup of scavenged potato skins and milk.

Pamya convulsed and ranted for days—she was a ballerina, pirouetting down the block, toe-dancing on fence posts; she was a baker kneading fresh rye into loaves for the Tsar, a rabbi in Jerusalem chanting Scripture by heart, a riveter forging weapons of iron. Old Sarrushka knew the only cure for her daughter, so she spread word begging new mothers to bring their babes.

For days women from all over Kiev—Jewish and Gypsy mothers hidden in Christian spare rooms and basements, in walls and cupboards of abandoned homes, Russian mothers, Ukrainian mothers—dragged themselves from birthing beds to bring their babies to Pamya, formed lines around the block desiring their children to receive Pamya's gift of a remembered husband or father, son or sister, mother or neighbor or cousin or greengrocer or dairyman or seamstress or even an unknown soldier or someone else's murdered grandma or auntie, a partisan, a Jew who had fled the Warsaw ghetto only to end up in Babi Yar, dead.

Pamya sensed that she held more memories from Jews to pass on than from others, but did not know whether baby Russian lips would attract only Russian spirits, whether Ukrainian infants would attract only Ukrainian pasts, or whether two related souls would actually repel like identically charged magnetic poles. She hid her inability to control the spark that leaped from her to newborn children, did not reveal her failure to discern whether the wide-eyed jolt of an infant she touched signaled ancestral recognition or delight at an exotic mixing of swarthy and fair.

Some Jewish mothers assumed that Pamya would impart only Jewish memories to their children, some Gypsy mothers assumed she would transfer only Gypsy spirits to theirs. Some Russian and Ukrainian mothers actually made a demand of purity, each concerned with preventing alien memories from polluting their children's future. But others— mothers long ago accustomed to passing ancient Tatar and Khazar milk in the flow from their European breasts—did not care, understood that someone would know their lost sisters and sons if only their children undertook to know another's.

After Pamya finally released all memories absorbed in the ravine and red river, after her teeth returned to white, her eyes lost their burgundy, her hair follicles again looked black and fit through the tines of a comb, after her limbs felt completely light and strong, she returned to the site of death to crawl among ten thousand more, repeated the cycle month after month. And once every month old Sarrushka would find her daughter on the Dnieper's shore, would carry Pamya home on her crooked back, each time bending deeper toward the ground until her nose plowed furrows in the earth on the path toward home and a waiting line of nursing mothers.

But one morning after Pamya had gone once again to the ravine, as old Sarrushka hobbled as usual toward the river's edge, her back now so bent and curved that she could see only the tops of her straw slippers, she tripped on the protruding root of a tree stump and fell, struck her head on a flat gray stone. Curled on her side, a dried, autumn gourd too long on the vine, old Sarrushka blew a kiss toward the river, knew that she could not wait for Pamya to crawl and find her, that she had strength only to grab the fringes of the translucent robed figure who appeared at her side, and to join her last breath to that of a passing breeze.

HAVING FINISHED her story, the girl with lapis eyes rose from the flat gray stone where she had been sitting, where she had been shifting uncomfortably and unwinding her braids throughout the telling of the tale. She thanked me for my attention, ran fingers through her freed hair, now thick and lush on her shoulders, and moved as though to leave.

"But what happened to Pamya?" I asked. "Did she survive the war? Did she ever have children of her own? And did she find her mother?"

The girl with lapis eyes kissed me on the cheek, raised her eyebrows and flashed a wry smile, turned and silently walked away, left me, alone, to contemplate both the sparkling tingle on my cheek and the gray stone where she had just been sitting, a stone now bearing a moist red spot.

MARK APELMAN grew up in New York City and now lives in Colorado. His short stories and essays have appeared in numerous literary magazines, including *American Literary Review, International Quarterly, The Laurel Review,* and *Pearl.* An attorney, Apelman is also associate fiction editor for the *High Plains Literary Review.* In 1999 he received a fiction fellowship from the Colorado Council on the Arts. "A Visitor's Guide to Berlin" won first place in *International Quarterly*'s 1998 Crossing Boundaries Fiction Contest.

A Visitor's Guide to Berlin

Mark Apelman

How to See the City

CONGRATULATIONS. By choosing this guide, you prove yourself a traveler, not a tourist. You go not merely to observe, but to participate. Suffer not the candy-coated lies of Fodor and Michelin. Step out from the safety of buses. Skip the museums. Tear up your maps. So what if you get lost? You will not lose yourself. A great energy is moving nearby. You are alive, a human being. Dive into the streets, dive into your own beating heart. Let yourself be part of the place, let it be part of you. Is that not *why* you travel?

You cannot start in the beginning. There is no beginning. Such a small city, really, so far off in the east, coiled on itself, swallowing its own history. Start anywhere. Walk out of your hotel in the morning after a hearty German breakfast. Stand on the street and stretch. Feel the sun on your face, the power in your arms, the unceasing motion of your blood. Close your eyes. Listen. The city is calling.

A Word of Caution

VISITORS to Berlin often report sudden bouts of uncontrolled weeping. On a warm afternoon in the Tiergarten, late at night by the River Spree, along the Ku'damm or on Alexanderplatz in East Berlin, it's not uncommon to find people huddled together, weeping. They come from every nation. Whether you arrive by plane into Flughafen Otto Lilienthal, tel. (w) 41011, or by train into Zoo Station, it helps to be ready when the tears come.

It is the past. The memories. Homeless memories drift through the city, searching for a mind like yours, a kind mind, an intelligent mind, a mind itself in search of something both magical and nameless. Like a piano tuner, who *knows* the sound of 440 vibrations per second, the memories know the beat of the hearts they seek. Their will to live is as strong as yours, and they need minds the way we need air.

They will become your memories. Soon you will lose the ability to distinguish them from your own memories. Perhaps you have already lost the ability. Perhaps you are already a host. It is possible that much of what you remember about your life never happened to you.

The Café Einstein

No TRIP to Berlin is complete without a visit to the Café Einstein. A Berlin institution, named for one of Germany's better-known Jews, the café is located in an elegant two-story brick building on Kurfürstenstrasse near the Tiergarten. The coffee is strong, the service efficient, and there's a quiet backyard patio where you can enjoy the summer air. Café Einstein is famed for its delicious cakes and pastries.

Say "*Ein Stück Linzer Torte, bitte,*" and prepare your buds for a taste to remember.

One morning at the Café Einstein I sat outside with a cup of coffee and a cherry danish, working on your *Visitor's Guide to Berlin*. Sparrows hopped through the courtyard, pecking at crumbs. Young Germans sat at the wrought-iron tables, drinking coffee and chain-smoking cigarettes, talking intensely in the animated style of the European café.

An old woman walked into the courtyard and sat at the table next to mine. She wore a turquoise pin and a sleeveless black cashmere sweater, the kind you don't see much anymore.

When I looked up a minute later she was staring at the books and maps spread out on my table. I smiled. "I'm writing a guidebook," I said, speaking German.

"I *lived* here," she answered, in English. I tried to place her accent. First language German, but something else, too. South Africa maybe.

"So," she said, "a writer. I have something to show you. For your book."

"Let me make an educated guess," I said when we were on the street. "You grew up here. You had to leave. You went to Johannesburg."

"Sydney. I went to Sydney. Anything else you want to guess?"

She steered toward the Tiergarten. German and Turkish families picnicked on the grass. Couples strolled through the park, holding hands. A group of kids played soccer; nearby a tiny boy in an oversize sweatshirt down to his knees stood clapping. At a large oak tree near the path the woman stopped. "Here," she said. "Right here, under this tree. I'm sure of it."

"Sure of what? There's nothing here," I said. I didn't tell her that every tree in Berlin was cut for firewood during the war. I didn't tell her she was older than any tree in the park.

"Where Franz kissed me. Under this tree. There was a bench here. Put it in your book."

"It's not a novel. It's a guidebook, you know—museums, hotels, tourist stuff."

"You have to tell the stories," she said. She glared at me, and I felt I had done something wrong. "They have to know the *stories*." She actually stomped her foot on the grass. Then something caught my eye and I saw, on the soft, wrinkled underside of her forearm, a faded blue tattoo.

She watched me. "So," she said, "you can see I did not go directly to Sydney."

I looked around to see if anyone was watching. She leaned against the rough bark of the tree and looked at the ground, down where the bench used to be. "Now put it in your book. Greta Rosenthal, Franz Alexander, the Tiergarten, Berlin, May nineteen thirty-eight."

She seemed to forget I was there. She closed her eyes and it was 1938, before the war, and she was young, and Franz had just kissed her—it tasted sweet—and he was handsome, and he was in love with her, and she let her body touch his, just a little, less than she wanted, more than she was supposed to, and she thought love must be the answer, the key to this vast unbearable sweet mysterious world. I touched her shoulder, felt the soft cashmere sweater, the knobby bone beneath. She lifted her hand and patted my fingers, but her eyes remained closed. I turned and walked away.

The Sky over Berlin

FOR THOSE of you with a thirst for adventure, walk down the hill from the State Library to the circus tents near Potsdammer Platz (admission ten DM). Watch the trapeze artists and lion tamers. See Herkules the strong man in his leopard-skin tights and Belinda, said to be the world's smallest lady. She stands just sixteen inches high in heels.

After the circus visit the netherworld across the street. See the tents and people living in old fighter planes and transport trucks. This strange and haunting part of Berlin is the setting for Wim Wenders's 1988 movie, *Wings of Desire*. The German title is *Himmel Über Berlin,* which translates literally as "heaven over Berlin" or "the sky over Berlin." The English title suggests a universal longing, but misses the particularity. This is a film about Berlin, a film in love with the sad, dreamy, strange, and lonely life of a city divided, split in two, cut off from the world, with nowhere to go but deeper into its own fractured self. Walk where Bruno Ganz, Solveig Dommartin, and Peter Falk walked.

Lothar and Astrid

IN THE RUSH to open the city, the Wall in this part of Berlin was simply cut into twenty-foot sections then lifted by crane and turned sideways to allow passage through. These sections remain, a concrete maze, adorned with colorful artwork and graffiti. This is a part of Berlin few visitors ever see, and one of the last places you can still find large pieces of the Wall. Enter the maze and marvel at some of the best Wall art in the world.

Look for the beautiful painting of a woman on the Wall near the rainbow-colored B-29 where Herkules lives. (Most afternoons you will find Herkules lifting weights on the wing of his plane.) Note the English words beneath the painting: ASTRID, WILL WE EVER BE TOGETHER? Admire the exquisite detail of the artist's work, the windblown hair, the right ear slightly higher than the left. See how the fine cheekbones shade down into the hollow of the cheek, suggesting in a single face the darkness and light that burn in us all.

The artist is the painter Lothar Simmins. See his work at the Berlin Art Museum (admission six DM, four with valid student ID). At the time Lothar was an art student, living away for the first time from his native Hanover. Astrid, the object of Lothar's love and desire, was a dancer from Amsterdam. She did not want Lothar's love. She did not want to make love to him. She considered it, knowing what it would mean to him. It would be easy. She could lead him to her flat, watch his face as she lifted off her sweater. In the end she rejected Lothar. "I'm sorry," she told him one chilly afternoon in the Tiergarten, "I don't love you." She lifted up on her toes to kiss his cheek. "And you know what? You don't love me."

Lothar painted Astrid that night, with only a yellow streetlamp to see by. He worked from memory. He did not see the late-night walkers who stopped to watch. He did not hear the East German guards and trucks on the other side of the Wall. He worked until the eastern sky grew pink. In Lothar's painting Astrid's eyes follow you wherever you go. The forward lean of her head gives the impression she has just asked you an important question and is waiting for your reply. The painting suggests a woman lovelier, perhaps, than others might find her, and this idealized portrayal may be why the magazine *Stern* put Astrid on the cover of its "Women of the Wall" issue.

All the next day Lothar wandered the streets of Berlin. He was exhausted but couldn't sleep. He was cold, but he didn't go back to the flat in Prenzlauerberg he shared with three other art students. That night he went down to the Spree and watched the glassy black water. He considered throwing himself in. He imagined being carried down to the quiet river bottom. He fell asleep on the grass by the water.

As it happened, the place Lothar slept (where the Spree runs past the Reichstag, on the south bank, near the French Consulate) was a place men go to find men. Sometime after midnight he felt a tug on his belt. He looked up and saw a man, smiling uncertainly, watching for signs of resistance. Lothar gave none. He wanted to be touched. He longed for the touch of another human being. The man knelt down as if in prayer, took Lothar in his mouth. After Lothar ceased to tremble and lay still, the man stroked Lothar's cheek and left.

All that night Lothar walked. Through the Tiergarten to the place where Astrid said she didn't love him and he didn't love her. *But I do love you,* he thought, *with all my soul.* He longed for her. He recited poetry. *Everything that in my youth ran nameless through my heart, I will name after you before the radiant altar of your shining hair, the altar crowned lightly by your breasts.*

Many years later Lothar saw that Astrid had been right. He hadn't loved *her,* and she'd been smart enough to see it. What he loved, needed, was to touch the cord that runs through everything. To find it, he followed the only path he knew, the path of a woman's body. But Astrid was not a path. She was Astrid, bone-standing on the earth. Atoms from the dawn of time were spinning in her eyes. He had offered her nothing. He felt like a fool.

Eventually Lothar did learn how to love a woman, but that story is beyond the scope of this, your *Visitor's Guide to Berlin*.

As for Astrid, she danced for ten years, for the Berliner Dance Ensemble. She gave birth to a child, a girl, but never married. In 1988 *Stern* ran "Women of the Wall" and Astrid's life became intolerable. Thousands of men saw Lothar's painting and fell in love with her, pinning their dreams onto her airy features. Besieged by pleas for the name of the real Astrid, *Stern* offered a reward to whoever found her. In his studio in Charlottenburg, Lothar read about the offer and threw the magazine in the trash; Hans Steiger, one of Lothar's roommates from art school, recognized Astrid and claimed the reward.

Astrid became famous then, her real face on the cover of every magazine. Men who had never met her offered huge fortunes for her hand. When she could no longer endure it, Astrid moved to the Azores, where she was rumored to be living with an Italian sailor. That, however, could not be confirmed, and the islanders are said to be fiercely protective of Astrid's privacy. Anyone traveling to the Azores to find her may wish to read *Astrid in the Azores* (Hamburg: Stern Pub. Co., 1990). It is requested, however, that her wish for privacy be respected.

Hashish in Berlin

IF YOU WISH to go even deeper into Berlin, consider hashish. This cannabis derivative is known to open the heart. Profound insight into the nature of people and things is also associated with the use of hashish. The paranoia and fear associated with other psychotropic drugs does not occur with hashish, making it an excellent drug for a walking tour of Berlin.

Hashish has a long and distinguished history. To prepare for your trip and learn more about the remarkable qualities of this drug, read Walter Benjamin's "Hashish in Marseilles" (in *Reflections,* New York: Harcourt

Brace Jovanovich, 1979) and Isabelle Eberhardt's *The Oblivion Seekers* (San Francisco: City Lights, 1978).

Finding hash in Berlin is easy. Stroll through Kreuzberg, the Turkish district. Find it on any street. Many young Germans live here, too. Buy from the Turks. They have better connections and are less apt to cut the product. Ibrahim (on the east side of Goetheplatz, near Leipzig Allée) offers excellent black hash at very reasonable prices.

Take the whole day. Do not hurry, please. To modulate the intensity of the drug, do not smoke it, but rather ingest a small amount orally (the size of a lemon drop is about right for the average person). Pick a sunny day, preferably a weekend, when the streets are full of people and the Tiergarten is crowded with picnicking families. For an hour you will feel no different. Then, just when you start to suspect Ibrahim, the drug will kick in.

Wander the streets of Berlin. Notice the sense of unreality that hangs over this city, the result, perhaps, of too many ghosts, too many memories searching for home. Feel the past. Walk down the Kaiserdamm, the insanely wide, treeless boulevard Hitler built for Nazi parades. You have seen the old black-and-white films of those parades, the endless stream of tanks and troops moving past huge cheering crowds, their right arms raised in Nazi salute. The people open their mouths, and blood pours out. A gang runs by, singing, "Everything is twice as nice when Jewish blood flows from the knife." A woman lifts a child onto her shoulders. "There he is! There's the Führer! Say 'Heil Hitler,' sweetheart."

And indeed, yes, it's true, there he is, across the Spree, Adolf himself, screaming and clenching his fist at the crowd. The sound is deafening. Hold your ears. A group of men link arms and dance around a bonfire of books. Flames light up the sky and sparkle in the river. Close your eyes. It's not happening! It's not happening! It's not happening!

The Jews of Berlin

THEY LIVE in Argentina now, in America, in Australia. They come back, some of them, fifty, sixty years later, to see the city of their youth. They recognize nothing. Everything they knew is gone. The streets have been destroyed, renamed, rerouted. They wander through the city, breathing the air of '96, remembering '36. They dream.

They are invisible. They float over the sidewalks, steering with invisible arms, gliding upright through old Berlin, banking hard around corners in their zeal to reach the past.

Samuel Chernow glides into East Berlin and up the creaky wooden steps of his old building. Inside, incredibly, he finds the furniture his parents left behind when they fled to Shanghai. "This is *mine*," he says to the East German family eating sausage and potatoes at the dining room table. "This belongs to *me*." He pounds the table. They hear nothing.

Elsbeth Jaffe floats into Zoo Station. She was nine years old on the day in 1936 that she learned she was leaving Berlin forever. "We're not wanted here," her father said. The family left their apartment with everything inside, even Dingo their dog. *Just shut the door and left, poof.* They drove to the station and abandoned their car. In the rush Elsbeth left her favorite doll behind. The next day they were in Holland, heading for Argentina. Now Elsbeth glides through the parking lot looking for her father's car, searching among the shiny new BMWs and Audis for a black 1936 Maybach with a doll in the back seat.

Moritz Levin goes to his old synagogue (on Oranienstrasse, near Marx-Engels Platz). The Nazis used it as a stable during the war. Today sunlight pours through stained-glass windows. Moritz steps forward into the light. He was supposed to have his bar mitzvah here on a Saturday in 1938, but that Friday was Kristallnacht. The synagogue was ruined. He rocks forward and back, the ancient Jewish motion of prayer. Listen to the murmur of his voice. He is reciting his bar mitzvah. Afterward he walks through a cold November rain back to the Hotel Metropol (single DM 225, double DM 280). He sleeps.

The Writer and the Editor

THE WORLD is bleeding. It has always bled. Skin is so easy to cut, and the world is so full of steel. Blood flows out through the holes steel makes, flows as you read, flows into the gutters and fields of the world. Whoever thought to give us hearts, then shielded us with skin: Must have liked pain. Must have intended us to live *in* the world. Must have had a very weird sense of humor.

The editor calls from America. "What is wrong with you?" he demands to know. "This isn't a guidebook. I don't know what it is."

The writer sits at the round table in his hotel room, watching CNN with the sound off. He didn't *want* to be pulled down by the past, Berlin's or his own. He didn't want that. Outside, the clouds hang dark, heavy with rain. The writer thinks the clouds are beautiful. They remind him of something from long ago, but what? He wishes he could remember. He says, "You haven't seen what I've seen."

"I don't care what you've seen," the editor says. "I want a guidebook. Addresses. Prices. Facts. I want facts. Don't you want to get paid?"

The writer watches the carnage of the day on CNN. This time it's Bosnians, mostly children, in makeshift hospital beds, staring at the camera. Their Slavic faces are broad and vacant. So many missing limbs, it would take three of them to put a body together. In the summer heat, flies feed on the moisture under their eyes, and the children make no effort to brush the flies away. The writer sighs, shuts his eyes, sits on the edge of his bed. He's glad the sound is off. He doesn't want to hear the words. He imagines a giant fish at the bottom of the ocean, eating away at the telephone wire. He imagines the aliens watching from outer space, laughing, crying maybe, whatever it is that aliens do. To the editor he says, "I'll do what I can, all right? I'll do what I can."

A great energy is moving nearby. Open your heart.

Selected Chronology

1929	*Threepenny Opera,* words by Bertolt Brecht, music by Kurt Weill.
1931	*The Blue Angel,* starring Marlene Dietrich.
September 3, 1931	On the night of her eighth birthday Greta Rosenthal falls asleep holding her new stuffed bear, listening to the piano from the neighbor's apartment.
1934	Albert Einstein leaves his position at the Kaiser Wilhelm Institute and flees to America.
Summer 1936	Jesse Owens wins four gold medals at the Berlin Summer Olympics.
May 14, 1938	Greta and Franz kiss in the Tiergarten.
May 21, 1938	Franz and his family leave Germany for England.
November 8, 1938	Moritz Levin nervously practices his bar mitzvah recitation.
November 9, 1938	Kristallnacht—the Night of Broken Glass.
March 8, 1941	Greta and her parents "relocated" to Poland.
1949	Chiang Kai-shek's Nationalist Kuomintang falls to Mao's Red Army. Chiang goes to Taiwan and establishes the Nationalist Republic of China. Samuel Chernow and his family leave Shanghai for the Philippines.
1951	Samuel and his family settle in Australia.
1961	Berlin becomes a divided city. Hungarian-born composer Gyorgy Ligeti calls West Berlin a "surrealistic cage": only those inside are free.
1963	John F. Kennedy stands by the Wall, says, *"Ich bin ein Berliner,"* and the locals laugh to hear it, because a Berliner is a jelly doughnut. Several months later, in Dallas, John Kennedy is assassinated.

1971	*Cabaret,* starring Liza Minnelli.
November 1978	Astrid says she doesn't love Lothar. Lothar paints her on the Wall.
February 14, 1986	Samuel Chernow dies, Melbourne, Australia.
October 1988	*Stern* runs "Women of the Wall," featuring Lothar's painting of Astrid on the cover. Within a month the magazine receives more than eight hundred pleas for her address.
November 9, 1988	Moritz Levin returns to Berlin from his home in Los Angeles and recites his bar mitzvah.
November 9, 1989	Fifty-one years to the day after Kristallnacht, the Berlin Wall comes down. In his house on Marien-strasse, Heinz Mueller rummages in the basement until he finds the old hammer he used to smash windows on the Night of Broken Glass. He hobbles down to the Wall and takes an angry whack at the graffiti-covered concrete.
April 1990	Astrid moves to the Azores.
October 26, 1990	Buenos Aires, Argentina: Elsbeth Jaffe celebrates the birth of her third grandchild, Jaime Federico Moreno.
1991	Wim Wenders films *Until the End of the World,* with William Hurt as Sam Farber, Solveig Dommartin as Claire, and Sam Neill as Gene, who says, "I believe in the magic and the healing power of words, and of stories."
May 1996	Greta returns to Germany. Reviewing confiscated Nazi records, she learns that her mother and father died on October 14, 1942, at Theresienstadt. At the Jewish cemetery she orders a headstone with the dates of birth and death of her parents and the words WHOEVER LIVES IN MEMORY IS NOT DEAD.

A native of Brooklyn, STEVEN SHER now lives in Corvallis, Oregon. He is the author of eight books of poetry and short fiction, most recently the poetry collection *Flying Through Glass* (Outloudbooks, 2000). His poetry collection *Traveler's Advisory* (Trout Creek Press, 1994) was a finalist for the Oregon Book Awards. Sher's work has appeared in more than 150 U.S. and international magazines and journals, including *Midstream, Olam, Prairie Schooner, Response, European Judaism, The Jerusalem Review,* and *Jewish Affairs* (South Africa), as well as in several anthologies, such as *Blood to Remember: American Poets on the Holocaust* (Texas Tech University Press).

Tsuris

STEVEN SHER

"HOW DO YOU EXPLAIN the dinosaurs?"

The question catches Rabbi Rosenberg off guard, absorbed in his lesson. He tries to go on, but the sight of the cynical child smiling, slouched in his seat on the aisle, stops him in midthought. All the children are attentive now, staring curiously at the strange rabbi in black who appears before them as if from outer space these autumn afternoons. His lesson flies out of his head.

"What do you mean?" he asks, certain he has fallen into another of Berger's traps. The boy has been nothing but trouble this first week of Hebrew school. Rabbi Rosenberg reminds himself he's doing a mitzvah instructing such needy children, finds them already worlds away from what he has to teach. He has seen the worst make games of smacking boys across the head, girls gossiping behind their *Siddurim*. And if not this restlessness there is their boredom to contend with, for the children have already sat a full day in the public schools. And if not the boredom there is always their unfounded dread of learning, for these students, in their young minds, have better things to do with their free time. But the parents do insist their children attend. It is the only leverage the rabbi has over the class.

"If Jews believe the world is five thousand seven hundred and fifty-two years old," continues Berger, "how come scientists say the dinosaurs lived millions of years ago?" Berger smugly folds his arms across his chest.

Rabbi Rosenberg studies the child, considering his answer as if it must contain a cure for the boy's lack of respect. The yarmulke is crooked on Berger's head and will fall to the floor several times before the end of the class. His shirt balloons out of his pants at the waist. And Berger's sneaker laces are untied, his feet stretched in the aisle, so it appears the boy would like nothing better than to kick off his shoes into the center of the room, as if he were home in his bed, just to get the other students laughing.

"Has anyone ever heard the term *tsuris?*" asks Rabbi Rosenberg. Most of the class snickers at the strange-sounding word. The light goes on in one or two faces, a sign of recognition. "It's a Yiddish word meaning 'trouble.' And what's most interesting about *tsuris* is that it's very similar to *saurus,* as in brontosaurus, tyrannosaurus, or stegosaurus. In fact it was a Jew who gave the dinosaurs their name."

Rabbi Rosenberg sits straight faced on the edge of the desk in front of the room. Rubbing his bearded chin, he basks in their rare full yet skeptical attention, unwilling to say anything just yet that might diminish it. Even Berger has sat up straighter in his chair, pulled his legs in from the aisle. His arms have dropped, like a tiring fighter, onto his thighs.

Finally he draws a breath and plunges ahead into the silence. "We Jews," Rabbi Rosenberg begins, "were leaving Egypt, about to enter the land that had been promised our ancestors, when Hashem decided to test us. The people, who were really scared, had heard the land we would inherit was inhabited by giants. Of course they were afraid to go any farther. But

Hashem told them not to fear for He would fight on their behalf. Being a doubting bunch, they decided to first send in spies."

Berger seems interested in the story, the instigator silenced, so Rabbi Rosenberg proceeds.

"Twelve spies were sent out from the camp. Everyone hoped for the best. But as soon as they set foot in the land, they saw something more huge and terrible than anything they knew. *Tsuris,* yelled the bravest, Caleb, as the others ran for cover behind some rocks. A giant reptile, longer than a dozen men laid head to foot, was passing within hearing range. But the spies got lucky. The *tsuris* was too busy eating leaves and grass to bother with unappetizing people. It went on by without so much as a look in their direction.

"It took some time for Caleb to gather the spies to continue on their mission. Several had already run away. Yet he convinced those who remained, once their bravery returned, to scout ahead with him.

"Soon they came to a hill where they could see for many miles in all directions. In the distance to the west another *tsuris* was feeding on the carcass of a smaller creature. A group of *tsuris* roamed the desert to the east. To the north great herds of stampeding *tsuris* whipped up clouds of swirling dirt like a plague waiting to settle.

"And then a roar, like the snap of an Egyptian's whip or the thunder jumping from the clouds, snuck up from behind. Flashing its meat-ripping teeth, the hideous beast approached them.

"*Gehakta tsuris,* screamed their leader—which in Yiddish means 'really big trouble,'" Rabbi Rosenberg explains. "And it was certainly the biggest flesh eater of them all. Naturally they fled. But Caleb, who stumbled and fell at the giant's feet, was left behind.

"When the spies returned to camp, they told of the terrible *tsuris* in the land and how they had escaped it. Sadly, they reported that poor Caleb had perished so that they might survive and warn the others not to come.

"But you know what? A day later Caleb appeared without even a scratch. The people gathered around him, anxious to hear his gory tale. Instead he told how Hashem had kept his word. *There I was,* Caleb explained, *armed with nothing but my pitiful staff, no more than a toothpick compared to those huge sharp teeth. Just as I was about to become the beast's reluctant dinner, a miracle occurred. A ball of fire flew down from the night sky and struck the* gehakta tsuris *dead. Surely God will likewise drive the other giants from the land.* Caleb pleaded with the people to pack their things and proceed at once.

"The trouble was, no one listened to him. The other spies had seen these giants, too, and they were scared out of their wits. Not a single one would dare return to the land so long as there were *tsuris* there.

"The Torah tells how the Jewish people, because they ignored Caleb, were left to wander in the wilderness for forty years. An entire generation of doubting adults slowly died out. Caleb, though, was allowed to live, to set foot in the land again, inheriting that very ground where he had met the *gehakta tsuris.* But after forty years there were no giants left to fear. New tests of faith replaced the old. The *tsuris* had become extinct."

Rabbi Rosenberg claps his hands one time to signal that he is done and stands facing the silent class. He is ready to return to their lesson. Scanning the room for one objection, his eyes lock on Berger, allowing the boy a final rebuttal.

"Does the Torah really mention dinosaurs? In school they tell us that they lived long before people." Berger sits back in his chair, less sure of himself. His legs are underneath his seat. He seems smaller than before, having been reduced by curiosity.

Some giggles circulate and Rabbi Rosenberg shushes them. When someone keeps on talking in the back of the room, he slaps the top of his desk to silence the child. All heads snap back in line.

"The Torah warns of giants in the land. It chronicles how the others perished, except for Caleb and Joshua, because they doubted that Hashem would help them." Rabbi Rosenberg insists, "You will have to read it for yourself, interpret it for yourself. Create new midrash that make sense to you. Not everything is as clear as you would have it. Not everything is known."

As Rabbi Rosenberg resumes the lesson, his resistance to these children seems to lift. His soul is lighter than at any time since he began commuting to this shul. His spirits begin to soar. His feet are barely touching the floor. Because his heart is open to them now, his eyes more easily forgive the petty things he sees.

Again there's Berger, turning around in his seat, looking for more trouble. And so soon, the rabbi sighs. But the boy has turned to quiet someone in the row behind him. Once he is done he sits attentive in his seat, no feet in the aisle, no arms locked in flagrant provocation across his chest, an empty vessel waiting to be filled.

Rabbi Rosenberg is frozen with amazement. He smiles though he cannot speak. He nods his head—a miracle indeed. The greater *tsuris* he has known within this room exists no more.

TERESA PORZECANSKI of Uruguay is the author of eight short-story collections, five novels, and a book of poetry. Her work has been translated into English, Dutch, German, and French. Two of her novellas, *Sun Inventions* and *Perfumes of Carthage,* have recently been published in English by University of New Mexico Press, and many of her short stories have appeared in English in anthologies such as *Short Stories by Latin American Women: The Magic and the Real* (Arte Publico Press, 1990) and *The Global Anthology of Jewish Women Writers* (Micah Publications, 1990). Porzecanski has also published extensively in the social sciences and is the winner of various awards and fellowships, including a Fulbright Scholarship and a Guggenheim Fellowship. The following are new translations of two of her stories.

LOUISE POPKIN holds a Ph.D. in Spanish and Latin American literature and is a lecturer in Spanish at the Harvard University Division of Continuing Education. Her translations of Latin American prose, poetry, and drama—particularly from Uruguay and Argentina— have appeared in a number of anthologies and in literary journals such as *Triquarterly, Kenyon Review, Mid-American Review,* and *Beacons.* She resides in Montevideo, Uruguay, for part of each year.

The Seder

TERESA PORZECANSKI

Translated from the Spanish by Louise Popkin

WHAT COULD BE SIMPLER than following those familiar directions: Singe and scrub a chicken carefully, thoroughly scrape its limbs and torso, then place its feet, giblets, and dead body in a pot along with water and a sliced onion. Bring to a boil and skim. Add celery, parsley, peeled and sliced carrots, leeks, and salt. Simmer for an hour and a half, or until the chicken shows signs of tenderness and almost of life again, by shivering under the prongs of a fork.

Yet there I stood, at a loss and utterly defenseless, before the stiff, dismembered corpse of that chicken I had brought home dead from the market: on the one hand its head and extremities, amputated and bagged in transparent plastic, and on the other the gummy, fattened torso that had maybe almost managed to fly.

For a long time—ages ago—the knowledge that a beheading was imminent had sent me scurrying from the kitchen: those chickens were alive when they showed up under Grandma Estherina's merciless knife. "I'll kill myself," I would think as she tried to keep me from fleeing, "or I'll refuse to eat, and then I'll hold a funeral for the chickens." But none of that ever happened. Time placed things in perspective, softening outlines and blurring details.

Just as I was about to beat some egg yolks, I noticed the impropriety of the cucumbers lying there on the countertop looking forlorn: some were small and lopsided; others, large and swollen. I lifted the mixer out of the bowl and watched limp stalactites droop from its blades. Something about those cucumbers—their brazen freedom of form—struck me as malicious, as if my *tante*'s recipe were a magic spell, a deliberate attempt to overwhelm my heavy heart.

I wondered exactly what it meant to buy proper cucumbers—neither too large (if their flesh turned soggy, their flavor would be ruined beyond repair), nor too small (if they fermented too quickly, you wouldn't get that crackle of flesh against palate); in short, what might qualify as a perfect cucumber? Exactly what did it mean to add a "handful" of salt to the brine; how much was a "handful," as opposed to a "fistful"? And were those drops of distilled vinegar to be added with the right hand, or the left? To make things even more complicated, maybe before, maybe after, my *tante* suggested pouring the whole concoction into a container—preferably a large wooden barrel already aged by lots of slow fermentation—and packing the washed cucumbers one right on top of the other, so that no pockets of air remained and they couldn't go floating around in their bath of brackish slime. Finally you were supposed to weight the whole mixture down by placing a clean, flat stone directly into the container: this would both compress the cucumbers and make doubly sure they couldn't fly off anywhere. Next you had to wait ten days to two weeks; let the whole mishmash steep slowly in a warm place (though never in direct sunlight); keep a close watch on what would soon be sheer delight cooked in its own process of putrefaction; and wait.

Then one fine day (surprise!) you'd wake up absolutely sure—what made you so sure was something no one in all those generations of pickle-making housewives had managed to explain—that the pickles were ready to eat. So you'd uncover the container, which by then had most likely attained the status of cult object; and, skimming off the layers of scum floating on its clouded surface, you'd confidently proceed to taste one. If on the first bite it offered a bit of resistance and emitted a slight crunch, you'd have passed the test; as a reward you'd be secretly blessed with membership in an elite sisterhood of illustrious guardians of flavor.

There was also the matter of those white cabbages, finely shredded and destined for lengthy stays in the hidden depths of the ancestral barrels. And those succulent matzoh balls, swimming in luscious chicken broth flecked with perfect rounds of golden fat. Each dish was a miniature landscape as old as the earth itself, meant to endure, hidden and mysterious, behind its cryptic recipe.

In a hasty gesture I wiped my brow with the palm of my hand. There was no time just now for remembering. I'd buy the pickles at Malke's shop, even if they didn't have that venerable flavor. And the chicken. And maybe the fish, as well. My father's sisters, at age eighty, probably wouldn't notice the difference. Delighted to be temporarily free of the yoke of widowhood, as in previous years they would join us for the seder and take their stand against slavery in the ancient land of the pharaohs. For them the Pesach meal would be as magnificent as ever: on a linen tablecloth trimmed with macramé, a gift from an otherwise forgotten cousin, the twinkling candles would stand erect, gracing the food with the scant happiness of our lives, the briefest of glimmers.

I looked around the kitchen at two in the afternoon. The autumn sun dwelling on the countertop seemed daunted by the unremitting daily routine. The chickpeas and carrots lay scattered about; the boiling sugars and syrups seemed to collapse into tiny whirlpools. And that outrageous pile of gadgets designed to crush, slice, grind, squeeze, pierce, sat waiting for my hands to proceed with the transformation of matter. . . .

*

I can remember hearing my children in the next room, traveling to far-away places, imitating the sound of a train moving off into the distance along shadowy tracks. As I burst into tears over the matzoh balls, I understood what was really happening. Suddenly overcome with awe, I bowed before the chicken's stiff body, which lay bathed now in a haze of silvery light. As a ghostly halo formed a crown over it, I felt my own sweat dripping slowly onto the beets. So it had been since the days of my grandmothers and theirs—generations of women all gathering for the seder, reborn before my very eyes, in those beloved, ancient flavors that came welling up out of the past. A very distant past.

Rochel Eisips

Teresa Porzecanski

Translated from the Spanish by Louise Popkin

AND THAT'S WHY I'M STILL carrying that damn letter around in my pocket. Just knowing it's there, I have a restless urge to rub its crumpled envelope between my fingers. So I slip my hand in gingerly, like I'm afraid of springing a trap. I'm really hoping it won't be there, that I'll feel the flabby emptiness of that pocket clinging to my hand.

Still, as I head home in the noisy seven o'clock crush with an unintelligible hum zigzagging through my ears, and I'm overcome by the feeling—the absolute certainty—that I'm about to keel over, I go straight for that envelope, quickly locate it in my jacket, and touching it brings me a calm, almost bountiful, sense of well-being.

I repeat Rochel Eisips's name to myself as if I could see her again, sitting there with her arms flapping, and I read it over and over in that Hebrew script, faded now, as if little by little whoever wrote it had forgotten how to form the ancient letters, and a labyrinth of undecipherable symbols had escaped from his pen. The rest of the envelope is a mass of fingerprints, a jumble of ridges, crisscrossing back and forth.

For what led me to Rochel Eisips was an ambiguous address given me by a Lithuanian shoemaker, a man of few words, who vaguely recalled once having a distant relative by that name, paralyzed or hard of hearing or close to death, probably the mother of some distant nephew he barely knew, or was it the son of a despicable aunt who worked in some bank with an impossible name, third floor, loan department. . . . And I met the old man, in turn, through a lonely seamstress, whose specialty was sewing lapels on suit jackets, and whose address I got from an ex-milliner, who remembered that in her *pension* on Calle Blandengues she had once had a neighbor by the name of Rochel Eisips, a cook, who might still be alive and kicking.

All that so I could end up in the presence of this musty, infinitely ancient woman who, opening one extremely leery eye, snapped at me in the stale air of the hallway: "And why would anyone want to see me? Me, of all people. . . ."

The nurse didn't bother to answer. She glanced at me sideways, the left corner of her mouth curling into a complicitous sneer. Then, exactly a minute later, with a cavalier shrug of the shoulders, she took off casually down the ice-cold hallway and left me standing there in front of the wheelchair.

And so we were alone, Rochel Eisips and I, just the two of us, in the orphaned bleakness of that rest home. It was then that the old woman motioned me into a chair and settled comfortably into hers, and I realized we were somewhere beyond time.

"In Jerusalem," I murmured . . . "In the City of Stone, the very oldest part of the Old City," I continued, "an elderly rug merchant handed me a letter with your name on it, and no address. 'It's really urgent,' he said. 'Make sure it reaches a woman called Rochel Eisips as soon as possible.'"

"Ah, so . . . ," the old woman mused, her accent a blend of assorted times and places: "a City of Stone, you say, and very, very old?" Then, as if some radical thought had suddenly crossed her mind, she begged, "Go on, please, I want to hear the whole story."

Whether it was her deafness or that sleepy way she had of looking at me, something told me she would never understand.

"I have a letter for you," I repeated firmly. "It's from a man who sells rugs in Jerusalem."

But all at once, from deep inside her, a new voice emerged, remote and resonant, repeating her own questions over and over, as she unraveled a bewildering story shaped in the far reaches of her memory. Then, as if struck by some plausible truth, Rochel Eisips invented laughter. Laughter that rose up out of the pit of her stomach, as if something inside her had suddenly opened wide, giving birth to a whirl of light and harmony.

"Of course I know you, Annele," she declared with her newfound voice. "You think I could forget my oldest grandchild, the skinniest of my daughter Frieda's girls? Why, you're the spitting image of your mother, who died in Latvia. And those eyes . . . you got them from that fool of a father of yours. May they both rest in peace. Amen."

"No," I exclaimed, startled. "Look, I'm not your granddaughter. I'm not related to you at all. I just came to bring this letter." And I held out the envelope, which struck me as incongruous—downright absurd—in that gloomy place.

"Letter?" she laughed, waving it away. "What letter?" Now I could see her almost toothless gums, sopping wet like those of a newborn. "Who needs a letter of introduction from you?" she continued. "How could I possibly forget you, Annele . . . after all those times I fed you and told you stories, while your mother was back in Latvia looking for that fool she married? He wasn't about to budge from Riga . . . oh, no, they'd have to come for him. Well, they came for both of them. In 'thirty-nine."

Unexpectedly the old lady's infinite age had dwindled. Her whole body had filled out now, and an incipient youthfulness seemed to emanate from her small but shining eyes and from her smile, which grew increasingly idyllic as the barely comprehensible words came tumbling out one on top of another, fairly gushing from between her soft, frothy, baby gums. And through her, all her long-departed relatives trooped back toward life, a loving frenzy of apparitions, sustained by Rochel Eisips's radiant, glistening eyes.

Yet again I managed to gasp: "That old man I ran into in a rug shop . . . When I told him I was headed back to Montevideo, he scribbled this note, and asked me—begged me—to deliver it to a woman called Rochel Eisips. 'It's urgent,' he said, 'Rochel Eisips.'"

But now a group of Cossacks had ransacked the house where she was born, set fire to her parents trapped inside, made off with all the religious objects. And then her aunt, a peddler of pastries in a market in Vitebsk, had raised the orphan on her own. And now it was January of 1922, and Rochel Eisips was disembarking in Montevideo with just a pair of shoes and the clothes on her back, quite enough for a cook on a country estate in Colonia, who eventually moved to Montevideo, Calle Blandengues, Room Number 8, where she bore five studious children by a ghostly husband, who had passed on.

It was getting late, and Rochel Eisips was still telling stories. There was something vaguely liturgical about the rhythm and intonation of her words. Over and over the Cossacks murdered her parents, and the aunt from Vitebsk baked her pastries to sell in the market. Then a boat would appear on the horizon in Montevideo and a fifteen-year-old with a kerchief tied under her chin would step onto the pier, vanish amid heaps of dishes and kitchen utensils, and later on become pregnant and bear five studious children. What had it all been but this ceaseless, impromptu recounting, in the fabulesque ebb and flow of untold afternoons?

But in other versions it was Rochel Eisips who peddled pastries in the market, only not in Vitebsk, but in Vilna; and her parents were killed by some Polish thugs, not in a fire set by Cossacks. Then it was her aunt who would arrive in America, with just the clothes on her back and those shoes; and it was the five children who bore Rochel Eisips.

I don't know why I didn't leave, but I had to stay. I sat there hour after hour, spellbound, until it was totally dark and Rochel Eisips seemed to settle down. Then, as two perfunctory, overweight nurses wheeled her off, her chair glided by without a squeak. And she was on her way for the last time, her head tilted, her eyes still sparkling, and those baby gums of hers, still opening and closing and babbling. . . .

So that's why that crumpled letter is sitting there in my pocket, unopened. That's why I haven't been able to deliver it. I'm not quite sure why I've held on to it, or why I've kept it right where I put it in the first place. Perhaps I'm just afraid to open it, lest I discover that Rochel Eisips is still here, and that she carries me within. And that the two of us are forever doomed to drift gently, irrevocably bound one to the other.

Born in Morocco, RUTH KNAFO SETTON moved to the United States as a child and later lived in Israel for several years. Her novel *The Road to Fez* was just published by Counterpoint Press. The recipient of fellowships from the National Endowment for the Arts, PEN, Sewanee Writers Conference, Great River Arts Institute, Wesleyan Writers Conference, Pennsylvania Council on the Arts, and Yaddo, Knafo Setton is writer in residence for the Berman Center for Jewish Studies at Lehigh University. Her poetry and prose have appeared in many literary journals and anthologies, including *Luna, International Quarterly,* and *ForPoetry.*

The Cat Garden

RUTH KNAFO SETTON

To TAKE AWAY THE EVIL EYE, my mom, Vanille, sits on a chair facing you and sets out a long cloth of blue felt and a needle. She mumbles names of rabbis and prayers in Hebrew and Arabic. She touches you and moves the needle on the cloth. With each round of prayer and touch we get closer to the needle. After, when prayer, touch, and needle meet on the cloth, she pours a pinch of salt on you. Soon you'll be doing this for others, she tells me. And when I shake my head in horror, she smiles and says, It's in the blood, my girl, you can fight anything but the blood.

I WALKED in on a healing. The three of them: my mother and her two assistants, Canelle and Aviv, bent over a woman lying on the living room sofa. Her flowered housedress lifted to reveal a fat, swollen leg with bursting purple veins. A sad splotched leg with a thick ankle and toes round as marbles. A leg that seems to stand for the hopelessness of this town, of our lives. Is this what it means to become a woman? To end up fat and shrunken and helpless, legs blotched and pale and scarred with veins, black-and-blue marks, scabs and sores, swollen thick useless legs. The foot is so tiny and round, fleshy and tiny—a little foot that doesn't look as if it could hold up this fat woman. My mother sits on a chair at the side of the sofa and presses her palms along the leg—from thigh to ankle. Aviv crouches at her side, her pet, ready to hand her whatever she needs. Canelle stands behind my mother, looking down at the woman. I can't see Canelle's expression, but I can imagine it: the same mixture of tenderness and compassion she bestows on everyone. She's mumbling prayers in Arabic and Hebrew in a low voice that makes the words fall like a waterfall. My mother, white hair pulled back into a tight bun, is intent on the woman's leg, her hands moving, searching for the tingles under the flesh, the electric current that vibrates, that marks the connection. The woman moans softly, as if she's falling asleep.

I stand motionless in the doorway, wondering if I've stumbled onto a movie set, another era, a time that isn't mine. This woman can't be my mother. I feel no bond to her. I don't know her. I don't recognize her. I don't like the smells here, of Canelle's Moroccan cooking: *kzboor* and cumin and *za'atar* and fresh *na'ana* growing wild outside the window. A white butterfly flutters in, hovers for a second on the sill, over Mom's herb plants, then flutters back out.

Mom holds out her hand. Aviv gives her a bottle of *araq*. She tilts her head back and drinks, gargles it, and spits it out on the woman's leg.

I catch my breath in a gasp. Only Aviv sees me. He shakes his head and turns back. My mother swallows the anise liquor again and spits it again, sending a spray over the woman's leg.

I am afraid suddenly to move, to breathe too hard, to cough. If I disturb the air, the tableau will disappear and leave me hovering in dark space, alone.

How do I find my way home? That's the question. I thought it was about becoming a woman and finding love. I don't even want to become a woman, and I doubt I'll ever fall in love. I just want to go home, to somewhere familiar, where my reflection in the mirror doesn't come as a constant surprise. I'm already forgetting what I looked like before I got here, Dad's face, my room.

The white butterfly returns, flutters. Outside, kids scream in a game, loud Hebrew I don't understand, a game I'll never play. I am fourteen. I want to die.

EACH TIME I walk, dazed and reddened (after reading all day) as if I've spent the day burning under the sun, I go closer to the ruins of Beit She'an. I already know it is a seven-thousand-year-old city that was destroyed in an earthquake in 749 C.E. That archaeologists are digging it up, layer by layer, uncovering a vast civilization, a world that existed beneath ours. There is a great amphitheater where men wrestled with wild animals, or gladiators fought each other. Mom tells me that when she was a girl in Morocco, her mother taught her that the earth sits on the horns of a bull, which stands on a fish that is in water, which is on wind, and the wind itself is on an empty place, a void that only God knows. An earthquake is caused when the bull gets tired or restless and shifts the earth from one horn to another.

As I walk I know Aviv follows me, even though I only caught sight of him once. I turned swiftly and saw him in a crowd of boys playing soccer in a field. I knew it was him, recognized his eternal blue-and-green-striped T-shirt. What is his problem? I asked Mom, blundering on through her frown: I mean, is he deaf and dumb, or retarded, or what? He gives me the creeps.

For a second I thought she was going to hit me, but she didn't: her hands are lethal, I guess, like a boxer's fists. She squeezed them together until the knuckles stood out white and red. She nodded and walked away, which I interpreted to mean: follow me.

I followed her downstairs and outside the apartment building—like all the others in Beit She'an, identical beige blocks rising in the sky. The only touch I like: every apartment has a balcony. The women hang their carpets over the iron railings and beat them. The long-lashed men sit and smoke, staring between the railings as if they're in jail, their coils of smoke drifting through, freer than they are. Kids play games, girls dress their dolls and look down at me when I walk past, sometimes yell in Hebrew. Housewives call to each other across the balconies and rows of laundry, carry on long conversations that wake me every morning. I crouch on the balcony and read, often stopping in the middle of a paragraph—to watch the sun light and dark on the page—to wonder about how Jane heard Mr. Rochester even though they were miles apart, or how the dancing girl, Cigarette, seduced the soldiers in the French Foreign Legion, or why Sam Spade is like God. Why the resolution of a mystery is so satisfying, the only sort of book that truly ends, that doesn't send off associations of future possibilities for the characters, unforeseen combinations. That is the summer I decide to become a detective: Jo Becker, Private Detective. Like Philip Marlowe and Sam Spade, I will enter worlds soft and ripe with corruption and, with my blazing honesty and courage, will restore order. I will close people's books for them, allow them to say: *the end,* with an air of finality, knowing that the problem has been solved, the question answered.

Mom leads me to the kitchen garden in back of our building. Weeds, tangled with stalks of *na'ana, luisa,* and *shiba* (for tea, remedies, and spells), and daisies and oleander, bleached and forlorn, searching for water. There has been no rain since I arrived. The air is so dry it snaps like a paper clip. I think of my father's dour voice as he said good-bye at the airport: You're going to the Promised Land. Behave! Don't let your mother fill your head with nonsense!

When I picture his face now, it's in the center of one of his round hex signs, like a medallion: his gaunt pale face surrounded by rosettes and blue birds of happiness.

A low stone wall extends a few feet, starts in the center of the garden and leads nowhere, has no gate, no earthly reason I can determine for existing. A mystery! My mother sits on the wall and gestures for me to do the same. We sit quietly for a few minutes. The garden is filled with loads of garbage, bags of refuse, fruit peels, coffee grounds, cigarette butts, empty juice and beer bottles, plastic milk cartons. Most of the bags are ripped, the contents strewn across the dry dirt. Cats lurk in the shadows of the bags. One orange cat is so thin that he is crouched in a permanent arch. I wonder if he is the one I hear cry in the night, outside my window. The rotting garbage, the glassy shimmer of heat as the sun beats on our bare heads, the starving cats slouching toward us make me dizzy, as if I'm about to throw up.

. . . and the Prince said, let me go with you please! I have to see the earth!

I squint at her. The wild froth of long white hair shading the olive skin, the black gown: the way I imagine a Finnish witch. Her dark eyes look past me, over my head.

So Omar, the Guardian of the Gate, let him slip through the slit that led out of the Rose Balloon, and the Prince fell to earth. It was raining, the ground was muddy, the colors so bright—after living in a rose-colored balloon in which everything was shades of pink—he could hardly see at first. So this was earth. Omar made him promise to return in twenty-four hours to the red wheelbarrow (which was how he brought supplies back to the Balloon—like Israel, they had to import nearly everything). The Prince was so excited he barely listened, and was off and running before Omar was through. The rain tasted delicious, wet and slippery, on the tongue. He laughed as he ran through the mud until he came to a stone wall—something like this one. Except it went all the way around a garden. He opened the gate and entered. A shady kitchen garden. The door to the house opened, and the Prince hid behind a tree to watch.

Is this why she brought me here? I wonder. To tell me a story? As if I'm still a kid, and she's making up for not being with me all these years?

A cook with a white cap and apron threw out scraps of food leftovers. Before she even went back inside and shut the door, cats were on the food.

Like these, I say, looking down at the cats beneath my feet dangling in sandals. Brand new Nimrod sandals with two black straps, just like the girl soldiers in the army wear. My feet look strange, long, brown. Desert feet. Cigarette dancing barefoot in the Sahara.

Like these, Mom says. But not as hungry, because they got fed more regularly. Here people eat their food to the bone. What they throw out is truly garbage, not fit for animals. The cats in Morocco were hungry, too. Wherever you have poor people, you have skinny hungry cats.

She leaves me to ponder that while she lights a cigarette. She's started smoking here. I don't remember her smoking when she lived with Dad and me. She smokes Royal cigarettes: they smell as nauseating as the garbage, leaving off a thick sick-sweet odor. I prefer the smell of Time, which most of the long-lashed men smoke. They also smoke a nameless brand that is sold for a few *agorot* in the shuk and gives off a burned-rubber smell. I picked up a stub on one of my walks and tore it apart (for evidence): a few tobacco leaves, grass, a couple of crushed twigs, even a pebble.

After they filled themselves, the cats perched on the stone wall and stared straight ahead. Like this. Cigarette in the corner of her mouth, she puts both hands in front of her—like paws—and stares glassily ahead. The Prince watched them. These must be the inhabitants of earth, he thought. I will do as they do. He perched himself on the stone wall the way they did, stared ahead, and didn't move. Until the cook threw out scraps of food. He scrounged with the others. He lost track of time. In the Rose Balloon no one had a watch or clock. Time passed the way it does when you leave it alone: back and forward, sideways and circling, or just stopping for a while. He jumped down for the food with the cats and returned to the wall and stared the rest of the time. He might have stayed there forever if a little girl named Flora hadn't wandered into the garden one day and seen him and started laughing. What are you doing up there? she asked.

He didn't know what to answer so he followed her out of the garden. As soon as he found himself on the dirt road again he remembered his life in the Rose Balloon, and Omar the Guardian of the Gate, who must be worried, and his parents and family and everyone in the Balloon. He started running back down the road until he came to the red wheelbarrow. Luckily it was the time of month that Omar came to earth to collect supplies. He was so relieved to see the Prince he didn't scold him, only pushed him up and through the slit into the Balloon again. After he washed and dressed in his royal robes, the Prince held a press conference for the inhabitants of the Balloon. Everyone crowded around him to hear the truth about earth. He stood in front of the round pink flag, behind a dais. He spoke in a low, important voice: It is very wet there, he said. The colors are brighter than you can imagine—all sorts of reds and pinks, shades I've never seen before. The ground clings to you and tries to suck you down. There is a garden. The Queen of Earth wears a pale pink crown when she feeds the humans. They're smaller than we imagined, hairier, with great unblinking eyes. They lick themselves clean, and their language is composed of howls and snarls. They grab for the food, but the rest of the time they sit and ponder the mysteries of the universe. Only one of them talks, the Princess, who is also the only one allowed to enter and leave the garden. They don't touch. I don't think they know what love is. They're a great bore. I never want to go back.

OF COURSE I know what she's trying to tell me. Don't jump to conclusions. Don't form judgments about Israel and your mother on this visit to Beit She'an. But like the Prince, I've seen nothing else. And apart from this little story, she keeps me at a distance. I'm sure she's hiding something. The story was a warning. Whatever you discover, don't judge me harshly.

I want to tell her: You left Dad and me to come here and play doctor with all these poor gullible people. Was it worth it? My life against theirs? You be the judge. Mom.

LOOK AT what the Prince didn't see, Mom says, gesturing around the garden. The bee, for example. A small saint, it makes sweet honey and knows everything. You can predict the weather by the sound of its humming. You must never kill a bee, Jo. Treat it kindly: like us, it's a prisoner in its own skin. And the cats. They have *baraka,* a kind of magic power. They clean themselves and say prayers every day. You don't want to get on the wrong side of a cat. And the oleander growing over there. Look for the ones that cluster with four leaves instead of the usual three. You can use them to fight the evil eye. Look at the stones we're sitting on. Small, insignificant, but, like everything else, they contain a universe of meaning. And the sun—no, don't look directly at it! And never point to it. Look down instead, at the herbs I am growing: *kzboor, h'rmel, zafran, sheeba, luisa*—each with its own strength and use. And I haven't even mentioned the air. The way it hangs over us in layers, as if God is baking a cake over our heads. The clouds are the icing on top. You can almost taste it. And the breeze you feel when you shut your eyes: the way it carries heat and flowers and dust right to your nose. And the ground, which gives us fruit and grass. Each grain of earth, each speck of dirt, singing its own song. And the birds and ants and the path that winds around the building. And the carob growing at the side. And the pomegranates and cherries growing wild. And the fig tree. I haven't even begun, and it's already time to go in. But you'll learn, my girl, that what is most true is wordless.

CANELLE IS SO pretty, she shimmers with gold heat. Hair, eyes, skin: every part of her gold dusted. Mom watches her proudly, as if the beauty is her doing. I think Mom has a God complex. Canelle is an orphan, like Aviv. Vanille is their mother more than mine. She named them both. Canelle means "cinnamon," because of the gold that bounces off her, the tart-sweet spiciness of her. Aviv, because he is my age and she finds him beautiful, the promise of spring. Both refuse to tell me their original names. With Vanille they have been reborn. Their names—vanilla, cinnamon, spring—wind around me, a green breeze whispering a secret I can't quite hear.

THERE ARE many mysteries to solve here. The women who come to Mom with cheating husbands, sons who steal, daughters who slip out at night and return at dawn (like the twelve dancing princesses), virgin births, madness and strange spells found under a pillow. They ask her for amulets, holy words (blessed by the saint, her invisible partner in this business), tiny vials of crushed powders and liquids. They ask her dream questions and wait for her interpretations with anxious eyes and nervous hands. She helps them fight the evil eye with silver earrings, scraps of blue cloth, henna paste smeared on their foreheads. They bring her their uncontrollable daughters: one with coarse black hair, a shrunken skull face, and half her teeth missing. A young bride comes in nervously, shyly wonders why it is that she's been married six months already and hasn't gotten pregnant yet. Later, in the kitchen, Mom tells Canelle about it while I pretend to read. He never entered her, she says. Neither of them knew how to do it! He thought if he rubbed against her, it was enough.

I hear Canelle's laugh, but Mom sounds sad. They have no idea, she says. We're not born with knowledge. We know nothing.

The conversation is significant. I note it in my new graph-lined notebook (bought at the town square, in Marcelle's shop—Marcelle with the swollen purple legs), but like my other clues, like the dead-end stone wall, it leads nowhere. Conversations are hushed, carried on in whispers. Canelle and Mom break off as soon as they hear me approach. And Aviv is always silent, watching me with huge hungry eyes. I snap at him, ugly words in Hebrew I am learning, push past him to make him move aside. He comes to embody the dead end that is this town, this summer: the utter blankness in his stupid face. A beautiful boy, isn't he? Mom asks Canelle, as she rubs a sour-smelling clear lotion on his cheeks. Gold dusted like Canelle's, but darker, thinner. I make a rude sound. How can stupid be beautiful? How can an empty face charm? When I fall in love— *if* I ever do—it will be with someone I can talk to, someone devilish and dangerous and wise, like Sam Spade.

I PEEK IN from the hallway. The pale fat man who works in the shoe store—the one who measured my feet for the Nimrods—sits on the chair facing Mom. He stands and opens his short-sleeved dark blue shirt. I lean in farther to see his chest. It's vast, luminous, a pale pink ocean of flesh, with jutting boobs. Oh shit, he's got tits! They're actually bigger than mine! They point out and up, with perky nipples. Mom's hand covers one breast. He's mumbling under his breath. She shushes him and continues exploring. I take a step into the room. *I have to see this.* If a man and a woman can both have breasts, *what does it mean?* Aviv glances up from his crouched position at Mom's legs. Gives me one of his yearning looks. Or is he telling me to clear out? I can't read his eyes. Suddenly nothing makes sense. No one. Not him or Mom or the man-woman. Or even me, spying on them.

A LAZY SHABBAT afternoon. Mom is having her afternoon meeting with the saint in the shrine—what I call the small bedroom where she communes with his holiness. Canelle is having a nap in her room. Aviv is off somewhere, skulking around, his cot neatly folded in the corner of the living room. The smell of *dafina* still lingers in the apartment, even with the windows and balcony doors open—or it's the *dafina* from all the other apartments wafting in. I drifted off to sleep myself, lying on the sofa, leaning against the arm, staring up from *The Maltese Falcon* (my third time through), as if Sam Spade smiled back at me from the wooden plaque of Jerusalem, as if the spires of the Gold City on the Hill reflect the hills and boozy splendor of San Francisco. I will move there as soon as I'm old enough. I hate Virginville, and I hate Beit She'an even more. I'll start my own private detective agency on Turk Street, a name that makes me think of incense, spices, bazaars, the Middle East . . . I come to, and the apartment is silent. I am crouched in a corner of the couch, neck twisted, one leg asleep. I drop my book and get to my feet, stretch, and shake out the tingles in my leg. I think of Mom's remedy for your foot falling asleep: put four matches between the toes and a little spit above each toe.

Right.

The pale air hovers at the window, as if waiting for an invitation to enter. I walk softly on my stiff leather Nimrods. (You have to walk in the sea to soften them. I'll take you to the beach at Acre next Shabbat, next Shabbat, next Shabbat.) I stop at the closed door to the shrine. Behind this door lives the saint. Even Mom admits he's not here all the time. He comes at night, only sometimes in the afternoon. He doesn't speak to me in words, but I understand his language.

He gave it to her with his tongue, Canelle told me, shocking me with her crudity. Her large pure eyes glowing on me. Yes, with his tongue: he kissed your mother and passed her his knowledge and power. Saliva contains *baraka,* especially in holy men. Your mother is a holy woman: her saliva contains *baraka.* That's why everyone comes to her.

Mom retreats to this small room to meditate, to ask him questions for which she has no answer, to help her with the most difficult cases. The room is forbidden to all of us, even Canelle. But I've peeked in. It reminds me of a Chinese or Mexican restaurant: gaudy, with red and green lanterns, plastic flowers, wax figurines and candles. Photographs, newspaper articles, even a small baby photo of me are pasted on the wall. A cot—stern, white, spotless—nearly fills the room. More a long closet than a room. One small window that is always open to a green tree, its leaves and branches fighting to get inside. A low table holds scissors, needles, balls of wax, pen and paper, matches, glue, a broken mirror. Three *hamsas* hang above the table. Two Hebrew scrolls tacked up slap the wall lightly as the branches struggle through the opening. A framed photograph of a rabbi with a long white beard and furious dark eyes. The room smells of incense, candles, oranges. She does not smoke in this room. At night I often hear her rise and come here. At night is when the saint and I talk, she told me once. You don't understand. Never mind. When you're older, I'll explain.

I also smell sweat in the room, human sweat. Jacob wrestled with God and became Israel, Canelle tells me solemnly. Your mother wrestles with her spirit.

Who wins? I ask her.

Both of them. They both come out stronger.

I press my ear to the door and hear a faint murmur. She's talking to the saint, maybe wrestling with him right now. I've got to see this. See if my mother is absolutely wacko, as my dad thinks she is. Or if there actually is something there. I shut my eyes hard, then pull down the door handle soundlessly, as far as it will go, and push the door slightly. A narrow opening. The murmur grows louder. I squeeze farther and peer through the narrow opening.

She's not alone. Canelle is in there with her. They're sitting on the cot in their underwear, white bras and panties. Fighting in Arabic. I don't understand a word, but the sound and rhythm of the language flows through my veins. I *know* it intimately, profoundly, without having the slightest idea what is being said. Vanille is angry, face distorted, as she snarls in a low, spitting voice at Canelle, who hides her face and cries. My mother looks up and sees me. An endless moment while we stare at each other. She clears her throat and says, in a strange, thick voice: It's nothing important. Just an argument. To clear the air.

Canelle lifts her head and looks at me with large wet eyes, and I feel a strange stirring inside me. Something mysterious and uncomfortable, as if my heart and lungs are suddenly too large for my chest.

I FOLLOW an American tourist group through the ruins of the seven-thousand-year-old city. We sit on the steps of the amphitheater and each have our private dreams. Then we climb to the top, where we are hit with a hot wind of grit and dust. I touch my face and feel the grit. The top of the hill reveals the vista of the city. The streets and baths and temples. The fountain and pottery workshop. The Byzantine mosaic floors and Roman columns. As we climb back down the tourists sing "Guantanamera!"

Humming through the verses they don't know. Laughing at themselves, at the intense heat, the ruined residences and dreams, the absurdity of being here in Israel, wearing identical red caps, posed in dutiful awe. The group leader's cap flies from his head and over the cliff, whirls madly like a dying mosquito, before it disappears. He looks back at the group, holds out his arms in surrender, and says: Everybody! The refrain picks up again: "Guantanamera!"

I leave them and stumble down a dirt path where they are still excavating, an area marked: DANGER! KEEP OUT! I duck into an opening in a wall of dirt. In spite of the heat, I am shivering. I hug myself in the dark cave, lick the sweat off my arms, smash my nose and mouth against the dirt and rocks. *I don't ever want to leave this place. I belong here.* It is suddenly so clear, the answer I searched for: the need, the desire, the question mark in the air. I need to stay *here,* under the ground, in the ruins. Another earthquake will come and sweep me under. In a thousand years they'll dig and find traces of me beneath the rubble. These are not ruins. It's all lies, what we believe, what we think we see. The amphitheater is whole, the mosaics bright and vivid, people still stroll down Palladis Street greeting each other in the baths, bowing to each other in the temple, sitting spellbound in the theater. They've been jostling me since I arrived. I breathe them, hear them, feel the whispers and rustles of air as they pass by me, bump right into me without seeing me. A rumble of stones and dirt. The air stirs. They're here, right now, behind me, around me. I turn around.

Aviv enters, breathing hard and fast. Emitting an electric hum, he leads me by the hand in the dark to a world that isn't his or mine, deeper into a cave we have to crawl into—small and dark, like him, with his peculiar smell of nuts and earth. We lie on the ground sideways, facing each other. He lifts my hand and makes me touch his face, runs my fingers up and down and across his warm cheeks and forehead. He's still humming, vibrating, beneath my fingers. Over and over, he rubs my palm against his thin lips, pushes my fingertips into his open mouth. His teeth grate against each other, make an odd clicking sound, capture my fingers and bite. I can't give you a miracle, I tell him, but he doesn't hear me, too far gone, eyes scrunched together, digging my hand, my whole fist, into his mouth. I let out a yowl, long and hungry and terrible as the cat outside my window at night. The earth moves, tilts, back and forth beneath us. Drops of water fall, the spirits breathing down our faces, drenching us with sweat, shaking us upside down. A rainbow curves on the wall behind him, crowning him with a scroll of radiant light. As if there is no end, and this is only the beginning.

Finland's Marjatta Koskinen is an essayist, journalist, fiction writer, and painter. After working and teaching in the field of social work, Koskinen studied journalism and began writing fiction. She won first place in the Tampere Region writing competition, and stories of hers have appeared in three Finnish anthologies. One of her short stories, "Death of a Cabbalist," was published in English in *Beacons*. This is the first English-language publication of "Dies Irae."

Jill Timbers, an escort-interpreter for Finnish leaders invited by the U.S. Information Agency, has lived in Finland, Belgium, and Germany. She holds degrees in English literature, comparative literature, and information and library science. Her translations from Finnish and her articles about translation have appeared in *Beacons, Translation Review, Michigan Academician, Nordic Women Writers* (Garland Publishing), and elsewhere.

Dies Irae

MARJATTA KOSKINEN

Translated from the Finnish by Jill Timbers

IT ALL STARTED WHEN . . .

Mirjami tried to hold on to the dream, but the conscientiously wound alarm clock did not relent. It always rang at the wrong time, in the middle of the most exciting dream. Has anyone done a study of just how much health is wasted due to the imposition of inappropriate work hours? Not to mention the accidents, the arguments . . . okay, okay, if I have to, I have to. Money decides all. Let them die and let them gripe, just so long as they're productive! And again . . . soon I'll have forgotten the dream.

Mirjami closed her eyes and tried to remember. Experience had taught her this was dangerous on a workday morning. Nothing guaranteed sleep better than trying to remember dreams.

....

A TOWN . . . an old town . . . Was there anything familiar about it? No—
and yet, everything so distinct. Stone houses on both sides, beautiful
ones, the way houses used to be. A stony street, a rise, a church at the
top, baroque style . . . small columns in the tower, green patinated roof.
But—were there any people in the whole dream?

"MOM! YOU'RE going to be late!"

Minna at the door. Had tried to call from the kitchen. "You're not going to make your usual shift, anyway. Dad's left already."

"And didn't wake me?"

"Of course not. He said each person takes care of his own business.
Tea's on the table. I can clean up."

How fortunate the girl is this big, starting to assume responsibility.
Mirjami bolted some food and tried to slap some color onto her poor
winter-paled face. If only we used veils here, too, at least in winter.

"I won't be home till seven because of choir," the girl called from the
table.

Yes, yes. She already has her own comings and goings. But why is there
choir on a Monday already?

"Silly, you're all mixed up! This is Thursday! Dreams again?"

"So tomorrow . . ."

"Yup, Friday, and the next morning you can sleep in."

"Ahhh!"

"Tell me!"

MIRJAMI DUG her ticket out of her pocketbook as she ran and glanced
at the dark street to see if she'd dropped anything. Luckily there were
others at the bus stop, because the bus was already coming. Before she
stepped onto the bus she tried to take deep breaths so she wouldn't pant

anymore once inside. Mirjami looked to see if there were any acquaintances on the bus, some sort of beacon toward which to aim. She didn't see any, but luckily there were open seats. Halfway down she noticed a man watching her advance. Maybe someone she'd met somewhere and ought to say hi to? No, he wasn't, but still . . .

A whole bench still open. She could sit by the window. A good place to collapse, doze a little longer. You could see the bus reflected in the window, its walls, the seats with their occupants. Mirjami searched the window reflection for the people sitting midway, looked a moment, then closed her eyes. She opened them at stops when more people got on. Fortunately the intervals between stops were still long. Only at the third stop did empty seats begin to run out.

A young man came up the aisle. He threw off his hood of imitation fur and tossed his longish black hair back with a sharp motion. Maybe still a schoolboy. Seems somehow nervous, or perhaps just more susceptible than most? As he neared, an impossible thought abruptly struck Mirjami: it was as if she were seeing her own face approach! The boy stopped next to her as if considering, looked around, and sat down beside her. What is this— the dream still? Me here—and that one there, the boy? Mirjami did not have the nerve to look directly at him. She just glanced sideways enough to confirm her perception of the moment before. She turned her gaze to the mirror bus and noticed that the man in the middle had turned his head sideways, was straining to see, found their bench. He looked at them both for a moment, the boy and her, and then turned to face forward again.

THIS ISN'T real anymore. Mirjami closed her eyes. But instead of darkness there were pictures behind her closed lids. The dream city returned, she was there. Would she see anyone now? Over there someone is coming. . . . She jumped when somebody pressed the signal bell.

The boy got off before the center. The midway man took his leave one stop before Mirjami. Before he rose he turned his head sideways. His nose was long and thin, like his whole face; his hair was black like that of the boy who had just been there. As he was leaving he turned all the way around and looked at her. A vestige of some repeated childhood nightmare hit Mirjami.

That day and the next few days Mirjami kept replaying in her mind the morning events and her dream and trying to find some explanation for them, but gradually she forgot. Finland's cold and dark demanded all her strength. It was enough just trying to make it through the mornings from Monday to Friday.

MIRJAMI STOOD numb in the midst of the darkness. Darkness that again felt as impenetrable as the heart of winter. A few February days had already offered a preview of spring. Humbug, like all advertising, Mirjami thought dejectedly. The darkness had summoned all the infernal forces to its aid: wind whipped, sleet lashed—there's your spring for you! Right in the face!

The bags were squeezing her fingers, and the throngs of Friday grocery shoppers in the store made her mood worse. Mirjami had thought she would make the earlier bus, which ran more often, on a rush-hour schedule. But as luck would have it, it left. While she was standing in the checkout line behind shopping carts stuffed to overflowing. What would one of the skeleton children on the TV news, or his mother, feel if they saw these prodigal loads? Probably nothing. Their minds would simply refuse to believe. After all, the child doesn't even feel the fly in his eye.

The buses pushed the mass into the market square. Like ants on an ant hill, rushing here and there. Mirjami noticed a hunched figure behind her in the shadow of a roof pillar. His hood was pulled up to shield his head, his body sought shelter in the rest of the coat. The figure moved to see the station's illuminated clock. Mirjami recognized the youth. His face looked even thinner than before. Was it the cold or the fluorescent lamps that gave his face a blue look? The youth's expression held both suffering and a slight smile.

At last. The bus sped around a curve into the market square. Ticket quickly into the entry machine and the driver had already stepped on the gas again. After a long straight stretch the bus came to a stop where many passengers changed buses. Shivering creatures dripping water and snow pushed their way in. Why even look at them, strangers all?

Sleet lashed the window. Outside, people with their umbrellas were pushing forward toward whatever their destination. In one direction the wind drove against them, in the other it pushed from behind, and sometimes blew an umbrella inside out. The bus stayed at the stop longer than usual. Someone must be buying a ticket. The driver would of course repay the delay by starting up with a great jerk and taking the curves at top speed. What unfortunate . . .

The newcomer had gotten his ticket and grabbed the first fixed handhold with his free hand, barely managing to keep his balance. He looked around and noticed Mirjami. The bench on the other side of the aisle was unoccupied. The man stopped, but before he sat down, he looked at something in the back section of the bus. He put his purchases down on the aisle-side seat and sat himself at a slight angle on the seat next to the window.

The morning of months earlier came back to Mirjami in full detail. The dream, too. Once again a dome of unreality descended over everything. Did the never-ending sleet trickling down the window belong inside the dome, or outside it?

From overhead could be heard first softly, then soon quite loudly: "Somewhere across the ocean somewhere there's a land. . . ." Mirjami turned to look at the driver. The back of the neck of a man nearing the end of middle age flushed. In the mirror she could see a small smile spread across his face. "Oh if someday I could ever reach that fairy-tale land I would never fly away. . . ." That was it, exactly. Somewhere it's got to be different. In heaven, in fairy-tale land, over the ocean. For him, too, who drives the suburb route back and forth, back and forth.

They had gone a long way without stopping. The first shrill sounding of the signal bell announced the start of the emptying phase. The thin-faced boy was among those getting off. His departure was followed from the neighboring seat as well. Then it was Mirjami's turn. As she went, she felt the stare from the window like a weight.

At night Mirjami had nightmares.

"IF ONLY we could go abroad again!" Mirjami leaned her cheek on her hand between sips of tea. "But I guess we can't afford it. Just paying for the walls forever."

"Why don't you go, if you want to?" the girl said indifferently. "I for one am going to work all summer as a gardener."

"There's travel money enough for one person. And it doesn't look as if anyone else wants to go," the man said from behind the newspaper.

"I wonder if somebody would go along. I don't suppose all alone . . ."

"Why not? More exciting." The girl spoke with a teenager's know-it-all confidence. "They're just laughable, those middle-aged ladies who move around as a group."

"So I'm . . ."

"Sorry! Not you, thank goodness. But I bet you remember when you were with Hanna. One of you wanted to see one thing, the other, something else; one wanted to sleep, the other wanted to go into town."

Mirjami remembered.

"How about if I took part of my vacation in the fall. It's still warm in mid-Europe then, but there are concerts and everything."

"Whatever. It's fine with me," the man said.

And her daughter: "Makes no difference to me."

But it does to me, Mirjami thought. That way I can make summer last, and shorten the accursed darkness.

IF ONLY this, too, were just a dream. And me, home in bed. Here I am now on the deck of a half-empty ship in the fog. The wind has dried the rain at least, but with promise of hours of tossing ahead. And that, Mirjami would withstand poorly.

What if she got her things from the cabin and rushed off the boat while there was still time? But the money, thrown away? And the laughter, at home, at work. No, let's go on with it . . .

On the open sea the fog abruptly disappeared. The wind was still strong, but a blue ocean did not seem at all as threatening as a gray. On the contrary. Even the wind felt joyful now. Her regret vanished. Now it was beginning, the long-awaited journey.

A TRAIN carried the travelers from Travemünde to Lübeck. Mirjami took a taxi from the station, although the hotel was within walking distance, judging from the map. She had not been able to sleep well on the ship and was now feeling not the least bit energetic.

When she saw the hotel she was grateful for her decision. At the travel agency she had wished for a romantic old hotel, but this . . . She threw a hasty glance at her luggage and her outfit as she tried to trip daintily into the lobby, escorted by taxi driver and doorman. Luckily she had bought new, though it had been painful. But the old had been worn out.

"*Guten Tag,* madame." And a laser glance.

Papers filled out, keys happily in hand.

"We hope you enjoy your stay, madame."

The room was straight out of some grandiose dream.

THE HOTEL was located next to a large park. Paths crisscrossed beneath the leafy trees, and arched bridges led over brooks whose waters rippled toward the stream that cut through town. In that direction the park opened into a sun-warmed grassy opening. It is different here, full summer still. Mothers sat on playground benches, watching children busy playing in the sand and on the equipment. Some warm, unhurried childhood feeling came to mind. Nowadays at home you only saw tense superbeings herding children to and from caregivers.

She had wanted to head for the old town. Aha, over there. Her friend had said you just have to watch the church towers, there were enough of them. Lübeck had stayed intact relatively well through the war. Over there were the famous salt lofts and the town gate. Where first? Perhaps the market square—no—to the oldest church, after all.

It seemed as if even the sun had vanished near the cathedral. She certainly would not come here in the dark. Even the ghosts were surely a thousand years old. Part of the church had been destroyed and the ruins remained, jutting up. Inside it was quiet. Mirjami shivered under the thick church vaults.

She hurried toward the market square and people.

EVENING MUSIC in St. Mary's. Marienkirche—like a graceful maiden stretching upward toward sacred heights. You could almost imagine the stars peeking through the small tapered windows in the roof, their shape repeated lower down in the giant windows' noble form. She had entered the church early in order to look around before the concert began. But people began to stream in early, too. The performers must be well known. It would be best to find a good seat and keep looking at the church from there.

Music swelled through the colonnade. Eyes and ears conveyed pleasure and harmony.

The organist had judged right. People jumped when the trumpets of doom shook the church: *Dies Irae*—Day of Wrath. Far removed from peace and joy.

Fragments came to mind: "I was hungry and you didn't . . . sick and in prison, naked, and you . . . take away from me the clamor of your hymns!" This magnificent monument, too—built with the harsh toil of people who lived in want. To honor God—hardly! To honor the princes, rather, for them to sit and be worshipped where all could see.

Mirjami started to hate it all. The well-fed people around her, even the lovely church itself. Day of Wrath. Whether it comes in the form of God sitting in judgment or as the end to patience of the oppressed and persecuted, the day will come.

Were anyone else's thoughts here following a similar path? Did this well-to-do crowd even remember where they were? Just another concert . . .

Mirjami gave a start.

A little farther forward a dark head turned slowly sideways . . . more, tried to look back. What? How—how can it be possible?

Mirjami listened to the rest of the concert as in a dream.

When they were leaving the church, she did not even try to escape. The same feeling as in a nightmare: pointless to run, you'll never get away. She moved forward toward the door and as she went she knew she would soon hear, "Excuse me, but . . ."

THEY WALKED toward the medieval restaurant.

Why are you here? A meeting. And me, just clearing my head, escaping the fall. Me, too, actually. Darkness suffocates.

Tension melted with the candle flames and the people's good cheer. They hardly needed wine, they were able to sing without it just fine. What a peculiar contradiction in these people—strange extremes: violence— gentleness, anguish—happiness, evil—kindness, wisdom—absurdity. Does a person contain another universe within himself, herself?

"Dreams and children's imagination tell of that universe."

"But an adult fears his own reach, his outmost limits. He invents ex- planations."

"And projects his fears onto other people, onto the different."

Evening slid into night.

"Tomorrow there's a Bach concert in Hamburg. Will you go?"

"Of course, if it's Bach."

"We'll have time to look around the city a bit before we go into the church."

In this direction there was an area that had not been much damaged during the war. In spots you could imagine yourself walking through a Hanseatic city of long ago. It was quiet. People had withdrawn to rest as the dusk deepened. The night town would not be on the move until late.

APPARENTLY THEY were already late, for the street leading to the church was empty. They walked quickly, and Mirjami almost tripped trying to see the church in all its splendor. Spotlights illuminated the steeple, the baroque colonnade on the crest—baroque . . . Mirjami stopped abruptly and grasped the man's arm, groping for support.

"It—it was this!"

The words came haltingly, her teeth chattered.

The man had not yet understood anything when they heard running footsteps approaching. Mirjami gripped his arm harder and stared past the church.

"Let's get going," the man said, trying to pull Mirjami into motion. Her feet started to obey, finally breaking into a run.

When they reached the door they saw a boy who seemed to be running on his last strength. Some distance behind him two skinheads were coming at the same pace. Or maybe there were even more of them coming.

The boy was almost in front of them when they suddenly realized who they were seeing: the boy from the suburban bus. Without thinking or speaking the man grabbed the boy firmly, and Mirjami said, "Come!"

The boy almost wrenched himself loose but then he realized he had heard his own language, and he let himself be pulled into the church. Like a limp bundle.

Had the skinheads noticed?

The ticket sellers in the church foyer buzzed angrily. There was also an old man in an usher's suit among them. He seemed to grasp the situation quickly.

"Go on into the church. I'll keep an eye on the situation. If they stay hanging around, I'll call the police."

The old man sighed and went on softly, "So sad. Is it starting again already? I remember one time before the war, in front of this church . . . a whole Jewish family . . . The child was a boy. Hoodlums like those had found out they were Jews. I couldn't look. And the police sided with those criminals. I guess you know."

THEY BOUGHT tickets, one for the boy, too, and quietly entered the church. To the side, where it was dark. They sat each on one side of the boy. Mirjami tried to make her own trembling stop. She tried to concentrate, to listen.

The St. Matthew Passion? In the fall? But Bach at his best. Maybe just pieces.

". . . The sun too clothes itself in pain, the curtain tears, the rock splits, the earth trembles, and graves open, when they see the Creator dead." The master had lived the agony deeply and was transmitting it just as rendingly to his listeners.

They walked the boy back to the student dorm. "Why were they chasing you?"

"They were shouting, 'Jew, look at the kike!' They were threatening to kill."

YES. IT was here.

CYRILLE FLEISCHMAN of Paris, France, began his writing career with stories for the French Jewish press. Many of his stories are set in the Jewish quarter of Paris's Marais district. Since 1987 Fleischman has published seven books of fiction, including the short-story collection *Nouveaux rendez-vous au métro Saint-Paul* (Le Dilettante, 1994), which was awarded a prize by the Académie Française in 1995. English translations of his stories have appeared in *Partisan Review, Yale French Studies,* and *Shofar,* and one of his stories recently appeared in the Polish periodical *Midrasz,* in Warsaw. "One Day, Victor Hugo . . ." is from his prizewinning collection.

AVRIEL GOLDBERGER, formerly a professor of French at Hofstra University, has published translations of Madame de Staël's novels *Corinne* and *Delphine* and her memoir, *Ten Years of Exile.* Goldberger's translation of Emilie Carle's autobiography, *A Life of Her Own,* won a place on many of 1991's lists of notable books in the United States and the United Kingdom. The recipient of numerous grants, including a Fulbright Scholarship and a grant from the National Endowment for the Humanities, Dr. Goldberger was in 1988 named a Knight of the Order of Arts and Letters by the French government.

One Day, Victor Hugo . . .

CYRILLE FLEISCHMAN

Translated from the French by Avriel Goldberger

ZALMAN LESERIK SUBSCRIBED to a Yiddish paper that came by mail. Even so, around ten-thirty he would go down to the newsstand to buy a daily paper in French. Simply to have a better idea of how world events might reverberate in his private life. Not that Leserik was famous. But this was a man who had sold magazines and secondhand books at the markets of the Paris region and who, since retirement, now as always, attached the greatest importance to the printed word. Besides, when he stopped working, he had given up his van but kept the major part of his stock. So that between what he hadn't sold and the newspapers he bought daily, he was certainly one of the men in the neighborhood with the greatest number of printed characters under his eyes.

That particular day, when he left his building, instead of going straight to the newsstand near the metro he stopped at the drugstore to buy a bottle of oil of paraffin. The medicine prescribed by his new doctor hadn't worked, and he'd decided to go back to products he knew.

As a result, there in the pharmacy Zalman Leserik met Simon Rikof, who wanted something for a cough. They exchanged a few words.

When it came time to say good-bye and Leserik announced that he was going for his paper, Rikof observed pleasantly: "Don't get me wrong, Zalman, but what are you going to do with all those papers, all those books, when you're dead? I hear from the maid, who comes to my place, too, that your place is stuffed with them. You'd be better off playing pinochle. Come on, I'm inviting you."

Leserik was unresponsive. He knew that Rikof spent his time with a few other retired men in a café near the metro. But for him it held no interest. He just asked: "And you, so you don't read?"

"Never! My wife tells me when she hears something interesting in town. That's enough for me."

"Then how—without reading a paper—could you know what will happen?"

Rikof had a good laugh. "You think the end of the world, it'll be printed three days ahead of time in the classified ads of *Unzer Wort* or *France-Soir?*"

Annoyed, Leserik would rather have left it at that. "Stay well," he called out as he left the drugstore with his little bottle of paraffin sticking out of a small paper bag.

But Rikof didn't let him off the hook, he ran after him. "Tell me, I forgot to ask you just now, you wouldn't have, maybe, a few old novels for me from your stock? It's not for me, or my wife, it's for my grandson who's ruining his eyes with a bunch of writers his father has no choice but to buy him at the Bazaar de l'Hôtel de Ville . . ."

With a vague gesture Leserik replied only: "Let him go to the library, to city hall!"

Simon Rikof tugged at his sleeve: "That's the way you talk to someone who has a grandson who wants to improve his mind with old books that are absolutely no use to you?"

Leserik shrugged and without a word started walking. The other man followed him.

By now they were in front of the newsstand where, as luck would have it, they met Bertolt Frisnach, a hairdresser they both knew. He was looking for change in his pant pocket to pay for a movie magazine.

"You've heard what I have to listen to for my grandson?" asked Rikof, taking him to witness.

Bertolt Frisnach turned around politely and said hello to Leserik, then Rikof, before asking the latter: "Your grandson is sick?"

"No," Leserik broke in, irritated. "He wants me to give him books that belong to me. Do I come into your home asking for a wig or scissors?"

"Why are you talking about a wig?" said the startled Bertolt Frisnach, who was bald and sensitive. He was only five foot two, but he was an impulsive man, and pointed his rolled-up magazine at Leserik's chest. "Zalman, if you want to joke around with me, you'll do it all by yourself!"

Rikof watched the scene with his arms crossed, triumphant. He addressed the hairdresser: "See what I was telling you?"

Leserik turned to Frisnach to explain: "I was giving an example. We weren't talking about you. We were talking about books, education . . . What do I know? Things that have nothing to do with you. Don't take it the wrong way."

"Because I'm not cultured? Because I don't read? Because *I* don't buy newspapers?" said the little hairdresser, irritated again.

"A newspaper with naked women, that's not the same thing," Leserik answered pleasantly, pointing to the movie magazine Frisnach was brandishing.

They were about to continue when, right near them, stopped Victor Hugo, who had lived on the Place des Vosges for a long time and who, even though unquestionably dead, was also on his way to buy a newspaper at the stand near metro St-Paul.

Hugo looked the way he always did and wore a kind of frock coat. Still, even the hairdresser was surprised. Zalman, enraptured, was the first to react. "You wouldn't happen to be Monsieur Victor Hugo who has a museum on the Place des Vosges? I think you are, aren't you? I have at least twenty-five books of yours at my place! *The Human Condition, Les Misérables* . . . who knows what else. Good books in any case!"

"I don't remember all those titles anymore," said Hugo, rubbing his ear. "Tell me instead, my friends: Why are you arguing? Didn't I hear something about reading? Culture? Naked women? Your conversation sounds fascinating to me. Are you interested in table turning and séances as well?"

Bertolt Frisnach turned all the way around to study Victor Hugo closer. "Excuse me, I'm a turning chair in a barbershop myself, like you say, but the last time I saw you was at the movies."

"Really? In what film?" asked Hugo, interested.

Leserik thrust Frisnach aside before he could answer and firmly took Hugo by the elbow, pulling him along on a forced march: "These are people who don't read literature!" he explained. "Come look around my place instead. I'll show you my whole library with all your books and more besides. I live right near here."

Hugo went along with him. They had already gone four or five meters when Rikof caught up. "Wait a minute!" he called.

He spoke to Hugo: "I don't want to bother you, Monsieur Victor Hugo, but couldn't you come say a few words to my grandson who goes to lycée Charlemagne? Afterward, if he puts what you said in his homework, he's sure to get a good mark."

"Let him read my books. He'll certainly find an appropriate quotation," answered Victor Hugo, smiling.

Rikof shrugged: "A spoken word, it's more important than what's in a book. Since you're already here, how could it bother you to come to my place for a cup of tea? I'll phone my grandson to come by. That way he'll see you. It would really be good for his schoolwork."

Zalman Leserik was about to pull Hugo by the sleeve to keep him from listening to Simon Rikof, when, after some hesitation, the little hairdresser approached. "Monsieur Hugo, would you happen to have a photograph on you? With an autograph? In my beauty shop I have already, with a dedication, from Marcel Cohen, the boxer. If I had yours, too, over the cash register, it would be great for my customers."

Victor Hugo raised his arms. "Very sorry," he said.

He turned to the other two. "Come to think of it, it's a little late in the morning for visiting. I'll pick up my newspaper and go back to the museum."

He nodded: "Good day, dear friends, good day."

Zalman, distressed to see him leave, clutched Hugo's arm in an almost despairing gesture. Genuinely distressed, he asked: "But, seriously, in your opinion, do novels and all that really make a person more intelligent?"

Victor Hugo sighed: "The novel, since you ask, may indeed be a necessity. However, what is important, truly important, is poetry!"

The three of them shook their heads, without really understanding but solemnly, because this man speaking had a museum to his name. Then they watched Victor Hugo toddle along toward the newspaper stand near the metro. On his way back, when he passed them again, the great man gave them a friendly wave with his paper. Overtaking them, he repeated: "Poetry. Remember, my friends: poetry . . ."

At one point he turned around.

Already a little too far away to be heard distinctly, he added, still waving his paper: "You will understand later on, dear friends. But you, too, were poetry."

And he left . . . until next time.

YIZHAK OREN's work is known for its dislocation of reality and exploration of the paradoxical, whimsical, and fantastic. Born in Siberia in 1918, Oren lived in China until his family emigrated to Palestine in 1936. During the British Mandate he worked paving roads and for the British Army, and later studied literature, philosophy, and history at the Hebrew University. More than a dozen of his novels, short-story collections, and essay collections have been published in Hebrew. His work has been translated into Russian, French, and Italian; his collection *The Imaginary Number* was published in English in 1986 (Benmir Books). Oren is the chief editor of the *Encyclopedia Judaica* in Russian and the recipient of several literary prizes.

The Cat Man

YIZHAK OREN

Translated from the Hebrew by Yael Politis

THIS MORNING THE ANNOUNCEMENT of Yuri Tchestnov's death in Moscow was published in the papers. So, Yuri Tchestnov has passed away. Thus I am no longer bound by the oath of silence I swore to him. Tchestnov's death places the opposite obligation upon me—to speak out. Since the day he tragically lost his wife he remained single, and he had no children. Therefore, I have no reason to fear that his family might be harmed by these words that I now put into writing, even if they may some day be published.

Tchestnov achieved fame as the world's most distinguished anthropologist by his discovery in northern Siberia of *Homo felis,* the Cat Man. I had the good fortune to meet him at one of the international anthropology conventions. All were eager to hear him speak, but although his lecture was to be the highlight of the convention, he did not present it. At least not in public. At the time designated for his lecture it was announced that he was ill. Most delegates demanded that the lecture be rescheduled, but, surprisingly, the delegation from the Soviet Union insisted that the original schedule be kept. Tchestnov had missed his opportunity.

The next evening I met Tchestnov in a restaurant. A pale yellowness tinged his cheeks and cast a Mongol-like expression on his wide-jawed face. A half-full cup of tea stood on the table in front of him. He sat alone and no one from his delegation approached him.

"Do you mind if I join you?" I asked in Russian, indicating the chair opposite him. His table was in one of the far corners of the restaurant.

"Not at all," he mumbled, lowered his eyes, and sipped his tea.

To me, he paid no attention.

I smiled and said:

> My only friend comes every eve,
> Reflected in my cup of wine.

This was a quotation from a famous poem by the Russian poet Blok.

I had the feeling that this quotation, cited in his native language, attracted his interest. Then, out of the blue, he said: "Are you Jewish?"

"Yes," I said. "From Israel."

"Ah, from Israel!" I felt desire on his part to continue our conversation. Little did I realize that this moment was to be the beginning of a trust that allowed me to learn the circumstances surrounding his discovery of Homo Felis.

"Let's go out to the garden," he suggested, and got up. As he rose I noticed how tall and powerfully built he was.

We went out to the garden, headed toward the nearest bench, and on the way I thought of all that I had heard about Russian Jews seeking contact with Israelis. His face now bore a stronger resemblance to that of a Mongolian. I was trying to decide if he was Jewish.

I anticipated questions about life in Israel, and prepared to give him a brief survey of our struggles and achievements. As we settled onto the bench I returned his earlier question to me, and asked:

"Are you Jewish?"

"No."

"Russian?"

"Not entirely. My father was a Russian and my mother a Buryat."

"What's that?"

"The Buryats are Mongolian people who live in northern Siberia."

I expressed my disappointment about his cancelled lecture. He rose. "I will tell you all about *Homo felis,* but promise me that whatever you hear this evening will remain only with you." He spoke with emotion, as one who needed to unburden himself.

"I'm not used to taking vows," I said, "especially when I don't know their significance."

"Promise!" he insisted.

I was anxious to hear about *Homo felis* so I gave him my word. But even as I was making this pledge I resolved not to keep it. Scientific ethics do not permit keeping important discoveries to oneself and, for the sake of scientific progress, I was willing to break a vow. However, after I heard what he had to say I changed my mind. As long as Tchestnov walked the face of the earth, his secret was buried in my heart.

This is what Tchestnov told me:

> The first rumors about the existence of a wild man in the *taiga* forests reached me in 1950. At that time I was with my wife, visiting my mother in one of the small Buryat towns in north-eastern Siberia. During her life my mother almost never set foot out of the town where she was born, but after I left home I would from time to time come to visit and spend a few weeks with her in the spring or early summer. This time my wife, who was also an anthropologist, was with me.
>
> At first my wife and I did not credit the stories we had heard about a wild giant wandering through the forest accompanied by a wolf, and preying on every creature that crossed their

path. However, after questioning some of the local inhabitants, these rumors began to rouse my curiosity, although I still considered them to be fantasies. An ancient Buryat woodsman who must already have been a relic when I was a child, and now, after the passing of forty years, was still magnificently powerful, took it upon himself to track the vestiges of this mysterious creature and to lead us to him.

We were three when we left: the old man, my wife, and myself. My wife was experienced in travel under difficult conditions—for years she had taken part in my scientific expeditions, many of which were dangerous.

We equipped ourselves with a hide sewn to serve as a tent, rifles, food, and fuel. We carried this load on our backs, with the bulk upon the shoulders of the old Buryat guide.

Toward dusk we would stop at a clearing. We would put up the hide tent and build a fire. It was summertime, but the nights were still chilly and damp due to an abundance of water from the Siberian glaciers melting in the last days of spring and drenching the earth.

Those who have never seen a primordial forest in the far north in the beginning of summer will never know the primeval feeling it evokes in the traveler. Everything that lives or blossoms bursts forth from the earth in all its natural power, filling every mortal with elation. I mention this only to emphasize the contrast between the wonderful beginning of this journey and its tragic end.

Four nights we slept in the forest. On the morning of the fifth day we chanced upon a trail. There were two kinds of tracks: the footprints of a man, and near them the tracks of some animal.

The face of the old man displayed satisfaction and terror at the same time; satisfaction that his stories were borne out, and terror . . . Yes, there was reason to be terrified.

It looked as if the animal tracks were made by a wolf. Wolves are not rare in the northern forests. The wonder was that the

wolf's tracks never parted from those of the man himself. This
was no ordinary man. His foot was almost twice as large as the
average.

My wife gave me a curious look.

It happened in the morning. In the afternoon of that day my
wife would be dead.

We continued on our way for about two hours. Then the
tracks vanished, and we stopped.

At that instant, a wolf sprang from the thick of the forest and
attacked my wife. My rifle was raised but I don't remember if
I managed to pull the trigger. Before I knew what happened to
my wife, a powerful blow struck me and threw me to the
ground. The image of a horrifying giant, whose face was covered with wildly grown hair, passed before my eyes for a moment. Then it seems another heavy blow struck me and I lost
consciousness.

When I regained my senses I was stretched out in the tent.
The Buryat took care of me. My wife was nowhere to be seen
and the Buryat said he did not know where she was. I was too
weak to be able to search for her, but as I was led away I
vowed that I would return as soon as possible or try to send a
search party for her. I did not know at that time that she had
been killed in the encounter and that the wolf had partly devoured her.

The events that followed are known to the world. It proved
impossible for me to get a search party for my wife, and it
took me two weeks to recover and assemble an expedition
myself. We were a well-equipped group of fifteen members
when we returned to the scene of the disaster. To make it
short: we discovered *Homo felis* and in a fierce fight against the
clawing and snarling beast succeeded in overwhelming him
and forcing him into a cage. The characteristics of *Homo felis*
are no doubt familiar to you from the scientific publications.
You know the enormous dimensions of his limbs, the structure

of his skull, which resembles that of a link between man and ape, his long teeth, sharp fangs. We also found the horrible remains of my wife and buried them in a simple ceremony.

With the actual capture of the mystery creature, yours truly, Yuri Tchestnov, had made the greatest contribution to anthropology since the existence of that science: a living prehistoric man, not a skull or a bunch of bones. The journals wrote that Tchestnov had brought honor to his homeland.

There is one aspect of the Cat Man you do not know. About it I did not publish a word. Only I and the former chief of my Institute know it. In a few minutes another will know—you. I was forbidden to mention it to anyone. And I have already made you promise that the secret will remain with you.

The captured *Homo felis* lived in a large cage in the courtyard of the Anthropological Institute. I moved into a building in the same courtyard. I investigated, measured and drew up detailed scientific reports.

Homo felis cooperated. He ate heartily and gained weight. In a short time he allowed me to come near him. I would enter his cage and carry out my examinations without objections on his part. At times his expression—an expression of great sadness—would astonish me, although that expression is characteristic of some animals, including beasts of prey. I had gained his trust, but I myself still behaved according to the principle "respect him but suspect him."

As the days passed I felt a gradual change in my prisoner. I watched him closely. It seemed that he was slowly gaining human nature, perhaps regaining it, as if reversing a possible original metamorphosis *into* "prehistoric" man. Even his deep-seated growls seemed to change their pitch and sound more human.

One day I was crossing the courtyard on my way home with a large framed portrait of my late wife which I was about to hang on the wall in my room. As I stopped in front of the cage of the Cat Man, he reached out from behind the bars and seized the picture from under my arm, held it in his hands, gazed at it, and his expression changed to that of a human being.

Suddenly I heard *Homo felis* speak. I could not believe my ears. He opened his mouth and asked in Russian: 'Your wife?'

Yes, the Cat Man could speak—and Russian at that! And when I recovered from my surprise, he settled down and told me his life story.

He was born, he told me, in eastern Poland to a wealthy Jewish family. He was a delicate boy, talented, meditative, and a dreamer. As he approached adolescence he was taken with a strange disease, apparently one of those diseases related to ele- phantiasis: his limbs became extraordinarily large, he grew to a height of about eight feet, and his features became distorted, almost animal-like. Keep in mind the publications of the An- thropological Institute; remember the photographs—these are all authentic. All efforts to cure him were in vain. But this ex- traordinary growth had no effect on his character or his men- tal and emotional traits. He was still a sensitive young man of intellect and spirit. Only his physical power increased extraor- dinarily. He could bend nails with his fingers, and with his fists could have killed a horse with one blow. After he graduated from high school he studied law at the university and at that time became a member of the Communist party. When the Germans invaded Poland he was sent to an extermination camp and suffered there for four years. He survived because the Nazis treated him as a circus freak and used him for their amusement. He lived to see the liberation, and when he was freed he went to Russia, continued his studies and was an out- standing student.

When the State of Israel was established, warm feelings to- ward his people were aroused in him. I don't know how he expressed these feelings, but the Soviet authorities disapproved of something he said or did. He was arrested and sent to a concentration camp in Siberia. His body saved him again.

Because of his strength and proficiency as a wood cutter, he won the right to receive his meals from the first pot (that is to say, his portion was twice as large as that of those workers whose output did not reach the quota), and soon was put in charge of a group of workers.

One day he went out to the forest with his group and never returned to the camp. The sight of weak and starving people who were driven near death, trying to fill the output quota at back-breaking labor, and under a regime which since his youth he had believed would redeem mankind, had shocked him profoundly. Disgust with everything called Russian filled him.

Together with a German shepherd guard dog, which had become his companion in the camp, he escaped to the thick of the forest and resolved to become a hermit. From then on, he lived off the plants of the forest or wild animals that he hunted together with his dog. Eventually he became like a prehistoric man and his dog like a wild wolf.

All the while the Cat Man was telling me, Tchestnov, his story he kept his eyes on the portrait of my wife. I remembered my wife's remains that we had found on the day that the man was captured.

It seemed that he read my thoughts. He said to me: "I didn't touch her. The dog devoured her."

I opened the door of the cage. Then I went to my rooms, got a razor blade, brought it to him and said: "Go to the bathroom and shave."

He left, I sat in his cage and waited. When he did not return, I knew what I had expected had happened. I went to the bathroom and found him lying on the floor in a pool of blood. The razor was stuck in his neck.

I called the police. Afterward I went to the head of the Institute and told him the story. I was ordered to keep silent. I was forbidden to mention or to put into writing what I have told you now. The muzzle was placed on me because the Soviet

Academy did not want the embarrassment of having to admit that the celebrated prehistoric man was nothing but a Jew who had escaped their camp. And now you know why yesterday I could not force myself to deliver before an international audience a paper on *Homo felis* which would have perpetuated the official version—a lie!

I did not ask Tchestnov the obvious question why he had told *me* the story. But there was another question which I *did* ask him:

"Why was the man called *Homo felis*—that is, the Cat Man? There is no similarity between him and a cat. Neither have I found an explanation in any scientific publication."

"It was done at my request. It was the only request the Institute complied with."

"Which means?"

"The man's name was Katz. *Katz* in Yiddish means cat. I wanted to commemorate his name."

I laughed and said: "You have been misled, professor. Yes, *katz* in the language of Eastern European Jews means cat, but the name Katz is an acronym of two Hebrew words: *Kohen-Tsedek,* the priest of justice."

As I left Tchestnov I could not help but reflect on the reasons why he had told the story to *me*. Was it because he felt that Katz's life story had special significance to a Jew, to an Israeli?

JOHN SHEPLEY's short stories and essays have appeared in numerous publications in the United States and Italy—*Paris Review, Southern Review, Massachusetts Review, Corriere dell'adda* (Milan), *I Quaderni della crisi* (Florence), *The Best American Short Stories of 1956* (Houghton Mifflin, 1956), *The Quixote Anthology* (Grosset & Dunlap, 1961), *The Best from Fantasy and Science Fiction* (Doubleday, 1959, 1967), and elsewhere. He has translated more than a dozen books from the Italian, including works by Alberto Savinio, Beppe Fenoglio, and Pier Paolo Pasolini. For his translation of Pasolini's *Roman Nights and Other Stories* (Marlboro, 1986), Shepley was the first person to receive the Italian government's Italo Calvino Translation Award. He currently lives in New York City.

A Golem in Prague

JOHN SHEPLEY

My substance was not hid from thee,
when I was made in secret,
and curiously wrought in the lowest
parts of the earth.

PSALM 139:15

A GOLEM IN PRAGUE? Well, of course, where else would
it be? And how did it get there? Quite simply. Under the arcades on Uvoz
Street, at the point where it descends into Nerudova, a woman raised her
arm in a gesture of violence toward her companion, and at that moment
a golem appeared on the sidewalk.

Not, perhaps, a perfect golem. For that you need an ecstatic rabbi,
well versed in kabbalistic lore and the *Book of Creation,* one who knows
all the proper incantations and the secret name of God. That the secret
name of God is known to this angry, buxom Czech woman, who has just
knocked down a bearded young man on crutches, seized one of them
out from under him, and is threatening to brain him with it, seems

unlikely to say the least. Yet all things considered, she has done remarkably well. But so engrossed is she as she lifts her arm with the crutch over the man's supine body that she can have no idea of what she has inadvertently created. In the final analysis the golem, a mute observer, must create itself.

Re-create might be the better word. For such is the golem's lack of confidence, the mark of how unsure it is of itself, that it comes not only with the requisite Hebrew letters—EMET or "truth"—inscribed on its forehead, but with the *shem hameforash* bearing the holy name in its mouth, as though it needed both these talismans to justify its existence when one would have been enough. And indeed, standing there patiently on the sidewalk and awaiting the commands of its *shiksa* mistress, the golem is visibly confused. It is getting, as we say, mixed signals.

Certainly the scene being enacted in its presence is bewildering enough. Various explanations suggest themselves. The man may be drunk. Anyway he looks it: his eyes are mournful and dazed, his movements unsteady, even for a cripple on crutches. The woman, who no doubt works her fingers to the bone taking care of him, has momentarily lost all patience. Perhaps later she will be remorseful, cry, and caress his head in her lap. On the other hand this may be a regular pattern of mistreatment, no matter how sorry she feels about it afterward. Perhaps she is the reason he drinks; perhaps (worst thought of all) his disabled state is the result of her abuse, and his revenge takes the form of further provocation: an endless round of reciprocal aggression and humiliation. Is he her husband, her brother, her lover? No telling. It is one of those finite human dramas incomprehensible to God and the angels, let alone to a clay android of limited intelligence and sensitivity.

The sky is overcast, the air heavy with the threat of rain. With no commands forthcoming, the golem might be expected to dissolve back into the haze of legend from which it has reluctantly emerged. But no, this golem has already risked too much; its feet are planted firmly on the pavement and now are anxious to move. Still, having been conjured up and now finding itself footloose in Prague, it has no idea where it wants to go, no recollection of anywhere it might have been before, nor any reason to return there.

This is not to say that golems have no memory. A submerged trickle of something, like water in the mud at the bottom of the Vltava, flows steadily through what, for lack of a better word, we must call the golem's mind. Hesitantly, with a lingering sense of transgression, it leaves the shelter of the arcade and one by one descends the steps into Nerudova Street. Already it has grown a few inches in height, a sign of renewed self-assurance. The first drops spatter on the pavement and people hastily put up umbrellas or run for cover. The golem proceeds downhill, placing one foot ahead of the other as though afraid of toppling over, and it has every cause for concern that the rain may impair its clay exterior.

With the years of Communism safely behind it and investments pouring in from the West, Prague, too, has come back to life. There is an air of activity and bustle, a sense of purpose long delayed and as yet undefined. The facades of the historical buildings along Nerudova Street are being renovated or restored, and the golem is able to take refuge, briefly, under a scaffolding. But the space is contested by several citizens crowding in to escape the rain, and after a little uneasy jostling the golem relinquishes its place and continues on its way. Golems are essentially shy, timid creatures, and this one is no exception. Though prone on occasion to fits of temperament and sudden displays of brute strength, they neither seek nor welcome confrontation. Fortunately it is only a brief shower.

At the bottom of Nerudova lies Malostranske Square, and here the golem is faced with more choices than it is prepared to deal with. Where shall it go? The back of the church of St. Mikulas says nothing to it. High up on one side rise the castle and the cathedral of St. Vitus; on the other the Petrin Hill, which is more or less where it has just come from. Kampa Island? To get there it must cross a small footbridge. The golem is starting to have a dim recollection of these places, less a memory than a kind of dull inner reverberation, signifying little more than an uneasy recognition of their existence. It walks around the neighborhood, past foreign embassies, Renaissance palaces with sgraffito facades, gardens with statues and stucco decorations, and always comes back to Malostranske. Several times it has approached the Charles Bridge, but the broad flowing expanse of the Vltava terrifies it, and it is unwilling to venture across.

Whether prompted by a whim, or guided by some sort of unconscious purpose, the golem boards the Number 22 tram. It has no ticket, of course, and no money to buy one, nor would it know how or where to buy a ticket if it had the money. Having no ticket, however, is not a problem peculiar to golems. Though threatened with surprise checks by plainclothes inspectors, and stiff fines if caught, many citizens of Prague apparently take their chances and ride free on public transportation. As the tram ascends a curve, a recorded voice informs the riders in several languages that they are passing through an area with a high concentration of pickpockets. Women hold their purses and shoulder bags more tightly, men compulsively feel for their wallets, but the golem receives this news impassively. To say that it has no pockets to be picked is only stating the obvious, but there is a deeper significance to its indifference. The truth is that it has no sense of private property and no feeling for the anxieties of those who do.

At Vypich the golem, still in the grip of some inevitable purpose it does not pretend to understand, changes to the 174 bus, which takes it to the outlying suburb of Stodulky. Beyond what was once a rural village with a wooden church loom monumental housing units. Boards are laid across the mud of the unpaved streets, but the golem does not make use of them as it descends from the bus and tramps resolutely on. A group of children, engrossed in kicking a ball over a scrubby patch of earth, doesn't even look up as the golem approaches, but two stray dogs begin barking. One then lets out a howl and flees in terror, but the other stands its ground and even gives a tentative wag of its tail. There is a Cultural Center or People's House, unfinished and already falling into decay, alongside a structure apparently intended as a cinema, but no sign of stores or food markets. Even a golem, who requires no nourishment to sustain it, might conceivably divine some sort of failure here, a lack of foresight, a combination of skewed priorities and faulty planning if not an actual collapse of history. But whether or not the Communist bureaucrats learned anything from this abortive project, it has nothing to teach the golem, who draws no conclusions and simply turns its back, takes another bus to the terminus of Nove Butovice, and there transfers to the metro for the return journey to downtown Prague.

The metro is another achievement of the Communist era, and this one can be called a success. These vast underground caverns and tunnels speak to something in the golem's nature, resonate in its being, and for a time it feels comfortable, in its element. It takes pleasure in the dank air, the subdued light, the hollow echoes and reverberations as the train appears, the recorded chimes and clear tones of a woman's voice punctually announcing each station. Such is its renewed sense of well-being that the golem grows several more inches in height between Nove Butovice and the central station of Mustek. Here it might linger forever and never again look upon the light of day. But apprehensive as they are in bright light, golems are not necessarily at home in the dark, either: it may be part of their nature to oscillate constantly between one and the other. It gets off the train at Mustek and makes its way up several levels by stairs and escalator. Outside, where once again a thin drizzle is falling, it immediately gets lost in a maze of streets. Does it occur to the golem that by taking the circuitous route from Malostranske to Vypich, Stodulky, and Nove Butovice, it has successfully circumvented its fear and arrived in the center of Prague without crossing the Charles Bridge? That in itself should be cause for celebration.

Wencelas Square, with its fresh crop of drunks, muggers, and prostitutes, is, one is told, a place to avoid at night. But the free market has also brought a number of daytime scandals. Crime syndicates have sprung up, extortion rackets are rife, and just last week a hired assassin confessed to the kidnapping and murder of a businessman who had sought to renege on his protection payments. There is danger in the air, a climate of menace palpable enough for a golem, though the situation has its comic side. In this same week a number of frightened entrepreneurs, in an effort to throw their predators off the track, have gone so far as to fake their own obituaries and publish them in the newspapers. The muddy eyes light up in a twinkle, the clay lips part in a ghostly smile, for even a golem is not wholly devoid of a sense of humor, albeit a rudimentary one.

Actually the golem feels no kinship with these people, nor is there any reason why it should. The gangsters and their hapless prey, who by certain standards might be seen as more or less interchangeable—no, they cannot be golems. Golems have been known to run amok, but they are never corrupted by money. Furthermore, it has even been said that during the Communist period all of Prague was ruled by golems; that the huge statue of Stalin, long since toppled, was itself a monstrous golem. Nothing could be farther from the truth. Humanoid clods perhaps, but *golems,* with the name of God in their mouths and TRUTH inscribed on their foreheads?—certainly not.

The golem plods on. Though it may seem to be going haphazardly in circles, these circles must inevitably lead somewhere, to what it dimly perceives as its destination. Sunshine and rain showers continue to alternate. Celetna Street, with its shops and taverns, has been refurbished in pastel shades of yellow, pink, and green, and these pretty, candy-box colors make the golem blink. It mingles with the busy throng of tourists in the Old Town Square, and on the stroke of the hour stops to view the clock tower, where a skeleton jiggles an hourglass and rings a bell, while high overhead a procession of apostles skitters around a track. There is no way of knowing what impression all this makes on the golem.

The square is full of souvenir stalls festooned with T-shirts, hundreds of which bear the likeness of one Franz Kafka, late citizen of Prague. But this means nothing to the illiterate golem, who, no doubt like many of the tourists, has never heard of Franz Kafka. Still, it cannot help noting that the tragic features printed on the T-shirts bear a passing resemblance to those of the crippled man knocked down on the sidewalk by its own creatrix. Among the countless mass-produced objects for sale there are even small clay golems, but somehow it fails to recognize these lifeless totems as miniature replicas of itself.

It is while perambulating along Parizska, a broad avenue whose name if not its appearance suggests a kind of Belle Epoque elegance, that one literally stumbles—three steps down—on the ghetto. Waves of memory break over the golem, and yet it hardly recognizes the place. First of all, it is so much smaller, as though it had shrunk like a desiccated plant. The golem, of course, has never heard of slum clearance or urban renewal, even if carried out a hundred years ago, but if it were capable of putting all this into words, it might say that this erstwhile tangle of twisting streets, with its overhanging roofs and sagging doorways, its blind alleys and furtive passages, has somehow been smoothed out by a huge clay thumb. Once it was poor, now it's impoverished, if you see the distinction. It has become tidy, not to say quaint. Where are the peddlers and tavern owners, the disputatious rabbis and raucous students, the companies of actors? . . . Of tourists there are plenty, there's no mistaking them. Although as usual it lacks a proper ticket, the golem joins the throng pushing its way into the Old New Synagogue, and the doorkeepers, perhaps intimidated by its unyielding bulk, make no effort to stop it. Each male sightseer is handed a provisional yarmulke, a flattened cone of paper to put on his head. The golem, too, receives one and follows suit. But the paper is slippery and keeps falling off its head, it must hold it clumsily in place with its hand, and it is not alone in this predicament. All the men are having the same difficulty, including a guide lecturing a group of Spanish tourists, who must steady his yarmulke with one hand while gesturing all around him with the other.

The sound of Spanish being spoken stirs something in the golem, a dim recollection of court intrigue among rival Hapsburg factions at which it could hardly have been present. But there had been a learned rabbi who was a friend of the emperor Rudolf, the two of them were said to spend hours together discussing alchemical distinctions of spirit and flesh, and all this had somehow figured in the cabal, like a silvery thread running through one of the Flemish tapestries adorning the emperor's study. The guide points out the faint remains of medieval frescoes on the walls, along with inscriptions evoking the Psalms, and launches into a discourse on the symbolism of the number twelve, but the golem, distracted for the moment by the dimmest of historical echoes, cannot begin to follow his explanation.

The gravestones in the cemetery stick up helter-skelter, tilting crazily this way and that. The golem, hemmed in by tourists, makes the circuit along a narrow path. Although the last burial took place over two hundred years ago, in this tightly circumscribed space the dead from previous centuries lie in layers. But with live humanity pressing from behind, there is no time to stop and ponder this geological stratification. The living toss pebbles on the graves in a sign of respect for the dead; the golem, more massive and clumsy than ever, finds it hard to stoop and pick up a pebble. It has no choice but to break off one of its own fingers and drop it on a grave.

In the Pinkas Synagogue a sallow, longhaired youth is engaged in transcribing 77,297 names on the wall. It is a memorial to Czech Jews killed by the Nazis, but the golem, whose historical memory has proved so defective, cannot be asked to remember the worst. It is painstaking work, this exercise in patient calligraphy, which the golem, its curiosity overtaken by a sudden sense of foreboding, stops to admire. The nearsighted boy dips his brush, brings his eyes to within a few centimeters of the wall, and slowly traces each name in smooth, minute strokes. Already he may have done seven thousand names . . . which means he has barely started. How long will it take him to finish?

Other questions come thick and fast, like a swarm of insects, as the golem leaves the ghetto and heads for the embankment of the Vltava. How many thousands from Prague alone? The golem has no aptitude for figures, no capacity to fathom or even conceive such calculations. Any mathematical excursus would go quite over its head, and yet it is now in the grip of the full horror of existence. Its heart is not clay but ashes, and there is a taste of ashes in its mouth. *Death,* in its Hebrew spelling, is only one superfluous letter removed from *truth,* and the golem is longing for someone to erase that letter from its forehead or take away the *shem* with the ineffable name.

Without a qualm, guided by the instincts of a homing pigeon, it tramps across the Charles Bridge. All the saints shift uneasily on their pedestals as the golem passes, but it pays no attention. Indeed, it is scarcely aware of the flowing river, which had so terrified it before; its foolish panic has given way to grim determination. It reaches Malostranske Square and begins the ascent of Nerudova Street.

What now of the man on crutches and the irate woman? Despite the shocks it has sustained, the golem has not given up trying to grapple with the inexplicable. Matter and spirit, mud and air—such are the dichotomies it has been called upon to reconcile, and the battle has been a losing one from the start. Adam himself was a golem for the first twelve hours of his existence, before he received a soul, and even so he was vouchsafed a vision of all future generations. But this golem, cut off from the past and marooned in the present, can see no future, either for humanity or itself. Its poor tellurian head is still groping in the darkness and getting hopelessly muddled. Yet it must eventually dawn on even the most obtuse of golems that it is here by default, sailing, as it were, under false colors, that its claims to existence are null and void, and that the quotidian sickness and violence of human beings are not enough to justify its reappearance in the world.

No less an authority than Gershom Scholem reminds us that, strictly speaking, a golem's life does not outlast the ecstasy of its creator. It is only in the popular imagination that golems achieve some sort of independent existence, move freely hither and yon, do mundane chores like hauling water and chopping wood, and sally bravely forth to the defense of the Jewish community in times of danger. Needless to say, traipsing about Prague like a tourist was never foreseen as part of their agenda. And the time it takes to walk in a circle around one's creation while reciting 221 alphabets (or in reverse to undo the fruits of one's labor) can easily be compressed into a second, a moment of rapture, more than enough, say, to raise a weapon and bring it crashing down on another's skull. Thus furious *shiksas* and ecstatic rabbis have perhaps one, if only one, thing in common: they are both "beside themselves," as the saying goes. Their transport rises in direct proportion to the rush of adrenaline. In both, moreover, the thalamus and the medulla oblongata can be seen to usurp the function of the neocortex. Beyond that, who can say?

The golem, having walked in many smaller circles, has now come full circle. There under the arcades of Uvoz Street, at the point where it runs into Nerudova, a woman brandishes a crutch over a man cringing on the sidewalk. His dazed eyes look upward in terror and contrition, while she towers above him with all the determination of a punishing angel. But the golem sees only the crutch, a glowing baton tinged with sacramental fire. It descends in an arc and the golem crumbles thankfully into dust.

YAKOV SHECHTER grew up in Odessa, Ukraine, then studied in Kurgan, Siberia. To increase his chances for obtaining permission to emigrate to Israel, Shechter abandoned his graduate studies and moved to Vilnius, Lithuania, where emigration conditions were generally easier. In Vilnius, however, the Soviet authorities refused him permission. After six years as a refusenik, he was finally permitted to emigrate to Israel in 1987. His first book, *If I Forget* (1985), details the history of a destroyed Lithuanian village; his second, *Your People* (1990), explores the way in which Jewish survivors dealt with Lithuanians involved in the Holocaust. Shechter's short stories have appeared in Russian-language publications in Israel and the United States, and a collection of his short stories, *Chessboard Escapades of Gingerbread Rabbits,* appeared in Russian in 1998. He has also edited two books of poetry: *Poets of Greater Tel Aviv* (1997) and *Levantine Crown* (1999). "Midday" is his first short story to appear in English.

DANIEL M. JAFFE has translated numerous Russian short stories and essays as well as the Russian-Israeli novel *Here Comes the Messiah!* by Dina Rubina (Zephyr Press, 2000). In 1999, he received a Massachusetts Cultural Council Professional Development Grant in support of his literary translation work.

Midday

Yakov Shechter

Translated from the Russian by Daniel M. Jaffe

COLD WATER RAN OFF the yellowed headstones of the kabbalist cemetery. Jets of rain pelted umbrella ribs and, scattering in drops, flowed into boots. Lifting their legs, tourists traipsed around Safed like starved herons. No vacancies in the hotels.

Dan returned to the bus station. The schedule board's long list of destinations soothed him. To get lost among the footfalls and noise, to slip into the thick of unknown faces. To hell with the friendly kibbutz cats beneath the bougainvillea.

The bus for Rosh Pinna would depart in four minutes. Not even knowing why, Dan bought a ticket, climbed into the last seat, and pulled down the shade. Rosh Pinna . . . Where could you hide among twenty inhabitants and five cows?

The bus set sail, swayed on the mountain road's turns. Storm clouds lingered overhead; the evening sun ran back and forth from one side to the other until settling on the back window.

Twilight oozed from mountain crevices; fantastical shadows rose up toward the bus. First they resembled giants sprawling across the earth, then the fluttering wings of enormous birds. In the vain play of darkness and light Dan searched out a sign, a clue, even a hint. A decision hovered about, and this foreboding, as relentless as a cramp, led him along behind.

He lifted the shade. Cars coming toward them turned on their headlights.

If the world, thought Dan, is an indivisible, harmonious whole, then the answer to every question can be found in any speck of dust. One need merely learn how to look and the answer will arrive by itself.

It was dark and quiet in Rosh Pinna. Dan knocked on the first door and inquired about a room. They gave him a detailed, convoluted explanation although, as it turned out, the house was just around the bend.

He put his things away, lay back on the pillow, and fell instantly asleep, shivering sometimes as if from mosquito bites. The forgotten radio softly played brisk marches.

It rained all night. The wind whirled dead foliage under the lamppost by the wicker gate, and quavering shadows danced across Dan's face.

He awoke before dawn. From the depths of the house—a barely audible drip of water; a warm darkness lay across the bed. He turned on the lamp after twisting its neck down so that the shade lay nearly flat against the desk's yellow-polished surface. The prime minister looked out mournfully from a photograph; in the semidarkness his face seemed almost likable. Dan winked at the premier and put the photograph away.

He ate breakfast on the veranda. The rain stopped, steam rose from porous stones on the mountain slope. Dan slid his fingers along the teacup's side; the heat of the warmed faience soaked into his palm, penetrating to his hand's very core, to the pink, tubular darkness of his bones.

A white cat played in the drying grass. The cat was acting out a hunt: he stole carefully near, froze with uplifted paw as if fearing to scare off a wild fowl, then, fluffing his tail, sprang onto the harmless wood chip and, in celebration of victory, snarled with triumph and gloating. Noticing Dan, he spread his whiskers wide, ran up onto the veranda, and began to purr in a small unctuous voice. Dan tossed him a healthy slice of sausage; the cat stood for a second, dumbfounded, not believing his good fortune; coming to, he seized the sausage and immediately disappeared.

The landlady came for the tray. Pink skin showed through hair the color of antique silver; a long skirt half hid her dirt-soiled sneakers.

"It's the rain's doing," she said, noticing his glance. "It eats away at the mountain, brings dirt right into the garden."

Her hands, strewn with splashes of old-age liver spots, were quick and agile.

"Yes, of course," he echoed. "It's the rain."

"My name's Clara," the landlady said.

Dan didn't answer.

Cheerful sunshine tickled the trunk of a terebinth tree. Patches of light glided slowly along the veranda's stone tiles like lazy jellyfish. Dan pulled a small case from his jacket pocket and set it on the table. A carving flowed gently across the brown lid. Depressions and reliefs interwove in adverse, wavering lines; little tears of congealed lacquer hung at the corners. The uneven run of notches and scratches resembled a coded message, as vague as crosshatches in timber. A silent appeal, despairing and hopeless, like a bottle tossed from a sinking ship.

Intermittent breaths of shame had led the carver's hand, concealing in the scattering of tiny pockmarks and flourishes an entreaty for salvation.

HE WOULDN'T be seeing his father again. Never, even in that terrible final minute before burial when they ask for someone to identify the body, when they pull back the sheet. They'd even denied him this.

His sister had telephoned from B'nei Brak a day after the funeral. She asked forgiveness, but Father had made the decision long before.

He'd died in the morning, after returning from synagogue. He bent down for a fallen spoon, but could not straighten back up. Dan imagined clearly how everything had happened, saw the face with its eyes, sunken after a night spent over books. It had also been morning when they parted, ten years ago.

"The Lord won't permit it," his father said after hearing Dan's decision. "To turn a nation of rabbis and kabbalists into a throng of soldiers, prostitutes, and semiliterate peasants? He won't permit it.

"You want to be with them. Then go, break your neck. But remember, when the deception explodes, the monster begins to devour its own tail."

"You've come for a rest, have you?" the landlady asserted, wheeling in the lunch cart.

Dan hastily took the case off the table and tried to smile.

"The baron's garden isn't far from here," the landlady continued, arranging the dishes, "a real one, a hundred years old; my little bushes are no match for it. Worth having a look."

Dan remained silent.

Drops of fat nervously circled the soup's surface. A lone dill stem whirled among the waves; hot liquid masses, fleeing the cold edges of the dish, tossed it from side to side ruthlessly, endlessly, mercilessly.

Dan lifted the dish by an edge and rocked it carefully. The small movement of soup turned into a disaster for the stem. A gigantic wave covered half the sky; lumps of cauliflower, raised from the bottom, overwhelmed the stem and dragged it below to the dense murky depths.

A garden, thought Dan. To press my back against thick bark, to merge with the unhurried movement of a treetop and take to humming in unison, sucking up its life force, its miraculous, invisible strength.

He smiled at the landlady in gratitude, sincerely now, didn't shift his eyes aside.

"Drop in on the museum," she added, "a very interesting museum. And don't worry about lunch, nothing will happen to it. Go work up an appetite, I'll reheat it."

Dan glanced at his watch, a double-lidded, antique pocket watch.

Midday. He went outside. Rosh Pinna seemed uninhabited. A shaggy mongrel, sprawled out, dozed right on the cobblestone road.

An old wall of porous limestone shale surrounded the garden. Lemon-colored butterflies warmed themselves on mossy stones. Dan walked through the garden, lifting a broken fern branch. Moisture from the night's rain lingered in the thick underside of the fern's leaves; oblong beetles with black spots on red backs advanced quickly on little feet, scurried between glittering drops.

A bench beneath a cypress seemed completely dry. Dan examined it closely: creases in the wooden seat had suspiciously darkened. He carefully settled on the edge and pressed his shoulder against the tree trunk.

The treetop rustled gently overhead; its branches creaked hoarsely; as if gasping, pigeons cooed. A breeze, swimming through peeled birch-bark underbrush, whistled softly. Then there was the melody of lonely brown bees and mouse tails flashing among fallen leaves, a mournful dirge of abandoned molehills and dead, dry burrs. The garden resembled music one could feel with one's hands.

Dan lightly touched the cypress trunk. An ant ran out from under the ragged bark and, twisting its antennas in confusion, took to its heels.

IT TURNED out there was only a photography exhibit at the museum.

The caretaker, a stocky young lady in overly tight jeans, was glad for a visitor.

"Rosh Pinna is the most beautiful town in Israel," she began, after barely managing to return his greeting, "and its history is just as wonderful as the Galilean Hills surrounding us!"

Dan loved museums. Through their glass displays life held itself out as logical and orderly; the only remaining surprise lay in the senselessness of human deeds. He usually let tour guides' explanations pass in one ear and out the other; it wasn't the facts of history that interested him, but the flavor of the times. Magnesium shadows on old photographs, the half-worn gold of medals: the mechanism of history could be understood through its component parts. For Dan it was something akin to a gigantic watch: day and night, like interlocking gears, ground time down into colorless, weightless dust.

Sometimes Dan noticed the absence of a mainspring and, annoyed at the exhibit curators' negligence, would search among the exhibits, would turn to the tour guides. After repeated questions and evasive explanations, Dan would realize that it wasn't a question of the laziness or carelessness of museum employees. The mainspring was missing from history itself, from honest-to-goodness real life. Troubled, he would spend a long time standing before an exhibit's glass, mentally setting the mainspring in place. The exit from tragic situations nearly always turned out to be simple, and therefore twice as humiliating for luckless humanity.

The girl, the caretaker, continued to chirp, carrying on with her sweet nonsense, a jumble of canvas pioneer tents and dried earth dunes. Now her voice shot upward, now it dropped nearly to a tragic whisper.

A little birdie, thought Dan, a young, trusting, chick.

He turned away from the photographs and took to examining the guide. Up close her stoutness wasn't at all disturbing—something homey lay hidden within that tightly stuffed bolster pillow beneath the jeans, something cozy, like a sleeping kitten.

The girl blushed: "Why are you scrutinizing me that way?" she asked, taking several steps back. "I'm not an exhibit yet."

"You're not related to that one over there, with the spade?" Dan pointed at random to one of the photographs. "You look so much alike."

The girl sighed. "You knew, you already knew. Somebody around here managed to tell you."

"I give you my word, I just guessed."

"It's my grandfather, the Galilee's best watchmaker."

Dan stared the girl in the eye. Dark, shining olives, a mix of mistrust and the desire to explain, to spurt out—come on, a real, live, bona fide, piquant story like that, how could you possibly keep it quiet?

"So that's your grandfather . . . but what's a watchmaker doing with a spade?"

She led him to a large photograph of old Rosh Pinna. Tiled roofs; the familiar slope of the Golan Heights, not changed at all in eighty years.

She carefully touched her pointer to a rooftop chimney.

"You see this house on the outskirts? The administrator forbade Grandpa from building within the settlement's pale. In those days Rothschild's administrator arranged everything. The baron gave money to settle Palestine, and each newcomer received a small loan from his agency. The loan was meant to be repaid, but in the entire history of the settlement process, not a single person did so. In fact, the baron didn't really expect repayment. The only one whom they forced to give everything back, down to the last agora, was my grandfather."

A naive kitten, Dan thought, you so like to convert family legend into genuine history.

"My name's Dan," he said. "And yours is . . ."

"Dina."

He liked the girl more and more. There was something electric in her, a psychic ectoplasm, a form of energy unknown to science. And the skin of her face—sleek, swarthy skin without coarse pores, pimples, or dark spots, slippery and cool like Syrian silk.

"A tribe of Bedouins used to wander around near Rosh Pinna. They'd steal cows, trample crops, dig up meters and meters of trees. Then the administrator let the Bedouins use the settlement's well. He thought they'd stop stealing in exchange for water. The Bedouins started driving in flocks of sheep and pailing out all the water, down to the last drop. It would take half a day for the well to fill up again. Grandfather considered this unfair, so he wrote a letter to the baron. The letter never left Rosh Pinna—the postmaster gave it to the administrator, and he accused Grandpa of stealing agricultural supplies. The court sentenced him to three months' corrective labor. A photographer showed up right then, took pictures of the well and Bedouins for the newspaper. Grandfather had piled sheep dung on the town square in front of the well and wound up caught in the lens."

Already dark outside. Night had fallen suddenly, thick darkness rising higher than the highest mountains. She got them there through a perfectly legitimate path, in good time and as was her right, but a basic injustice showed through her gloomy triumph, like someone slapping you across the cheek yet not allowing you to cry.

The wreckage of the house was overgrown with gorse; shrub branches quivered against the remains of rooftops. Old Rosh Pinna lay in ruins, the third generation of settlers having left the uncomfortable mountaintop bungalows and descended to the valley. Blocks of villas under roofs of red-flagstone tiles framed neat rows of streetlamps.

"My mother was born here." Dina stroked stones wet with mist. "Our family lived in this house for almost forty years, until the administrator turned Grandpa over to the English. They came at night, a squadron of British police from Safed, broke in the door, smashed dishes, ripped up floorboards. They were looking for weapons but found nothing except an old Turkish saber on the wall. They arrested Grandpa and took him away to Safed. He died a week later from the beatings."

A night bird cried out. The cold whirlpool of silence gave a flinch; a bat darted out of the ruins and went off into the dark.

The clap of its wings resembled the feeble applause of relatives in support of a prime minister who just lost. A blue star fell from heaven and rolled behind Mount Hermon.

"An angel," said Dina. "Oh, if only to know where it's heading and what its name is."

"Angels don't like excessive familiarity," Dan answered. "They fulfill the orders of those calling their names, but then they exact revenge, hit a weak spot."

"How interesting!" Dina exclaimed, taking him under the arm. "Where did you learn that?"

"I studied in a yeshiva . . . a long time ago when I was religious."

Her hand felt firm and hot. Carefully clasping her elbow, Dan realized that he was suddenly in love, had gotten himself into a real mess, had fallen the way the young do—recklessly, foolishly. A languid sweetness began to flow within, ancient worn-out words stirred in his mouth, tickled his palate and tongue. His past life suddenly seemed a reckless demolition of spirit, and the act that he was to commit—a loathsome and useless undertaking. By the time Dan carefully lifted her elbow, he'd already begun singing, whirling around, dashing about with bells and whistles; tears of emotion—the betrayers—had already started filling his eyes.

"How cold," he said, rubbing his palms as if trying to warm himself. "Come, I'll walk you back."

Cooled cobblestones tickled underfoot. Right before new Rosh Pinna, asphalt replaced them.

"Where have you been staying?"

"At Clara's."

Dina flinched.

"Clara is that administrator's daughter. Strange how everything's interrelated."

The bushes along the road mumbled like actors who'd forgotten their lines. The moon rose, superimposing two solitary shadows onto one another.

"To abandon a house," Dan finally uttered, "is like felling a garden or hanging a dog. Like trees, a house sends its roots into your very heart. And can a heart truly be changed?"

At the gate Dina again took him under the arm. "My dear"—her voice held more a motherly warmth than the agitation of a spurned girl— "don't torture yourself, don't tear yourself up inside. This, too, will pass, I promise. This, too, will pass."

Dan walked home through new Rosh Pinna, by thick fences of white plastic and garbage bins in special bays. Tears rolled down his cheeks.

"Why," he whispered, "why do you run from normal human feelings, from a calm, stable life? Only the abyss attracts you, a nonexistent duty you thought up by yourself. Or maybe you're the one doing the summoning, and you yourself are the abyss, and that other abyss is traipsing around you along your fragile edge, along your slippery, crumbling path.

"To marry Dina, to settle here, on the slope of the Galilean Hills and live, just to live, without the commotion and crush of irresoluble problems. Let others worry about the people's welfare and the state's, look after the nation's fate." He'll just watch Dina's figure become heavier, their children grow up, the sun rise.

Dan threw back his head. Stars winked and wept in the black vault, witnesses and accomplices, true distant friends.

"Whoever weeps at night——" he recalled, "the stars weep with him."

A LIGHT BURNED on the veranda. The landlady had not yet gone to sleep.

"Supper?"

Setting down a book in an old-fashioned cloth binding, she rose gently from her rocking chair.

"No really, it's late already. But thanks for the museum, it was truly interesting." Dan slowed. "You don't look like your father at all, much less than Dina."

Clara smiled. "Our Dina's a dreamer, a writer. She makes up stories and tests them out on trusting tourists. She writes up the ones that work best. She's already put out two books that way."

Dan set his hand on the back of the chair. "Why, why does she do it?" His fingers turned white from pressure.

Clara began to laugh. "Now don't go getting angry; writers are like little kids. Games are more important to them than real life. Nobody in Rosh Pinna's surprised anymore, they know what to expect, so she goes and pesters tourists."

"Good night."

Dan turned and went to his room. His favorite books were waiting curled up cozily on the desk. Dan looked at his watch. Midday. No. Midnight. He pressed the watch to his ear. It had stopped. Dan opened at random the first book he reached and took to reading.

> They led the Yeshiva boys over to a ditch and lined them up single file.
>
> The rabbi asked the officer for a few more minutes. The officer glanced at his watch, a double-lidded, antique pocket watch, and agreed.
>
> "When the High Priest slaughtered a sacrifice," the rabbi said, his voice hoarse from a cold, "the condition of his soul was equal to the sharpness of the knife. Uncertainty or fear would spoil the offering just the way a serrated edge would. Today we ascend to the altar, and whether or not the Jewish people will revive after the war depends upon us. We must bear this sacrifice with purity and calm of soul, without despair or torment, so that it shall be accepted."
>
> The rabbi walked along the single file. He stood beside each one for part of a second and gave a stare into the eyes. Reaching the end he turned and stated in a calm voice: "You may begin."

Dan set the book down. All was clear and bright, as if lit by dozens of funeral candles.

"A sacrifice must be pure," he repeated, pacing around the room, "and the watch must be repaired. No matter the cost, the watch must be repaired."

He went out to the kitchen and, trying not to make noise, washed his hands thoroughly. Returning to his room, he sat at the desk and with a decisive movement, withdrew the case.

A few minutes passed—heavy, like leaden bullets of days gone by. The case glistened nervously; shadows from the leaves continued their dance on the pillow's white linen. Dan moved the book to the edge of the desk and drew a silver candlestick over to the prime minister's portrait.

A freshness tugged at the half-open window; lightning flashed soundlessly, once, again, a soft peal shook the glass. And his heart felt heavy, unbearably wretched and vile, as if thousands of cats were clawing and biting his soul's invisible flesh.

Rain started to pound, to batter the window. The noise resembled a staccato drumroll, summoning to a lowering of the flag or calling to an execution.

Dan hid the case in his pocket and dashed out of the house. The desk lamp's yellow circle scared him; Dan ran under the sharp sprays of rain, trying to get so wet and tired that he could return without fear to his room, where, on the middle of the desk, the silver candlestick shone and glistened.

Cold drops glided down Dan's face. He caught them with his lips and kissed them. Just a minute ago, in the unattainable heights, they'd been tickling angel wings, but now were pouring into his wide-open mouth, becoming part of his body.

"Rain," he whispered on the run, "is the only living thread; join, weave me with heaven, rain, rain, rain . . ."

He returned near morning, took off his wet clothes, and, rubbing himself briskly, painstakingly, with a towel, collapsed into bed. By the time the first morning bird started its windowsill reveille, Dan was already asleep, having covered his head with the blanket, shivering occasionally as if from mosquito bites.

It was late when he awoke. On the floor, beneath the open window, lay a puddle of water smelling bitterly of autumn. Dan ate lunch on the veranda, observing the hilltops swimming in clouds of warm air.

Yesterday's cat was sitting on the drying flat of a rock and washing himself. Dan called to him, but the cat just scornfully sniffed. Dan tossed a piece of sausage, trying to get closer to the rock. The cat sprang to the damp grass and left, fastidiously shaking off his paws after each step.

At three in the afternoon Dan brought a notebook from his room and wrote a poem.

On the midday terrace,
Where sun spittle
Flows with slobber,
A breeze, hopeless yet pungent,
Tugs at terebinth twigs.
It's only midday on the watch,
Still too early to die.

Pink clouds were swimming over Rosh Pinna just before sunset. Filled with sweet bliss and languor, they hid behind the mountain slope, then darkness set in. Dan sat for another forty minutes, watching the quivering lights of the Golan Heights settlements. His kibbutz was not visible; Mount Hermon's spurs were covered in rows of tidy bungalows under roofs of red-flagstone tiles. He had planted the first trees, leveled land for foundations, laid the road. Thirty settlers, pioneers, the first little seeds.

Deception, it's all deception, he thought. Liars: both those who sent us here ten years ago, and those who've decided to return the land today. But he wasn't a marionette, not some spineless rag doll. He'd blow up his own house with his own two hands, would chop down the trees. The Syrians would get only ruins, a second Kuneitra . . .

It had turned cold. Dan stood and went to his room. Switched on the light, took his identity papers, and ripped them carefully up. Those he couldn't rip he cut with scissors into strips and flushed down the toilet. Then he took his time washing his hands, shaving, dressing in clean clothes. At seven in the evening he sat down at the desk, withdrew a black candle from the case, and stuck it in the candlestick. The candle burned evenly and quietly, giving off a scent resembling the fragrance of saffron. Dan opened a book and uttered a name.

THE PRIME minister ended his speech with a salty joke. Women smiled, covering their embarrassment with the congress's programs, men burst out laughing, looked at the premier lovingly. He was theirs, flesh of their flesh, speaking plainly and openly in such a folksy way.

Shills clapped their hands and the auditorium chimed in, answered with an endless ovation. The premier carefully gathered his papers into a stack and headed to the exit. On the stairs spilled with the yellow floodlights he suddenly moaned and, turning pale, grabbed onto the banister.

"What happened?" The colloquium leader ran over to him. "What, what is it, what, what?"

"Everything's all right." The premier shook his head. "Everything's all right now."

He shook his head again, as if freeing it from an invisible net trap, and, letting go of the banister, moved on.

AMID THE hysteria of the preelection campaign, news of the death of an unknown tourist passed without notice. He had no identity papers, his fingerprints didn't appear in any criminal files. They took his body to Safed, to the district hospital. The postmortem revealed death by massive heart attack, a highly unlikely occurrence at such an age, but possible. The police opened a case purely for the sake of formality since, strictly speaking, there was no case. The unknown man was buried in the cemetery at Safed, not far from the headstone of the baron's former administrator. Aside from the grave diggers at Chevra-Kadisha, only the Rosh Pinna museum caretaker walked behind the coffin. A funeral candle lit by her hand burned at the grave for twenty-nine days, but no one paid attention to that, either. The candle was extinguished only on the thirtieth day when the flame flickered and went out from a light breeze resembling a puff from the wings of a passing angel.

DEBORAH SHOUSE lives in the Kansas City area, where she works as a teacher, creativity coach, and editor. Her writing has appeared in numerous magazines, including *Tikkun, Ms., Woman's Day, Family Circle,* and *Reader's Digest,* as well as in various anthologies, such as *Chicken Soup for the Mother's Soul* (Health Communications Press, 1997), *In Loving Testimony* (Crossing Press, 1996), and *I Am Becoming the Woman I've Wanted* (Papier Maché Press, 1994). The author of several business books, including *Breaking the Ice* (Skillpath, 1996), Shouse is a frequent speaker, in both academic and business circles, on the subject of creative expression.

A Portrait of Angels

Deborah Shouse

"But Rabbi," Anna said, "I know I saw him. He's been peeking in the living room window at me. He's tall and not at all well behaved. I thought angels were supposed to have halos around them."

"Maybe this is a peeping man," the rabbi said. In his dark study, his hands looked the tallowy shade of a wax museum.

"Ah, I knew you would think that." Anna rose, feeling the tug of arthritis that kept her from dancing around her living room in the dusky sweet surrendered part of the evening. "But he was standing in my marigolds. And he didn't leave footprints."

The rabbi leaned back in his chair and put his second finger beside his nose.

In this very room, exactly seven years ago, Anna had risen from her chair and walked over to him. Like a teenager, she sat on his lap and kissed him. The angel had been inside her then, prodding her, poking her in the belly, in the breasts, despite her thinking, No, I'm married, it's unseemly. The angel shoved her onto the rebbe's lap and pressed together their juicy lip flesh, the secret slash of tongue against tongue, the accidental clash of teeth. After a few minutes she had gotten up, sat back in her chair, and resumed talking about her problem: her husband, Isaac, no longer cared about her.

"Really, Anna, an angel is just a part of yourself." The rabbi's voice was thick with Russian, each word a tangled forest.

Anna liked the translucent corrugated look of his hands. His eyes were dim with cataract.

"Rabbi, how can it be myself when I see this man, like a Chasid man only with an onion-bald head, zipping behind trees, peeking into my window? Once I found him sitting on my toilet. Only he is not a solid man because the light shines through him and he walks above the ground and his feet are blurs of light. He is an angel and I want you to tell me what to do about it."

Like something fragile unfolding, the rabbi stood and steadied himself with the arms of his chair.

"I have studied angels," he said. "The Bible implies that God uses them to show us parts of ourself. Ask this angel what he has for you, Anna."

The rabbi walked to the bookshelf and Anna saw how the furniture was positioned to support him: from the chair to the table was two steps, the length of the bookcase to the wingback chair was five steps, and near the door was a small table, perfect for steadying an uneasy body.

"I hoped the angel would come here with me," Anna said, following him to his bookshelf. "Then you could have a look at him."

The rabbi smiled as if she were a child who still believed in fairy people. Did he remember her lips? she wondered. They had never discussed that odd action of hers. Yet she had felt his fire, his desire, so different from her husband's. And now that Isaac had passed on, what if she reached out to the rabbi, only more gently this time? She knew other widow ladies brought him macaroons and packets of loose black tea. Had any of the other members of the senior division of the Temple Sisterhood ever kissed him?

"I brought some soup for you," she told him as she put on her coat. "It's on the stove."

Once a month she brought him food, and once a month she sat across from him in his study and talked about whatever was on her mind. She imagined Oprah coming to tape the old lady and the old rabbi talking angels. What did Oprah think of angels? Anna wondered. Maybe everyone had them. Maybe angels were one of those secret things, like alcoholic parents, dirty underwear, and grown children on drugs.

As Anna walked home two boys on bicycles whizzed by her. A long lean girl, blond hair flying, tanned skin taut underneath a lime-green halter top and green shorts, skated by, her body drinking up the sidewalk. Anna moved her hips from side to side, as though she, too, could drink up the sidewalk. She knew she looked like a wizened crone. Only her angel knew how she felt inside: lively, dancing, ready for adventure.

EVEN THOUGH Isaac had been gone for three years, the house still smelled of his Ben Gay, Mogen David wine, and stacks of old newspapers. His last years he had taken to hoarding things, burying pieces of candy under newspapers, hiding the crusts of sandwich in the folds of his chair. He was again a survivor, trapped in the concentration camp, and he imagined Anna as the captor.

Anna turned the radio to jazz and went into the kitchen, to make Friday-night blintzes. Anna wondered if her angel would ever appear in front of people. In the Bible angels spoke. But so far her angel was silent.

Anna was moving her hands through the cottage cheese mixture when the doorbell rang. Sheldon, her neighbor, stood at the door, holding a drooping daffodil.

"I was wandering lonely as a cloud," Sheldon said. He was in his fifties and newly retired, part of a downsizing or right-sizing or something.

"Come in," Anna said. Sheldon had dropped in often during the past years. Anna liked the comfortable cynicism he brought.

She brewed decaf and wiped her hands on her apron. She remembered how it felt to be newly separated from work, a mixture of swelling excitement, like a balloon rising into clouds, and then a narrowing fear, of the long day fat in front of her and not a mark on its languorous hide.

For a while Sheldon sat silently. Isaac used to call Sheldon deceptive.

"You look at him, you listen to him, and still, you know nothing," Isaac had said.

Anna looked at Sheldon's face and liked its mystery.

"I've been hearing voices," Sheldon said. In his royal blue warm-up suit, he looked as though he had gone to Sears and asked, What do retired people wear?

Anna felt a surge of interest. "What do they say?"

"A man's voice says, 'What are you doing, where are you going, are you in charge of things or are they?'"

"I guess I should be glad my angel is silent," Anna said.

Sheldon looked at her. "Your angel? You mean, Isaac?"

"No, I mean the angel who keeps popping up around here."

Anna twisted her fingers together and watched Sheldon. She knew he was thinking that she was getting old; her vision, maybe it was clouded. Isaac would have thought the same thing. Neither of them could understand how real, how implacable her angel was.

"So what do you do when you hear the voices?" Anna asked, to stir up the silence. She put both hands around her coffee cup. If Sheldon noticed her tremble, he'd assume she was dotty. Even as a girl she'd had this tremble. Her fork shook when she brought food to her mouth. Her first boyfriend had fallen in love with her over it and because of that, she never minded the occasional splats of spaghetti sauce or spurts of soup.

"If no one's around, I shout, 'Go away. Leave me alone,'" Sheldon said. "But I wonder if I'm doing the right thing. You are friends with that old rabbi. Would he talk to me about it?"

"Yes," Anna said. "But he's a rational man. The voices sound mystical."

She went back to the counter. She spread the cottage cheese on the dough while Sheldon rinsed out his mug.

"I can't get used to Mavis being gone," Sheldon said. He leaned against the counter, his arms folded.

"Where did she go?" Anna asked. Sheldon's wife, Mavis, was a loud woman, always dashing places. One week her hair was brilliant red, the next lemony blond.

"She's down in Florida," Sheldon said. "She says she's leaving me, she's not coming back." He fumbled at his hips, trying to hide his hands in non-existent pockets.

Anna turned from folding the dough and saw her angel, standing on the stove.

"Be careful. It might be hot," she said, speaking slowly so her angel could understand.

"Of course it's hot down south," Sheldon said. "Mavis wears bikinis all over town, even to the grocery store."

Anna stared at her angel. She had never seen him so close, and the fine lines of his face reminded her of spring rain.

"What do you want of me?" Anna asked the angel, holding out her hands. She had read that creatures from other planets were often scared by voice tones and gestures. She didn't want to frighten a divine presence.

"What if I spent the night with you sometime?" Sheldon said. "Not for sex, you understand, but to have someone near."

As Sheldon moved closer, the angel faded away.

"I've always admired you," Sheldon said.

His breath in her face felt like a swallow of warm Passover wine. How delicious to have a body nestled near, Anna thought. The charm of arms to hold her, the comfort of a leg over hers.

"Of course we would wear pajamas," he said.

"Of course," Anna said.

Anna imagined a hand running over her silk nightgown, down the eroded hills of her breasts and the rich mesa of her stomach.

Sheldon was the right size to fit spoonwise with her, the right amount of padding and lean. He was also attached to a wife.

Sheldon put his palms on her cheeks and looked into her eyes. A secret wind swept through her. Would Sheldon kiss? she wondered. Kissing would be such a dessert, such a bonus.

Then the grease on the stove popped.

"I need to finish my cooking," she said, her heart fast as a new baby's. "Do you want to sit and eat?"

Sheldon nodded.

Anna scooped out the blintzes and patted them extra dry. Men like Sheldon were usually on a low-fat diet.

Sheldon sliced across the blintz with his knife and stuffed a large bite into his mouth. While he ate Anna watched his lips, imagining the taste of him.

When Sheldon stood up to leave, Anna saw the angel hovering behind him, blocking Sheldon's path. She wondered what would happen if Sheldon collided with her angel? Would her angel be shattered, smashed, burst into shards of light? Or would Sheldon emerge glowing, shining with a delicious softness?

"Come over here," Anna said. "I will wrap the leftover blintzes for you."

Sheldon tapped his fingers against the counter while Anna fumbled with the plastic wrap. Sheldon's hand on the counter seemed something *traif,* forbidden. Yet she had touched so many difficult things in her life, a wounded snake, a bloody child, a dead husband.

Sheldon took the blintzes and walked right through the angel and out the door.

"Where are you?" Anna asked the angel. She knelt and felt around on the floor. But there were only the soft remainders of flour, the stickiness of a spilled egg.

After Anna cleaned the kitchen she got out the Sabbath candlesticks and two new candles, smooth and white as brides. The flame bruised the air as Anna murmured the Sabbath blessing.

Usually she sat and read in front of the candlesticks.

But the words in her book seemed dry as unbuttered matzo. A breeze teased the flames, coaxing smoke out of them.

Then she saw her angel's legs, dancing on the tips of those flames. A rabbi's robe swirled around his ankles. The robe looked real, so black and lustrous, that Anna knew it would catch fire. She reached out to tug her angel down to safety but her hand grabbed air and the fire singed her wrist.

For some moments she cradled her wrist and watched the angel. No matter how deep his robe dipped into the fire, it stayed whole and pure.

Anna's wrist ached as she dialed the rabbi. He answered on the seventh ring.

"The angel is still here," Anna said. "Sheldon walked right through him."

"The angel is part of you, Anna." The rabbi sounded quietly patient. "Have you been ignoring yourself?"

Anna thought of Sheldon's hands cupping the flame of her face. She remembered the rabbi's long-ago kiss.

"I'd like to come over," she said.

"You would be most welcome," the rabbi answered.

It was a sin to blow out the Sabbath candles, so she carried them with her. The night was an unopened envelope. She walked slowly, the candles flickering, the flames slurring the dark.

I must look like a crazy woman, she thought.

The rabbi's door was unlocked. Had he walked through the house to open it for her, she wondered, or did he not use locks?

Anna went to the study. The rabbi sat in his chair and behind him stood her angel.

"I see you have met my angel," Anna said.

"I am preparing to," the rebbe said. He stood, holding one hand out to her and steadying himself with the other.

Anna set the candles on the table. The rebbe's gentle arms enfolded her like God's blessing. She felt her angel touching her head, filling her with a silent jubilant light. That light flowed through her with the rebbe's kiss.

The rebbe's face had the coolness and sorrow of the Kol Nidre but his mouth held warmth and celebration. Anna sighed and moved her lips slowly against his, as if murmuring a prayer.

LATER ANNA didn't know if the Sabbath candles had burned out or if her angel had taken them, to light his way.

One of Mexico's most prominent writers, ANGELINA MUÑIZ-HUBERMAN was born in France and spent her early childhood in Cuba. After learning that she was a distant descendant of Sephardic survivors of the Inquisition, and after engaging in a period of contemplation, she underwent formal conversion to Judaism. She is the author of thirteen books of fiction, six books of essays, and five books of poetry. Much of her work transforms myth and explores kabbalist mysticism and spirituality. Her work can be found in English in such anthologies as *King David's Harp: Autobiographical Essays by Jewish Latin American Writers* (University of New Mexico Press, 1999), *Passion, Memory and Identity* (University of New Mexico Press, 1999), and *The Oxford Book of Jewish Stories* (Oxford University Press, 1998). Muñiz-Huberman is professor of comparative literature at the National Autonomous University of Mexico, is a fellow of the Mexican National Endowment for Creative Artists, and has won numerous literary awards.

ANDREA G. LABINGER has taught Spanish-language and Latin American literature at Simmons College; the University of Notre Dame; Indiana University, South Bend; and the University of La Verne, California, where she currently directs the University Honors Program. She has translated the work of numerous Latin American writers including Sabina Berman (Mexico), Alicia Steimberg (Argentina), and Carlos Cerda (Chile).

The Tower of Gallipoli

Angelina Muñiz-Huberman

Translated from the Spanish by Andrea G. Labinger

FROM THE SMALL OPENING in the window, through the bars, he looked down below, far below, at the rippling blue-green of the sea. And he felt nostalgic. Nostalgic. For not being able to plunge his body into the calming waters. For not being able to refresh his face and feel the salt on his lips. And the light breeze on his skin. As when he strolled the sands of Gaza. As when he first met Nathan. Nathan. The prophet. The beautiful. The perfect. And they would walk, together, and talk about the visions of this earth and of that sky. Nostalgic. For his present sadness was healed only when his voice escaped in ancient canticles.

And the voice flew. The voice filtered between the cracks in the door with its well-oiled locks and hinges. The voice, between the polished bars of the high window, flew toward luminous space. Toward that unattainable horizon of threaded sounds. Suspended. One coupled with another. Whoever passed by the foot of the tower would say: "Sabbatai is sad again and sings." "Once again, Sabbatai, prisoner and prey of melancholy."

What to do in the spacious cell, amid embroidered cushions and carpets with lush, interwoven colors? With his lute at his side. Well tuned. Beckoning delight and sound.

What to do, in silence, in solitude, but to remember the voice of God? And intone the canticles. The ones his ancestors carried with them into exile.

Would that his voice might reach the sultan's ears and that the sultan might take pity and decide to pardon him. Because God, God surely must have pardoned him.

Had God, indeed, pardoned him? With such ravings and such incongruity. And his sins and his violations. His memories and his lapses. His rages and his mildness. The straight and the twisted: Where was the ray of light dividing these?

First came the visions: the clarity, so clear that it blinds. And the darkness: so dark that it blinds. The word that is dictated to him and that he obeys: fleeing serpent-word: fire dragon-word. That which he must and must not do. Speak to the people: create comfort for pain. The story, the tale, the legend, so that reality might be well constructed and have nothing to do with the facts. So that everything might be interpreted conveniently. And then to see the tears of the believers, the faithful, those who are dragged along the roads, not by God's decree, but rather by kings who cannot see the glance of eyes other than their own.

Then, after the visions and the stories and the tears and the roads, mercy and love for each of the afflicted. "No. You are not alone. God has given you His shadow in which you may take refuge. The shadow of God is the exile of God Who understands your exile as man on earth. Do not hide. Do not deny your name, although you may not possess or know it: guard it, for the day will come. No matter what you do, you will still be you."

And Sabbatai loved and was merciful. The sky opened up for him luminously and the rays descended in parallel and oblique lines. Behold the image reflected in creation. Among the clouds and red sunsets. Before the Wall, in Jerusalem. In the fertile land of the Nile. On the sands of Gaza.

Only the canticle washes away his sadness. Now, in the prison of Gallipoli. In the high tower.

But at other times Sabbatai ceased to be Sabbatai. He pronounced the words backward and, like the golem, was destroyed. He locked himself away in the most remote corner, unable to see either God or man. It was a kind of enervation. A body that no longer knows itself and renounces its pulsing. A brain that disturbs order and thought, and enters instead into chaos and retraction. A shaking of each fragment of dislocated muscle, of exalted nerve. Such disturbances. Such mouthfuls of air. Such absolute impieties. Sabbatai is not Sabbatai.

Sabbatai runs through the streets, shouting: "I am not I." "God is not God." "He is not He." "I am not the Messiah." "Yes, I am the Messiah." "Let no one honor the Commandments." "The Commandments are false." "The end of time is here." "Babylon, monstrous, arises." "The Four Horses bray evil. The Four Horses kick out goodness." And he falls exhausted to the ground and good Nathan picks him up in his arms, drying his sweaty body with a white cloth and whispering words of love. Sabbatai is carried to his room. Carefully placed in bed. Covered with fine linen sheets. Beneath his head—the head that spins and agitates—the goose-down pillow and soft, frayed fabric. Sabbatai will rest. He will sleep the sleep of the just and the mad. He will not know. He will not remember. His awakening will be the passage to another world where there are no words, where there is no struggle: a void, yes: forgetfulness, too. His body languid and his mind paralyzed. Not an utterance from his mouth: nor a twitch of his fingers. But he isn't dead. Sabbatai is not dead. He appears to be. But he is not. Days may go by. Weeks. Months. In absolute silence. With nothing to do. Or to say. Like a weak, mechanical being. A golem of badly baked mud. A body barely carved from wood. A shapeless stone. Water that spills from a glass. A sound that bounces from wall to wall. An echo without an echo. A rainbow lacking a pact with God. And

Nathan at his side: caressing his forehead, changing his garments, carrying food to his mouth, giving him drink, seizing his hand to kiss. And Sabbatai, so far away.

Until the day when he awakens. When his eyes once again find the pupil reflected in them. When he recovers his speech. When he is reborn: a child who opens his eyes and sobs. "Who am I?" he asks. "You are You," Nathan replies. "You, God." "I, God." Nathan exults: "Yes. You. The Messiah. The Messiah has been born." And he throws open the shutters: Let the sun pour in through the window. The Messiah has been born again.

Sabbatai arises. He peers out the window and the sun doesn't blind him: at last, the son of the sun. And instead of speaking, he sings: "I am I."

Sabbatai, locked in the high tower of Gallipoli, sifts through his memory. Countless boats had come to greet him the day he docked in Smyrna. They covered the entire port. And the crowd packed the docks. "The Savior has come." They brought him offerings: incense and myrrh and gold. And flowers of the fields. And delicacies. And sacramental wine. But nothing was for him. The sultan's soldiers were waiting for him. They had been warned that the new arrival was planning a revolt. And Sabbatai was arrested, his hands tied behind his back.

In the high tower he was a prisoner like other legendary prisoners. But the sultan took pity on him and permitted the people to bring him gifts and allowed them to visit him and have the musicians come to play for him. It is said that, secretly, the sultan himself visited him and that they spoke of matters concerning heaven and earth. And that between the two of them there was love.

When Sabbatai awoke from those moments of slumber, his desire was to commit paradoxical acts. That is what Nathan and his disciples and his followers called them. Because Sabbatai committed all sorts of extravagant deeds and all sorts of excesses. He broke the rules and threw himself into sacrifices of his own devising. He mixed up the prayers. He neglected the Sabbath obligations. He was impure. He ripped up curtains and yanked the tablecloths from the tables. He blew out all the candles and would have set forests afire if Nathan had not gently, but firmly, stayed his arm. He ate forbidden foods and spilled wine on the floor.

And the more outrages he committed, the more ardent his believers grew, and the more they loved him. Nathan, his prophet, explained it thus: "He must expiate with his own flesh the sins others do not dare commit. He must descend to the deepest circles of despair and plunge himself into mire and corrupt his soul. In order to rise up later. To rise up to the Eternal. To the One Who awaits him. To the Throne. To the divine Carriage."

Sabbatai repented. He cried on the shoulder of his friend, Nathan. His beloved. And they caressed one another. And Sabbatai grew calm once more.

Sabbatai, he of the beautiful voice, had sung an ancient Sephardic ballad in the Smyrna synagogue. And returned it to the divine, and profane love became the love of heaven. Travelers, merchants, clergy of every cult came to hear him and described the enchantment of his song in their journals. And so the "Ballad of Lovely Melisenda" became the ballad of love consummated in God. The lovers' bed became the divine bed, and the signs of the body became the signs of the emanation of light.

> Down the banks of a river
> and up the slope of a valley.

Sabbatai sang once again from the tower of Gallipoli, and all those passing by lost their will and neglected their chores. Sabbatai changed the words, and the song always had a different beginning, so that no one repeated it the same way: there were as many versions as there were singers.

But profanation occupied his thoughts. To commit every forbidden act: dishonor, slander, inversion, debasement, offense, blasphemy. And as for committing them, he had. Even the most intimate ones: with parents and with wives and with children. Nothing was left untouched.

The only one remaining was the violation of God. And this act, too, he would commit.

Here: in the tower of Gallipoli.

With that sea air filtering between the bars.

And that wedge of magnanimous sky.

Surrounded by azure and white.

THE GREATEST of violations: to deny God: to change his religion. To announce his apostasy to the world. To send a message to the sultan: that he should come to see him: that he will accept his divine word.

And the celebrations will be countless. Indescribable. The sultan will hold a public conversion ceremony. The true religion will be affirmed. Sabbatai will become the sultan's protégé. His voice will intone songs from the minaret. He will leave the tower of Gallipoli.

And Nathan? What will Nathan have to say? How must he adjust his theory so as to remain loyal to his messiah? Or will he no longer be able to?

Nathan will be expelled and detested. He will wander from town to town, from city to city, from port to port. No one will give him bread or water. But he will always find some faithful believer to help him, to hide him, or to warn him in time to let him escape from his persecutors. And he will continue to write and preach, and the sect will not be extinguished. Despite the fact that Nathan of Gaza will then be called Satan of Gaza.

All this appears in a vision to Sabbatai, locked inside the tower of Gallipoli. And he foresees the end and his death. And how Nathan will fight to see him and to lay his warm hand on his tormented brow one last time. Sabbatai will always doubt, and the absence of his soul's physician will bring on his melancholy.

SABBATAI CANNOT endure imprisonment. He bangs his head against the walls and rattles the iron bars. Nathan cannot disembark in Smyrna.

Sabbatai recalls walking to the Smyrna synagogue, holding his father's hand. His small steps multiplying his father's. The terror of becoming lost among such large bodies, among the voices and the prayers. Of not recognizing anything and not knowing what to say. Eyes wide open. Suffocation and faintness.

Terror that paralyzes. Terror of everything. If only Nathan were at his side. Nathan, in whom he could confide every word: the end of the world: the greatest misfortunes. To gaze at his perfect features. The harmonious movement of his body.

The emptiness again. Spinning in a powerful internal dance. The letters run over one another. They have lost their luminosity. They no longer come together to find the name of God. It is the chaos before the great, divine contraction. Origin no longer exists. Nor matter. Nor the four elements. It is the pure, singular idea of God. The indefinable. The unpronounceable.

Sabbatai is the void of God. His incorporeality is the emptiness of his mind.

If his mind runs away and escapes him, God, too, runs away and escapes him.

His abandonment is one of the soul. His body shakes in spasms and oblivion. God rushes out.

Not even the tiniest space between one letter and another, between one sound and another, can be filled with the greatness of God.

What, then, is the greatness of God that has halted the precise mechanism of his mind?

FROM THE tower of Gallipoli, Sabbatai Zevi sinks his gaze into the immense sea and would be content to be a single one of its drops.

DINA RUBINA grew up in Tashkent, Uzbekistan, and moved to Moscow in 1984. In 1990 she emigrated to Israel, but following a recent appointment by the Jewish Agency she has returned to Moscow as the agency's director of the Department of Cultural Relations. Rubina is a best-selling author of two novels and more than half a dozen collections of short fiction. Her work has been translated into twelve languages including English, French, German, Spanish, Dutch, Bulgarian, and Uzbek; has been adapted for radio, stage, television, and film; and was twice nominated for the prestigious Russian Booker Prize. Her collection of short stories *The Double-Barreled Name* won the Arye Dulchin Award in Israel; the French translation of this collection was voted, by a network of independent French bookstores, one of the best books of the 1996 season. Rubina's most famous novel, *Here Comes the Messiah!*, a satire of Russian émigré life in Israel as well as an exploration of contemporary Israeli spirituality, was published in English in 2000 (Zephyr Press). This is the first time that "Apples from Shlitzbutter's Garden" is being published in English.

DANIEL M. JAFFE has translated numerous Russian short stories and essays as well as the Russian-Israeli novel *Here Comes the Messiah!* by Dina Rubina (Zephyr Press, 2000). In 1999, he received a Massachusetts Cultural Council Professional Development Grant in support of his literary translation work.

Apples from Shlitzbutter's Garden

DINA RUBINA

Translated from the Russian by Daniel M. Jaffe

I OFTEN FLEW TO Moscow in those days.

For some reason I just had to gulp the exhaust fume whirlwinds of Domodedova Airport, gallop via the express bus to the very city that, back then, seemed the center of the universe, and busy myself with nonsense for about a week: hang around editorial offices, drop in a couple times at a mediocre theater for whatever show happened to be playing, kill a few evenings in the smoke-filled House of Writers, and finally, while perspiring profusely in the wine press of GUM Department Store, fulfill requests by neighbors and friends. For some reason, in a word, to erase an entire week from my quiet sensible life.

Right before one such mad foray to Moscow, when spring caused my southern city to overflow with the passion of bursting buds, when I suddenly lost the energy for daily life in my wretched cell during the first thaw and I urgently bought a ticket for the day after next—right before the trip a writer friend telephoned, a pleasant fellow and his own man.

"They say you're flying to Moscow?" he asked without an accent. He also wrote in Russian, but it was strange: his Uzbek accent came alive on paper, and mischievously hovered over his tediously correct phrases.

"I sure am!" I exclaimed into the phone, already fixated upon the incoherent buzz of Domodedova, the greedy joy of nighttime Moscow conversations.

"As a favor, eh . . ." he said. "Take a story of mine to a particular magazine. Eh?"

"No problem, of course I'll take it." In those days I willingly undertook to fulfill any commission; my energy was boundless. "What kind of magazine is it?"

"It just so happens, you know, that there's a Jewish-language magazine. I want to submit one of my stories to them."

Surprised, I stopped short.

"You see," my friend said, rushing to fill in the awkward pause, "they just gotta be interested in it. The story's—I won't feign modesty here—brilliant. On a Jewish theme. . . ." and, inasmuch as the puzzled pause at my end of the phone kept dragging on, he elaborated: "It's about our neighbor, the cobbler, Uncle Misha. After all, I grew up in an Uzbek-style courtyard—all sorts lived there with us. My neighbor, Uncle Misha, is such a funny guy, Jewish . . . they just gotta be interested in it. The theme is friendship among peoples, nationalities. As you well know, that's an important subject these days . . . multiculturalism, internationalism, and all."

"I understand," I said finally. "But doesn't that magazine come out in Yiddish?"

"They'll translate it!" he, inspired, assured me. "It's to their benefit! Chock-full of hard-core internationalism! They'll translate it. You can tell them to deduct the cost from my account."

"All right," I said and, not holding back, added cautiously: "I've got to admit this is an unexpected dimension of your oeuvre. Why are you doing it?"

"I felt like it," he explained in an unsuspecting voice. He was a guileless fellow.

I read the story on the airplane. Partly out of curiosity, partly because I'd forgotten to bring something to read, and I just couldn't do without distractions on a flight. The fact of the matter is that halfway there, somewhere over the Aral Sea or the Kara Kum desert, when the stewardess is clearing away each tray with its barely nibbled yellowish cucumber, and when drowsiness overcomes the average Aeroflot hostage and shakes his poor head back and forth on the deliberately uncomfortable headrest, at that very moment a single wild thought usually descends upon me with innocent simplicity and schizophrenic clarity. How *strange* it actually is, I think, not comprehending . . . We're *so high* . . . I'm still an earthly being, all the way down to the earthly trembling in my knees, to the earthly nausea in my chest—how dare I show up here before my time and look, with foreign, living eyes, through the small round window at such blinding calm? What do I need it for? An earthly triviality—to travel as quickly as possible from one end of the country to the other. What for? For earthly trivialities . . . I think, How dare I?—while inside some dull earthly instrument—to rattle, shake, vomit into my otherworldly abode of wisps. How dare I so impudently run ahead and tear off the veil with a foolish, mischievous hand?

In a word, I usually take a good detective novel aboard. But this time, having forgotten the book at home, I willy-nilly pulled a red packet from my bag, the packet with the Tashkent writer's story, and I read through it rather quickly. This story "on a Jewish theme" made quite a keen impression. It was written as a monologue. A Jewish cobbler drops in for a minute on his neighbor, an Uzbek. A few phrases about routine things, and—little by little—the cobbler recalls his entire life, tragicomically, the way such characters typically do, and shares his misfortunes with his neighbor friend; in particular, the burdensome misfortune of his dissolute son's departure for Israel.

At this point I realized that everything would work out just fine for the story, that they'd publish it. I carefully tied up the string around the red packet, hid it in my bag, and turned to the window. The airplane, shuddering, hung over a fondant-icing plain of clouds, through which sun-dazzled sugarloafs poked here and there. That's good, I thought automatically, I've got to remember that—sugarloaf clouds.

No, I had no doubt that my friend's story would be published, and in a Jewish magazine, at that.

What a curious time it was: depicting Jews in current literature wasn't so much considered forbidden as undesirable or—to phrase it better—not quite proper. If one were to analogize to the venereal-disease realm (and, for some reason, this is precisely the realm where the analogy begs to be placed), then for example: not syphilis, no, but a certain unpleasant fungus.

In any event, it was during that particular period that a certain popular magazine's chaste editorial pencil turned the fool Izzy Silverman in one of my stories into the fool Petya Sidorov.

For a time, given my congenital meticulousness, I tried to figure out the motives behind my hero's ethnic rebirth, and concluded that it could be explained variously: for example, as an attempt by the editor to assure readers that we don't have any silver men cavorting in our country; or maybe as an attempt to save the reputation of the author, whom some reader or other might unfoundedly suspect of being in sympathy with a Silverman even though a total fool. In another story the editorial hand, without wavering, simply crossed out the name Lazar, thereby repudiating the very fact of the character's existence. However, Lazar insisted upon continuing to live for a long time, which, per my nontheological worldview, injected an added spurt of irony into the situation.

In only one situation was the hero permitted to be Jewish: when he branded those who had abandoned Russia for Israel as good-for-nothing traitors. Here the hero found himself with boundless opportunities for monologues, dialogues, and epilogues, here he tied himself up in knots so as to prove his devotion to his Native Land, his hatred of the turncoats, and his cherished desire to possess as little Jewishness as possible—and if only the Motherland would permit, then he'd unburden himself of this unpleasantness altogether.

In a word, that epoch already known as the epoch of Stagnation—I, sensitive in my perceptions of the world, imagine some kind of huge, slovenly bedridden societal body, veins filled with stagnant, sluggishly flowing blood, impotently supplying vessels of the brain for its valuable activity.

Of course in today's wonderful epoch of general Glasnost and openness the issue is taking a different turn. For example, recently at a leading magazine that instills broad ideas of democratization into various levels of social consciousness, they even suggested that in one of my stories I change a Petrov to a Shapiro! However—whether my personal character had become spoiled over the years, or whether exhaustion, having conquered youthful irony, had corroded my soul—I just couldn't accept such a precious gift. Later, when it was already in galleys, two young, clever, and extremely progressive editors smelted the restless Petrov-Shapiro into the neutral Habibilov.

Oh, my homeland!

The editorial manipulations of heroes' surnames automatically reminds me of how one of our family knickknacks was renamed; specifically—a clay dragon with fangs and a tongue lolling out like that of a racing dachshund; a dragon with the household nickname of Sashka Ibrahimov.

Ibrahimov stood staunchly on the television on four squat, dachshund-like paws, under one of which—the left hind paw—we usually stuck important papers: receipts, official certificates, and even five- and ten-ruble notes for household items.

Ibrahimov retained his Turkic-sounding name for a rather long time, until my son entered the phase of assimilating unprintable expressions. It was a rather difficult phase for the family when, time and again, behind sofas and wardrobes, various locutions were found scrawled on the wallpaper. "Take your notebook," I, in a fit of temper, advised my second-grader, "and write to your heart's content!" He took the notebook, but those unprintable wails of the soul sometimes broke free from notebook captivity. Once, while dusting Ibrahimov, I discovered on his left hind paw the ink-written: "S. O. Bitch."

"You're being silly," I said bitterly to the little louse, "you could have used better code, for example—Son of a B."

Need one even say that poor Ibrahimov was instantly renamed So-bitchee, thereby acquiring a certain Chinese flavor. In time this evolved into the musical So-la-bitchi-to, and then flowed smoothly into the Latin American, or the Mexican, if not the Spanish, La-bitchita.

"Where did I stick the official certificate from the Housing Authority?"

"Look under La-bitchita. . . ."

That year spring—stormy, humid—fell upon Moscow too early and roughly, like a groom, grown stupid from waiting, after his wedding. Dragging my heavy bag to the express-bus stop, unbuttoning my coat at the entrance, I cursed the weather, then myself, and even my parents, who'd convinced me to wear this damned sheepskin coat: "Moscow, you know, isn't Asia; they get sudden frosts."

I don't remember anymore who'd brought the coat from the expanses of Krasnodar's steppe, which, as is well known, has a reputation for animal husbandry. The coat turned out to be sneaky, with a false bottom: from the outside—deliciously natural, soft, well-tanned suede—it looked quite elegant. But underneath, that is, from the inside, that is to say on the fur side—there was no fur. Instead of noble sheepskin, the clever artisans had sewn a lining of some sort of nap flagrantly resembling quilted padding. All this rigmarole was crowned with a collar of innocently shining artificial fur, and when the collar was flipped up, it surrounded my head with a truly banal halo of romanticism.

I even have a photograph of me in the coat with the collar flipped up, actually a good photograph, the "real me," before a background of autumn trees; I look like a Chilean patriot in the deplorable conditions of underground life, or like a counterrevolutionary White Guardsman before an execution that would be excused by history. In any case, this photograph promoted my publications, even abroad. And if one were to add that recently the Englishwoman Rosamund Barnett, having imprudently arrived in Russia to face winter in a tweed jacket, wore such a coat in Moscow all winter long, one could say that this sheepskin coat has its own personal history.

In winter nowadays the coat hangs in a corner of the entryway: I put it on when I've got to ride to the Butyrsky market for potatoes.

But that year the legendary coat had just been bought, and, although three months of winter wear had made its quilted padding tangle in dirty clumps, on the outside it still looked perfectly respectable.

The trick was simply to carefully fold up the coat's skirt when sitting in offices and to ignore, at coatrooms, the grimaces of the coatcheck women who had the poor habit of throwing clothes onto the counter with the lining face-out.

A bus drove up. The conductress with a red pouch on her fat belly checked tickets from the passengers, all drained by the bathhouse heat; the bus taxied onto the highway, picked up speed; birch twigs banged against the windows, and the funnel of Moscow life started spinning me, drawing me in, and absorbing me, not to cast me out for a week, after an especially long, scattered, and useless day begun in the House of Writers and concluded somewhere in the backyards of Izmailova, in the stuffy cluttered quarters of a fashionable theater director, whose friends brought me to celebrate his name day . . .

In the morning, scowling and sneezing while pulling on a sweater permeated by the smell of yesterday's cigarette smoke, I thought: All right, enough swinish behavior, an entire week down the drain, you're coming undone at the seams—why did you come here looking for trouble in the first place?

While packing my bag I stumbled across the packet with the Tashkent writer's story and suddenly remembered that I still had to drop in on some (damn him, and me, too, with my promises!) Jewish magazine, which meant that I'd barely have time to catch a flight.

Not stopping my swearing, I called some Moscow acquaintances—nobody had the least idea where that editorial office was. Finally, someone remembered the street . . .Yeah, it's there, only I don't know the number, go and check all the nameplates.

Pulling on that very coat and taking my bag, I dragged myself to the airport ticket office.

The woman at the cashier's window paged through my soiled, tattered internal passport with dismay, time and again looking up suddenly from the photograph to my face, not mustering the energy, apparently, to believe that this ancient document belonged not to a pensioner who for the last decade had been doing battle with local courts and regional councils, but to a young, fresh-cheeked person.

Oh boy, it's true: I had no respect for the document. No respect—not so much for the document itself as for the social institution as such.

Here I can't resist the temptation of telling about my friend Lutefull, an outstanding Uzbek poet who's been living without an internal passport for thirty years now. When I tell this to people, they usually ask: "How so? Did he lose it?"

"Why do you say—lost?" I exclaim with secret ecstasy. "Never got one in the first place."

"But how can that be?" they ask. "So how does he get an Aeroflot ticket?"

"He doesn't fly," I answer in an inspired tone, "he lives on the outskirts of Tashkent, writes well-crafted verse, and cultivates a rare kind of grape."

"Oh, come now, come now!" they say, growing agitated. "And a residence permit, and—"

"What sort of residence permit!" I interrupt, affecting a happy naïveté. "He lives in a house built by his own grandfather, with his three brothers and fifteen nieces and nephews."

"Get out of here!" irritably exclaim my conversationalists, who all have internal passports and residence permits. "That just doesn't happen . . . a respectable person, publishes poetry . . . Besides, there's a regional police inspector who requires—"

"What kind of inspector are you talking about!" I sing out in scornful rapture. "The inspector is Uncle Rauf, Lutefull's older brother's wife's second cousin on her father's side." And I swear, I don't know which pleases me more: my friend's poetic talent or his existence beyond society's conceptualization.

It was unexpectedly simple to buy a ticket for the night flight. Already sensing that icy, midflight height anxiety, I left my bag in the checkroom and, with the red packet under my arm, stepped out into the wearying midday sun. Truth to tell, I had nothing left to do in Moscow whatsoever, other than to fix up someone else's story with a Jewish magazine. I dove into the airport metro station and, about twenty minutes later, surfacing at the right station, plodded along the sunny side of the street, peering at nameplates.

The damned sheepskin coat embraced me on all sides like a heavy compress; it was dangerous to take it off because the insidious April wind was whistling through the gate. Yet to unfasten the coat also made no sense at all—the lining already resembled either a worn-out loofah, an old goat's beard, or the tangled inside of a quilted blanket.

I walked, sluggishly moving my feet (a wild week in Moscow plus post-winter vitamin deficiency, plus the insulated coat), and just as sluggishly thought about how to present my friend's story at the editorial office.

First of all, it was essential to explain right away that the writer was Uzbek; this was very important as a strengthening of ties among national ethnic groups. At the same time I had to elaborate that the story was actually written in Russian, lest they fear the need to fuss with a double-level translation. And it was absolutely imperative to say straight off that a Jewish theme predominates, otherwise why this whole song and dance . . . The complexity lay in trying to convey all this baloney in one concise sentence.

I shuffled along the street and mentally polished a single solitary sentence that, like a retractable tape measure, contained all necessary information.

"How do you do," I'd say in an easy voice, "here you go, I've brought a Jewish-themed story written in Russian by an Uzbek author."

Yes, just like that. Simple. Calm, not at all giving away that I'm also a person of letters; that's irrelevant. I'm not a person of letters at all, exactly the opposite. An accountant, for example. He asked me, so I'm dropping it off. I'll hand over the manuscript and head back home from Moscow.

Having finally found the right nameplate, I shoved open the door and entered the editorial quarters. A gloomy room appeared beyond a damp, dark dressing area; rather spacious, somewhat akin to a hall, with two wardrobes—specimens of bureaucratic furniture from the beginning of the century—and a huge empty desk, spattered with ink and nicked up as if by careless schoolboys' pocketknives. There were several chairs, not a single one matching another, all as though brought in from various homes.

A somber man poorly rendered in oil colors stared at me from the wall. The man resembled our neighbor, Danny Moiseevich, a tedious, slow, and ornery old man. He was quite blind; when addressing you, he spoke while resting his gaze at the ground, but then he suddenly lifted his eyes (unfocused, old, and feeble) and it seemed as if he were looking not at you but somewhere into the ages: one eye's gaze escaping into past ages of pogroms and smoking crematoria; the other's into a future age even more, perhaps, frightening. His gaze was epic, biblical, terrifying; the Lord's gaze at Sodom and Gomorrah, then with a hoarse voice he'd utter some nonsense or other like: "Would you know, neighbor dear, if the Housing Authority's going to cease their hot-water shenanigans?"

Approaching the portrait, I read that it was Mendel Moshe Sforim. One should read a bit of Jewish literature, I thought in embarrassment—swinish behavior, of course, on my part.

Yiddish galleys lay in a heap on the desk's corner. I took a sidelong glance at the choppy script—those hatchets, twisted twig lashes—a script having passed into Yiddish from ancient Hebrew—as severe as weathered cliffs rustling in millennial winds, whistling through the whips of agelong persecutions, squeezed out like funeral wails in the language of the Bible, residing from the beginning of this century in the lethargic dream of Psalms said in prayer. On top of the pile lay a note, weighted down by a red pencil and written by same in Russian: "Shlitzbutter! For God's sake, what a mess you created by not waiting for the galleys!"

All was quiet. So, I thought in annoyance, am I going to have to loaf around much longer in this Pale of Settlement?

Finally, from the depths of the dark corridor I heard steps and women's voices. One—justifying itself; the other—disdainfully imperious.

". . . So I've always got to wear pants," the self-justifying voice patiently explained, "because I have plump legs."

"Plump?" exclaimed the imperious voice. "What—better they should be skinny? Your teeth you want to pick with them?"

Two figures appeared. I instantly christened one—a young but already puffy woman with submissive eyes—the Sacrificial Cow. The other was plump, too, but in a different way—sturdily knocked together, a solid block. She was clanging with earrings, bracelets, beads; she wiggled her brows, which grew together on the bridge of her nose, somehow reminiscent of a downy goose, and she resembled the Queen of Sheba, although I'd never seen a rendering of the latter, and such a rendering is not likely to have been preserved.

Spotting me, the women stopped, looked at each other. The Sacrificial Cow saddened and somehow tucked up her legs, thrusting her bust forward in greeting, and the Queen of Sheba, jiggling her millstone earrings and bracelets, asked in imperious singsong: "Ma-ay I he-elp you?"

"How do you do?" I said in a natural tone, precisely as planned. "Here you go, I've brought a Jewish-themed story written in Russian by an Uzbek author."

Instead of sending me to the seventeenth room at the end of the corridor so as to register the manuscript, or saying in a frozen voice, "Well, leave it . . . and we'll respond in three months"—in other words, the way it's usually done in normal editorial offices—the women looked at each other and, whereas the Sacrificial Cow's gaze acquired an even more doleful shade, the Queen of Sheba wiggled her goosey eyebrows. "Vos?" she said and then, with a quiver and clang, repeated, "Ma-ay I he-elp you?"

I should mention that while composing my phrase of introduction, and appreciating the ample share of idiocy crammed into it, I somehow hadn't counted on using it with frequency. However, while rehearsing, I became so used to it that I could no longer break it up or explain the situation otherwise. "How do you do?" I repeated louder and more articulately. "Here you go, I've brought a Jewish-themed story written in Russian by an Uzbek author."

An awkward pause.

"And with whom did he make arrangements?" the Queen of Sheba suddenly asked, looking at me with suspicion.

I pointed at myself. "With me."

"And who are you?" she asked in the very same tone.

"An accountant," I muttered, languishing in my coat.

"And?"

I became enraged—I'd had it: the heat, Moscow, the torpor of this editorial staff. At the same moment I remembered that this magazine was Jewish, after all, so one ought to be answering a question with a question.

"What do you mean—and?" I answered.

"And what's he—also an accountant?" she asked, decidedly displeased.

"Why do you say an accountant?" I answered. "He's a writer. An Uzbek."

"And so?"

"And so he wrote a story. In Russian. Jewish themed."

"And why did he do it?"

"He felt like it," I said, pulling out the red packet. "Forgive me, I'm in a hurry. The author's address is noted here."

"So he—what—hasn't made arrangements with anyone at all?" she repeated, not taking the packet from me.

I flew into a total rage. "And just who was he supposed to make arrangements with? What do you have here, a special system of contacts? In other editorial offices you show up, drop off, leave," I continued, revealing an inside knowledge of literary magazines that was strange for an accountant. "But with you people I stand around for half an hour, then you interrogate me and nearly body-search me as if I'm carrying a bomb! You don't need a new manuscript? Good-bye!"

"Stop!" Sheba exclaimed in a sonorous voice, extending her palm in regal gesture. "Follow me."

"What for?"

"Follow me!" she repeated and, grabbing the pile of galleys, went farther down the corridor, clanging, rustling, clicking her heels, and swinging her sweeping hips that resembled the sounding board of a rich Italian double bass.

I unbuttoned the coat and trailed along the dark corridor after the Queen. We turned right, then left. For God's sake, are they trying to save money on electricity?

"Careful, there are three steps down!" Sheba cautioned with inexplicable pride, as if she were speaking about a large marble fountain faced with Alexandrian mosaic. "Don't fall," and she opened a door to a square room with two windows overlooking a courtyard; it was bright and quiet inside. A thick, stuffy sort of apple scent filled the room, and I saw almost instantly a sack in the corner, packed to the top with palely luminescent Golden Delicious apples.

My heart gave a quiet start in my chest and began swinging, like the pendulum of Grandma's Paul Bourré grandfather clock, among ungraspable images of survivors of all the wars, pogroms, revolutions, and evacuations. My heart gave a quiet start and began swinging because five Golden Delicious apple trees grew in my grandfather's yard in the Kashgarka Market cul-de-sac, Tashkent's old Babylonian neighborhood. The Queen of Sheba's solid block of a back obstructed my view of who was sitting at the desk. I was shielded behind that back as completely as behind a breakwater against the wind.

The Queen shook her heavy bijouterie and said in Yiddish: "Grisha, enough combing your bald spot. A ledger clerk in a sheepskin coat has shown up with some Turk in Italian-lined clothing."

"Speak Russian," an old voice said in Yiddish. "How many times do I have to tell you! We don't know where in the provinces this ledger clerk will want to gab about chauvinism."

I stood in confused silence during this dialogue, for I was struck by the realization that I was *understanding* Yiddish. Fifteen years had passed since I was forever listening to Grandma and Grandpa, and I assumed that I'd long since forgotten that completely useless language—poor chattel in the eternal wanderer's burlap sack.

"You don't know your native tongue!" raged Grandma. I was sitting cross-legged in an armchair and lazily waving a bitten apple: Grandma was interrupting my reading of Kashtanka: *An auburn puppy—a mix of dachshund and mongrel—with a snout looking a lot like a fox's, ran back and forth on the sidewalk and nervously glanced from side to side—*

"You should study your native language!"

Now and then she stopped and, crying, lifting now one chilled paw, now the other, tried to figure out how she could have come to be lost.

"You see two Yidn walking and talking—go after them. Listen and learn a few words!"

On a tram once I undertook to learn Yiddish through Grandma's method. Two old Jewish ladies were sitting in front of me and mournfully discussing a grown-up son's behavior.

"Vos does he macht now?" one asked.

"He gelebt di arbait," the other answered dolefully, to which the first exclaimed in a fit of temper: "What a louse!"

I got up and jumped off at the next stop. No, I didn't want to learn this language of mine. And I sincerely assumed that I didn't know it.

Once, however, I was fooling around outside when Grandma yelled from the window that I should run over to Aunt Riva's and ask for a cup of vegetable oil. Aunt Riva, a small bug-eyed old woman, lived with her daughter in a neighboring Uzbek courtyard, in a room over a grape arbor. Clambering up the ancient wooden staircase and calling Aunt Riva, I fired off Grandma's request, hopping impatiently about since Grandma had called me at the height of a game.

"Wait a minute," said the old woman, and she went deep into her cool room. The arbor was entwined with grapevines, and green runners were tickling my naked legs. Wasps crawled lazily along the cracked wooden banister.

I heard Aunt Riva's voice: "Musya, Racheleh's Dinochka has dropped in for some oil, but we're down to our last bottle."

"No, then—tell her no," answered Musya's voice. I tore off some grape runners, stuck them in my mouth, and scampered down the stairs.

"Hey, wait a minute!" the old woman called to me from upstairs. She was holding a cup that was a third filled with oil. "Where are you running?"

"But you said there wasn't any oil." The tartness of the grape runners made my mouth pucker.

The old woman screwed up her eyes in surprise: "What's with you— you understand Yiddish?"

I blushed, muttered something, and darted to the gate . . .

. . . But now I was understanding it all, I hadn't forgotten a thing—not a single word, not an inflection. What had always seemed foreign and totally useless turns out to have dwelt tenaciously in the depths of my unconscious. I just stood there in my coat, hastily fastened in the light, and remained silent.

Finally the Queen of Sheba stepped aside, and I saw a very elderly man with an emaciated face and vast bald spot under a bright sunny glare playing from the window. That subdued halo over the emaciated face, wizened like an overripe cucumber, imparted a kind of holy, great-martyr quality to the man. The Great Martyr was sitting at a desk with a telephone receiver propped against his gray cheekbone and gnawing a Golden Delicious. A heap of tempting sandwiches towered on a plate in front of him. The Great Martyr fixed his gaze on me, bit off a yellow piece of the Golden Delicious, and said tenderly, "May I help you?"

Realizing that now, for the third time, I was about to utter the idiotic phrase I'd prepared, feeling my total impotence like a wild squirrel doomed to spin in a wheel, I took a deep breath and said, "I've brought a story. By an Uzbek author. In Russian; Jewish themed."

The Great Martyr chewed the piece well and then just as benevolently asked, "And with whom did he make arrangements?"

A swooning nausea rose in my throat.

"With me," I said quietly, dulled now by the heat.

"And you are?"

"An accountant." It seemed that they still had the radiator on in the office.

"How nice." He tilted his head aside, wiping his bald spot beneath the halo, turned the apple core this way and that, checking if there was any succulent fruit left, finally tossed the core into a wastebasket under the desk, and asked in a cordial tone, "And is the Uzbek an accountant as well?"

"Why an accountant?" I said, rooted to the spot. "He's a writer."

"Aha . . ." He took an interest in my coat. "And whereabouts has he settled down, this Uzbek? In the north?"

"Why in the north?" I said, posing another blunt question. "Tashkent's in the south, you know."

"Grisha, it's my impression," the Queen of Sheba chimed in, in Yiddish, "that this little girl's mameleh never carried her to full term."

"Speak Russian!" Grisha reminded sluggishly.

"Not at all to term," the stubborn Sheba continued in Russian, "maybe four months short." And she smiled at me reassuringly.

"So!" Grisha said, setting the telephone receiver onto the base. "He's an Uzbek writer."

"But the story's written on a Jewish theme," I reminded him, "although in Russian."

"And why did he do it?" asked Grisha with interest.

"He felt like it."

We fell silent.

"Ideologically, the story's irreproachable," I added, losing patience; even an accountant, with all his stick-to-itiveness, excusably loses patience under chaotic circumstances.

"That's good," Grisha agreed.

"The hero's an elderly cobbler, doesn't want to go to Israel."

"Correct behavior," Grisha said, getting aroused.

But without wiping that reassuring smile from her seductive lips, the Queen of Sheba said in Yiddish, "Who needs him, the old mule——"

"Anna Grigorevna," Grisha interrupted sternly, not glancing in the Queen's direction. "It seems that Shlitzbutter's in need of the galleys."

"Yes he is, he's coming," Sheba answered without wiggling her brows.

"Here's what I would tell you." Grisha stood from his desk; he turned out to be a gaunt, tall old man with disproportionately huge fists, onto which the sun's glare had migrated from his bald spot. "Now more than ever we need the theme of condemning those departures. You, as I understand, are an eastern person, so listen and tell the following to everyone in the east: Soviet Jewish patriots irately condemn those renegades, that wretched part of our nation that rips bloody ties from one's native land and streams to the land of some supposed forefathers or other."

Apparently Grisha had gained skill at such performances. He spoke heatedly, with conviction, waving a great fist in the whirl of the sun's glare. Just a shame that the Queen of Sheba spoiled the image with a gentle tapping of her fist in time to Grisha's speech. And to tell the truth, standing there in my coat, I wasn't in the mood for speeches.

"What is it they've left and forgotten back there?" Grisha demanded in a threatening voice. "And what will they find, all those degenerates and traitors? Harmful Zionist propaganda! Bluff and myth!"

"Steak and roast beef," muttered the Queen of Sheba, brushing crumbs off her skirt.

At that moment something strange happened to me. Melting in my buttoned-up coat, stupefied from the vision of Grisha's gleaming fist and the desire to seize an apple from the desk and bite into its springy flesh, I suddenly unstuck my lips and said in a weak voice, "Yidn! You either accept this peacemaker's work, or you let me go for God's sake already."

When I realized that, without intending to at all, I'd said all this in Yiddish, I felt a shakiness in my knees. Both windows listed to one side, turned into spindly wedges, shot up to the ceiling; all I managed to feel was them grabbing me under the arms and setting me on a chair.

Here I'll digress again . . .

Similar strange events had occurred to me two or three times before—when, temporarily losing control over my own thought-speech apparatus, I flew down a swooning echoing well and surfaced in a totally unexpected place, in the most unforeseeable shape.

For example, during ninth-grade physics class, a temporary separation of body from soul befell me: while my body remained at my desk, my soul flew out the window and did two smooth turns over the athletic field.

During my college years I once was dozing in an armchair in front of the softly cooing television. It was one of those light, fleeting drowsy moments when soothing household voices alternate, the day's impressions take shape and slip away. From the kitchen Mama called out to Father; he answered something quietly.

"Are you acquainted with Juan Rodriquez?" asked a cordial female voice. "Isn't it true that he's a highly suitable señor? He fattens up young pigs on his farm and next year hopes to acquire two bulls to increase the size of his herd of cows."

Hearing the information about worthy Señor Rodriquez, I opened my eyes and satisfied myself that the show *Spanish Language Study: Second Year* was airing on television.

"Señor Rodriquez's spouse is also named Juana," the announcer, smiling, said in Spanish.

I felt a chill of deep-seated, atavistic horror and, of course, instantly ceased understanding the announcer, which was completely natural, since I'd never tried to learn a single word of Spanish in my entire life.

It's interesting that I never told any of my close friends about these occurrences and only once, on a train, finding myself in a compartment with a linguistics scholar, did I ask how science might explain such phenomena. The linguist explained his dissertation in great detail, then dove into the thicket of psychology. In a word, I understood that a faculty of protolanguage lives within all people, and under hypnosis or a semihypnotic state our brains can get up to the devil knows what.

During that moment when I took in at a glance the spindly wedges of window shooting up to the ceiling, and under the intensifying fragrance of apples, I flew down a swooning echoing well and surfaced in a painfully familiar place; looking around, I realized that I was standing at the threshold of Grandpa's barn, in the quiet and green Kashgarka Market cul-de-sac. I knew in an instant that I was begging Grandpa for a fifty-kopeck piece for the movies, and the silly lazy dog Naida, not recognizing her own people, was tearing at the chain and raging at the gate.

"Do you know why I feed this meshuganeh creature?" Grandpa asked me in a melancholy voice. He was introducing order deep within the barn: puttering around, moving stacks of old newspapers tied up with twine. In the corner of the barn stood a sack filled to the brim with the pale, lemon-colored peels of Golden Delicious apples.

"C'mon, they're showing *Lemonade Joe,*" I whined, shifting from one bare foot to the other right where, on the barn's clay floor, a hot slanted square of sunlight fell from the doorway.

"Mameleh, come on, you know how it is," Grandpa softly reminded from the clouds of gold dust rising in the depths of the barn. "Because you climbed in through the window and didn't listen to Grandma, there's no way no how du geen in the movies."

That was Grandma's punishment; I knew, too, that as crazy about me as he was, dear Grandpa would waver sooner or later. Therefore I'd besieged him in the barn and howled, hopping barefoot on the sun-hot clay floor.

"You haven't seen what a great film it is!" I started in for the fifth time.

"No I haven't," Grandpa agreed, "and I've survived."

"You don't understand a thing! A really incredible film. You're old, you don't need anything."

"What I ne-ed," Grandpa sang, groaning from the weight of another stack of newspapers, "is for you to stop being such a fo-olish girl. Eight years old—you're a big girl already, mameleh, and you want to go to that lemonade idiooot for the third time."

"I'll go nuts here, like your Naida!" I howled, drained of arguments. "I'll die, understand? I'll croak right here, understand? You have, maybe, some spare grandchildren?"

Curious how a Jewish accent appeared two hours after my parents settled me into Market Alley for summer vacation, and how it disappeared without a trace ten minutes after the start of roll call at the beginning of the school year.

One had to acknowledge that Naida was a fool, but not that big a one. She was tearing at her chain and spewing curses because my friends were propped up against the fence, banging it with their bare heels. They were reminding me that there was little time left before the show. Naida was going crazy, melancholy Grandpa was trying to raise me, and I was pestering him for a fifty-kopeck piece.

Grandma stepped onto the porch of the house—to pour out slops or toss grain for the chickens. She looked down the end of the yard where I was engaged in hand-to-hand combat with Grandpa and cried out, "Duvid, don't feel sorry for our little Mongol warrior! She'll get to go to the movies today! But first let her macht di arbait peeling the potatoes!"

"Didn't I already take out the garbage today?!" I hollered, all upset. "It's my vacation! I'm not your coolie."

"You're not a coolie, you're a Mongol warrior!" Grandma answered cheerfully from the porch and went inside.

Outside, somebody's naked heels were beating a tap dance against the fence. Naida was tearing at her chain, puffing out her chest like a drunken sailor in a tavern. I gave a howl and, in a frenzy, stomped my foot on the barn floor.

Grandpa impatiently moved the last two stacks of old newspapers and said, "He should guzzle lemonade till he bursts, that American fool, making a child suffer so!" He dug into the pocket of his dusty old man's trousers with the fly forever fastened by a single button, grabbed some change, and said, "There. Take it, mameleh."

From deep in the barn he stretched his palm to me, that hand so worn out by life. Three fifteen-kopeck coins and a dull, brown five-kopeck piece, as worn out and old as Grandpa's palm. Good Lord, how many of these fifty-kopeck pieces did I wring out of his meager pension!

Grandpa stood in the clouds of gold dust and stretched out the change to me. It smelled of apples, of old newspaper dust, burlap sacks, old rags. I wiped my tears and snot and moved toward him to take the money. But Grandpa, hiding his eyes, suddenly backed up, mixing with the dust in the depths of the barn. I was left standing alone in the doorway, and the door wasn't even there anymore, nor the barn; it had disintegrated in a swirl of dust, and only the delicately wafting aroma of Golden Delicious apples kept hovering over me . . .

"Make her some air!"

"I am."

"Do it harder. It's from the heat. Didn't I ask you to call where you were supposed to and tell them to finally stop heating the editorial office like a bathhouse?"

"What are you talking—a bathhouse, when she's the one in a sheepskin coat! I've never met such an idiot. Why isn't she in felt-lined boots, for that matter?"

"Quiet, that's enough. Make her some air!"

"I am."

The Queen of Sheba was working over me, shaking her entire body like a tzaddik in prayer, fanning me with the red packet containing the Tashkent writer's story.

"That's enough. Thank you," I muttered.

Grisha leaned his apostolic bald spot toward me and asked, "Di bist a yiddishka?"

"Who else would I be but a Jew?" I snapped weakly.

"So why are you trying to pull the wool over everyone's eyes with this Uzbek business?"

"I'm not! I've truly brought a story written in Russian by an Uzbek on—"

"Enough," he said. "We've already heard that. Here, eat a sandwich."

He held a sandwich under my nose. I took it automatically. My coat lay on a chair, lining face-out so that the dirty quilting bristled in all directions. I glanced away from it and took a bite of the sandwich.

"So what do you do in Tashkent?" asked Grisha.

"I live there," I answered, digging into the sandwich. I suddenly realized that I hadn't eaten breakfast, thinking to grab a bite at the airport cafeteria, but somehow I never ended up there.

"Dear Lord," said Grisha with a sigh, "but You've scattered us all over the earth." He opened a bottle of mineral water and poured it, spurting, into a glass. "Drink. You were on your last legs, fainting from hunger like that. What are you, a poor student?"

"No, I'm an accountant!" I exclaimed energetically, for some reason resisting ultimate exposure.

"Eat some more . . . There was a time when many of our people lived in Tashkent . . . How is it now?"

"There's a heap of us," I mumbled, setting in on a second sandwich. "Although lots have been leaving in recent years."

"Yes," he said, saddening somewhat. "People are leaving." And it wasn't clear exactly what was causing him pain: whether the leak of Jewish population abroad or the impossibility of following the example of this group of renegades.

"Whoever has brains in his head, has them!" piped in the Queen of Sheba enigmatically and triumphantly, as though she'd been trying to prove something to Grisha for a long time.

"Will you take Shlitzbutter's galleys already!" he ordered Sheba.

"Fine," she said calmly, settling down onto a chair. "Five minutes without the galleys won't kill Shlitzbutter."

I was getting the distinct impression that, after business hours, she'd be fulfilling some other sort of duty for Grisha.

"And what took you off to Tashkent?" he asked.

I was offended. "What do you mean—'what took you'? I was born and live there. You think life's worse in Tashkent than in your crazy Moscow? I wasn't the one taken off to Tashkent, but my parents. After being wounded, my father ended up in a hospital and stayed there. Mom, Grandma, and Grandpa were evacuated there. Actually, they're from Ukraine."

"Ah! From Ukraine!" he livened up. "Have an apple. This kind's called Golden Delicious. And where did they live in Ukraine?"

"Near Poltava." With postwinter greediness I bit into the tart juicy flesh. "Maybe you know it—there was a small town near Poltava—Zolotonosha."

"Listen to her telling me!" Grisha suddenly shouted in a frightening voice. "She's telling me about Zolotonosha! She came from Asia in a sheepskin coat and tells me—me!—where Zolotonosha is!"

He ran out from behind his desk, grabbed me by the shoulders, and shook so hard that a piece of apple I'd bitten off flew onto the desk.

"Kindeleh mantz! How often with these here very legs did I run all over Zolotonosha, without boots on those dirt paths, for seventeen years yet! And you're telling me?"

He ran around the room in a strange sort of frenzy.

"Ay-ay-ay!" he exclaimed. "Ay-ay-ay, what an encounter!" Although to my way of thinking, there was nothing all that supernatural in our encounter. "Your last name!" He stopped.

I stopped short. My Grandpa's last name was the same as that of such a famous poet that I generally avoid boasting about it. "Zhukovsky," I finally admitted.

Grisha slapped his bald spot.

"You're Uncle David's granddaughter?" he cried and, turning to the Queen of Sheba, said, "She's Uncle David's granddaughter!"

Perplexed, I caught the look from frenzied Grisha to the Queen of Sheba, who sat with an expression on her face of an enthralled spectator at a play's climactic moment. Her fluffy goose-down eyebrows crawled up her forehead and trembled, wriggled.

"Ha! The Zhukovskys!" Grisha cried triumphantly. "She's telling me about the Zhukovskys! And here we lived gate by gate—you know how many years? Don't even try! More years than you've lived on this earth . . . They all had that last name—it means 'black beetles,' you know?—because they were all dark like Gypsies, all except Frieda . . . the Zhukovskys! They had Gypsy blood, the real thing, nomadic." He waved a hand at me. "This one probably doesn't even know—"

"Why wouldn't I know!" I felt insulted. "I know all about it. Great-Grandpa spotted her in a tavern at a fair, fell in love, and brought her to town. They say she was stunning."

"Precisely. I knew her as an old woman. After that Gypsy, every woman born was stunning." Grisha then held out his hand in my direction as if illustrating that I was an example of the Zhukovsky breed of women. I stopped chewing and, sitting up straight in the chair, squared my shoulders. The Queen of Sheba burst out laughing.

"I knew each of David's three daughters. They were known even in Poltava!" He stopped. "Whose are you? Asyechka's? Friedochka's?"

"I'm Rita's."

"Rita was a bit younger. How old was she when the war started?"

"Mama? Fifteen."

"I don't really remember her as well. You see, right before the war, I went to study in Kharkov. And why? Because Frieda didn't choose me but Sashka Bezrukov. God but I was in love with her, like some dumbstruck shmegegeleh! I never found deep green eyes like that again my whole life. Tell me, does she still have such big green eyes?"

I choked on a bite and set the uneaten sandwich aside on the desk.

"Listen, how she used to play the mandolin—Friedochka! 'The Patriots' March!' 'We're born in order to turn a fairy tale into reality-y-y-y-y.' Making that vibrato with a pick . . . Here now—everything—fall into a swoon . . . It's all right before my eyes: she's sitting with her auburn curls tossed down her back, her eyes just like grapes . . . the mandolin on her knees . . . 'We're born'—with a pick . . . a Shulamit! Asya and Rita—they were beautiful, too, you can't say otherwise, but Friedochka, the middle child— a Shulamit! The fool didn't choose me, but Sashka Bezrukova. What she saw in that Sashka, I'll never understand to this day . . . Ay-ay-ay what an encounter! So!" he sat down at his desk. "Tell me about everyone!"

"About whom—everyone?" I asked quietly. "Didn't you ever return to Zolotonosha after the war?"

"That's exactly the point—no! You see, I was demobilized after the fighting, and I'm thinking, Where should I make my way to—after all, none of my family were left . . . I met a girl on the train, a Muscovite . . . So . . . love showed up on my doorstep. A family, so . . . Writing, even in the army I was writing . . . Then I sort of wheedled my way into literature. And now, you know, so few really know Yiddish."

"Of course," I muttered. "I see."

"And your people were hurled way out there! Boy, to Tashkent . . . Uncle David probably died already?"

"Yes, fifteen years ago."

"Cancer?"

"Yes, lung cancer. Grandma—later."

He nodded, grief stricken—the mortality of human beings.

"And what about Frieda—how is she, where? She must be some lady, oy-ey-ey, a paragon, right? Children, grandchildren, right? Got really fat, Friedochka, eh?"

I couldn't look at Grisha, I felt so badly for him.

"No," I said slowly. "Frieda—no . . . she hasn't gotten really fat . . . The Germans hanged Frieda."

I lifted my eyes. Grisha was staring at me with a stunned look. His face reminded me of a wizened plaster cast of a cucumber. I could have remained quiet about the rest. But for decades the family history had taken the form of a simple story and wouldn't bear chopped-off endings. Now, so many years later, I think—What kind of cruel demon instigated me to lay out the entire awful truth before that old man, what need did I have to shock him and ravage the memory of his youth?

"They say that a German major fell in love with her and . . . well, she could have remained alive on a certain folding cot . . . But Frieda, well, you know . . . she always had a wildly strong character . . . In short, before they hanged her, they chased her, naked, down the highway for ten kilometers—rifle butts in her back."

I moved my eyes away from Grisha's wizened face. The yellow peel of a Golden Delicious shone so sweetly in the corner.

The door squeaked open. With mournful eyes the Sacrificial Cow appeared in the crack. She said in a timid voice, "Shlitzbutter is still asking for the galleys of his article on raising internationalist consciousness."

Grisha made a silent gesture, and the Sacrificial Cow, frightened, shut the door. He slowly shifted his gaze to the window and, for several minutes, stared in a strange, fixed way at a puffy cloud stuck onto the middle of the smooth blue.

"It's a nice day," he said, his voice far away. "A real nice day." And for a few minutes he shuffled some papers on his desk.

"You eat, eat," he said, suddenly remembering. "Here, have an apple. This kind's called—"

"Golden Delicious," I muttered.

The Queen of Sheba wiped a corner of her dress along the india ink mascara dripping from her lashes. Her earrings and bracelets rattled softly.

"Whoever has brains in his head," she repeated weightily, "has them."

"Take Shlitzbutter his galleys!" Grisha bellowed. She took the pile of papers from the corner of the desk and, before leaving, said with a sigh, "That Shlitzbutter has tortured everyone with his capacity for work."

Grisha and I remained silent.

"Why didn't she join her family in the evacuation?" he squeezed out.

"Because, because . . . she couldn't tear herself away from Sashka . . . She ran off and hid in a barn. But by that time they were already shooting on the outskirts. Until the very last minute Grandpa kept running and shouting: 'Friedochka, my daughter! Have pity on your family, you louse!' Then he silently harnessed the horse—after all, he had two other daughters on his hands, and Asya was expecting a child. It was his duty to save them . . . Grandpa punished himself the rest of his life: 'I should have wound her hair around a fist and not let her take a single step. I should have beaten her with a belt until she bled!' which sounded so funny since Grandpa was such a softy. You know, as a child it was easy for me to wheedle a fifty-kopeck piece out of him for the movies, no matter how severely I was being punished."

"Sure, sure . . ." Grisha suddenly muttered, "sure, the cup has been drained dry, don't I always say that? But I continued living here, and I want to die here, so everybody leave me in peace!" He pointlessly shifted some papers around his desk, pens, the case for his glasses.

"Oy, just don't give me that story of Moses leading us in the desert for forty years so that a generation of slaves would die off!" He threw up a palm as if to prevent a flow of oratory from me, although I hadn't intended to say anything at all—for goodness' sake!—on this subject I knew absolutely nothing about.

"I don't need it! I'm the slave who's not worth leading anywhere. I, with your permission, will lie down right here, under a little bush, and will die on this very land that's maybe damned—no argument from me!—three times over!"

He kept speaking more and more quickly, agitatedly, and mournfully; I couldn't grasp to whom he was directing all this or why, for that matter, he was addressing the door through which the Queen of Sheba had exited.

"You're all young, you've got your whole lives ahead of you, fine! As for me, just let me breathe three more years between my first and second heart attacks. And after you bury me in Vostrekovskoye Cemetery—go revive the nation and be well, but I've revived all I could during this life . . . Yes," he continued, staring at me, "yes I'm an old mule, and I have no national-ethnic consciousness. For example, I cry when I hear Ukrainian songs. When I hear 'The Patriots' March' I cry, too, like an old mule, because Frieda played that march on the mandolin, vibrato with a pick. So to hell with my national-ethnic consciousness! You have it, you young people, go and be well, I always say, right? If you find the strength to bury your father alive—go ahead, and may God even help you!"

"Who is she—your daughter?" I finally guessed, nodding at the door.

"So who did you think?" he exclaimed, offended. "Just tell me, tell me, I can't remember anything anymore: Here I am—wounded three times and then, under Stalin's anticosmopolitan campaign, gracing a prison cot like some spy. So tell me: Am I a hero or an old fool?"

I smiled in embarrassment. Not giving me a chance to answer, the Queen of Sheba returned. I sustained a respectful pause and asked, "So will you take the story? Otherwise I've got to catch a plane."

"Don't ask foolish questions! David's granddaughter comes to me forty years after my youth and I—for David's granddaughter!—shouldn't publish some story?"

"You'll still have to work a little on the phrasing when you translate it," I cautioned, stepping out of my accountant's role.

"Don't worry!" he assured me, gloomy now. "We'll embalm it so well, this masterpiece, that the author himself wouldn't recognize it in its coffin."

I started saying good-bye.

"Pack the child some sandwiches!" he ordered Sheba in a tone like Solomon ordering one of the less quick-witted among his wives. "Throw in some apples!"

"Thank you, but what for?" I said, trying to fend them off.

"They're apples from Shlitzbutter's garden!" the Queen of Sheba said triumphantly, as if speaking of apples from the Garden of Eden. "This Shlitzbutter has tortured everyone with his apples."

I started pulling on my coat—what else was I supposed to do with it? Pensively, Grisha said: "Southern peoples freeze in our climate."

Right before leaving that stuffy room, I turned. Sitting at his desk, Grisha was again reminiscent of a great emaciated martyr and looking at me with a long, protective stare.

"What you're to be commended for," he said, "is for mastering a difficult profession. Such a profession will never let you down."

"Good-bye," I said.

"Zay gezunt," he answered sternly.

I stepped outside. It had rained a bit, but the sun was already drying up the asphalt where, like snippets of lace, dead rain worms lay scattered around. I've got to remember this, I pointed out to myself automatically, rain worms like snippets of lace; I've got to remember this.

Rush hour was in full swing, and the street gurgled with whirlpools of long and short lines, traffic jams here and there, crashes at intersections; my fellow citizens with the imprint of eternal worries on their faces were streaming—where? Where were they streaming, like spawning fish?

The bag with apples was tugging at my hand, the coat was stubbornly heating up my body, but my soul, rent in two, felt cold in the crowd of my compatriots.

An auburn puppy—a mix of dachshund and mongrel . . . ran back and forth on the sidewalk . . .

I shuffled to the subway, nervously glancing at the faces of onrushing passersby, and for the first time made an effort to feel—whose am I, whose?

I felt nothing.

I just guessed, perhaps, that this personal, inner feeling of blood tie was not something that could be foisted onto somebody. That at times it arrives late, maybe too late; at other times in those final minutes when, defenseless, you're being chased down a highway. By rifle butts. In the back.

Born in Memphis, Tennessee, STEVE STERN currently lives in Saratoga Springs, New York, where he teaches fiction writing, Jewish folklore, and Yiddish literature at Skidmore College. He is the author of half a dozen books of fiction, including the short-story collections *Lazar Malkin Enters Heaven* (Viking, 1986) and *The Wedding Jester* (Graywolf Press, 1999), for which Stern won a National Jewish Book Award. Known for his Jewish fabulist fiction, Stern has also written the children's books *Mickey and the Golem* and *Hershel and the Beast*. Many of Stern's stories, including "The Tale of a Kite," are set in a mythical Jewish neighborhood in Memphis.

The Tale of a Kite

STEVE STERN

IT'S SAFE TO SAY THAT WE JEWS of North Main Street are a progressive people. I don't mean to suggest we have any patience with freethinkers, like that crowd down at Thompson's Café; tolerant within limits, we're quick to let subversive elements know where they stand. Observant (within reason), we keep the Sabbath after our fashion, though the Saturday competition won't allow us to close our stores. We keep the holidays faithfully, and are regular in attending our modest little synagogue on Market Square. But we're foremost an enterprising bunch, proud of our contribution to the local economy. Even our secondhand shops contain up-to-date inventories, such as stylish automobile capes for the ladies, astrakhan overcoats for gentlemen—and our jewelers, tailors, and watchmakers are famous all over town. Boss Crump and his heelers, who gave us a dispensation to stay open on Sundays, have declared more than once in our presence, "Our sheenies are good sheenies!" So you can imagine how it unsettles us to hear that Rabbi Shmelke, head of that gang of fanatics over on Auction Street, has begun to fly.

We see him strolling by the river, if you can call it strolling. Because the old man, brittle as a dead leaf, doesn't so much walk as permit himself to be dragged by disciples at either elbow. A mournful soul on a stick, that's Rabbi Shmelke; comes a big wind and his bones will be scattered to powder. His eyes above his foggy pince-nez are a rheumy residue in an otherwise parchment face, his beard (Ostrow calls it his "lunatic fringe") an ashen broom gnawed by mice. Living mostly on air and the strained generosity of in-laws, his followers are not much more presentable. Recently transplanted from Shpink, some Godforsaken Old-World backwater that no doubt sent them packing, Shmelke and his band of crackpots are a royal embarrassment to our community.

We citizens of Hebrew extraction set great store by our friendly relations with our gentile neighbors. One thing we don't need is religious zealots poisoning the peaceable atmosphere. They're an eyesore and a liability, Shmelke's crew, a threat to our good name, seizing every least excuse to make a spectacle. They pray conspicuously in questionable attire, dance with their holy books in the street, their doddering leader, if he speaks at all, talking in riddles. No wonder we judge him to be frankly insane.

It's my own son Ziggy, the *kaddish,* who first brings me word of Shmelke's alleged levitation. Then it's a measure of his excitement that, in reporting what he's seen, he also reveals he's skipped Hebrew school to see it. This fact is as troubling to me as his claims for the Shpinker's airborne faculty, which I naturally discount. He's always been a good boy, Ziggy, quiet and obedient, if a little withdrawn, and it's unheard of that he should play truant from his Talmud Torah class. Not yet bar mitzvah'd, the kid has already begun to make himself useful around the store, and I look forward to the day he comes into the business as my partner. (I've got a sign made up in anticipation of the event: J. Zipper & Son, Spirits and Fine

Wines.) So his conduct is distressing on several counts, not the least of which is how it shows the fanatics' adverse influence on our youth.

"Papa!" exclaims Ziggy, bursting through the door from the street— since when does Ziggy burst? "Papa, Rabbi Shmelke can fly!"

"Shah!" I bark. "Can't you see I'm with a customer?" This is my friend and colleague Harry Nussbaum, proprietor of Memphis Bridge Cigars, whose factory supports better than fifteen employees and is located right here on North Main. Peeling bills from a bankroll as thick as a bible, Nussbaum's in the process of purchasing a case of Passover wine. (From this don't conclude that I'm some exclusively kosher concern; I carry also your vintage clarets and sparkling burgundies, blended whiskeys and sour mash for the yokels, brandies, cordials, brut champagnes—you name it.)

Nussbaum winces, clamping horsey teeth around an unlit cigar. "Shomething ought to be done about thosh people," he mutters, and I heartily concur. As respected men of commerce, we both belong to the executive board of the North Main Street Improvement Committee, which some say is like an Old Country *kahal*. We chafe at the association, regarding ourselves rather as boosters, watchdogs for the welfare of our district. It's a responsibility we don't take lightly.

When Nussbaum leaves, I turn to Ziggy, his jaw still agape, eyes bugging from his outsize head. Not from my side of the family does he get such a head, bobbling in his turtleneck like a pumpkin in an eggcup. You'd think it was stuffed full of wishes and big ideas, Ziggy's head, though to my knowledge it remains largely vacant.

"You ought to be ashamed of yourself."

"But, Papa, I seen it." Breathless, he twists his academy cap in his hands. "We was on the roof and we peeped through the skylight. First he starts to pray, then all of a sudden his feet don't touch the floor . . ."

"I said, enough!"

Then right away I'm sorry I raised my voice. I should be sorry? But like I say, Ziggy has always been a pliant kid, kind of an amiable mediocrity. Not what you'd call fanciful—where others dream, Ziggy merely sleeps—I'm puzzled he should wait till his twelfth year to carry such tales. I fear he's fallen in with a bad crowd.

Still, it bothers me that I've made him sulk. Between my son and me there have never been secrets—what's to keep secret?—and I don't like how my temper has stung him into furtiveness. But lest he should think I've relented, I'm quick to add, "And never let me hear you played hooky from *cheder* again."

And that, for the time being, is that.

But at our weekly meeting of the Improvement Committee—to whose board I'm automatically appointed on account of my merchant's credentials—the issue comes up again. It seems that others of our children have conceived a fascination for the Shpinker screwballs, and as a consequence are becoming wayward in their habits. Even our chairman Irving Ostrow of Ostrow's Men's Furnishings, in the tasteful showroom of which we are assembled—even his own son Hershel, known as an exemplary scholar, has lately been delinquent in his studies.

"He hangs around that Auction Street shtibl," says an incredulous Ostrow, referring to the Chasids' sanctuary above Klotwog's feed store. "I ask him why and he tells me, like the mountains should tremble"— Ostrow pauses to sip his laxative tea—"'Papa,' he says, 'the Shpinker rebbe can fly.' 'Rebbe' he calls him, like an *alter kocker*!"

"Godhelpus!" we groan in one voice—Nussbaum, myself, Benny Rosen of Rosen's Delicatessen—having heard this particular rumor once too often. We're all of a single mind in our distaste for such fictions—all save old Kaminsky, the synagogue beadle ("Come-insky" we call him for his greetings at the door to the shul), who keeps the minutes of our councils.

"Maybe the Shmelke, he puts on the children a spell," he suggests out of turn, which is the sort of hokum you'd expect from a beadle.

At length we resolve to nip the thing in the bud. We pass along our apprehensions to the courtly Rabbi Fein, who runs the religious school in the synagogue basement. At our urgency he lets it be known from the pulpit that fraternizing with Chasids, who are after all no better than heretics, can be hazardous to the soul. He hints at physical consequences as well, such as warts and blindness. After that nothing is heard for a while about the goings on in the little hall above the feed store that serves as the Shpinkers' sanctuary.

What does persist, however, is a certain (what you might call) bohemianism that's begun to manifest itself among even the best of our young. Take for instance the owlish Hershel Ostrow: in what he no doubt supposes a subtle affectation—though who does he think he's fooling?—he's taken to wearing his father's worn-out homburg; and Mindy Dreyfus, the jeweler's son, has assumed the Prince Albert coat his papa has kept in mothballs since his greenhorn days. A few of the older boys sport incipient beards like the characters who conspire to make bombs at Thompson's Café, where in my opinion they'd be better off. Even my Ziggy, whom we trust to get his own hair cut, he talks Plott the barber into leaving the locks at his temples. He tries to hide them under his cap, which he's begun to wear in the house, though they spiral out like untended runners.

But it's not so much their outward signs of eccentricity as their increasing remoteness that gets under our skin. Even when they're present at meals or their after-school jobs, their minds seem to be elsewhere. This goes as well for Ziggy, never much of a noise to begin with, whose silence these days smacks more of wistful longing than merely having nothing to say.

"Mama," I frown at my wife Ethel, who's shuffling about the kitchen of our apartment over the liquor store. I'm enjoying her superb golden broth, afloat with eyes of fat that gleam beneath the gas lamp like a peacock's tail; but I nevertheless force a frown. "Mama, give a look on your son."

A good-natured, capable woman, my Ethel, with a figure like a brick mikveh, as they say, she seldom sits down at meals. She prefers to eat on the run, sampling critical spoonfuls as she scoots back and forth between the table and the coal-burning range. At my suggestion, however, she pauses, pretending to have just noticed Ziggy, who's toying absently with his food.

"My son? You mean this one with the confetti over his ears?" She bends to tease his sidelocks, then straightens, shaking her head. "This one ain't mine. Mine the fairies must of carried him off and left this in his place." She ladles more soup into the bowl he's scarcely touched. "Hey, stranger, eat your knaidel."

Still his mother's child, Ziggy is cajoled from his meditations into a grudging grin, which I fight hard against finding infectious. Surrendering, I make a joke: "Mama, I think the ship you came over on is called the *Ess Ess Mein Kind.*"

COMES THE auspicious day of Mr. Crump's visit to North Main Street. This is the political boss's bimonthly progress, when he collects his thank-yous (usually in the form of merchandise) from a grateful Jewish constituency. We have good reason to be grateful, since in exchange for votes and assorted spoils, the Red Snapper, as he's called, has waived the blue laws for our district. He also looks the other way with respect to child labor and the dry law that would have put yours truly out of business. Ordinarily Boss Crump and his entourage, including his hand-picked mayor du jour, like to tour the individual shops, receiving the tributes his *shwartze* valet shleps out to a waiting limousine. But today, tradition notwithstanding, we're drawn out-of-doors by the mild April weather, where we've put together a more formal welcome.

When the chrome-plated Belgian-Minerva pulls to the curb, we're assembled in front of Ridblatt's Bakery on the corner of Jackson Avenue and North Main. Irving Ostrow is offering a brace of suits from his emporium, as solemnly as a fireman presenting a rescued child, while Benny Rosen appears to be wrestling a string of salamis. Harry Nussbaum renders up a bale of cigars, myself a case of schnapps, and Rabbi Fein a ready blessing along with his perennial bread and salt. Puffed and officious in his dual capacity as neighborhood ward heeler and committee chair, Ostrow has also prepared an address: "We citizens of North

Main Street pledge to be a feather in the fedora of Mayor Huey, I mean Blunt . . ." (Because who can keep straight Mr. Crump's succession of puppet mayors?)

Behind us, under the bakery awning, Mickey Panitz is ready to strike up his *klezmer* orchestra; igniting his flash powder, a photographer from the *Commercial Appeal* ducks beneath a black hood. Everyone (with the exception, of course, of the Shpinker zealots, who lack all civic pride) has turned out for the event, lending North Main Street a holiday feel. We bask in Boss Crump's approval, who salutes us with a touch to the rim of his rakish straw skimmer, his smile scattering a galaxy of freckles. This is why what happens next, behind the backs of our visitors, seems doubly shameful, violating as it does such a banner afternoon.

At first we tell ourselves we don't see what we see; we think, maybe a plume of smoke. But looks askance at one another confirm that, not only do we share the same hallucination, but that the hallucination gives every evidence of being real. Even from such a distance it's hard to deny it: Around the corner of the next block, something is emerging from the roof of the railroad tenement that houses the Shpinker shtibl. It's a wispy black and gray something that rises out of a propped-open skylight like vapor from an uncorked bottle. Escaping, it climbs into the cloudless sky and hovers over North Main Street, beard and belted caftan aflutter. There's a fur hat resembling the rotary brush of a chimney sweep, a pair of dun-stockinged ankles (to one of which a rope is attached) as spindly as the handles on a scroll. Then it's clear that, risen above the telephone wires and trolley lines, above the water tanks, Rabbi Shmelke floats in a doleful ecstasy.

We begin talking anxiously and at cross-purposes about mutual understanding through public sanitation, and so forth. We crank hands left and right, while Mickey Panitz leads his band in a dirgelike rendition of "Dixie." In this way we keep our notables distracted until we can pack them off (photojournalist and all) in their sable limousine. Then, without once looking up again, we repair to Ostrow's Men's Furnishings and convene an extraordinary meeting of the Improvement Committee.

Shooting his sleeves to show flashy cufflinks, Ostrow submits a resolution: "I hereby resolve we dispatch to the Shpinkers a *delegatz*, with the ultimatum they should stop making a nuisance, which it's degrading already to decent citizens, or face a forceable outkicking from the neighborhood. All in agreement say oy."

The only dissenting voice is the one with no vote.

"Your honors know best," this from Kaminsky, a greenhorn till his dying day, "but ain't it what you call a miracle, this flying rebbe?"

For such irrelevance we decide it also wouldn't hurt to find a new secretary.

En route across the road to the shtibl, in the company of my fellows, I give thanks for small blessings. At least my Ziggy was telling the truth about Shmelke. Though I'm thinking that, with truths like this, it's maybe better he should learn to lie.

We trudge up narrow stairs from the street, pound on a flimsy door, and are admitted by one of Shmelke's unwashed. The dim room lists slightly like the deck of a ship, tilted toward windows that glow from a half-light filtering through the lowered shades. There's a film of dust in the air that lends the graininess of a photogravure to the bearded men seated at the long table, swaying over God-only-knows-what back-numbered lore. By the wall there's an ark stuffed with scrolls, a shelf of moldering books, spice boxes, tarnished candelabra, amulets against the evil eye.

It's all here, I think, all the blind superstition of our ancestors preserved in amber. But how did it manage to follow us over an ocean to such a far-flung outpost as Tennessee? Let the goyim see a room like this, with a ram's horn in place of a clock on the wall, with the *shnorrers* wrapped in their paraphernalia mumbling hocus-pocus instead of being gainfully employed, and right away the rumors start. The yids are poisoning the water, pishing on communion wafers, murdering Christian children for their blood. Right away somebody's quoting the *Protocols of Zion*. A room like this, give or take one flying rebbe, can upset the delicate balance of the entire American enterprise.

Returned at least in body from the clouds, old Shmelke sits at the head of the table, dispensing his shopworn wisdom. An unlikely source of authority, he appears little more substantial than the lemon shaft pouring over him from the open skylight.

"It is permitted to consult with the guardian spirits of oil and eggs . . . ," he intones, pausing between syllables to suck on a piece of halvah; an "Ahhh" goes up from disciples who lean forward to catch any crumbs. ". . . But sometimes the spirits give false answers." Another sadder but wiser "Ahhh."

When our eyes adjust to the murk, we notice that the ranks of the Shpinkers (who until now have scarcely numbered enough for a *minyan*) have swelled. They've been joined this afternoon, during Hebrew school hours no less, by a contingent of the sons of North Main Street, my own included. He's standing in his cockeyed academy cap, scrunched between nodding Chasids on the rebbe's left side. To my horror Ziggy, who's shown little enough aptitude for the things of this world, never mind the other, is also nodding to beat the band.

"Home!" I shout, finding myself in four-part harmony with the other committee members. Our outrage since entering having been compounded with interest, we won't be ignored anymore. But while some of the boys do indeed leave their places and make reluctantly for the door, others stand their ground. Among them is Ostrow's brainy son Hershel and my nebbish, that never before disobeyed.

Having turned toward us as one, the disciples look back to their *tzaddik,* who God forbid should interrupt his discourse on our account. Then Hershel steps forth to confront us, pince-nez identical to Shmelke's perched on his nose. "You see," he explains in hushed tones, though nobody asked him, "figuratively speaking, the rebbe is climbing Jacob's Ladder. Each rung corresponds to a letter of tetragrammaton, which in turn corresponds to a level of the soul . . ." And bubkes-bobkes, spouting the gibberish they must've brainwashed him into repeating. I look at Ostrow who's reaching for his heart pills.

Then who should pipe up but the pipsqueak himself, come around to tug at my sleeve. "Papa," like he can't decide whether he should plead or insist, "if they don't hold him down by the rope, Rabbi Shmelke can fly away to paradise."

I can hardly believe this is my son. What did I do wrong that he should chase after moth-eaten *yiddishe* swamis? Did he ever want for anything? Didn't I take him on high holidays to a sensible synagogue, where I showed him how to mouth the prayers nobody remembers the meaning of? Haven't I guaranteed him the life the good Lord intends him for?

Not ordinarily combative, when the occasion calls for it I can speak my mind. To the papery old man whom I hold personally accountable, I ask point-blank, "What have you done to my child?"

Diverted at last from his table-talk, Rabbi Shmelke cocks his tallowy head; he seems aware for perhaps the first time of the presence among his faithful of uninvited hangers-on.

"Gay avek!" he croaks at the remaining boys. "Go away." When nobody budges, he lifts a shaggy brow, shrugs his helplessness. Then he resumes in a voice like a violin strung with cobweb, "Allow me to tell you a story . . ."

"A story, a story!" The disciples wag their heads, all of them clearly idiots.

The rebbe commences some foolishness about how the patriarch Isaac's soul went on vacation while his body remained under his father's knife. Along with the others I find myself unable to stop listening, until I feel another tug at my sleeve.

"Papa," Ziggy's whispering, Adam's apple bobbing like a golf ball in a fountain, "they have to let him out the roof or he bumps his head on the ceiling."

"Do I know you?" I say, shaking him off. Then I abruptly turn on my heel and exit, swearing vengeance. I'm down the stairs and already crossing Auction Street, when I realize that my colleagues have joined me in my mortification. I suggest that drastic measures are in order, and as my anger has lent me an unaccustomed cachet, all say aye.

They agree there's not a minute to lose, since every day we become more estranged from our sons. (Or should I say sons and daughters, because you can't exclude old Kaminsky's orphaned granddaughter Ida, a wild girl with an unhealthy passion for books.)

But days pass and Rabbi Fein complains that even with the threat of his ruler, not to mention his assistant Nachum (whom the boys call Knock 'em), he can't keep his pupils in Hebrew class. Beyond our command now, our children are turning their backs on opportunity in favor of emulating certifiable cranks. They grow bolder, more and more of them exhibiting a freakish behavior they no longer make any pretense to conceal. For them rebellion is a costume party. They revel in the anomalous touch, some adopting muskrat caps (out of season) to approximate the Chasid's fur *shtreimel*. Milton Rosen wears a mackintosh that doubles for a caftan, the dumb Herman Wolf uses alphabet blocks for phylacteries. My own Ziggy has taken to picking his shirttails into ritual tassels.

He still turns up periodically for meals, silent affairs at which even Ethel is powerless to humor us. For his own good I lock him in his bedroom after dinner, but he climbs out the window, the little pisher, and scrambles down the fire escape. "Not from my side of the family does he get such a streak of defiance," I tell Ethel, who seems curiously resigned. "I think maybe comes the fairies to take him back again," she says, but am I worried? All right, so I'm worried, but I'm confident that, once the Shpinkers have been summarily dealt with, my son will return to the fold, tail between legs.

Still the problem remains: What precisely should we do? Time passes and the Shpinkers give no indication of developing a civic conscience; neither do they show any discretion when it comes to aiding their blithering rebbe to fly. (If you want to dignify what he does as flying; because in midair he's as bent and deflated as he is on Earth, so wilted you have to wonder if he even knows he's left the ground.) In response to their antics, those of us with any self-respect have stopped looking up.

Of course we have our spies, like Old Man Kaminsky who has nothing better to do than ogle the skies. He tells us that three times a day, morning, noon, and evening, rain or shine, and sometimes nonstop on Shabbos, Shmelke hovers above the chimneys. He marks us from a distance like some wizened dirigible, a sign designating our community as the haven of screwballs and extremists. We're told that instead of studying (a harmless enough endeavor in itself), the shiftless Shpinkers now spend their time testing various grades of rope. From the clothesline purchased at Hekkie's Hardware on Commerce Street, they've graduated to hawser obtained from steamboat chandlers down at the levee. They've taken to braiding lengths of rope, to splicing and paying them out through the skylight, so that Shmelke can float ever higher.

Occasionally they might maneuver their rebbe in fishtails and cunning loop-the-loops, causing him to soar and dive; they might send him into electrical storms from which he returns with fluorescent bones. Sometimes, diminished to a mote, the old man disappears in the clouds, only to be reeled back carrying gifts—snuffboxes and kiddush cups made of alloys never seen on this planet before.

Or so says Old Man Kaminsky, whom we dismiss as having also fallen under Shmelke's mind control. We're thankful, in any case, that the Shpinkers now fly their *tzaddik* high enough that he's ceased to be a serious distraction. (At first the yokels, come to town for the Saturday market, had mistaken him for an advertising ploy, their sons taking potshots with peashooters.) But out-of-sight isn't necessarily to say that the rebbe is out-of-mind, though we've gotten used to keeping our noses to the ground. We've begun to forget about him, to forget the problems with our young. What problems? Given the fundamental impossibility of the whole situation, we start to embrace the conviction that his flights are pure fantasy.

Then Ziggy breaks his trancelike silence to drop a bombshell. "I'm studying for *bar mitzvah* with Rabbi Shmelke," he announces, as Ethel spoons more calf's-foot jelly onto my plate. But while his voice issues the challenge, Ziggy's face, in the shadow of his academy cap, shows he's still testing the water.

Ethel's brisket, tender and savory as it is, sticks in my gorge. I want to tell him the *tzaddik*'s a figment of his imagination and let that be an end to it, but Ziggy's earnestness suggests the tactic won't work.

"What's wrong," I ask, clearing my throat with what emerges as a seismic roar, "ahemmm . . . what's wrong with Rabbi Fein?"

"He ain't as holy."

Directly the heartburn sets in. "And what's holy got to do with it?"

Ziggy looks at me as if my question is hardly deserving of an answer. Condescending to explain, however, he finds it necessary to dismount his high horse, doffing his cap to scratch his bulbous head. "Holy means, you know, like scare . . . I mean sacred."

"Unh-hnh," I say, folding my arms and biting my tongue. Now I'm the soul of patience, which makes him nervous.

"You know, *sacred*," he reasserts, the emphasis for his own sake rather than mine.

"Ahhh," I nod in benign understanding, enjoying how his resolve begins to crack.

"That's right," pursues Ziggy, and tries again to fly in the face of my infernal tolerance, lacking wings, "like magic."

I'm still nodding, so he repeats himself in case I didn't hear.

"Oh sure, ma-a-agic," I reply, with the good humor of a parent introduced to his child's imaginary friend.

Flustered to the point of fighting back tears, Ziggy nevertheless refuses to surrender, retreating instead behind a wall of hostility.

"You wouldn't know magic if it dumped a load on your head!"

You have to hand it to the kid, the way he persists in his folly; I never would have thought him capable of such high *mishegoss*. But when the admiration passes, I'm fit to be tied; I'm on my feet, jerking him by the scrawny shoulders, his head whipping back and forth until I think I'm maybe shaking it clear of humbug.

"I'll magic you!" I shout. "Who's your father anyway, that feeble-minded old scarecrow or me? Remember me, Jacob Zipper, that works like a dog so his son can be a person?" Then I see how he's staring daggers; you could puncture your conscience on such daggers, and so I pipe down.

I turn to Ethel cooling her backside against the hardwood icebox, an oven mitten pressed to her cheek. "So whose side are you on?" I appeal.

She gives me a look. "This is a contest already?"

But tempted as I am to make peace, I feel they've forced my hand; I cuff the boy's ear for good measure and tell my wife, "I don't know him anymore, he's not my son."

UNDERSTAND, it's a tense time; the news from the Old Country is bad. In Kiev they've got a Jew on trial for blood libel, and over here folks are grumbling about swarms of Hebrews washing onto our shores. Some even blame the wreck of the Titanic on the fact that there were Guggenheims onboard. It's a climate created by ignorance, which will surely pass with the coming enlightened age—when our sons will have proved how indispensable we are. But in the meantime we must keep order in our own house.

At the next meeting of the North Main Street Improvement Committee I propose that the time is ripe to act.

Ostrow and the others stir peevishly, their hibernation disturbed. "Act? What act?" It seems they never heard of fanatics in our bosom or the corruption of our youth.

"Wake up!" I exhort them. "We got a problem!"

Slowly, scratching protuberant bellies and unshaven jaws, they begin to snap out of it; they swill sarsaparilla, light cigars, overcoming a collective amnesia to ask me what we should do.

"Am I the chairman?" I protest. "Ostrow's the chairman." But it's clear that my robust agitation has prompted them to look to me for leadership, and I'm damned if I don't feel equal to the test.

"Cut off the head from the body," I'm suddenly inspired to say, "and your monster is kaput."

At sundown the following evening the executive board of the Improvement Committee rounds the corner into Auction Street. There's a softness in the air, the stench of the river temporarily overwhelmed by potted chicken wafting from the windows over the shops. It's a pleasant evening for a stroll, but not for us, who must stay fixed on the critical business at hand. We're all of one mind, I tell myself, though yours truly has been elected to carry the hedge shears—donated for the deed by Hekkie Schatz of Hekkie's Hardware. Ostrow our titular chair, Nussbaum the treasurer, Benny Rosen the whatsit, all have deferred the honor to me, by virtue of what's perceived as my greater indignation.

This time we don't knock but burst into the dusty shtibl. As it turns out our timing is perfect: A knot of disciples—it appears that several are needed to function as anchors—are unravelling the rope beneath the open skylight. Rising into the lemon shaft (now turning primrose), his feet in their felt slippers arched like fins, Rabbi Shmelke chants the *Amidah* prayer: "*Baruch atoh Adonoy,* blessed art Thou, our God and God of our Fathers . . ."

The Shpinkers start at our headlong entrance. Then gauging our intentions by the sharp implement I make no attempt to hide, they begin to reel their rebbe back in. My colleagues urge me to do something quick, but I'm frozen to the spot; though Shmelke's descending, I'm still struck with the wonder of watching him rise. "Decease!" cries Ostrow, to no effect whatsoever; then he and the others shove me forward.

Still I dig in my heels. Disoriented, I have the sensation that the room is topsy-turvy; above is below and vice versa. Standing on the ceiling as the rebbe is hauled up from the depths, we're in danger of coming unglued, of tumbling headfirst through the skylight. I worry for our delinquent sons, who now outnumber the Shpinkers, and in their fantastic getups are almost indistinguishable from the original bunch. Among them, of course, is Ziggy, elflocks curling like bedsprings from under his cap, perched on a chair for the better view.

Then the room rights itself. Holding the handles of the hedge shears, I could say that I'm gripping the wings of a predatory bird, its mind independent of my own. I could say I only hang on for dear life, while it's the shears themselves that swoop forth to bite the rope in two. But the truth is, I do it of my own free will. And when the rope goes slack—think of a serpent when the swami stops playing his pipe—I thrill at the gasps that are exhaled ("Ahhh") all around. After which: quiet, as old Shmelke, still chanting, floats leisurely upward again, into the primrose light that is deepening to plum.

When he's out of sight, my Ziggy is the first to take the initiative— because that's the type of person we Zippers are. The rascal, he bolts for the open window followed by a frantic mob. I too am swept into the general exodus, finding myself somehow impelled over the sill out onto the fire escape. With the others I rush up the clattering stairs behind (incidentally) Ida Kaminsky, who's been hiding there to watch the proceedings. I reach the roof just in time to see my son, never an athletic boy—nor an impulsive or a headstrong or a rebellious one, never to my knowledge any of these—I see him swarm up the slippery pane of the inclined skylight (which slams shut after) and leap for the rope. Whether he means to drag the old man down or hitch a ride, I can't say, but latched onto the dangling cord, he begins, with legs still cycling, to rise along with the crackpot saint.

Then uttering some complicated mystical war cry, Hershel Ostrow, holding onto his homburg, follows Ziggy's lead. With his free hand Hershel grabs my boy's kicking right foot, and I thank God when I see them losing altitude, but this is only a temporary reversal. Because it seems that Rabbi Shmelke, handicaps notwithstanding, has only to warble louder, adjusting the pitch of his prayer to gain height. I console myself that if he continues ascending, the fragile old man will come apart in the sky; the boys will plummet beneath his disembodied leg. Or Ziggy, whose leap I don't believe in the first place, unable to endure the burden of his companion, will let go. I assure myself that none of this is happening.

From beside me the wild Ida Kaminsky has flung herself onto Hershel's ankle, her skirt flaring to show off bloomers—which make a nice ribbon for the tail of a human kite. But even with her the concatenation doesn't end: The shambling Sanford Nussbaum and Mindy Dreyfus, the halfwit Herman Wolf, Rabbi Fein's own pious Abie in his prayer shawl, Milton Rosen in his mackintosh, all take their turn. Eventually every bad seed of North Main Street is fastened to the chain of renegade children trailing in the wake of old Shmelke's ecstasy.

One of the rebbe's zealots, having mounted a chimney pot, makes a leap at the flying parade, but for him they're already out of reach. Then another tries and also fails. Is it because, in wanting to pull their *tzaddik* back to the earth, his followers are heavy with a ballast of desire? This seems perfectly logical to me, sharing as I do the Chasids' despair.

Which is why I shout "Ziggy, come back! All is forgiven!" and make to jump into the air. In that instant I imagine I grab hold and am carried aloft with the kids. The tin roofs, the trolley lines, the brand new electric streetlights in their five-globed lamps, swiftly recede, their incandescence humbled by the torched western sky. Across the river the sunset is more radiant than a red flare over a herring barrel, dripping sparks—all the brighter as it's soon to be extinguished by dark clouds swollen with history rolling in from the east. Then just as we're about to sail beyond those clouds, I come back to myself, a stout man and no match for gravity.

CREDITS

Apelman, Mark, "A Visitor's Guide to Berlin," © 1999 by Mark Apelman. Previously published in *International Quarterly,* 1999.

Boroson, Rebecca, "The Roussalka," © 1993 by Rebecca Boroson. Previously published in *J: The Guide to Jewish Living in Northern New Jersey,* 1993-94.

DeVidas Kirchheimer, Gloria, "A Case of Dementia," © by 1984 Gloria DeVidas Kirchheimer. Previously published in *North American Review* (1984), *Shaking Eve's Tree* (Jewish Publication Society, 1990), and *Goodbye, Evil Eye* (Holmes & Meier, 2000).

Fleischman, Cyrille, "Victor Hugo, un jour." Published in *Nouveaux rendez-vous au métro Saint-Paul,* © 1994 by Le Dilettante. "One Day, Victor Hugo . . ." translation © 2001 by Avriel Goldberger.